KU-172-160

Mysterious letters are discovered in the victim's belongings, strange links to the foreign office and why do the clues keep coming back to the assassination of a Baltic king?

As Flora closes in on the killer, it soon becomes clear she is no longer safe in London, but will her husband Bunny be able to get to her before it's too late?

For Alexandra – who is stronger that she seems, braver than she believes, more beautiful than she imagines and more loved than she knows.

And, as she looked around, she saw how Death, the consoler,
Laying his hand upon many a heart, had healed it forever.

from 'Evangeline' by Henry Wadsworth Longfellow

Chapter 1

Flora alighted onto the platform into clouds of white smoke from the steam engine that hissed beneath the massive iron and glass canopy of Waterloo Station. Porters darted between travellers pushing squeaky-wheeled trolleys loaded with luggage towards the line of hansom cabs that waited beside the platform; the odours of hot horseflesh wet leather and manure mixed with the sweet fragrance of dried lavender from the flower seller's stalls.

Flora handed her maid a portmanteau, then followed in the wake of the porter who had careened off with their luggage, her neck craned to keep him in sight. Disembarking passengers jostled on the platform as Flora carved her way through ladies in wide hats and harassed looking nurses holding dawdling children by the hand. The soot smuts on their faces reminded her of childhood train journeys spent with her head stuck out of the window, eyes narrowed against the wind as it tugged at her hair; something every child should do at least once.

Sally hurried along the platform beside her, the bag hefted on one hand and three hatboxes bouncing like balloons on their strings in the other.

Suitcases bumped Flora's shins, their owners making no effort to move aside, reducing her progress to a series of shuffling steps and starts. Spotting a gap in the crowd, she dodged between two slow-moving matrons, only to collide with a man in a black homburg hurrying in the opposite direction. He barely paused to apologize, simply lifted his hat an inch before disappearing into the crowd.

Flora glared at the miscreant over her shoulder, muttering at his lack of manners as her turn arrived at the barrier.

The guard clipped their tickets with a machine hung around his neck, releasing them into the arched cathedral roof of the main hall. Coming to an uncertain halt as the crowd disbursed into the vast expanse of the station, she glanced up at the monochrome, four-sided clock that hung from the ceiling,

'He said he would be here to meet us.' She bit her lip as the first pangs of anxiety gnawed at her. 'Our train arrived on time, so where is he?'

What if he had forgotten her? Would she be able to find his apartment unaided?

'He must have been held up.' Sally transferred the cumbersome bag to her other hand, flexing her fingers with a grimace. 'Don't fret, Miss Flora, I expect he'll be here directly.'

'I'm not fretting.' Flora fidgeted, irritated at having been so transparent. 'I'm merely surprised he isn't here waiting for us.' For the tenth time since leaving Richmond, she wondered if it had been wise to agree to this visit on her own; misgivings her husband had dismissed.

'I would accompany you, my love, but I've a complicated legal case on at the moment. After all, William is hardly a stranger; you've known him all your life.' His reasoning had not acknowledged her anxiety at all.

'Perhaps.' *Though not as my father*, a voice inside her head reminded her. The last time she had seen William, her behaviour had been less than cordial. When the truth of her parentage had come to light, she had laid the blame squarely on him, fairly or not. Circumstances had kept them apart since then, though his invitation to stay at his London apartment

2

came as no surprise, but one Flora had thus far avoided. Now she would have to prepare herself to face him all over again.

'Where'd that porter go?' Sally dropped the portmanteau at Flora's feet with a relieved grunt. 'I'll have something to say if he's run off with our luggage.'

'I very much doubt that. He has a job to do, and not everyone is disreputable.'

'You weren't dragged up in Flower and Dean Street,' Sally muttered darkly. 'Can't trust no one down there.'

Flora pretended not to hear, immune to Sally's tendency for drama and a belief that lurid stories of a childhood in Whitechapel gave her notoriety among those who had led more affluent lives; a judgement made on virtually everyone. Flora raised herself on tiptoe, her eyes narrowed in an effort to locate the porter's face among the noise, smoke, and clamour of the busy station that had begun to make her head pound.

'There it is!' Sally pointed to where Flora's elephant grey trunk with its military style fastenings sat on a trolley, their porter idling in conversation with the news seller, apparently confident of his fee.

Sally hurried towards him, her voice raised in protest as she heaved the bag she carried onto the trunk, piling the hatboxes on top. The largest tumbled off again and rolled across the concourse floor. With a theatrical groan and slump of her shoulders, she gave chase and after a tussle with an urchin boy who got there first, grudgingly parted with a coin before stomping back to the trolley and returned the box to the pile.

'Mrs Harrington?' An unfamiliar voice drew Flora's attention from the comic sight of her annoyed maid to where a man stood a few feet away; a bowler hat held in both hands at waist level.

'Yes, I'm Mrs Harrington.' She gave the concourse a final, swift glance in a last effort to locate William, then turned to the young man. 'May I help you?'

She judged him to be somewhere in his mid-twenties, and definitely someone she had never met before. Standing an inch or two taller than she, with a compact, but substantial build. Symmetrical features sat beneath arched brows with startling eyes so dark, the pupils looked the same colour as the irises.

'And who might you be then?' Sally stepped between Flora and the stranger, her chin lifted in challenge.

'My name is Peter Gordon.' He took in Sally's belligerent expression with a wry smile of amusement. 'I'm an associate of Mr William Osborne; he sent me to meet you.'

Flora had expected him to have an accent to go with his Mediterranean looks, but his diction was pure Home Counties.

'Can yer prove it?' Sally demanded.

'Sally,' Flora warned, sotto voce. 'Although my maid does have a point, sir. I was not expecting to be met by a stranger.' Despite her uneasiness, there was something compelling about him.

'But of course.' He withdrew a rectangle of pasteboard from an inside pocket and handed it to her.

William's name was embossed in black cursive script. She read the line beneath and stared at him, confused. 'It says here he's a "Secretary to the Foreign Office?" To her knowledge, William had spent most of his life on estates and plantations all over the world. She had never imagined him as a civil servant.

'Indeed so, Madam. I'm Mr Osborne's assistant, and all I know is that his duties prevent his presence here. I'm sure he'll make everything clear in due course.'

4

'I suppose it cannot be helped.' Flora sighed, disappointed.

'Is this your luggage?' Mr Gordon eyed the trolley, then without waiting for her response, clicked his fingers to attract the porter's attention. 'I've a cab waiting if you'll follow me.'

He took a step toward the exit, then halted, one eyebrow raised at Sally who stood in his way.

Sally returned his silent request to stand aside by standing her ground, her wide brown eyes narrowed on Mr Gordon's black ones, while passengers swept past them towards the exits, shrill whistles sounded and engines chuntered into the station.

Flora rolled her eyes but offered no comment, speculating on which of them would yield first.

Finally, Mr Gordon gave a resigned sigh, skirted round Sally and set off across the busy concourse.

'I'd watch that one if I were you, Missus,' Sally whispered when he was out of earshot. 'He looks foreign to me.'

'I cannot imagine there's any reason to be distrustful if William sent him.' Flora slanted an irritated, sideways look at her. 'Maybe he simply isn't used to being challenged by saucy lady's maids? Incidentally, you were quite rude to him just then.'

Sally sniffed, but ignored the reprimand. 'Still, I always keeps a hatpin sharpened for these occasions.'

'We'd better go, or we'll lose him.' Flora gestured her to follow, while at the same time wondered what she meant by "these occasions" but was too tired to make an issue of it.

Beneath the wrought iron canopy of the Praed Street entrance, the wide main road was crowded with hansom cabs, private carriages, and carts. It was barely four in the afternoon, but the gaslights had already been lit, their sulphurous light barely penetrating the fog, giving the street an eerie quality.

Mr Gordon stood beside a gleaming black motor taxi, the luggage piled at his feet. Unlike a hansom, the driver's seat was located beneath an open-sided canopy over the front tyres instead of perched at a precarious angle above the rear.

'Where's the 'orse?' Sally eyed the vehicle with suspicion, alarm flattening her vowels. 'I've never been in one o' those.'

'Really, Sally,' Flora chided. 'This is one of the French-built Prunels.' She turned a smile on Mr Gordon, delighted with his look of surprised admiration at her knowledge. 'My husband is convinced motor cars are no longer a strange novelty. That they will take over from the horse-drawn hansoms completely in the next few years.'

'Are you sure it's safe?' Sally's brown eyes narrowed and she took a step backward.

'Sally, really! You've seen Mr Bunny's motor car a dozen times.' Flora called over her shoulder as she climbed inside, 'Come along. It's freezing out here.'

'Still, don't like 'em,' Sally grunted, but obeyed, tugging the hatboxes onto her lap.

The door slammed shut leaving Mr Gordon on the pavement, a hazy figure illuminated by the yellow arc of a street light.

'Are you not coming with us?' Flora asked through the lowered window.

'Ah no.' He stood to attention, his hands behind his back. 'My instructions were to see you safely into a taxi. However, should you arrive at Prince Albert Mansions before Mr Osborne, his butler, Randall, expects you.' At his curt wave, the driver pulled away from the kerb, straight into the path of a horse-drawn hansom cab.

Flora made a grab for the leather strap above her head, wincing at Sally's high-pitched shriek as the taxi steered expertly out of the vehicle's path.

With disaster successfully averted, Flora inhaled a relieved breath and looked back through the rear window at the receding station. The pavement stood empty with no sign of Mr Gordon.

Chapter 2

'Are you sure we're still in London?' Sally pressed her nose against the window, wide-eyed at the expanse of parkland set behind black railings. 'We might be in the country.' The grass had died off to winter brown and a layer of grey mist hovered at the tree line.

'That's Hyde Park.' Flora eased closer to share the view. 'Have you never been here before?' Sally's rapid shake of her head came as a surprise, but then what reason would a girl from Whitechapel have to venture into this part of London. 'It must be quite different from where you come from?'

'Nothing but soot and filth down there, hardly a tree or flower to be seen. Is this where Mr William lives?'

'On the other side of the park in Knightsbridge, yes. I expect the driver will take us all the way round, so you'll get to see a more elegant side of your home town, Sally. There's a picturesque lake in the middle with ducks and a charming bridge which I'll take you to see while we are here.'

'Mr William must be very rich to live here,' she said, adding gleefully, 'Richer than the old Missus at any rate.'

A smile tugged at Flora's mouth in silent agreement as she scooted across the seat. Since Beatrice Harrington's discovery that Flora was not the daughter of a butler, but William Osborne, wealthy brother of a countess, she was deprived of the pleasure of looking down on Flora for reasons of her lowly background.

'Miss Flora? Might I ask you something?'

'Depends what it is.' Flora shot a look at the driver, hoping Sally wasn't going to be indiscreet, though the man did not appear to be listening.

'Is Mr William really your dad?' Sally whispered.

Goodness, can the girl mind-read? 'Yes, Sally, he is.' Not that she expected to keep it secret in a house full of servants, though Sally was the only one with the nerve to ask outright.

'That came as a surprise to me, Missus, 'cos the housekeeper told me you was raised by a butler.'

'I was, Sally. I had no knowledge that Riordan Maguire wasn't my real father until a year ago, and no, I don't intend to explain the circumstances.' She turned to stare out of her side of the taxi, hoping Sally might lose interest in the subject.

'Don't have to.' Sally sniffed. 'The cook told me all about it. Mr William is Lady Vaughn's brother, ain't he?'

'*Isn't* he. And as I have already said, I'm not going to explain.'

'And *I* said you didn't have to, so's I'm telling you what I heard.' She kept her voice to a discreet whisper. 'You wouldn't want outright lies doing the rounds in the servants' hall, would you?'

'Well, no, but—' Flora broke off, aware she had been outmanoeuvred. 'Thank you, Sally.' *I think.* Flora had not yet cultivated that mixture of disdain and distance the aristocracy used with regard to their servants, though neither avoidance nor sharp reprimand worked with the girl.

'So.' Sally huffed a breath and settled her hands in her lap. 'Your mother married the head butler because you were on the way?'

Aware she was already on entirely the wrong path with Sally, Flora decided she could hardly make things worse so might as well be candid. 'My mother died when I was six and

Riordan Maguire raised me. And yes, he was the Vaughn's head butler.' She did not bother to explain that Lily Maguire had disappeared, a fact which would make no difference. Flora harboured no regrets about her life, other than the fact she had been lied to for most of it.

'You should count yerself lucky, Missus. I was one of ten and none of us knew who our dads were.' Sally rubbed condensation from the window with one hand. 'At least you've been given a chance to know yours.'

'I suppose that's one way of looking at the situation,' Flora replied.

The taxi halted outside the wide façade of a building that stretched across several shop fronts. 'Prince Albert Mansions, Miss. That's right ain't it?' the driver addressed her over one shoulder

'Is this the place?' Sally ducked her head and peered through the window on Flora's side, her eyes wide. 'It looks like a hotel.'

'Indeed it does,' Flora murmured, her earlier anxiety reappearing. 'And yes, thank you, driver.'

Five storeys high, Prince Albert Mansions was built of pristine, cream coloured stonework, its wide windows set in arched embrasures declaring it to be newer than the surrounding buildings, having yet to take on the layer of black soot characteristic of most city structures.

The double set of glazed doors swung open but instead of a uniformed doorman, William appeared at a run, took the front steps at a sideways leap and tugged open the taxi door.

'I'm so sorry I wasn't at the station to meet you, Flora.' Pulling her bodily from the cab, he encircled her waist with one arm and held her free hand with the other. 'Had this tiresome meeting I could not get out of. Gordon found you all right then, did he?' Without waiting for her response, he guided her up the short flight of steps, through the front doors and into a lobby that could have graced one of the city's best hotels.

'Um, yes, he was most - helpful.' Flora's breath left her at his unexpected exuberance, which also helped dispel some of her nerves.

She had forgotten how handsome he was, with his thick, conker-red hair brushed straight back from a strong brow revealing silver wings at his temples that were thicker than at their last meeting; the only sign that he was in his early forties. His permanently tanned skin set off intelligent green eyes that sparkled with some private amusement, though just then they seemed troubled. A tiny crease sat at the bridge of his nose as he guided her through the glazed doors into a lobby which resembled one of the city's most elaborate hotels. Marbled floors that stretched to a curved and thickly carpeted staircase that wound to the floors above, each with a gallery that looked down onto the central lobby.

'Thank you, Dunne.' William nodded to a barrel-chested porter, who held open the door. 'If you would collect Mrs Harrington's luggage from the taxi. Oh, and pay the man would you? I'll settle up with you later.'

'With pleasure, Mr Osborne.' He saluted them both with a hand raised to his peaked cap.

'Excellent fellow, he'll obtain anything you need,' William said as the porter scurried outside. 'My apartment is on this floor and to the left. Do hope you like it. Bought the place without even seeing it, but when the agent said it was near the Park, I couldn't resist.' He chattered on as he led her to a shiny black door set in an alcove off to the left of the lobby.

Flora watched him covertly from the corner of her eye, surprised by his nervousness, evident by his rapid, clipped speech and the way he seemed unable to meet her eye; something she did too when anxious.

'This is a beautiful building.' Her voice shook, knowing they shared something so personal stirred sharp emotion. Perhaps they were connected by more than words after all. She had always regarded him as her employer's younger brother, a handsome, elusive figure who came into her life, or rather the Vaughn's lives for an entertaining few weeks, then left again on his travels with barely a word.

This familiar, more human side of him made her think she could see him as a parent after all, not simply the man who had dismantled what she had thought was her life.

'It is rather grand, isn't it?' He gave the high ceilings and marbled floor and walls a sweeping glance. 'So glad you like it, so far that is. Now, do come inside and see the rest of my domain. I hope you find everything to your taste.'

'*My* taste? Surely you didn't buy this apartment purely with me in mind?' she asked, only half-joking.

'Would that worry you?' He halted at a black door that stood invitingly ajar, his boyish grin accentuating tiny white lines in his deep tan beside his eyes.

She shook her head, unsure quite what to say with Sally present and the porter due back any second with her bags.

'I was happy to live as a gypsy up until this point, however now I have settled into regular employment, it seemed the right time to have a home of my own. This is Randall.' William indicated the spare, wiry man with sparse grey hair who took her coat at the apartment door. Of a similar height to Flora, and several inches shorter than William, that he addressed his shoes while murmuring a brief greeting made Flora think her late father could have shown him a thing or two about how to greet visitors. This thought accompanied a sharp pang below her ribcage that reminded her William was her father and that Riordan Maguire, the man who had raised her, had died more than a year before.

The manservant melted into the shadows with their coats as William led her into a brightly lit hallway with doors at intervals on either side, each room beyond filled with pristine furniture in pale woods and pastel painted walls, polished gilt mirrors, crystal chandeliers and the sculptures and artwork William had brought back from his travels abroad.

The space smelled of beeswax polish overlaid with a floral scent which must have been artificially introduced, for the season was too late for flowers and too early for festive wreaths. Idly, she wondered if William would decorate the apartment with holly and laurel, or ignore Christmas altogether and spend it at Cleeve Abbey?

'Come into the sitting room.' He ushered her through a door on their left, following behind into a large, but comfortable room with three primrose and gold sofas set in a horseshoe shaped arrangement around a faux Adam fireplace.

Flora couldn't help smiling as having selected one of the brocade-covered sofas, he fussed around her with cushions and moved a table closer to accommodate her bag. Instead of taking a chair opposite, he slid onto the upholstery beside her, from where the musk and sandalwood fragrance of his cologne filled her senses. For the first time since she had left Richmond, she stopped worrying that their first encounter would be formal and difficult. He took her hand in his once more, his warm grip reassuring her he too had been looking forward to her visit but was at the same time apprehensive.

'You didn't answer my question,' Flora said. 'About buying this place for me.'

He shrugged. 'Perhaps I did, in a way. I wanted somewhere for you to come and visit, although thus far you have refused all my invitations.'

'We saw each other when Bunny and I came to Cleeve Abbey for Lady Vaughn's house party last Christmas.'

'That was almost a year ago and the house was so full of guests, I barely managed to get five minutes with you alone.'

'I suppose so.' That she had contrived to be surrounded by others on that occasion filled her with hot shame. A few weeks before the house party, Riordan had been killed, and since then, her emotions had fluctuated between rage at him for having lied to her all her life, and grief at his loss which meant she could never demand he explain.

The disappearance of her mother when she was small had been tragedy enough, but to discover she was the result of a liaison between Lady Vaughn's younger brother and her lady's maid had left her confused; untethered to the life she had always believed in, resulting in Flora's resistance to a meaningful relationship with him.

She searched his face, seeing in his expression a need to make amends, so decided not to mention that if it were not for her husband's persistence, she would not be there at all.

'After all, Flora,' Bunny had said. 'He has his own side of the story to tell, which might surprise you.'

Flora had doubted that, but seeing William looking so boyish and eager to please, made her re-think that statement.

'I hope you understand why I kept away,' she began, experiencing a need to justify herself. 'I needed time to mourn for Riordan. He was the only father I knew.'

'Of course.' William's smile did not falter, but he released her hand and moved slightly along the squab, raw hurt in his eyes.

'What made you choose an apartment in the city? I thought you regarded Cleeve Abbey as your home.' Flora forced brightness into her voice as she acknowledged the fact she might have misjudged him. He wasn't simply paying lip service to the fact she was his daughter, he really wanted her here.

'I have rooms there, true, but purely as a guest,' William explained, giving the room a slow, possessive sweep with his eyes. 'This is my home now and although the country is perfect for relaxation, the comfort and ease of living here suits me.'

'Like these lights?' Flora blinked beneath the glare of the stark yellow of the glass fitments on the walls that were over bright and unnervingly silent without the perpetual hiss of gas jets.

'You'll get used to them. We have every modern convenience here. The boiler room provides hot water on demand for the whole building, and on Randall's night off, I can even order something from the kitchens for supper if I wish. I have twelve rooms here altogether, two of which are occupied by Randall.' He slapped his thighs and rose. 'Speaking of Randall, I expect he's helped your maid unpack by now, or if not, she's aware of the layout of your room. What say I show you where you will stay this week before we have tea?'

'I cannot wait.' She rested her hand in his outstretched one and allowed him to lead her into the hall again, where they retraced their steps past the front door and along another corridor.

'For future reference,' William said. 'Turn right at the front door to reach your room, while mine is on the left at the other end. The drawing room, sitting room, dining room, and study are in between.'

'Here we are.' He paused at the last door and pushed it open with a flourish. 'Well, what do you think?'

Flora preceded him into a room decorated in cream, gold and palest grey that sported a floor-to-ceiling window onto the front drive giving a view of St George's Place with Hyde Park beyond. A gilded arch separated the vast bed from a sitting area made up of a small sofa and an armchair beneath the window. A door to one side of the bed led to a dressing room lined with shelves and a long hanging rail, while another opened into a private bathroom complete with a cast-iron claw-footed bath.

William hovered on the threshold, his eyes wary, almost as if he expected her to be disappointed.

'It's – unbelievable.' Flora gasped, her hands clasped in front of her. 'I have never seen anything so beautiful. Marie Antoinette would have been jealous.'

'Oh, I'm so glad.' William exhaled in a rush. 'I didn't know if you would like the colour scheme, or if the bed was too ornate.' He indicated the vast, high bed with a gilt-edged headboard upholstered in creamy silk. 'If the mattress is too soft, I could-'

'I'm sure it's the most comfortable bed I have ever slept in. It's certainly the most beautiful.'

The house on the Thames at Richmond, though elegant and comfortable, was not hers. Despite Bunny and his mother being equal owners, somehow her mother-in-law's influence dominated each room. Sometimes Flora wondered if she would ever feel truly at home there.

'I hope you won't tell Bunny that, or he might not let you come again.' He laughed with what was evident relief, but broke off as Sally emerged from the dressing room, her bold stride halted when she saw them.

'Sorry, Missus, that Randall says I'm to finish the unpacking before I can have me tea. He's a bit of a stickler by the looks of it.' She smoothed her hands down her skirt, her cheekbones tinged with red beneath William's scrutiny.

'He'll have to adjust to having a female in the house.' William cleared his throat as if unsure how to address her. 'I've had the room next door set out as a bedroom for you, er, Sally is it? It's quite small, but I hope will be adequate.'

'Aw don't you worry 'bout me, Mister William.' Sally waved him away. 'I've slept on a washing line slung between the walls afore now. Didn't know what a real bed felt like 'till I came to live at Miss Flora's.' She flung open the lid of Flora's trunk and hefted a pile of petticoats in her arms. 'I'll be off presently and out of your way. Could do with a cuppa.'

'Thank you, Sally, and I'll see you later.' Flora gently guided a bemused William back out into the hall and pulled the door closed.

'Did she mean that? About the washing line?' William asked a hand lifted to indicate the closed door.'

'I believe she used it more as a euphemism.' Flora smiled.

'Ah, yes I see. She's quite er-adequate is she, as a personal maid?' William sounded sceptical.

'Sally's brighter than she appears, although she tends to speak as she finds.'

'Hmmm. In my experience, that's merely an excuse to be unspeakably rude.'

'You could be right, but in Sally's case, I don't mind it.' Flora had always regarded her maid's straightforward manner as more interesting than the 'yes ma'am', 'no ma'am' blandness Beatrice Harrington demanded from her servants. It was her mother-in-law's open disapproval of Sally that made Flora determined to keep her. 'She might be somewhat unconventional, but she suits me very well,' Flora said as William continued to stare at the bedroom door as if he was trying to see through it.

'I see, well.' He rubbed his hands together. 'Randall is nearby if you need anything, and a maid of all work comes in the mornings to do the housework. She lives here as well.' At her enquiring look he rushed on. 'Not in the apartment, but in quarters on the lower floor. This building was constructed with bachelors like me in mind and some lone occupants share domestic staff.'

'That sounds very practical.'

The rattle of crockery from along the hall made William smile and extend one hand. 'Ah, our afternoon tea is ready. Shall we?'

Chapter 3

Flora stepped from the warmth of the lobby into the chill night air outside the apartment building, her breath forming droplets of moisture on her fur collar. Fog shrouded the darkened street and turned moving pedestrians into shadows, her breath billowing in a white cloud as William handed her into a horse-drawn hansom. The greenish glow of the street lights were no more than disembodied balls of light that seemed to float in the mist.

'Blast.' William halted with his foot on the step and slapped each of his overcoat pockets in turn. 'Forgotten my opera glasses. Make yourself comfortable, Flora, I won't be a moment.' With a brief, backward wave, he turned and sped back into the building.

Settling into the seat, Flora availed herself of the blanket provided and tugged the rough wool across her knees, her attention to her right, where Hyde Park stretched away towards the Serpentine lake, the tops of the trees poking through the layer of grey fog.

The seconds stretched and she drummed her heels against the floor, unable to keep still. A motor taxi chuntered by, but apart from a cough from the driver above her head and the solitary clop of a shifted hoof, the street was quiet.

The entrance doors to the apartment building opened at last, bringing Flora upright in her seat, only for her to slump back again when she saw neither of the two figures who emerged from the building onto the top step was William.

Backlit by the stark electric lights of the lobby, a man in his early thirties led a woman by the elbow. He sported a moustache and had wayward light brown hair that could do with the attentions of a barber. Despite the bitter cold, he was clad only in trousers and shirtsleeves, as if he did not intend to stay outside long.

In contrast, the young woman was dressed for the street, the heaviness of her coat evident by the way it swayed in slow motion around her ankles as he propelled her into a brisk walk down the steps and out through the wrought iron gates. He halted on the pavement a few feet from the hansom and swung her around to face him, their features thrown into sharp relief by the streetlight overhead.

Flora sneaked a look at them from the side of the canopy, though all that was visible of the woman's face was a delicate chin beneath a wide-brimmed hat. Underneath the streetlight, her coat was a leaf green with black frogging down the front. A brooch pinned to the lapel that winked in the light caught Flora's eye. A circle of stones in two colours, too dark to distinguish, with a white flash across the centre.

'I don't know what you hope to gain by this harassment, Miss Lange,' the man snapped. 'Suffice it to say, this discussion is over. I don't expect to hear from you again.'

He must have assumed the cab was empty, for he made no attempt to lower his voice.

'In which case, I might well surprise you,' the woman replied, apparently immune to his anger. 'Until I get what I want, you may indeed see me again.' She inclined her head in a feminine, teasing gesture, then turned on her heel and strode away.

The man lingered on the street for a minute more; hands on his hips as he stared after the woman before hurrying back inside, almost colliding with William on his way out.

William moved to one side, his hat raised in greeting as the man nodded in acknowledgement and then disappeared into the apartment building.

'Sorry to keep you waiting, Flora. I hope you aren't too cold.' He scrambled into the seat beside her and closed the flaps over their knees.

'Not at all.' Flora flexed her numb fingers inside her gloves. 'Although that's the second time you've apologized to me within the hour. Are you sure my visit won't be an inconvenience?' She eased further away from him on the seat, aware she did not know him well enough for any physical contact, even accidental.

'Certainly not.' He rapped on the roof hatch. 'Theatre Royal, Haymarket please, driver.'

The hansom did a stomach-churning u-turn in the middle of the road, giving Flora a view of the young woman as she strode confidently along St George's Place away from the apartments, her head high and her bag swinging at her side. Whatever had taken place inside the apartment had not troubled her at all. Unlike the man she had seen, whose brooding expression as he stared after her told a different story.

'I hope you'll like the play,' William said, interrupting her thoughts. 'There's a fantasy in one act called *Shades of Night* on first, though the performance I really brought you to see is *Cousin Kate*, which begins at nine.'

'I'm looking forward to it.' She sneaked a look at his face, thrown into relief by the lamps that hung from the side of the cab.

He slanted her a sudden, enquiring, sideways look, and embarrassed to be caught staring, Flora tugged her coat collar against the sharp night air that flowed round the open cab.

Their driver plunged the cab into the heavier traffic circling Hyde Park Corner, ignoring a shouted curse from a tradesman's cart forced to a sharp halt to avoid a collision.

Flora returned William's smile and sent up a silent prayer that not every London cab journey would be quite so exhilarating.

*

Flora linked her arm through William's and joined the crowd disgorged onto the pavement by a constant stream of hansoms and motor taxis in front of a canopy supported by six Doric columns over the theatre entrance.

In the foyer, Flora parted with her cloak to a girl behind a desk, accepted the metal token in exchange and re-joined William in the lobby where patrons greeted each other with braying voices and false laughter. Ladies with coiffed heads adorned with flowers, ribbons or precious stones wound into their hair swept by on a swish of silk, leaving a cloud of perfume behind them. The entire room struck Flora as being a performance in itself, while a sweet, cloying smell of face powder mingled with pomade, overlaid with the spirit tang of the pre-theatre drinks served by obsequious waiters in black and white livery.

The doors flapped open at intervals to admit arriving patrons, their faces alight with anticipation of the coming evening, bringing with them a wave of cold air that blew through the entrance. An atmosphere of excitement prevailed as they greeted friends with air kisses and firm handshakes.

'I've never been here before.' Flora looked up at the ornamental ceiling with its gold leaf architraves and the massive crystal chandeliers that winked in the bright electric light. 'I've visited *Her Majesty's* opposite several times,' she added, hoping she didn't sound unsophisticated. 'But never this one.'

'There's been a theatre on this site for over a hundred and fifty years.' William handed a white five-pound note to the usherette who hovered beside the door, a pile of programs balanced in the crook of her arm. 'John Nash designed the original facade, but the inside has been altered several times since.' He broke off to press a gratuity into the girl's hand, oblivious of her longing smile at his retreating back, much to the annoyance of the queue of patrons waiting for programmes.

'The old girl is looking a little worn these days.' William indicated the peeling paint in the high corners and the faded red curtains with ragged fringes that hung in the doorways. 'I was fortunate to obtain tickets at all because the theatre is due to close soon for extensive refurbishments. I hope they don't change things too much as these rich, dark colours always remind me of boyhood Christmases when we were treated to outings to a play followed by tea at Fortnum's. Neecy always scoffed all the peppermints during the first act, and I was always blamed for the resultant squabble.'

'You call Lady Vaughn, "Neecy"?' Flora regarded him with surprise.

'Of course, I do.' He chuckled and leaned closer, his breath warm on her cheek. 'She's still my big sister, no matter how grand she gets.'

Flora's gaze snagged on the male half of a middle-aged couple who surreptitiously watched them out of the corner of his eye, his upright collar so high, he was forced to view the world down a patrician nose, while his female companion sneaked frequent looks at them over her shoulder.

'It appears we're a figure of interest.' Flora nodded towards them as the pair disappeared into the main hall.

'That's Rudi Carruthers.' William's mouth twitched into a mischievous smile. 'He pretended not to notice us, but I expect word will be all over the FO by tomorrow lunchtime that I'm escorting a young and beautiful lady around town.'

'Oh dear. I don't think I like the idea of your reputation being sullied on my account.' Flora's cheeks flamed in annoyance at people with little better to do than spread malicious gossip.

'Don't worry. I'll nip it in the bud in a day or two.' He winked. 'Ah! there's the bell for the start of the performance. Shall we take our seats?'

Flora started toward the door marked, *Stalls*, but William held her back. 'Not that way, I've booked one of the lower boxes for tonight's performance.'

'A treat indeed.' A thrill of excitement rushed through her as he guided her through the jostling crowds that gave off waves of 'Jicky' perfume and 'Floris' cologne. He led her up the stairs and along a carpeted corridor to a door that opened into a box draped with velvet swags and hangings held back with gold silken cords, set close to the proscenium. Four matching upholstered chairs set two on two in matching oxblood damask.

'This is lovely.' Flora peered over the low edge to the rapidly filling seats below, where jewels draped around ladies' necks and hung from delicate ears winked and flashed in the light from electric chandeliers. 'We're practically seated on the stage. Do we have this to ourselves?'

'Indeed we do. It was all they had available, but I quite like the exclusivity. The ghost of a former actor-manager has been seen in the wings.' William arranged his opera glasses and programme on the shelf in front of them.

'Name of John Buckstone. He was a friend of Dickens. He wears a beige coat and twill trousers and hangs about in the wings. He's been heard backstage rehearsing his lines, so if you happen to see him do let me know. I've never seen a ghost before.'

'I'll do no such thing.' Flora had no patience with fate, omens, or superstition. 'And if you're trying to frighten me, it's not working. I don't believe in ghosts.'

'Is this play as scandalous as the review in the *Daily Mail* says?' Flora tapped the programme against her lip. 'It said *Cousin Kate* featured a young lady jilted by an Irish lover who falls for a stranger on a train.' He frowned at her and she smiled. 'I confess to having read it before I left home.'

'Oh really,' William crossed one ankle over the other. 'And what did a Fleet Street hack have to say about it?'

'I cannot recall his name, but the man's apparently a guardian of good taste, because, in his opinion, ladies do not engage in flirtations in railway trains, nor follow that up with desperate love-making in empty country houses. At least, not without the formality of an introduction and without knowing each other's names.'

'Do you disapprove of flirtations in trains?' he asked, though his mocking smile told her otherwise.

'It depends, with whom and which train. For example, the 10.20 to Reading is too parochial for romance, whereas the Oriental Express to Venice might appeal.'

William's delighted laugh brought several looks their way from the stalls below them. 'I have to agree, the Paris Gare de l'Est is infinitely more romantic than the 8.30 am to Paddington. Hush now, the play is about to begin.'

*

The lights went up for the interval, greeted by enthusiastic clapping and a sudden rush for the aisles; the respectful quiet ceasing abruptly as everyone began talking at once.

'What do you think of it so far?' William idly flicked through the programme but discarded it when nothing appeared to catch his interest.

'Honestly?' Flora hesitated for a heartbeat. Was it rude to criticize a performance to which one had been invited? 'The plot is somewhat predictable, and it's a shame the cast are all wearing ordinary clothes. I would have liked to see some elaborate historic costumes. Like you, the theatre always makes me think of Christmas, the more festive the better.'

'Noted.' William held up a finger in emphasis. 'I'll be sure to book Goldsmith's *She Stoops to Conquer* next time. A play which is performed exactly as Sheridan would have arranged it.'

'The theatre is lovely, in a faded, old-fashioned sort of way.' She leaned forward in her seat, her arms folded on the ledge to watch ladies who strolled the aisles below them, their' hats piled high with artificial flowers, feathers, and ribbons.

'Care for a chocolate?' William bent to retrieve the lilac pasteboard box he had placed beneath his seat. 'They're violet creams.'

'No thank you, not that they aren't delicious, but I have already eaten two. Any more would spoil the dinner you promised me.'

Two men stood in the side aisle almost directly below them; both dark-haired and swarthy looking. She narrowed her eyes as something about one of them struck her as familiar, but all she could see of him was the top of his head. They seemed to be in earnest conversation, involving a good deal of finger pointing and expansive arm waving on both sides.

The bell rang for the resumption of the performance, but instead of taking their seats, only one of the men sat down. The other bore a strong resemblance to Mr Gordon, which made her follow his progress as he marched purposefully up the aisle. Before she could determine if it was indeed him or not, he had disappeared through the exit. Was William's assistant also a theatre lover and, if so, why was he leaving before the end of the performance?

There was no time to ponder the question as the lights dimmed, sending the patrons grouped in the aisles scurrying to their seats. The low roar of conversation diminished to the occasional cough and Flora relaxed back in her seat.

'What were you looking at just now with such fierce attention, Flora?' William asked.

'I thought I saw your Mr Gordon in the stalls, but I was probably mistaken.'

'I should think so. He left the office early due to some personal business on the other side of town, so he isn't likely to be here. Anyway, comedy theatre isn't really his style.'

'Apparently not as he has just left,' Flora murmured.

'What did you say?'

'Oh, nothing. I must have imagined it. I'm used to seeing people I know wherever I go in Richmond, but there must be thousands of men like him in the city.' She helped herself absently to another chocolate from the box on William's lap, though she didn't really want one. 'Now,' she said as the house lights dimmed to darkness. 'We shall see if Cousin Kate will accept her new suitor in the second half, or abandon him like she did her last?'

'She was jilted, Flora, that's somewhat different.'

'Then perhaps she wants revenge on the rest of mankind and will cast Mr Desmond into the abyss?'

'Sometimes,' William paused and gave an exaggerated shudder. 'You females make me exceedingly nervous.'

Chapter 4

The humid warmth of the restaurant enveloped Flora as William guided her into Elena's L'Etoile in Charlotte Street. Savoury aromas of cooked meat and hot bread stirred her hunger, reminding her she had not eaten since midday. The room was narrow, intimate rather than imposing, with twelve or so tables set around the walls, each of which seated four diners.

The waiter's assessing eyes swept over them, then came to rest on William where they lit up with recognition.

'Mr Osborne, how delightful to see you again. Your usual table?'

'That would be most agreeable, Francoise.' William allowed the waiter to take the lead, guiding Flora into an alcove at the rear, where a round table was set for two with a gleaming white cloth and a dizzying number of crystal glasses. A lone candle sat in a silver and glass holder in the centre of the table, the gentle hiss of a wall-mounted gas jet on the wall above.

The low light gave the place a funereal atmosphere, prompting William to whisper, 'Shall I order for you?'

'Thank you, no,' Flora perused a menu larger than a broadsheet. 'I prefer to make my own choices.'

'Quite so.' His wry smile told her she had been too strident. 'However, might I suggest you try the mushroom soufflé? It's a house speciality.'

Flora wrinkled her nose. Mushrooms were not to her taste; which William would have known had he played a larger part in her life. This unbidden thought shocked her in its intensity, for it was not William's fault she had grown up without him. She pushed down her resentment and summoned a bright smile. 'I'll have the chicken liver parfait, followed by the lamb in raspberry sauce.'

'The parfait sounds good.' William handed the menu back to the hovering waiter. 'I'll have that too, followed by the grilled salmon.' His choice of wine received an effusive compliment before the waiter bowed and retreated.

'Now, tell me.' William snapped open the napkin and laid it across his lap. 'Why did you not bring Bunny with you on this visit? My invitation included both of you.'

'He was going to come, but then this case came up. He said if he had any chance of becoming a partner in the law firm, he couldn't turn it down.'

'The fraud at the bank?' William nodded. 'I read about in *The Times*. He moves in illustrious circles these days.'

'I also felt that since we discovered—' she broke off, her cheeks burning.

'That I was your father?' He kept his voice low. 'I hope you don't regard me as an embarrassment?'

'No, not at all,' Flora rushed to reassure him. 'I never did.' She swallowed the lie, shamed by the anger she had felt at the time. For months she had hidden behind grief, not only for the death of Riordan Maguire but for having been kept in ignorance for so long. 'I admit it took some getting used to. I hope you understand that I first needed to mourn the man who had raised me.'

'I confess to a little jealousy, but naturally, I understood. How do you feel now?' Uncertainty stood in William's eyes. Eyes that so resembled her own, she couldn't help but stare, his face thrown into sharp relief by the light from the candle between them.

'I'm growing accustomed to it. I know why you and my mother made the decisions you did. Not that it's my place to criticize either of you.'

'Perhaps not, but you've had to live with the consequences of our actions.'

She was saved from a response by the return of the waiter with their first course. He fussed over the dishes, then made an elaborate show of pouring their wine, while Flora eyed her food hungrily, wishing he would go away.

'I've been fortunate,' Flora said when they were alone again. 'My husband has been wonderfully understanding. Some men would have been horrified to learn that their wife was the result of a liaison between a lady's maid and a member of her employer's family.' She groaned inwardly, aware she sounded petulant. Something she had promised herself she would not do, but she couldn't help herself.

'It wasn't a liaison, Flora.' His eyes pleaded for understanding. 'I loved your mother deeply.'

'Just not deeply enough,' she murmured under her breath.

His hand stilled on his wine glass indicating he had heard. He looked about to respond, but changed his mind and summoned a smile.

'How do you get on with Bunny's mother? I hear she's a formidable woman.'

'Er-she is.' Flora reached for her water glass and gulped a mouthful. Why couldn't she control her tongue? 'Beatrice is perfectly pleasant most of the time. She saves the barbed comments about governesses for when no one else is listening. Poor Bunny cannot understand why we aren't close friends.'

'Because he never sees it?'

'Exactly. I sense she's not quite sure how to treat me these days since she learned I was not, in fact, a butler's daughter.

She keeps asking when I'm going to invite her to Cleeve Abbey in order to introduce her to Lord and Lady Vaughn. I cannot count the number of times I have explained the prerogative is entirely theirs. It's not as if I have any influence over their social calendar.' She took her first bite of pâté, savouring the taste, which was rich and slightly sweet with a low note of herbs.

'That's an improvement of sorts,' William acceded. 'Although I detect a certain resentment on your part. Have you talked to Bunny about his mother?'

'Not directly.' Flora fidgeted, uncomfortable with the subject of her mother-in-law. 'It's her home too after all, and Bunny's very protective of her since she was widowed.'

'That was years ago, and doesn't mean he should allow her to trample over your self-respect.'

'No, he shouldn't. And he doesn't mean to, it's – awkward.' Flora rearranged her napkin. The real reason she did not want to appeal to Bunny to smooth her way with his mother, was so as not to appear weak in his eyes. Like most men, Bunny wanted, and deserved, his domestic life to be a well-ordered, efficient sanctuary, not a hotbed of dissent and resentment.

Whatever difficulties she experienced with Beatrice were hers alone and she would deal with them in her own way. 'I intend to establish my own truce with my mother-in-law as time goes on. If that proves impossible, then I'll simply make sure no one knows where I buried her.' She popped the last piece of toast into her mouth and chewed.

William's eyes flicked up and pinned her with a look filled with uncertain laughter.

'I'm teasing,' Flora added when the silence stretched.

'Of course, you are.' He exhaled in relief. 'But it ensures I shall take every care not to upset you.'

'You couldn't do that. After all, you and I have known each other all my life. I have very fond memories of those summers spent at the Abbey.'

'I like to think Bunny allowed you to come alone on this visit because he knew how much I've been looking forward to having my grown-up daughter to myself for a while.' His eyes twinkled and a smile touched his mouth. 'Do you remember you used to call me Uncle when you were young?'

'You're not my uncle, though, are you?' As soon as the words were said, she regretted them. She didn't know the full story as to what happened between her parents, thus it was possible she was being unfair in heaping all the blame onto William.

'No, I'm not.' He clamped his lips together, the subject hovering between them like a small grey cloud waiting to burst. 'What did you think of Miss Jeffreys?' he asked, pointedly changing the subject.

'She played the part of Kate beautifully, considering the overly dramatic script.'

William chuckled. 'I saw Miss Ellis at The Prince of Wales theatre last year and she was every bit as entertaining as this evening. Unfortunately, her divorce did nothing to enhance her reputation.'

'The scandal played out in the newspapers last year; it caused quite a stir.' She pressed one finger into her cheek and adopted her mother-in-law's fiercest expression. 'Actresses are disreputable enough,' Flora mimicked. 'Without compounding their lack of morals by divorcing their husbands.'

William spluttered on his wine and while he recovered, she added. 'I admire her for not accepting her husband's violent jealousy. I don't believe men have a right to abuse their wives.'

'Hmm, I see you're quite a progressive.' He dabbed at the red spots of spilled wine on the tablecloth with his napkin. 'I'd better watch what I say.'

'I hope you don't do any such thing. As for *Cousin Kate*, as a comedy with elements of farce, it works well.'

'Mr Cyril Maude would be sorry to hear his work damned with such faint praise,' William said. 'Among thespians he's considered a master of his class.'

'I meant the script, although Mr Maude's Heath Desmond was almost farcical. As for those menacing eyebrows, they put me in mind of an Italian gangster rather than an Irish Lothario. Had *I* been alone in an empty house when he walked in unannounced, I would have made use of those French windows and put as much space between us as possible.'

'They were a somewhat contrived plot device, I agree.' William laughed, a full-throated, genuinely amused laugh that drew other eyes in the restaurant towards them, just as it had in the theatre. 'Even that walrus of a man in the next box who told us off for laughing couldn't spoil it for me.'

'I couldn't help but think the playwright must be a misogynist.'

William looked up sharply, his knife halted above his plate. 'Now there's a controversial word. Some would say misogyny is merely the desire to reserve a specific role for the female gender. Preserve and cherish, not disparage.' He eased back as the waiter removed the empty plates and replaced them with their entrees.

'I see it as disparagement to assume women are so malleable they would accept an offer of marriage after one afternoon's acquaintance. It's too ridiculous to be taken seriously.'

'His view of the male species isn't much better. After all, Heath abandoned his fiancée two days before their wedding because he wanted to paint on the Sabbath.' He nodded at her plate. 'Lamb tasty enough for you?'

'Excellent.' Flora forked another piece of meat into her mouth, so tender that it required little chewing.

'How long did it take you to fall in love with Bunny?' he asked, apropos of nothing as far as she could tell.

'Longer than a train journey, but I wasn't engaged to someone else at the time.' She mopped up the sweet sauce with a fluffy potato, using the time to gauge whether or not he was teasing her. William was well aware she had met her husband on a steamship, and that their romance had blossomed during the voyage.

'I apologize, I wasn't trying to embarrass you. Didn't you both discover a murderer on your way back from New York after Amelia's wedding?'

'We did. Two in fact.' His eager expression demanded more, so she complied, giving him a summarized account of how she had discovered a dead body on the deck and insisted everyone was wrong that it had been an accident. 'I did receive help from a Pinkertons detective, not that I knew he was one at the time.'

'Have you always been fascinated with violent crime?' William asked, a smile in his voice.

'Never, though I admit the voyage was made more exciting by the race to find a killer before we reached England. Bunny wasn't quite so enthusiastic at first, but when the evidence began mounting up, he couldn't deny what was going on.'

'And he found you so fascinating, he proceeded to court you when the ship docked?'

'Yes. Not quite a shipboard romance, but almost. We've been married over two years now.'

The couple at the next table rose to leave, and something about the commanding way the man guided his companion out of the door reminded Flora of the scene she had witnessed outside the apartment.

'By the way, who is the gentleman from your building with sandy hair and a patchy moustache?' She picked up her wine glass, surprised to see it was empty and put it down again. Little wonder she was talking so much, though William appeared not to mind.

'Goodness!' William blinked, his wine glass halted in mid-air. 'Where did that come from?'

'He came out of the building while I was waiting for you to fetch your opera glasses. You passed him on your way out the second time. I assume he lives there too?'

'That was hours ago. What made you notice him in particular?'

'I was just curious.' Flora shrugged, in two minds whether to mention the young woman he had hustled out in such a hurry.

'Ginger and a 'tache, you say?' William considered a moment, then smiled. 'That's Arthur Crabbe. He lives at number eight on the floor above. With his wife,' he added as an afterthought. 'I expect you'll meet him before long. Nice chap. He works with me at the Foreign Office.'

Flora stilled for a second, relieved she had kept quiet about the woman. Mr Crabbe had addressed her as Miss Lange. *Definitely not his wife.*

'Which brings me to another subject.' William cleared his throat. 'A more difficult one for me, in that I'm afraid I'll be unexpectedly tied up this week at the office. We have a major crisis which I have to deal with, so I might not be able to spend as much time with you as I intended during your stay.'

'Oh, I see.' Flora tried to hide her disappointment. 'I was wondering about your work.' She remembered the pasteboard card Mr Gordon had given her which now sat in her dresser drawer in the apartment. 'I thought you managed cattle ranches in South Africa and Indian rubber plantations. How does that equip you for the civil service?'

'I don't know really.' He gave a nonchalant shrug which was entirely unconvincing. 'Perhaps having an earl for a brother-in-law helped.'

The waiter removed their plates, returning within seconds with oversized menus for dessert.

Flora declined, so William ordered coffee and brandy, both of which arrived so rapidly, she imagined they had overstayed their welcome, though one glance told her the restaurant was still half full.

'Is that really how it came about?' she asked when the waiter had gone. 'Or were you vetted over a gentleman's club luncheon and decreed a good fit for the corridors of Whitehall?'

'My, I had no idea how acerbic you can be.' He raised a cynical brow. 'I'll have to watch that, though I flatter myself you inherited that from me. In fact it wasn't only one luncheon, young lady. I had to attend two rather tedious dinners as well. Not to mention a banquet with the Austrian delegation.' He leaned closer, so the flame on the candle was reflected in his eyes. 'The government feels that due to my frequent travels in the Baltic, I possess valuable local knowledge which might be useful in the current situation.'

'What current situation?'

His eyes sharpened again, indicating their light banter was over and the conversation had taken a more serious route. 'Have you heard of something the press referred to as the *May Coup*?'

'Vaguely.' Flora frowned as she searched her memory. 'Something about murders in Belgrade, but not the details. Wasn't there a queen with a strange name I cannot for the moment recall?'

'Queen Draga, the Serbian word for "dearest".' William's smile faded as he swirled the dark liquid in the crystal bowl he held in one hand. 'In May, King Alexander and his wife were assassinated by their own security service. They were cornered in their bedchamber, both stabbed, and their bodies hurled over a second-floor balcony into the palace garden.'

'How awful.' Flora broke off from nibbling at a Florentine biscuit.

'Accounts vary, but a reliable source says when the king was pushed, he tried to hang onto the balcony by his fingertips, so they slashed his fingers off with a sword to make him let go.'

'Makes me glad I'm not royalty.' Flora shuddered, though she attributed that more to the brandy.

'Indeed. They killed the queen's brothers too, which wasn't much of a loss.' He snorted. 'Our government has recalled our ambassador in protest, and Balfour is still debating whether or not to impose sanctions against Serbia.'

'The Prime Minister? Goodness, you do move in exalted circles these days.' When he didn't respond, her smile faded. 'This is serious, isn't it?'

'I fear so.' William signalled the waiter to bring him another brandy, an enquiring brow raised at Flora.

'Not for me, thank you. I doubt I'll be able to finish this one. What are the government trying to do?'

'They have insisted the new king, Peter Karagergevich, should punish the Head of Security. A man called Dimitriević,' He took a breath. 'And please don't ask me to repeat either of those names. I'm not sure I pronounced them correctly.'

'I promise not to.' She smiled at this admission. 'I doubt the king would publicly expose the men who put him on the throne in the first place? That would hardly engender his people's trust.'

'Precisely, although rule by blood is never a good idea in my opinion. King Peter favours the Russians, which means the pro-Austrian nationalists are bound to step up their activities within Serbia, as well as Bosnia and Herzegovina. If we don't contain the situation, I wouldn't be surprised if Europe isn't at war by the next decade.'

'In that case, you must do what you have to,' Flora said, surprised by his candour as well as the turn the conversation had taken.

Lady Vaughn had always described her younger brother as the dreamer of the family who though capable, never settled to anything for long. Had Flora's mother rejected him because she too subscribed to the notion that he was not only fickle but unreliable? If only she could see him now; an impossible wish as Flora's mother had disappeared twenty years ago.

'Flora, I hope I haven't worried you with my mention of war.' William's soft voice broke into her thoughts. 'This is still a foreign problem which we hope to settle before it has any impact on this country.'

'No, not at all. And don't worry about me, I'm quite capable of amusing myself while you are busy.' Her initial nervousness at being alone in his company was replaced by disappointment that their time together might be limited.

'I'm annoyed about it too. I was so looking forward to getting to know you, but I didn't want to postpone this visit.'

'William, you've known me all my life.'

'As a governess to my nieces, not as my daughter. I like to think things have changed between us.'

'We'll still be able to spend the evenings together won't we?' Flora said, surprised by the plea in her own voice. The evening had gone so well and she no longer felt awkward in his company, which made her determined to make the best of whatever time he could spare.

'I sincerely hope so.' He replaced his glass on the table and covered her hand with his. 'Now, as that's the second yawn you've smothered in the last five minutes, I think it's time to take you home.' He scraped back his chair and rose. 'Besides, the waiters have been eyeing us for the last quarter hour from the kitchen door.'

Chapter 5

William waved down a passing hansom cab on the corner of Charlotte Street, by which time Flora was yawning in earnest. The rhythmic clop of horse's hooves sent her into a light doze on the journey back to Prince Albert Mansions. William nudged her awake as the cab drew to a halt at the kerb.

'I wonder what's going on over there?' He nodded towards an alley that ran down the side of a hotel on the corner.

'Hmm – where?' Flora murmured through a yawn, heaved upright and stretched her stiff neck muscles.

A knot of curious onlookers were being held back by several policemen; while another stood guard at the end of the street, feet apart and hands behind his back. A horse-drawn black police van stood beneath the greenish-blue glow from the gaslights at the end of the alley.

'Perhaps something has happened at the hotel next door?'

'I don't think so.' William leapt onto the pavement, handed the fare to the driver through the hatch in the roof, then extended a hand and helped her down the step. 'They've blocked the entrance to Old Barrack Yard.'

'A barracks?' Flora pulled her collar tighter against the icy wind that insinuated itself under her coat. 'Are there soldiers billeted there?'

'Not for the last seventy years. The barracks are unused now, but the building at the end of the alley was once the Duke of Wellington's officers' mess for the infantry regiment. It was so popular, even the last King George was a frequent visitor, so it was opened in '18 as a public house, called, I believe, The

Guardsman. After Waterloo, the name was changed to honour the Grenadier Guards who distinguished themselves there.'

'You *are* a fount of information, first theatres and now soldiers.' He greeted her comment with a sardonic lift of an eyebrow and hoping she had not offended him, added, 'Which delights me, in that I love London and its history is so rich, there's always something new to learn. And what better teacher than you.' She shivered as a gust of wind threated to remove her hat. 'Let's get inside, it's freezing out here.'

'That's far too much flattery, but you're forgiven.' William tucked her arm through his as they set off along the path lit by welcoming lights from the lobby where the porter stood holding open the door.

'What's happening in the street, Dunne?' William enquired of the porter as they stepped into the well-lit entrance.

'We've had a little bit of excitement this evening, sir.' The porter's eyes glinted as he prepared to share his superior knowledge. 'They've discovered the body of a young woman in the alley... Strangled.'

'Gracious, when did that happen?' Flora had been on her way to the apartment's front door but returned to the counter.

''Bout eleven or so. First I heard of it was the whistles.' Dunne scanned the desk with a frown. 'I have a card here from the detective in charge. Name of Maddox. He says he'll be here in the morning to interview all the residents who weren't at home this evening. Asks that everyone makes themselves available.' He held the card by a corner and held it out as if the idea of the residents being given orders from the constabulary was distasteful.

'Do the police know who the dead woman is?' William fingered the card thoughtfully.

'I'm thinking they don't know any more than I do, sir.' Dunne lowered his voice and looked past them towards the doors, though they were the only occupants. 'I doubt she was a lady of quality.'

'What makes you say that?' Flora asked in response to his smug, knowing expression.

'Stands to reason, Miss. There's nothing in the Yard but the school and The Grenadier public house.' His flabby chin telescoped into his neck. 'Everyone knows a lady wouldn't be seen there alone late at night. Unless she was up to no good, if you understand me.'

'What makes you think she was on her own?' Flora demanded 'There could have been someone with her. Have they questioned the other patrons?'

'Can't say, Miss. I just assumed—' the porter broke off, flushing.

'Exactly. It's slanderous to make assumptions without proof.'

'Thank you, Dunne.' William gripped Flora's upper arm. 'Come on, Flora. It's getting late.'

'I was only—'

'I know what you were doing,' he whispered, guiding her gently across the lobby to his front door. 'Perhaps the victim didn't require a champion, much less deserved one.'

'Even so.' Flora sniffed as he helped her out of her coat and hung it beside the front door.

'Would you like some cocoa or something before you retire?' William asked. 'I told Randall not to wait up but I could rouse him if you wish.'

'I wouldn't dream of it, and thank you, but no. I wouldn't mind your company for a little while though.' The thought that a woman had been brutally killed not fifty yards from

43

where they stood made Flora unwilling to be left alone, although her eyelids felt heavy and she had fallen asleep in the hansom. 'I cannot stop thinking about that poor woman they found.'

'Ah, yes. Dreadful business,' he spoke absently as if he had already forgotten about it. 'One doesn't expect such things to happen in Knightsbridge. Though not everyone regards this area as desirable. One of my more aristocratic neighbours moved out recently because of the underground station being constructed further down the street. She thought it would lower the tone.'

'She'll imagine she was proved right now there's been a murder here.' Flora fought another yawn, but lost. 'You're right, I ought to get to bed.

William escorted her along the corridor, and halted outside the door to her room. He looked about to hug her but at the last second, gave her shoulder a pat and dropped his arms to his sides. 'I wanted you to know that I'm really glad you're here, Flora.'

'So am I. Thank you for this evening, I really enjoyed myself.' She was about to add excluding the murder next door, but thought better of it. She pushed open her door, turning back at the last second before going inside. 'Goodnight, William.'

His parting smile didn't reach his eyes, which told her he didn't like the fact she called him by his given name.

'At last, Missus.' Sally's strident voice came from inside the room. 'I thought you were never coming. I'm yawnin' me 'ead off in 'ere.'

William frowned at the door, looked about to speak, then changed his mind, skirted a small wave and retraced his steps along the hall.

Flora stood watching him, annoyed with herself for being hurtful. She could hardly call him 'Uncle' anymore but was uncomfortable calling him anything else. Maybe she should mention it at breakfast? Or would that make the situation worse? Unable to reach a solution, she exhaled with a sigh and turned to matters over which she had some control.

'Now Sally,' she closed the door and leaned against it. 'We need to have another talk about when you should remain silent in company.'

*

'I don't want you to worry about what went on last night, Sally.' Flora attempted to sound reassuring as her maid dressed her the next morning. 'I imagine the porter keeps a wary eye open for strangers in the block.'

'I didn't know anything about it 'til those coppers came banging on the door.' Sally tutted as she arranged petticoats in the dressers drawers. 'Thought they was going to break in for a minute. Don't they know what doorbells are for?'

'Mr William thinks most of the residents were out last night,' Flora said. 'I take it the police questioned the staff?'

'Flatfoots crawling all over the place,' Sally completed her train of thought. 'Blagging cups of tea in the kitchen. Crafty lot.' She folded Flora's negligee, smoothing the silk with her hands. 'Anyway, in my experience, it ain't strangers who does people in.'

'*Aren't*, Sally,' Flora said automatically, though she couldn't fault her maid's logic. Even in her own experience, she found this to be true.

'Let me redo your hair, Miss Flora. It's all coming down at the back.' Sally tucked the negligee beneath a pillow, then positioned herself behind Flora's chair at the dresser.

'My fault, I'm afraid.' Flora relaxed into Sally's firm, busy hands. She had already been dressed once that morning, but at the last moment, had panicked that her grey silk was too dowdy and had insisted Sally bring out the green skirt and white blouse with pearl buttons, thus dislodging all the maid's hard work on her hair.

'Good play last night, were it?' Sally asked as she picked pins out of Flora's curls.

'The play was most enjoyable,' Flora chose not to correct her this time. 'Although not what you would call a glamorous show. The cast all wore ordinary clothes when I was looking forward to seeing some extravagant costumes.'

'Ordinary to you maybe, Missus, but not for the likes o' me.'

'You can drop the "poor little me" attitude.' Flora narrowed her eyes at Sally's sullen reflection in her dresser mirror. 'I was a governess before I married, don't forget.'

'Not likely to, not when the mistress keeps reminding all of us staff,' Sally muttered, then brighter. 'I went to the Vaudeville once to see that Marie Lloyd. Though we were sat right up in the gods, so it could've been Queen Alexandra for all I saw of 'er.'

An image of the Queen singing 'The Boy I Love is Up in the Gallery' to an enraptured audience sprang into Flora's head and she stifled a giggle.

*

Randall produced an impressive spread at breakfast, complete with hot and cold dishes, soft rolls, toast and two varieties of marmalade. 'To welcome you to Prince Albert Mansions, Miss,' he said when she exclaimed at the row of bubbling bain-maries on the sideboard.

'That's most thoughtful of you, Randall.' Flora took the chair he held out for her with relief, hoping he didn't notice the sudden wave of nausea evoked by the cloying smell of hot fat and cooked eggs. 'However, I doubt I'll do all this much justice. I'm still recovering from the excellent dinner we had last evening.'

'Don't worry about that, Miss Flora.'

Randall replenished the coffee pot from a kettle set above a flame, then poured another cup which he handed her. 'Mr Osborne always enjoys a hearty breakfast.'

'Indeed, I do.' William turned from the sideboard, a full coffee cup in one hand and a plate piled with toast in the other. 'Randall is trying to make me into a homebody with his excellent cooking.' William resumed his chair and reached for the butter dish. 'Did you sleep well, Flora? You look a little heavy-eyed.'

'Very well, it's just I'm still not accustomed to these electric lights.'

'I'm surprised Bunny's enthusiasm for new innovations hasn't extended to having electricity fitted in Richmond.'

'Believe me, he's tried, but his mother won't hear of it. In her opinion it's not only dangerous, but a conspiracy among scientists to control our brains. She feels the same way about wireless telegraphy.' The warm, yeasty smell of the basket of soft rolls on the table called to her and she helped herself to one.

'This coffee is excellent, Randall.' Flora hoped the compliment would compensate for her lack of appreciation for his food. The ploy appeared to work as the butler accompanied his parting bow with a slightly puffed out chest. 'Has there been any more news about that poor woman who died last night?' she asked when they were alone again.

'The police were back again early this morning, but by all accounts they have discovered very little.' William poured milk into his cup.

'Didn't anyone see anything?' Flora tore off a piece of roll and popped it into her mouth.

'Apparently not, and it was a bitterly cold night, so most of the staff stayed huddled round the fire in the communal sitting room.'

'Have they any idea yet who the dead woman was?'

Randall returned with a dish of blackcurrant jam that he placed at Flora's elbow.

'Another of my favourites, Randall. You must be psychic, or have you been doing your research?'

'I aim to please, Miss Flora.' He waggled his fingers in the air. 'And in answer to your question, I'm certain the victim wasn't from this building.' His expression became pained as if the notion of murder tainted his domain. 'The police think she might have been a member of the staff or maybe a guest of the Alexandra Hotel next door.' He broke off at the sound of the doorbell and turned to William, 'Excuse me, sir. Are you at home?'

William set down his cup. 'That's probably Gordon. Let him in, would you?' He consulted his half-hunter. 'I suppose I must hang about for a while until the police get here.'

'Randall seems well informed,' Flora said as the door closed.

'He has an impressive network of contacts in this building who keep him up to date. He ought to go into espionage.'

They were still smiling at this observation when Randall showed Mr Gordon into the room, looking much as he had the previous day. His black suit jacket buttoned to the neck, highly polished shoes and a leather briefcase held like a shield in front of him.

'Good morning, Mrs Harrington,' he greeted her with a half bow.

Flora returned his greeting, uncertain he was the same man she had seen at the theatre, dismissing it as unimportant. After all, why shouldn't he enjoy an evening of entertainment like anyone else? But then if so, why did he leave during the interval?

'Time for a coffee, Gordon?' William asked. 'We're expecting a visit from the constabulary this morning and might need to linger awhile.'

'Thank you, sir, no.' His tone gave the impression he had wasted enough time on niceties. 'You have a meeting with the Prime Minister this morning.' A look of panic entered Gordon's dark eyes as if changing the schedule at such short notice bordered on sacrilege. 'A meeting which is bound to extend through luncheon.'

'I cannot help that. There's been a murder right next door to this building. I have to make myself available to the police. Inconvenient certainly, but there's nothing I can do about it.'

Flora blinked, and peered at William over the rim of her cup.

'Sorry.' He flinched. 'Didn't mean to be insensitive. But it's all dashed awkward.'

'Might I make a suggestion, sir?' Mr Gordon cocked his head like an attentive blackbird. 'You could always dictate a statement recounting your movements last evening, which I could transcribe and deliver to the police station on your behalf.'

'Capital idea.' William crumpled his napkin and discarded it on the table. 'If this detective chap isn't content with that, I could always call in at Cannon Row later.' He rose and strode towards the door. 'Grab your notebook, Gordon, and we'll step into the study. Though I doubt you'll need one with your memory.' He gripped the doorknob, but at the last second turned back. 'I'm sorry, Flora. I forgot about today's meeting with Balfour. I probably won't be back for luncheon.'

'Don't worry about me.' Flora hid a surge of disappointment. 'I doubt I could compete with the Prime Minister in any case.'

She was halfway through her second cup of coffee when the doorbell sounded again. Randall's round, low tones drifted along the hall, followed by a pause, then William's voice.

Flora rose carefully and crept to the door, curious as to what this Inspector Maddox looked like. However, the man with William in the hallway was not a policeman but the sandy-haired neighbour with the thin moustache she had seen the evening before. What was his name? Cranley? No Crabbe.

Flora couldn't hear what they were saying, but as she strolled past them on her way to her room she bestowed a smile and a nod at the pair. Crabbe's boyish face was flushed and he spoke in a low rapid tone, while William listened, his head down and one hand cradling his chin.

'Ah, there you are, Flora.' William halted her. 'Come and meet Arthur Crabbe, my neighbour. Arthur, this is my daughter, Flora Harrington. She's come to stay with me for a few days.'

Flora took the man's outstretched hand with a benign smile. 'Nice to meet you.'

'A pleasure.' His gaze lingered on her for mere seconds, then slid away, evidently eager to resume his conversation with William.

Leaving them to their talk, Flora inclined her head and continued along the hall but had only gone a few paces when she heard the neighbour speak.

'I had no reason to connect the two incidents, but with another riot taking place last night, I couldn't help wondering if it was all of a piece '

Intrigued, she ducked into an alcove that contained her bedroom door.

'And as if to complicate things, if what the lady said is true, it looks like someone on the staff has been tot-hunting, sir,' Mr Crabbe continued.

'Have you any firm evidence which would confirm these theories, Crabbe?' William kept his voice low.

'No, just a feeling. But, sir, I-'

'We cannot act on feelings alone, Crabbe,' William interrupted, dismissing him.

A contrived clearing of a masculine throat from behind her brought Flora's head around to where Mr Gordon leaned nonchalantly against the doorframe of William's study. He stood with his arms crossed, his face an impassive mask, though his black eyes glinted with a mixture of amusement and triumph. Or was it a warning?

'Mr Gordon.' Flora pushed open her bedroom door, then before she could stop herself, asked, 'Did you enjoy Miss Jeffreys' performance last night?'

'I beg your pardon, Mrs Harrington?' He blinked as if the question was unexpected. 'I do not understand your meaning.'

'I'm sorry, I thought I saw you at the Theatre Royal.' She cast a look behind her but William and Mr Crabbe had moved away. 'I must have been mistaken.'

'Indeed you were. I do not frequent the theatre,' he replied carefully. 'Especially comedies. I find them too frivolous for my taste.'

'My apologies then. Good day to you.' She entered her room, closed the door quickly and leaned against it. Releasing a slow breath, she reminded herself to be more discreet in future.

Chapter 6

An hour after the departure of the taxi that took William and his assistant to Whitehall, there was still no sign of Inspector Maddox.

'Well, I don't intend to wait here all day.' Flora tossed the copy of *London Illustrated News* she had been reading onto a nearby table. 'Get your coat, Sally, we're going to Harrods.' Without her mother-in-law present to disapprove, she felt quite daring. 'I might even treat us to morning coffee at Fullers in Regent Street.'

'Straight away, Missus.' Sally shut a dresser drawer with a thump. 'Waiting around for flatfoots is no way to spend the morning.'

Beatrice Harrington derided the idea of women dining in public, despite the innovation of a tearoom like Fullers. Several such establishments had appeared in the city over the previous few years and, apart from Beatrice Harrington, no one thought less of the ladies who chose to frequent them without a male escort.

'I've never been in a real restaurant,' her maid said when she joined Flora at the front door. 'Leastways, not one with cloths on the tables and everything. Don't suppose a whelk stand at the local market counts.'

'No, I suppose it doesn't.' Flora emerged into the lobby, where Dunne turned from sorting the post into a bank of pigeonholes behind the counter.

'Good morning, Miss,' he greeted Flora breezily, aiming a vague nod in Sally's direction.

'Has there been any more information about last night's drama, Mr Dunne?' Flora asked.

'The maids can talk of nothing else this morning, Miss. Two have even threatened to give notice, afraid of being murdered in their beds.'

Flora smiled, bemused by the notion the world teemed with deranged maniacs out for blood when a more prosaic reason existed for most murders. 'Do the police know yet who the woman was?'

'No one seems to have known her.' The porter leaned his forearms on the desk, his hands folded together as if preparing for a gossip. 'The lad who brought the newspapers thought Cedric might have been up to his tricks.'

'Who's Cedric? Another resident?'

'No, Miss. Now there's a tale for you.' Dunne winked and beckoned Flora closer.

Sally hovered a few feet away, though her rigid shoulders gave away the fact she listened intently.

'About the time of Waterloo, I believe it was,' Dunne began, his ponderous manner of speech indicating they were in for a protracted bout of storytelling. 'When there was soldiers in the Yard, not that I could remember that far back, 'cos I wasn't even born then.'

Flora shifted her feet and eyed the main door, wishing he would get on with it.

'In those days, they used the cellar of *The Grenadier* as a gambling den. One night, a young subaltern, called Cedric, was caught cheating at cards, so his comrades gave him a beating. They must have got carried away as they ended up killing him.'

'That was harsh.' Flora winced. 'What happened to the men who killed him?'

'Nothing, so far as I know.' Dunne shrugged as if Flora had missed the point of the story. 'Every autumn since then, Cedric's ghost has been seen in the rooms of the pub and a long sighing moan drifts up from the cellar.'

'A ghost who strangles women?' Sally rolled her eyes and Flora smiled.

'Don't take my word for it.' The porter's mouth drooped in disappointment. 'There's plenty who'll confirm objects there disappear or are moved overnight. Tables and chairs rattle for no reason and a friend of mine said he heard footsteps overhead when he knew for certain there weren't no one there.'

'That's a fascinating story.' Flora gestured to Sally that it was time to go. 'Though, I doubt a ghost had anything to do with what happened last night.' She broke off as a young woman strode into the lobby. She wore a pale grey coat with a jaunty red felt hat on her fair curls, a sprig of green tucked into the hatband.

'Can I help you, Miss?' Dunne asked the newcomer.

'Might I leave some leaflets here for the residents?' She gave the porter a disarming smile and delved into a basket slung over her arm.

'That depends, Miss. What are they for?' He straightened from the desk, his eyes narrowed.

'This pamphlet outlines the aims of our society.' She slid a pile of leaflets in front of him. 'Including an invitation to our next meeting. Perhaps your residents might like to come along and see what we have to offer?' She cocked her head at Flora. 'Everyone is welcome.'

The porter glanced at the leaflet and immediately his face suffused with red. To Flora's horror, he snatched the pamphlets from the counter, circled the desk and thrust them into a wastepaper basket. 'Not in my building you don't. We don't want the likes of you round 'ere.'

Flora gasped, too shocked at his behaviour to offer any protest.

Ignoring her, Dunne grasped the young woman by the elbow and steered her towards the door, shoving her roughly outside. He closed the doors firmly then dusted off his hands as if he had handled something nasty.

Flora stared through the bevelled glass panel of the main door, where the young woman was still visible on the step. She appeared quite calm as she adjusted her hat, which had been dislodged in the scuffle. She strolled unhurriedly onto the drive, then turned and raked the façade of the building with a resigned smile.

'Surely that young lady didn't deserve to be treated so harshly, Mr Dunne?' Flora seethed. 'All she did was make a simple request, and very politely at that.'

'Hah! She's one of them, suffragists!' Dunne spat out the word as if it tasted bitter. 'Unnatural those women are. Can't have her disgraceful pamphlets where gentlemen reside. Votes for women, I ask you, never heard of such a thing.' He resumed his place behind his desk, retrieved his pile of letters and tapped them sharply on the countertop before going back to posting them through the pigeonholes.

'Miserable old sod,' Sally muttered to the porter's turned back.

Flora privately agreed as she strode to the wastepaper basket and retrieved one of the pamphlets. Only a few pages thick, the cover bore a drawing of a multi-branched tree topped by green foliage and labelled with towns around England; the whole set on a red background and the words,

National Union of Women's Suffrage Societies in bold black on white at the top.

Millicent Garett Fawcett's work in the Women's Suffrage Movement had always interested her, though she had yet to meet anyone closely involved.

By the time Flora glanced again through the front door panel, the woman had gone. Was she received everywhere she went with such hostility?

'Well, are we going or not, Missus?' Sally huffed with impatience. 'Wearing me coat indoors means I won't feel the benefit, or so me Mum always says.'

'Indeed, we are leaving right now.' Flora shook her thoughts free from the young lady, shoved the pamphlet into her coat pocket and pushed through the doors.

Flora set off along Knightsbridge where the shops had begun their preparations for Christmas, with small fir trees, their roots wrapped in wet sackcloth, set out by optimistic shopkeepers to tempt early revellers. Bow-fronted shop windows full of toys and plaster figures of angels with gold-tinted wings set in artificial snow scenes greeted them with each step.

Her thoughts drifted back to the night before and the scene she had witnesses between Mr Crabbe and the young woman. She had no reason to connect the two, but couldn't help wondering if that incident was related to what had happened in Old Barrack Yard later that night.

From what she had witnessed, it was evident that Mr Crabbe was intent on repelling Miss Lange, not pursuing her. In which case what had he meant when he had told William about, "two incidents"?

'Do you happen to know what "tot-hunting" is, Sally?' she asked, pulling her fur collar higher against the chill wind that made her nose run.

'Where'd did you hear an expression like that, Missus?' Sally blinked, her cheeks flushing an unbecoming red.

'I heard it somewhere.' Flora shrugged.

'It's what they call men who chase women,' Sally lowered her voice for the benefit of the pressing crowd. 'And in most cases catches them.'

'Thank you, Sally. That's exactly what I thought.'

Sally dawdled a few steps behind, exclaiming at each shop to point out the displays of jewellery, evening bags and scarves in every hue from sunshine yellow to rich, royal purple which hung between rows of beads. Tree ornaments beckoned from every storefront, sparkling with the promise of magic to brush away the drabness of everyday life for a few days a year.

A sharp, sweet smell emanated from string bags that bulged with oranges hung on hooks attached to the doorways, while others covered with cloves dangled from red ribbons, giving off a warm, festive smell that helped cover the more earthy odours from the carts and horses on the road.

Blood red holly and gleaming white mistletoe berries added spots of colour to bunches of greenery slung from market stalls piled high with produce outside shops and arcades.

The roar of traffic and the hoarse cries of the street hawkers were interspersed with the laughter of children, who pleaded with a parent or nanny to allow them to press their noses up against the shop windows to see the treasures inside.

Grocers' counters were piled with Christmas puddings and mince pies for those without resident cooks who had been preparing since November. Handmade chocolates, marzipan fruits, and humbugs wrapped up in striped red and green ribbons piled into baskets everywhere Flora looked. Crowded streets were made more impassable by the knots of people gathered on the pavements in front of shop windows to admire the exotic foods, tree ornaments, and gifts wrapped with brightly coloured paper. There was also the enticing smell of hot butter mixed with charcoal from the baked potato sellers, who did a roaring trade from the walkers dawdling along the pavement.

'They smell good, Missus,' Sally craned her head round to stare at a cart piled high with hot chestnuts. 'I wouldn't mind some of those.'

'Later, you've only just had your breakfast.'

Flora eased through the pressing crowd that seemed to thicken as she walked, many with brown parcels tucked under their arms or, in the case of the elegantly dressed ladies, were carried by maids who kept a regulatory three paces behind them. The festive atmosphere brought smiles to the dourest of faces as gentlemen slipped coins into the hands of the crossing sweeper as they passed; a rare sight indeed with Christmas still over two weeks away.

'Is this whole building one shop, Missus?' Sally asked, her neck craned to stare up at the towering façade of Charles Harrod's store, watched by a bemused doorman. Shoppers forced to walk around her glared in annoyance at the fascinated girl who stood frozen in the middle of the pavement.

'The store itself occupies the ground and first floor,' Flora explained. 'The other four floors are mansion apartments.'

'That's good because I don't much like heights.' Sally sidled up to Flora's shoulder. 'Is it true that there's a staircase inside that moves all by itself?'

'I think it's more complicated than that.' Flora had heard about this innovative contraption. 'It's more like a conveyor belt with a handrail. I don't see why we shouldn't take a look. If you pretend to be frightened and shake a little, they'll offer you a brandy at the top to settle your nerves.'

'Even better,' Sally beamed. 'Though who says I'll be pretending?'

Flora led the way through the series of halls, each one an Aladdin's cave of goods laid out to entice the most discerning eye. Ladies paraded between the rooms, exclaiming loudly, while uniformed girls dashed between cabinets to fetch items to show them.

'Look at all this grub!' Sally slowed her steps as Flora led her through the food hall where pheasants, turkeys, and geese hung from hooks above their heads, set beside vast pyramids of fruit and vegetables, some of which even Flora had not seen before.

'Don't dawdle, Sally,' Flora chided when her maid pressed her nose against a cabinet of cream cakes. 'I'm not buying food today. The hall I want is over there, the perfume department.'

Sally's gasp as she stepped through the archway reminded Flora of the first time she had visited Harrods with Riordan Maguire, a memory which made her throat burn. He had been gone over a year, but even a brief, passing memory caused sharp pain.

A full height hall extended into the roof through two storeys, with a gallery that ran round the top, below which two long rows of glass display cases were arranged opposite one another. The air filled with musk, roses, and sandalwood, from rows of crystal bottles in every colour, with names as famous as the fragrances they contained.

'Are those *real* palm trees?' Sally nodded at the rows of wide-leafed plants that fanned out between the shelves.

'I'm not sure. I think the ferns are attached to crepe-paper-covered posts and fastened to the cabinets to make them look like trees.'

'It's grand, just like the orchid house at Kew Gardens,' Sally observed.

'I suppose it does look a bit like that.' Flora regarded the long room with its glass lantern ceiling through Sally's eyes. 'As a special treat, would you like to try some of the perfumes?'

'May I?' Sally's eyes widened further.

'Of course. Don't let those haughty-looking girls behind the counter intimidate you. Many of them started off as housemaids.'

Taking her at her word, Sally proceeded to try out each of the colognes and perfume samples ranged along the counter.

'I think that's enough,' Flora whispered after the sixth bottle had been upended on Sally's wrist, a combination of herbal and floral scents making her cough. 'You smell like a flower shop.'

'But they are all so beautiful, Missus. I like this one best, I-oh—' A bottle of rose water tipped sideways, spilling precious perfume onto the glass-topped counter. As it dripped off the side and onto the floor, Sally's mortified face combined with the shop assistant's disdain as she mopped up the liquid prompted Flora to take pity on her maid.

'I wish to purchase the rose water,' Flora said, at which the assistant gave her an 'I should think so' look, which altered rapidly to a shocked start when Flora added, 'It's for my maid. I'll take a bottle of Violette as well,' Flora spoke down her nose in imitation of Beatrice when she addressed those she considered beneath her. 'No, not the small one, that one over there.'

'Certainly, Madam.' The assistant's disapproving expression transformed into an ingratiating smile. Flora watched her open a glass-fronted cabinet and take down a Baccarat bottle with silver embossed Greek figures encircling the base, hoping she had brought enough money with her, for the d'Orsay perfume was exquisite but ruinously expensive.

'You didn't have to do that, Miss Flora,' Sally whispered when Flora handed her the packages, neatly wrapped in pink tissue paper and silver ribbons.

'I didn't like the way that girl scowled at you,' Flora replied as they carved a path through the shoppers who filled the aisles between the display cases. 'She would have reacted very differently had *I* been the one who spilled her sample bottle.'

Knowing her mother-in-law's views on spoiling servants, Flora tried not to dwell on what Beatrice Harrington would have said had she known.

'Can we go on the elevator again?' Sally pleaded.

'No, you've been on it three times already and we're already on the ground floor. Now go and ask that doorman to hail a hansom. We're going to Regent Street next.'

The hansom darted through traffic around Hyde Park Corner, past Green Park and into Piccadilly, then took a left into Regent Street. They pulled up beside an ordinary-looking store, not dissimilar to the rest of the street, the only difference being the explosion of colour and variety of items on display in the windows. Red and black lacquered cabinets and armoires decorated with golden dragons occupied one large storefront. A row of paper lanterns in primary hues with Chinese characters in black strung across the front of the window. Jade figurines of serene-faced young women and men with plaited beards were set on delicate tables with gold legs that looked flimsy enough to be carried away on a stiff breeze.

'What is this place, Missus?' Sally's eyes widened as she stared through the glass.

'This is Mr Liberty's Store. I've never been here before, but I've read all about it in *The Lady*. He imports unusual items from places like Egypt, Asia, Morocco, and China to enhance the home. I doubt Mrs Harrington would agree, but I would love to have some of these at home. Wait until you see inside.'

Flora led her into a large hall filled with brightly coloured rugs draped in artistic layers over waist-high tables, interspersed with gilt vases and strangely shaped mirrors in all sizes.

'It's all very bright and, well, strange.' Sally started as she came up against a life-sized model of a giraffe. 'Folks want this stuff in their houses?'

'Of course, Eastern style is all the rage just now, and where else in London could you find it but here? Though perhaps I shall need to wait until Mister Bunny and I have our own house to furnish. Think how bright and cheerful a room would look dressed with turquoise and lilac instead of soil brown and sallow yellow.' She fingered a length of peacock blue brocade shot through with silver thread and on impulse, asked the nearest salesgirl to measure out ten yards of the silky fabric. Bunny adored that shade of blue on her and the metallic shine would add a magical quality to the gown she planned to have made.

'Cheerful certainly, Miss. But how would you sleep with all these bright colours around you all the time? It would give me an 'eadache.'

'I should love it.' Flora handed Sally the parcel of cloth and moved on through the store, issuing 'excuse me's' to ladies slow to step aside so she might examine the silks and coverlets that hung from the galleries on the upper floors; the vast hall a blaze of colour which shone in the subdued light from artistically placed oil lamps around the room.

'It's just like an Eastern Bazaar.' Flora craned her neck to take in the lengths of multicoloured voiles and calicos arranged to form a tented ceiling in one corner.

'I ain't never been to one 'o them.' Sally ran her fingers along a carpet on a waist-high pile, tracing the edges of the intricate pattern.

'*Haven't* been, Sally. Neither have I, but I'm certain that if ever I do, it will look just like this, if considerably warmer.'

'Do they really sit on cushions on the floor in those Eastern countries?' Sally pointed to a mountain of cushions in vast wicker baskets at the ends of rows.

'I imagine they must do.' Flora picked up a gold filigree lamp with an enamelled lid shaped like a minaret roof.

'Funny sort of thing to do if you ask me. What's wrong with proper chairs?' Sally sniffed.

Flora laughed, then glanced up at a clock on the wall. 'Goodness, it's almost time for luncheon and we haven't even had that coffee I promised.' She replaced the lamp and headed for the door. 'We had better get back to the apartment.'

*

'A shame we couldn't find a motor taxi, they have more space inside for parcels.' Flora piled her purchases into the corner of the seat of the hansom she had almost lost heart at finding in Regent Street.

Sally fidgeted, rearranging a square package wrapped in brown paper.

'Don't tear that one,' Flora warned. 'It's my new dress. I've never bought a store made one before, but I couldn't resist.'

'Sorry, Missus. These small ones were sticking into my back.'

The traffic in Regent Street crawled along, becoming no better by the time they reached Knightsbridge, the road lining the park crowded with motor cars, carts and horse-drawn hansoms in the gathering fog. A unique combination of fresh manure mingled with fumes from the engines made a unique smell which was, thankfully, dampened down by the cold winter air.

Flora could make out the corner of their building from where she sat and fretted at the fact they had moved no more than a few feet in the last ten minutes. 'Drop us here would you please,' she called through the overhead trap. 'Come on, Sally, we'll walk the rest of the way.'

Jostled by impatient walkers, Flora clutched her parcels tightly and scooted aside to avoid being tripped up by an elderly man with a walking stick. As she set off again, mumbling to herself about bad-mannered people, she glanced to her right, where the sign on the narrow alley beside the Alexandra Hotel proclaimed it to be Old Barrack Yard.

'That's where they found that woman.' She turned to see if Sally had heard her, but her maid was trapped behind three matrons in wide hats who took up the full width of the pavement, her head only just visible.

Flora waited for her maid to catch up, her attention still on the alley. Barely wide enough for a cart, scant light penetrated between the tall buildings on either side, the ground twisting sharply to the right as it stretched away into blackness. Was she killed right here in sight of the road, or further along the alley? Where did it go?

She summoned a picture in her head of the woman in the green coat with Mr Crabbe on the pavement the night before. His words of dismissal repeated in her head, then the lady's softer, more reasonable one saying he would be hearing from her again.

If she was the woman they had found, no one would be hearing from her now. Is that why she was killed? Did Mr Crabbe have anything to do with it?

'Sorry, I made you wait, Miss Flora.' Breathless, Sally reached her at last, the larger of the parcels under one arm and the others clutched to her chest. 'Some people don't have no manners.'

Flora smiled that it was no trouble, and with the prospect of a warm fire and hot coffee beckoning, she pushed all thoughts of the dead woman away and carried on to the entrance of William's building.

Chapter 7

'That policeman is here to see you, Miss.' The porter cut a glance at a serious-looking man who occupied one of the lobby sofas. In a brown tweed suit with a mustard stripe, he looked to be in his early thirties, his forearms on his knees and a black bowler hat on the seat beside him. The set of his shoulders indicated he had been there a while.

Flora released a sigh as thoughts of coffee and a welcome fire dissolved. She acknowledged Dunne with a curt nod of thanks; still mildly irritated by his earlier behaviour toward the suffragist.

The stranger balanced his hands on his knees and pushed himself to his feet while eyeing her with the look of someone accustomed to making snap judgements about people. 'Mrs Osborne, is it?'

He stood an inch or two taller than herself, well-built with shrewd brown eyes that held a look of weary annoyance as if he didn't appreciate being kept waiting. Flora was surprised at how handsome he was, though the effect was spoiled by the sight of the grey and mustard check suit beneath his overcoat. Was the man colour blind?

'Harrington actually, Mrs Harrington. I believe you wished to speak with me about what happened last night?'

'Uh-I did, yes,' he mumbled, flushing slightly, and coughed into a fist.

Flora flicked the porter a glance and wondered what gossip he might have imparted to make the man so uncomfortable.

'Despite being aware of my impending visit, you and Mr Osborne went out on separate errands this morning.' His tone did not quite amount to a reprimand but came close.

'Hardly an errand, Inspector,' Flora corrected him. 'Mr Osborne had an appointment with the Prime Minister.' She waited for his startled apology, but none came. 'As for myself, I had no idea when to expect you. Besides, I only arrived in London yesterday, so I doubt I have anything important to contribute to your investigation.'

'Even so,' he spoke slowly as if explaining to a child, 'this is a murder enquiry. You're required to make yourself available to the police. I also need a word with your maid.' He flicked a glance at Sally. 'I would have done so last night, but she refused to answer any of my questions without your permission.'

One of the parcels tucked beneath Flora's arm slipped and she shifted it higher, her head turned to frown at Sally, who stared back with blank innocence. This was the first Flora had heard about any refusal. No wonder Inspector Maddox was annoyed with them, he must think they had deliberately avoided him.

'Well, I'm available now, Inspector.' Flora regarded him steadily. 'Ask me whatever you like.'

'I'll take your purchases inside, shall I, Missus?' Sally tugged them from Flora's hands and moved off towards their apartment door.

'You don't mind if we talk here, do you, Inspector, er— I'm sorry, what was your name?' Flora employed a tactic her mother-in-law used on occasion to put lesser mortals in their place.

'Maddox. Detective Inspector Maddox,' he replied archly, enunciating each word as if to dare her to forget it a second time.

'Of course.' She took a seat on the sofa he had just vacated. 'Please, do sit.' She didn't appreciate being told off like a schoolgirl. Nor was she going to defend herself with the fact she had waited for over an hour for his appearance that morning.

He flicked back his overcoat and sat, knees splayed, though his raised eyebrow showed he had expected more reverence for a member of the police. Or perhaps fear.

'Have you discovered the victim's identity?' she asked, folding her hands demurely in her lap.

He paused in the act of producing a battered notebook and pencil from the pocket of his overcoat. 'Er-not yet, no.'

'When exactly was the woman discovered?'

He hesitated again, then inclined his head. 'The body was spotted when The Grenadier emptied at closing time.'

'I see. Do you believe she was killed when the public house closed, or earlier in the evening?'

He inhaled slowly before answering. 'We won't know until the post-mortem. The fog was heavy last night and she wasn't immediately obvious—' He broke off and flicked open his notebook. 'Mrs Harrington. Normal procedure is you answer *my* questions, not the other way around.'

'Of course,' she replied with no hint of apology. 'In which case, then please,' she lifted her hands from her lap in surrender, 'go ahead and ask.'

He coughed into a fist and peered at his notebook. 'What exactly is your relationship to Mr William Osborne?'

Flora hesitated, unsure of the relevance of such a question. How could she begin to explain the situation that existed between her and William? Nor did she wish to, not having got it straight in her own head. 'He's my father,' she replied, settling on the simple truth.

'Ah, I see.' He relaxed his shoulders as if he had anticipated a different response. 'Mr Osborne's manservant informed me that you both attended the theatre last evening? Might I ask which one?'

'The Theatre Royal in Haymarket. We left here at around seven forty-five. Mr Dunne, who summoned the cab, will confirm that.' She half expected him to demand the name of the play, but he merely nodded.

'And you returned, when?'

Flora thought for a moment. 'The performance ended at around ten-fifteen, after which we ate dinner in the West End, and arrived back here at around eleven-fifty.'

He scribbled something on the page, taking his time. 'Did you come straight home from the restaurant?'

'Yes.' Flora fidgeted. 'If the woman in the alley wasn't immediately detected, might she have been killed elsewhere and dumped outside the public-house?'

'Mrs Harrington.' He flicked a speck of dust from his striped trousers. 'I cannot possibly comment. And this interview is going to take twice the time required if you continue to ask me questions.'

'I apologize, I didn't intend to be difficult. I'm simply interested. After all murders don't happen that often do they? At least not in Knightsbridge.'

Flora glanced past his shoulder to where Sally stood at their open front door, a fist pressed to her mouth to stop herself from laughing.

'Now.' He poised his pencil ready over a page of his notebook. 'Did you see anyone enter or leave the apartment block at any time last night?'

'Well no, I didn't. I don't know anyone here, I-' she broke off as Arthur Crabbe's face jumped into her head, followed by that of the woman who had accompanied him. In any other situation, she wouldn't hesitate, but she was unwilling to implicate him. She would speak to William about it first, and if she was challenged at a later date, simply claim to have forgotten.

'Mrs Harrington?' Inspector Maddox prompted.

'I-I was just thinking. And no, I don't recall anyone.' She paused before asking, 'What did the victim look like?'

Resignation sat in the detective's eyes as he flicked back several pages in his notebook. 'A young female of approximately twenty-five years of age,' he recited in a monotone. 'Dark hair, medium height, wearing a black wool skirt, a white silk blouse, and a dark green woollen coat.' He snapped it shut again. 'Does that description remind you of anyone?'

'I-I don't think so.' A sudden chill ran through her as an image of the woman's brooch returned vividly. It couldn't have been the same woman, surely? 'Was there anything distinctive about her? A certain piece of jewellery perhaps?'

He narrowed his eyes before consulting the notebook again. 'No. She wore no jewellery at all apart from an engagement ring. In fact, her pockets were empty, with neither purse or handbag, which brings us to the conclusion it was a robbery gone wrong.' His eyes hardened into suspicion. 'Why do you ask?'

'No reason, other than I am trying to help, Inspector.' Flora swallowed, suddenly nervous. 'I cannot, I'm afraid. There must be thousands of women with green coats in London.'

'Precisely.' He scribbled something else on the page without looking up.

'You say it might have been a robbery?' A worm of doubt nagged at her. 'But she still wore an engagement ring?'

He consulted the notebook again, if reluctantly. 'Yes, here it is. Yellow gold, fourteen carat, one carat diamond.'

'Why would a robber have ignored that?'

'Rings, Mrs Harrington, are notoriously difficult to remove. Her attacker might have tried but given up in fear of being seen. Or maybe he simply didn't notice she wore one.' He frowned at the page in his hand. 'Ah, yes. She wore gloves.' He snapped the notebook shut with a final snap.

'And yet she was strangled,' Flora said, thoughtful. 'At least, that's the rumour going around the apartment building,' she added when he swung his head towards her and arched an eyebrow. 'Though surely robbers bash people over the head? I would not have thought many went in for throttling.'

'Indeed? And exactly how many killers have you apprehended, Mrs Harrington?'

Flora was on the verge of saying, 'Three at the last count,' but resisted. She doubted this man would be impressed by the fact, or was even likely to believe her. 'What conclusion have you reached, Inspector?'

He returned the notebook to his pocket, the interview apparently at an end. 'We handle quite a few acts of violence linked to alcoholic beverages in my business. You'd be surprised to learn how many men kill their wives or sweethearts after a few ales.'

'I thought you said it was a robbery?'

'Well – we are exploring several theories. It's early days as yet.'

'Is that so?' Flora narrowed her eyes, conscious she was being patronized. 'Well, Inspector, if that's all—' She rose, smoothing her coat from the waist with both hands.

'I haven't said the interview is over, Mrs Harrington.' When she didn't move, he clambered reluctantly to his feet.

'I must have misunderstood,' she replied unapologetic. 'What else do you wish to ask me?'

'Well – uh.' He flushed again. 'Actually, I think we've covered everything.'

Flora felt a surge of sympathy for him. He had all the presence of command, which in her case clearly wasn't working. 'Then I'll bid you a good day. And as you asked *so* nicely,' she called over her shoulder as she strode away, 'I'll send my maid out to speak with you.'

Chapter 8

Flora took tea that afternoon seated comfortably in a wing back chair beside a crackling fire, the only sounds a clop of hooves and the odd motor car horn from St George's Place beyond the window.

Having failed to find a suitable work of fiction in William's sparse library, she reverted to browsing the suffrage pamphlet she had rescued that morning from the lobby waste paper basket.

Belatedly, she recalled something the policeman had mentioned earlier. 'Sally? You didn't tell me you sent Inspector Maddox away last night.'

Sally looked up from mending a petticoat. 'I wasn't going to let some flatfoot question me when I didn't know nothing.' She shrugged. ''Sides, I had nothing to tell 'im. Still, don't.' She dipped her head back to her stitching.

'*Anything*, Sally. You didn't know *anything*.'

'That's what I said.' Sally sniffed.

'What questions did he ask you?'

'Same thing he asked you, I expect.' Sally drew her needle slowly through the delicate silk. 'He asked where I was last night, and if I saw anyone. As if I spent me evening staring out of the window with all that unpacking to do. Oh!' Her needle halted in mid-air. 'I did tell him about that Mr Gordon coming round when you was at the theatre.'

'Mr Gordon was here while William and I were out?' Flora frowned. 'I wonder why?'

'He told Randall he needed some papers from the study.' Sally tied off the thread and snapped it between her teeth. 'All togged up he was too. Like he was off out somewhere.'

'You weren't listening to his conversation with Randall by any chance?' Flora instilled reproach into her voice, but at the same time hoped her maid's curiosity matched her own.

'Course not.' Sally unravelled a bobbin and cut a length of white thread. 'That Randall asked me to see him to the door when he left.' She sniffed. 'Like I was some housemaid or something.'

Flora raised the pamphlet to conceal a smile. Sally didn't like taking orders from anyone but herself. 'Did Mr Gordon say anything to you when you saw him out?'

'Only that he would call again first thing this morning to accompany Mr Osborne to Whitehall.' Sally licked the end of the thread, one eye closed to insert the end through her needle. 'I told him that Mr William probably knew the way by now, him being a grown-up and all, but he just stared at me confused, like. Is he foreign or something?'

'It's possible, I suppose,' Flora mused, the thought having not occurred to her before now. She hadn't much liked the way Gordon stared at her when he'd caught her eavesdropping on William either. Although that was most probably guilt and entirely her own fault. 'Did he arrive before the police came about the murder?'

'Ages before.' Sally contemplated her left thumb, which exhibited a hangnail. 'Why, Missus? You don't think he was up to no good around in Old Barrack Yard do you?'

'No, I don't.' Flora went back to her leaflet, then something else occurred to her. 'Did he take anything from the study when he left?'

'Dunno.' Sally rummaged through her workbasket and exchanged the petticoat for another, smaller garment where the embroidery had unravelled. 'He had a briefcase when he arrived, so he could have.'

'Ah well, it's not my business, and I expect William knows all about it.' Flora frowned, uneasy with the idea of the enigmatic assistant having access to William's study. But if Randall didn't think it unusual, who was she to cast doubt?

'What's so interesting in that pamphlet, Miss Flora?' Sally nodded at the paper in Flora's hand. 'You've been reading it this last fifteen minutes.'

'It's quite fascinating, actually.' She laid the leaflet on her lap and reached for her teacup. 'According to this, the first serious campaign to obtain the right for women to vote began in eighteen sixty-five.'

'That so, Miss?' Sally raised a cynical eyebrow. 'Shame they haven't got anywhere then.'

'That's exactly what I thought until I read this pamphlet, but various women have campaigned for a change in the rights of women for over fifty years.' At Sally's non-committal grunt, she added. 'No really, this campaign is important and might affect all women one day. Especially if Mrs Garrett Fawcett manages to get a bill put through parliament, which seems to be what they are aiming for.'

'Huh! I doubt servants will ever get the vote.' Sally didn't bother to look up.

Flora didn't respond, but perhaps Sally had a point. The campaign was squarely aimed at married women with property and offered no incentives for either professionals or the serving classes to fight the cause. 'Maybe not yet, but we have to begin somewhere.'

Then something she had not noticed before made her bolt upright. Returning the teacup to the saucer, she brought the page closer. A red and green circle with a white flash across the centre sat inside the illustration of the tree; the words *National Union of Women's' Suffrage Societies* around the circumference. Like a badge.

The woman Mr Crabbe had escorted from the building wore a brooch like that. A sort of badge, albeit an elaborate one. Was she a suffragist too? Was that what she had argued about with Crabbe? Had Miss Lange tried to recruit Mrs Crabbe to the cause and her husband had objected?

She flicked to the next page, which displayed an announcement that the next meeting of the society was that evening at their headquarters in Victoria Street.

If Flora could contrive a way to attend, and the woman she had seen was there, she could stop worrying. That didn't help the poor creature found in Old Barrack Yard, but it would set Flora's mind at rest and thus exonerate Mr Crabbe.

A sharp knock on the door preceded the arrival of Randall. 'Excuse me, Miss Flora. Mr Osborne rang a few moments ago saying he regrets having been delayed at Whitehall and will not be home for dinner.'

'I see.' Flora's mood dipped a notch because the caller wasn't Bunny. They had only spoken once in the last thirty-six hours, a brief, unsatisfactory conversation to let him know she had arrived safely. 'Is Mr Osborne still on the line?' she asked in a tone brighter than she felt.

'No, Miss Flora. He was on his way to an important meeting.' His tone implied that Randall regarded his time too precious to be wasted carrying messages.

'In that case, please don't bother to prepare dinner for us. Sally and I will eat out.'

'As you wish.' His gaze briefly slid over Sally, his upper lip curled. Or had she imagined that?

'Well, Missus, that sounds good to me.' Sally hunched her shoulders in delight.

'I'm sorry to disappoint you, but I doubt it will be that exciting.' Flora waved the pamphlet in the air before discarding it onto the table. 'We're going to a meeting of the National Union of Women's Suffrage Societies.'

Sally's hands dropped into her lap, crushing the garment into a crumpled heap. 'Whatever for?'

'Don't scowl at me like that,' Flora chided, though a laugh bubbled into her throat. 'It might be interesting, not to mention educational. And it says here that refreshments are being served.'

Sally dipped her head to her sewing without a word, though disappointment emanated from her in waves.

*

'This is the place.' Flora stepped out of the cab on the corner of Victoria Street and Abbey Orchard Street, squinting up at a four-storey red-brick building, its upper floors disappearing into a layer of fog. 'Although had I known how long it might take to hail a cab, I would have asked Dunne to find one for us. I fear we are horribly late.'

'I tried to warn you, Missus.' Sally followed her into the entrance that straddled the corner. 'My uncle was a cab driver, and never picked up a woman off the street if she didn't have an escort. Said she couldn't be respectable.'

'How many relatives do you have, exactly?' Flora negotiated a lengthy corridor marked with handwritten notices proclaiming *NUWSS Meeting here Tonight* every few feet. 'You seem to possess an anecdote for every occasion involving at least one of them.'

'Lots,' Sally replied, 'but some of them I don't like to talk about.' She halted abruptly and tugged at Flora's sleeve. 'Are you sure I'm welcome here, Missus?' She indicated her smart but dyed black coat and crumpled hat that had seen better days. 'They'll be ladies in there.'

'To be honest, I'm not sure I should be here either. I don't intend staying long.' *Only long enough to reassure herself Miss Lange was alive and well.* She approached an angular woman who stood beside a half-open door who greeted them with a finger held to her thin, puckered lips.

'Hush, please. Miss Sharp is about to speak.' The woman turned away to rearrange a pile of posters on a table.

Flora murmured an apology and gestured to Sally to follow her into the hall. When her maid paused and poked her tongue out at the woman's turned back, Flora grabbed her upper arm and tugged her inside the door that flapped shut behind them.

The room Flora found herself in had long windows covered by heavy black curtains that cast a gloom that the row of gaslights arranged along the walls couldn't penetrate. Chairs had been laid out in regimental rows, most of which were occupied. A platform at the end held eight women sat on upright chairs set out in a semicircle. Their uniform of smart, dark jackets and plain hats made them all look like schoolteachers.

Bare floorboards creaked beneath Flora's feet and dust tickled her nose as she waved Sally into a chair on the back row. Her rear had scarcely connected with the hard wooden seat, when a woman on the platform rose and approached a lectern which bore a large version of the same emblem that graced the leaflet in Flora's pocket.

The speaker looked to be in her early thirties, a trim, upright figure garbed all in grey, with a long face and prominent nose. Her large, expressive eyes swept the room as she prepared to speak.

'Thank you for turning out on such a damp and foggy December evening,' she began, her clear round vowels echoing round the room. 'And for those of you who do not know me my name is Evelyn Sharp, and I have come here this evening to tell you about the Women's Social and Political Union, the reasons for which will soon become clear.'

'I knew she'd be a toff,' Sally whispered.

Flora nudged her into silence, her attention on the woman on the platform, entranced by her confidence and the passion in her commanding, almost masculine voice.

'I will begin with a brief introduction of our cause for those who are new to the society,' Miss Sharp continued. 'Mrs Charlotte Manning formed The Kensington Society in the spring of eighteen hundred and sixty-five. In April of the following year, we petitioned the government to instigate change in the law pertaining to the right of women to vote, receive education and own property. Despite the support of men such as Henry Fawcett and Mr Stuart Mill, both of whom are no longer with us, the bill was defeated by one hundred and ninety-six votes to seventy-three.'

A flurry of applause greeted this information, though Flora wondered why if there was no success to celebrate.

'Not until eighty-two did the Married Woman's Property Act grant us the right to keep our earnings,' Miss Sharp went on when the hall fell silent again. 'Even now, a wife is still regarded as one of her husband's possessions.'

A murmur of disgruntled agreement ran through the room, halted by Miss Sharp's raised arm.

'Not only that,' she slapped the lectern with a fist. 'We're expected to pay taxes on the businesses the new law permitted us to own, but we have no say in how those taxes are spent.'

Another flurry of clapping erupted, louder this time, accompanied by an occasional muted cheer.

Flora listened with growing realization that she had never given much thought to these issues before. As a governess, the cause offered her nothing, but now she was a married woman, one on which William had made a financial settlement which remained hers to spend as she wished, she decided to pay more attention.

Miss Sharp held up a hand for quiet. 'Our Society has affiliates all over the country with thousands of members, and yet we are no further forward in achieving our cause.' She gripped the lectern with both hands and leaned forward. 'Therefore, it's time for more direct action.'

The cheers grew louder, though an accompanying low murmur and a few bobbing heads in the front row indicated not everyone in the room was comfortable with this idea.

'What's she mean, Missus?' Sally raised her voice above the sudden clamour.

'I've no idea,' Flora whispered back. 'But I suspect she's about to explain.'

'I'm here to tell you,' Miss Sharp raised her voice to be heard, 'that Miss Emmeline Pankhurst advocates a more militant movement. To this end, she and her daughters Christabel and Sylvia have broken away from the National Union of Women's Suffrage Societies and formed instead the Women's Social and Political Union in Manchester.'

'Another breakaway group?' a lady called out in a high-pitched, tremulous voice. 'Is that really necessary? Not to mention unwise.'

'What exactly do you mean by militant?' a woman at the rear of the hall demanded.

'Indeed it is necessary and quite simple.' Miss Sharp looked at each of them in turn. 'We hand out leaflets and discuss our demands over tea in drawing rooms with disappointingly little result.' She clenched her fists on top of the lectern, the tendons in her neck strained. 'We refuse to be ignored any longer. We must bring our cause right into the heart of the government as well as the general populace, who regard us a bunch of weak-minded idealists.'

'We understand that Miss Sharp,' a slight lady with a clear complexion and wide eyes, asked from further along the platform who wore her amber hair twisted into a circular plait on top of her head. 'Kindly explain to us what Mrs Pankhurst intends to do that we, as a society, are not doing here in London?'

The murmurs began again, while heads nodded and the crowd conducted conversations among themselves.

'We plan to organize a campaign of civil disobedience,' Miss Sharp replied. 'This will comprise holding demonstrations outside public buildings, disrupt political meetings and smash windows in the Houses of Parliament building and the homes of anti-suffrage members. We shall stage hunger-strikes, and-.'

'Hah!' This from a stout woman in a flowery hat. 'Who'll give a fig if a bunch of women starve themselves?' Her baritone rumble sent a ripple of laughter through the hall.

'You're in too much of a hurry,' someone shouted. 'The Liberal party simply needs more time to debate the issue. They'll come around eventually.'

'Eventually isn't good enough.' Miss Sharp's narrow cheeks suffused with angry red. 'We must demonstrate the need for change through our continued presence in the public eye.' She lifted a fist into the air, and shouted, "Deeds Not Words!"

'What about our policy of non-militancy?' the same lady who had spoken before said, her voice calm. 'The Society has always sought change through official government channels. Through education and communication. We aren't vandals.'

Miss Sharp twisted her upper body and addressed the lady directly. 'Then perhaps it's time we became vandals, Mrs Fawcett if that is how you wish to see it.'

'Ah, so that's Millicent Fawcett?' Flora mused.

Millicent Garrett Fawcett and her husband, Henry, had practically begun the movement. Flora had read somewhere that Henry had been blinded in a shooting accident in his twenties, but he never allowed it to interfere with his career as a Member of Parliament. He had died almost twenty years ago, but his wife continued her quest alone. Flora had always admired her but never imagined she would see her in real life, the heady knowledge making her sit up straighter in her chair in order to absorb every word.

'Mrs Pankhurst believes we have been passive long enough.' Miss Sharp was talking again. 'If we want equality, we must be prepared to do what the men do – fight for it with our fists and the weapons at our disposal. Those who feel the same must do as I do and join the Women's Social and Political Union.'

'Don't like the sound o' that,' Sally muttered at Flora's side.

'I couldn't agree more,' Flora said out of the corner of her mouth. 'And judging by the look on the faces of those women on the platform, they don't either.'

Accompanied by enthusiastic clapping from one section of the hall, Miss Sharp returned to her seat, her position at the lectern replaced by Mrs Fawcett.

Though smaller and softer-voiced than the last speaker, the lady instantly commanded the attention of the hall as she announced notices about the societies' forthcoming meetings. This was followed by a call for the owner to claim an umbrella left behind at the last gathering, a formal farewell and the location of the promised refreshments, at which the meeting broke up amidst low murmurs of both excitement and dissent.

Flora lingered in the hall, searching faces for the dark-haired woman she had seen the night before, but there was no sign of her amongst the women who drifted to the table with its rows of white china cups and plates piled high with sandwiches, tiny iced fancies, and slices of fruit cake.

'Can we go in, Miss, I'm starving,' Sally whispered, eyeing a rapidly forming queue.

'I've no idea how you keep so scrawny,' Flora said, laughing. 'Your mind is never off food.'

'Yeah, well, you've never 'ad to go to bed 'ungry.' Sally's accent slipped a little, a quirk of hers when she talked of her deprived upbringing.

'Go on then,' Flora said.

Without further prompting, Sally joined the short queue that had formed, leaving Flora adrift among groups of all ages including girls, some with enthusiastic smiles, while others retained disapproving scowls. The one common denominator was the presence of flat, enamel badges attached to their coats. A dark red and green circle which sported the same emblem as on the banners around the walls. The brooch the woman outside Prince Albert Mansions had been wearing was of a similar design, but hers was more a piece of jewellery made up of individual coloured stones.

Flora chewed her bottom lip. Was she wasting her time?

Chapter 9

Flora began to wish she hadn't come as she stood amongst the knots of earnest-looking women, cups of tea held aloft as they chatted and laughed like old friends. She began to contemplate the futility of locating the dark-haired woman amongst all these strangers when a young woman sidled up to her, an enquiring look on her face.

'Good evening,' she tilted her head, smiling. 'I don't think I've seen you here before? Is this your first visit to the Society?' She wore a heather-coloured tailored suit and a white cotton blouse, her mass of frizzy fair hair drawn up into an untidy bun.

Flora instantly recognized her as the lady the porter had unceremoniously thrown out of Prince Albert Mansions that morning.

'Er-yes. I mean, no, you haven't seen me before, and indeed this is my first visit.' Flora rapidly searched for a credible reason for her being there. 'I was intrigued by your pamphlet, so I came to see what it was all about.'

'I'm very glad you did.' The woman switched the pile of papers she held to her left hand and thrust out her right. 'I'm Lydia Grey. But please do call me, Lydia, we're all a sisterhood here.'

'Flora Harrington pleased to meet you.' She took the dainty, gloved hand, surprised at the firm handshake on someone so slight.

'What did you think of Miss Sharp's speech, Mrs Harrington?' Lydia's expressive hazel eyes gleamed with enthusiasm.

'Flora, please. Well.' She hesitated, unsure what was expected of her. Unbounded enthusiasm or sceptical reserve? She opted for the truth. 'I'm still new to the idea of women's suffrage, so I need to find out more before I make up my mind. Miss Sharp was very, er—' she scrabbled for a suitable word but failed.

'I know exactly what you mean, and don't look so worried. No one expects you to commit to the cause at your first meeting.' She crept closer, throwing an almost furtive glance over one shoulder. 'I'm not at all sure about the idea of smashing windows and setting fire to property, though. It strikes me as counterproductive.'

'I tend to agree,' Flora said. 'The speaker was quite strident, wasn't she?' For a moment she had expected to be publicly denounced, but the woman simply smiled.

'Indeed.' Miss Grey broke off to acknowledge a buxom lady in peacock blue who swept by before continuing, 'politicians already think we're too weak-minded to make important decisions about who governs us. If we start destroying property and shouting slogans in Parliament, it will reinforce their opinion. And suppose someone should get hurt?'

'Exactly, and women aren't likely to be any more taken seriously with such behaviour.'

'Forgive me, but have we met?' Lydia asked suddenly. 'You look very familiar.' She studied Flora's face for several seconds before her eyes widened in pleased recognition. 'Oh, I remember now. You were in the lobby of that apartment building in Knightsbridge where I delivered the leaflets.'

'Yes, that's right. I do apologize for the porter's attitude. He was quite rude and I told him so.' Flora scrutinized two late arrivals, but when neither was familiar, she turned her attention back to her companion.

'Don't worry about that.' Lydia waved a hand. 'I've encountered far worse treatment. A butcher in Wilton Street threw a ham bone at me last week.'

'Really?' Flora gaped. 'That's quite dreadful.'

'Not as dreadful as women being treated as if we possess no more sense or intellect than a pet dog.' She paused, a tiny frown beneath her brows. 'You appear to be looking for someone. May I help?' Her childlike expression was so alluring in its sincerity, Flora felt a stab of guilt that she was about to mislead her.

'This may sound odd, but I cannot recall the name of the lady who first told me about the Society. I had forgotten about it until I saw your leaflet, which is what brought me here. What I do remember was the charming brooch she wore.' Flora indicated the enamel badge on Lydia's lapel. 'Similar to your own, but fashioned of red and green coloured stones which might be precious, but I couldn't be sure.'

Lydia's tinkling laugh interrupted her. 'That sounds like Evangeline Lange. She's one of our most staunch supporters and that brooch of hers is quite distinctive. She had it made specially. Are you one of her recruits?'

'In a way, yes.' Flora stumbled on the lie, her heartbeat quickening at the sound of the name; the same one Mr Crabbe had used. Was this Evangeline Lange the victim in the alley?

'I'm a friend of Evangeline's.' Lydia wrinkled her nose. 'Well, colleague actually. We both teach the daughters of gentlemen at Harriet Parker's Academy in Lowndes Square.'

'Is Evangeline here this evening?' She gave the room another sweeping glance.

'No, not yet.' Lydia's eyes clouded. 'Which is unusual, because she's always early for these meetings. I said she was keen, didn't I?'

'You did.' Flora fervently hoped Evangeline might still appear, proving her suspicions were wrong. Besides, even if she was the same woman, Flora had seen Miss Lange walk away down Knightsbridge with her own eyes, so why would she return to Old Barrack Yard?

'Did you come alone, Mrs Harrington?' Lydia asked.

'I beg pardon? Oh, no, I brought my maid with me.' Flora pointed out Sally, who had gained the front of the queue and was busy loading her plate.

'Very wise.' Lydia lowered her voice. 'However, as this is your first meeting, you are probably unaware that maids and companions wait in the anteroom next door.'

'I'm sorry, that did not occur to me.' Flora cast a worried look at Sally who balanced a cake on top of an already high pile of sandwiches.

An air of hypocrisy existed among these women, all of whom referred to themselves as a sisterhood and yet the gulf between the classes was starkly evident. Women's Suffrage concentrated on obtaining rights for those who owned property or had an income. It occurred to Flora her with some irony, that had she still been a governess, she too would probably be consigned to the servants' room.

'We don't all bring maids, of course,' Lydia said without a trace of envy. 'However, we tend to arrive in groups, for safety as well as to maintain our respectability. There have been some unpleasant incidents in the streets between society members and the public at times. She pressed Flora's arm in a gesture intended to be reassuring. 'You'll know next time.'

Flora nodded, not sure if there would be a next time.

'Dear me!' Lydia exclaimed. 'Here I am, chattering away, and you don't even have a cup of tea.' Before Flora could say that it wasn't necessary, that she was about to leave, Lydia approached a lady at the table who stood guard over a large teapot, returning with two brimming cups complete with tiny spoons and a single sugar lump balanced on each saucer.

'There you are. It's not exactly Earl Grey, I'm afraid but it's hot and wet.' Lydia broke off at the sound of a raised male voice at the other end of the room where a tall man in a black overcoat had appeared at the door and appeared to be arguing with Miss Sharp.

'I know she's here,' the man shouted. 'I demand you bring her to me.'

A young woman tried to calm him with a hand on his arm but he threw her off, his demand repeated. A second lady intervened in an attempt to calm the situation as heads turned in their direction and a low muttering began.

The man refused to be assuaged. His brows drew together in angry frustration as the ladies kept repeating that the person he sought was not there. 'It's disgraceful that you should encourage a respectable young woman to be out at all hours in such company.'

More uneasy murmurs circled the room until a fair young man strode towards them and took the older man to one side. After a brief, whispered conversation, the angry man seem to wilt. He stopped talking, and after several meek nods, he allowed the younger man to escort him from the room.

'What on earth was that all about?' Flora sipped from her cup, intrigued but not alarmed.

'I have no idea, though it's somewhat of a coincidence. You mentioning Evangeline, I mean.'

'Why is that?'

'Well, that man who was shouting the odds just now is her father. And the young man who seemed to be the only one who could calm him was Harry Flynn, her fiancé.'

'Indeed?' So her father was expecting her to be at the meeting too? And judging by his demands, he had no idea she wasn't there. It seemed Flora wasn't the only one concerned for Evangeline's welfare.

'Maybe that's the reason she decided not to turn up this evening,' Lydia said. 'If she has had a disagreement with Mr Lange about the society, maybe she simply wished to avoid a scene?'

Harry Flynn had returned to the room alone and had immediately attracted a crowd of eager young women around him. His fair hair gleamed and his handsome face sported a wide, 'it was nothing,' grin. Flora wasn't sure whether she liked him or not as he gave an air of being altogether too sure of himself.

A worm of unease crept up Flora's spine as he bathed in the effect he had on the ladies. Or perhaps he knew more about Evangeline's fate than her father or her friends? 'Her fiancé doesn't look at all worried.' Flora nodded in his direction.

'Harry?' Lydia's brows rose. 'I suppose you're right, which is odd as he told me earlier she would be here. Or maybe she knew Mr Lange would arrive and make a scene, so she's keeping away.'

'I didn't think of that.' Flora hoped she was right. 'Are there many gentlemen members in the Society?'

'A few, although I suspect some attend in the hope of meeting young ladies.' At Flora's enquiring look, Lydia smiled.

'Young men are intrigued by the idea of independent, strong-minded women, especially those who don't blush if a man so much as glances at them. You must know the sort.'

Flora did know, she was married to one. Bunny always told her he loved the fact she thought things out for herself instead of accepting whatever she was told. Instinctively, she glanced down at her left hand, relieved her wedding ring was concealed beneath her glove. She didn't want to have to explain her circumstances, especially if this was to be her only foray into the suffragist cause.

'Does Evangeline have many admirers?' Flora recalled the glossy dark hair and full mouth of the woman she had seen only briefly. Hardly a face to go unnoticed in any company.

'Not since she met Harry.' Lydia's voice dropped again. 'Though between you and me, I believe Evangeline is having second thoughts.' Her eyes flew open and she flushed. 'Oh dear. How indiscreet of me. We've only just met, and I'm already blurting out matters of a private nature. Do forgive me.'

'You can trust me not to betray your confidence.' Flora hoped Lydia's attack of conscience wouldn't discourage her runaway tongue. 'You and Evangeline are close friends?' She still clung to the hope Evangeline was alive and safe somewhere, but deep down she didn't quite believe it herself. Her father aside, Evangeline should have been at the meeting.

'She tells me everything. Well, almost. Her father disapproved of her working as a teacher, and, as you just witnessed, he likes the idea of her being a member of this society even less.'

'I should imagine that's difficult for her, not to mention restricting.' At Lydia's puzzled frown she went on, 'I mean, if I was afraid of upsetting my family I might become secretive about my movements.'

Lydia snorted. 'Evangeline does what she wants, no matter what her family say. I doubt she feels the need to deceive anyone. Of course, she's always been indulged, especially by Mr Lange. He adores her.'

In which case, why hide away from her father when she would only have to deal with him at home?

'And Harry?' Flora asked, while the young man held court to the group of young women, all of whom gazed back at him with admiring eyes.

'The match was arranged by their respective families.' Lydia turned to watch him, her head cocked. 'Harry's an easy-going sort, and besides, what man could object to Evangeline for a wife? She has poise, beauty, and money.' Lydia flushed and dipped her nose to her cup. 'Oh dear. That makes me sound envious, doesn't it?'

'A little envy of those with an unusual number of attributes is quite natural.' Their new friendship sat lightly between them, and Flora hoped she might see this charming young woman again. Then the thought struck her that if something had happened to her close friend and Flora turned out to be the bearer of bad news, Lydia might wish to avoid her association.

'Even so, I really should learn to keep my thoughts to myself.' Lydia bit her bottom lip and frowned at the door. 'But I'm more than a little concerned about Evangeline's absence tonight. Yesterday at school, she said she had something important to tell me.'

'So am I,' Flora murmured, too low for Lydia to hear, then louder. 'Do you know what it was about?'

'I'm not sure, but I expect – oh dear, Harry's spotted us. Give him a few seconds and he'll come over. You're a new and attractive face, and Harry likes those.'

As Lydia had predicted, Harry Flynn said something to the group of women, then backed away and made straight for them, his approach the loose-limbed, unhurried walk of a man confident of his welcome.

'Good evening, Harry,' Lydia greeted him with an air of resignation. 'I must congratulate you on your diplomacy with Mr Lange just now.'

'He's not difficult to manage. Chap's all bluff and bluster with women, but a brief word by a fellow and he calmed down.'

'He's looking for his daughter, I believe,' Flora said.

'Oh, excuse me, I almost forgot.' Lydia coughed and switched into hostess mode. 'Allow me to introduce you to Flora Harrington.'

'Pleased to meet you, Mr Flynn.' His eyes were a startling green, though his long thin nose, over a full lower lip, together with a small scar on his chin kept him from being conventionally handsome.

'This is Flora's first visit to the society,' Lydia explained. She looked about to add something more when Flora forestalled her.

'I came to hear Miss Sharp speak. She has some controversial ideas, don't you think?'

'She does indeed,' Harry, said, his voice low, rich and leisurely. 'I cannot imagine Miss Grey throwing rocks at windows, she's far too proper.' Beside him, Lydia stiffened, though Harry didn't appear to register he might have offended her. 'Evangeline, on the other hand, isn't afraid to break the rules.'

'Flora is a friend of Evangeline's,' Lydia said pointedly.

Harry's eyes lit for a second then darkened. 'I don't recall her ever mentioning you.'

'I'm more of an acquaintance.' Flora held her breath, hoping she wouldn't have to tell many more lies.

'I expected Evangeline to be here tonight, actually.' Harry gave the room a cursory glance. 'Which is what I was told before old man Lange got into such a state. Odd that she didn't inform me she wouldn't be coming.'

'When did you last see her?' Flora's suspicions that Evangeline was indeed the body in the alley took firmer root, but more than ever she hoped she was wrong. Though the fact Harry expected her that evening might remove him from the list of suspects. If his concern wasn't simply an act for everyone's benefit.

Harry's eyebrows lowered; the question seemed to confuse him. 'Well, I'm not quite sure. I believe it was yesterday.' He squeezed the bridge of his nose between finger and thumb. 'No, I remember now, it was the afternoon before. We went for luncheon at the Criterion in Piccadilly Circus, then she left and went home. At least, I think she went home. Actually,' his tone lowered, 'we had a slight disagreement and she left me at the table.'

'Disagreement?' Flora prompted, alert for contradictions but thus far she couldn't find any.

'Oh, it was nothing really. I suggested we set a date for the wedding, but Evangeline accused me of rushing things. Rushing things indeed, we're engaged aren't we?' A nerve flicked at the corner of his eye which suggested their disagreement might have been serious. 'By the time I had paid the bill and followed her onto the street, she was nowhere to be seen. I assumed she went home, but then she was pretty angry so might have asked the driver to take her to Victoria?'

'Why would she do that?' Flora asked, frowning.

Harry shrugged. 'Evie regularly flounces off to her godmother's in Brighton. Sometimes I think she does it to teach me a lesson.'

Or needs time away to sort out her feelings. Second thoughts Lydia had said.

'I see. Have you contacted this godmother to see if she's there?' Flora asked.

'She never stays there long,' Lydia interjected. 'As Harry said, it's something she does to get away from friction. She even keeps some clothes down there all prepared. Evie is nothing if not well organized.'

'And you haven't seen her since?' Flora asked. 'Not even to see if she had returned home safely?'

'Er no, but now you mention it, perhaps I should have.' Harry cast a swift glance at the door through which Mr Lange had disappeared. 'From what her father said just now they've been having ructions at home about her activities in the society. He asked me what I was doing here without her.' He scanned the room again as if something had occurred to him. 'Now you mention it, the last thing she said to me was that she was looking forward to hearing Miss Sharp speak.' He flushed and coughed. 'Well, actually that's not quite accurate. She called me a pompous bully and left the restaurant, so I suppose *that* was the last thing she said.'

Lydia giggled, while Flora studied his face closely, but neither worry nor anxiety sat in his expression. He certainly didn't appear like a man who was worried about how his actions might be interpreted. The way he kept scrutinizing the room also indicated he still hoped Evangeline might appear.

A slow dread had formed in the pit of Flora's stomach, though she dare not introduce what she really thought had happened. Evangeline might still walk through the door, although it was a hope which faded as the evening wore on.

'I doubt there's cause for alarm.' Harry's forehead lowered into a distracted frown as several people caught his eye and called out greetings. 'Evie's a sensible girl. After a good old chinwag with her godmother, she'll come round to the wedding idea.' He raised an arm in salute to another young man who stood with a plain girl dressed in navy blue. 'Oh, excuse me. A friend of mine looks as if he needs rescuing from that dreadful bore, Mabel Danvers.'

Flora watched him go, while she sympathized with the unfortunate Miss Danvers. 'He doesn't appear very upset about Evangeline's absence,' she said once he was out of earshot.

'As I said, Harry's easy-going.' Lydia shrugged. 'He doesn't get into a fug about anything.'

'Even bolting fiancées?' Flora asked.

'I wondered about that.' Lydia tapped her top lip with a finger. 'It's not like Evangeline to leave London in the middle of a school term. She's far too conscientious.' She started at something on the far side of the room. 'Would you excuse me? Miss Sharp is about to leave and I must say goodbye to her.' She pressed Flora's arm as she backed away. 'I do hope we meet again.'

Flora nodded her farewell, while she wondered what to do next; the question still unanswered as to whether Miss Evangeline Lange lay on a slab in a London police station, or was alive and well in Brighton.

'That toff doesn't have a clue, does he Missus?' Sally spoke at her shoulder. 'His intended disappears, and he's no idea.'

Flora jumped and swung to face her. 'I didn't see you there. And don't call everyone a toff. It's not only rude but inaccurate.' She slanted her eyes sideways at her. 'Did you hear much of what we were saying?'

'Enough to know you're worried about this Evangeline person. Who is she anyway?' Sally bit into a slice of fruit cake, leaving a line of dark crumbs on her top lip.

'I don't want you repeating this, Sally, and it may mean nothing at all, but—' Flora leaned closer, but hesitated. Would confiding her fears banish or reinforce them. 'I'm sure I saw this Miss Lange outside the apartment building last night. I have a feeling she's the woman they found in the alley.'

'The one who was murdered, you mean?' Sally's rounded eyes combined with the moustache of crumbs on her upper lip made her expression bizarrely comical.

'Hush!' Flora glanced over her shoulder, but no one was close enough to overhear. 'It might not be her.' She frowned at the plate in Sally's hand, empty now but for a few raisins. 'Did you eat that entire plate of food?'

Sally shrugged and licked her fingers. 'It's all free ain't it? And we're here legitimate like.'

'Sort of.' Flora took in the rapidly emptying room. 'Come on, it's time we went home. William will wonder where we've got to.' She took the plate from Sally and returned it to the table, then tugged her by the arm toward the door.

Outside on Victoria Street, two ladies who had descended the steps in front of them were being jostled on the pavement by a trio of laughing workmen.

'Part of the Sister'ood are ya?' one of the men yelled, shoving one lady roughly towards the kerb. 'You can be my sister any day.'

His companion released a burst of suggestive laughter, but the objects of their derision ignored them, quickening their pace as they hurried along the street and were swiftly swallowed up in the dense fog.

'Louts!' Flora muttered, impulse driving her several steps toward the men.

Sally pulled her back with a firm hand on her sleeve. 'No, Miss Flora. Don't draw attention to yourself. It's over now with no real trouble caused.'

The man who had catcalled was being jokingly punched by a companion, who slung a careless arm across the man's shoulders as they staggered across the road in a parody of a three-legged race.

'I suppose so,' Flora said. 'They're most likely drunk too, though that gives them no excuse to be disrespectful to women.'

'I've known less reason for men insulting ladies than being suffragists,' Sally muttered, tugging her scarf over the lower half of her face against the cold.

Beads of moisture formed on Flora's scarf as they waited for a hansom cab, her mind filled with queasy uncertainties. She had depended on the meeting quieting her fears for the woman in the green coat. The fact she now had met her friend, fiancé and a concerned, if angry, father hovering in the background contrived to make the situation more complicated.

Chapter 10

The temperature plummeted overnight, and by morning, the thin morning mist that hung over the city was already a thick, yellow-green layer that left a film of oily soot particles on every surface. Despite the efficient heating system in the apartment, Flora woke to find ice lined the inside of the windows, while a layer of frost rimed the skeletal trees in the park opposite. The boiler in her bathroom gushed hot water, but bathing proved less than pleasant as the frigid morning air cut to her bones.

'I hope there's a fire in the dining room, Sally.' Flora braced her hands on either side of her waist as her maid fastened the tiny row of buttons on her gown.

'There is, Missus. Randall got up early and there's one in the sitting room too.'

'We'll have a real 'pea souper' today.' William observed when Flora joined him for breakfast. 'I imagine it's worse in the East End, what with all those factories belching out coal smoke from dawn to dusk.'

'Isn't Knightsbridge considered the healthy part of the city?' Flora drew her shawl tighter around her shoulders as she sat. 'At least that's what the advertisements for the Alexandra Hotel tell us.'

'I've known it worse than this,' William peered at her over the top of his newspaper. 'The fog was so bad one year, over eleven thousand Londoners died of bronchitis. Eighty-six I think it was.'

'Apologies it's so cold this morning, sir.' Randall nudged the door open with a hip and hurried in, a dish of scrambled eggs and tomatoes balanced on a tray. He had apparently eschewed the bain-maries on this occasion. 'The pipes froze during the night, sir and they need time to thaw so as not to crack them.' He added more coal to the fire, poking the glowing coals with a brass poker until the flame broke through and spread. 'Imagine we'll need more coal today, sir.' He braced a hand on one knee and pushed himself upright. 'I'll bring more from the store.'

Thanking him with a nod, William set aside his paper and picked up his cutlery. 'Monet said, "*Without fog, London would not be a beautiful city. It is the fog that gives it its magnificent breadth.*"'

'Monet?' Flora picked at her scrambled eggs, frowning. They tasted smoky and slightly sour which made her think the fog had seeped into the kitchen. 'You mean those moody paintings of London landmarks that look as if you are viewing them through cotton wool?'

'That's one way of describing them.' William chuckled as he lifted the coffee pot in the air to offer her a cup.

'Monet must have had no sense of smell to see beauty in this.' She gave a vague wave towards the window, her cup held out for a refill. At least the coffee was drinkable.

'Did you find something to occupy yourself last evening, Flora?' William transferred half a tomato to his mouth and reached for the toast rack. 'You weren't too bored, I hope'

'Not bored at all. I went to a suffragist meeting,' Flora said carefully. Then before he could react, asked, 'Would you like some of this cherry conserve?' She slid the crystal pot across the tablecloth toward him. 'I bought it at Fortnum's, it's very good.'

'I would indeed.' He reached for the pot and examined the label. 'I'm not sure how I'll explain your excursion into women's rights to Bunny. He thinks he's entrusted you to a respectable pillar of society, not a radical.' William set his empty plate aside and spooned the rich, purple conserve onto a slice of toast.

'You won't have to explain anything.' Flora eyed him enviously as she nibbled her toast spread with a miniscule scraping of the conserve. She loved sweet things and hadn't been able to resist the decorative pot and its enticing contents, but her figure, not to mention her corset, wouldn't allow such indulgences. It was a source of frustration that William stayed so athletic no matter what he ate. 'Bunny doesn't disapprove of women's suffrage.' At least she didn't think so, but it wasn't a subject they had broached at any length. 'What is your opinion of women's rights?'

'I'm all for them, and don't look at me like that. Did you think I was a misogynist?' Flora started to stammer an answer but he cut her off. 'I'm joking, though I cannot help feeling that harassing the government into changing hundreds of years of traditional thinking in one stroke isn't the way to go.'

'At least that's one subject we shan't disagree on.' Flora abandoned the eggs which had begun to make her queasy and nibbled at a slice of dry toast.

'I tend to keep my opinions to myself whilst in the marbled halls of Dunbar Court. Can't be seen to be aligning myself with the Liberals.' He wiped his fingers on his napkin, streaking the white linen with a purple stain. 'What prompted you to attend one of their meetings?'

Flora chewed her toast slowly, giving her time to summon a suitable response which required no mention of Evangeline Lange. 'Yesterday, a young woman suffragist delivered leaflets to the building. Mr Dunne was extremely unpleasant to her.'

'Hmm, so you decided to champion her cause? Aren't those meetings full of middle-aged, unmarried bluestockings?' He accompanied this with a slow wink to show her he was teasing.

Flora didn't respond, instead, she cradled her cup in both hands, her eyes narrowed above the rim as she contemplated introducing him to Lydia, which was guaranteed to change that opinion. He was as susceptible to a pretty face and a breathless mode of speech as any man.

'Don't keep scowling at me, Flora. I've already said I'm in favour.' William topped up his coffee cup. 'I don't have the first idea of what a bluestocking looks like. Now, where was this meeting?'

'Sorry, I don't mean to. I'm a bit out of sorts today. Must be this awful fog. The meeting was in Victoria Street. At the headquarters of the National Union—'

'—of Women's Suffrage Societies,' William finished for her. 'I'm familiar with the various groups that have sprung up over the years. We, I mean the government, have to keep an eye on any organization which advocates a change in the order of things. In fact it's the perpetual name changes and fringe groups that convinces most of government that these women are too fickle to be taken seriously.'

'Strange you should say that.' Flora slowly lowered her coffee cup. 'A Miss Evelyn Sharp was the chief speaker last night and she said Emmeline Pankhurst has broken away from the NUWSS and started a Women's Social and Political Union in Manchester. Miss Sharp wants to form a similar group in London.'

'They want to be political now?' William raised a cynical eyebrow. 'Do they need a new name because they want to wear lilac flowers in their lapels instead of red ones?'

'That's a facetious statement.' Flora bridled though her mouth twitched. 'Actually, it's more alarming than that. They advocate taking more direct action against the government.'

'What sort of action?' William's benign smile faded.

Flora hesitated. If the Government were watching them, what these women were planning might be taken as a threat. One which William would be honour-bound to report. 'Will what I tell you be repeated in the offices of Whitehall and used against them?'

'Not necessarily.' His expression remained guarded, but his level of interest piqued. 'If this new group intend causing real trouble, they'll garner less sympathy for their cause than they do already.' He held the coffee pot in the air, an eyebrow raised in enquiry.

'In which case, I'm unable to put your mind at rest.' Flora slid her cup closer for a refill, then thought better of it when her stomach protested and shook her head. 'Miss Sharp talked of disrupting meetings in the Commons, and even smashing the windows of government officials' houses.'

'I don't like the sound of that.' William stirred his coffee with a rhythmic tinkling of silver on china. 'Destroying private property will simply make them into criminals.'

'I agree; I certainly shan't be chaining myself to any railings.'

'Glad to hear it. Although I sympathize with their frustration. Were you aware there are just as many people against women's suffrage as are in favour? Not all men have the right to vote either; almost sixty percent of those who pay low rents and don't own property for instance. Parliament won't give women the vote over the ordinary working man.'

'I knew not everyone could vote, but I had no idea the figure was that high.'

'It is, and I foresee no immediate change to that either. I understand the women's frustration after forty years of campaigning, but violence is not the way to sway public opinion.'

'Do you think women will ever get the vote?'

'I do, but by the natural evolution of a modern society – and patience.'

'That's a politician's answer,' Flora said. 'Promising everything will come to those who wait, but in the meantime giving away nothing.'

'Jam tomorrow, you mean?' William tapped his copy of *The Times* that sat, neatly ironed beside his plate. 'There's a report of the murder in Old Barrack Yard in the newspaper, together with an artist's sketch of the victim.'

'Does it say who she was?' Her more compassionate side hoped it looked nothing like Evangeline Lange.

'No, she still hasn't been named.' William pushed the paper towards her, where it lay beckoning on the tablecloth. 'Dreadful really. The report suggests that because she was found outside a public house, she must have dubious morals.'

'How could they make such an assumption?' Flora's cup clattered into its saucer and she reached for the newspaper.

The story of the body found in Old Barrack Yard hadn't even made the front page but occupied page five, beneath a small black headline that read, *'Woman Done to Death Outside Public House'*, below which was a pen-and-ink drawing of a female face with ill-defined features. Apart from the dark hair, the sketch bore little more than a passing resemblance to Miss Lange.

'That's hacks for you,' William said, distracting her. 'With no facts to hand they make them up. And if shades of the

Ripper can be included somewhere, even better. Sensationalism sells newspapers, I'm afraid.'

'Surely they don't imagine putting her fate down as a hazard of her employment means they need not investigate it properly?' Her knuckles whitened on the page as her ire rose. 'No one knows if she was a – a...' Flora searched for a suitable phrase. 'A lady of the night. She's still someone's daughter, wife, or sweetheart.'

'Don't upset yourself, Flora. After all, it isn't as if you knew her.'

'Why does everyone always say that?' Flora pouted. 'What does it matter whether she was a stranger or a close relative? She was a human being whose life has been cut prematurely short. I'm being a compassionate, concerned citizen.'

William's response was cut off at Randall's arrival with a thin pile of letters he placed beside William's plate, a single envelope next to Flora's. At the sound of the doorbell, he bowed quickly and left.

'That'll be Gordon, I expect.' William shuffled through the pile of letters. 'He's always dead on time.'

Flora' spirits lifted at the sight of Bunny's handwriting on the letter and momentarily the newspaper was forgotten. 'Your Mr Gordon is very conscientious, isn't he?' she said carefully, recalling what Sally had said about his late night visit. 'Are all your employees like him?'

'He does have an uncanny knack of being always available. Whenever I want a quiet moment in my office, somehow I always find him at the door. Why do you ask? Did he catch you doing something you would rather not reveal, Flora?'

'Well no, I—' Did he know she had eavesdropped on him and Arthur Crabbe yesterday?

'Don't answer that,' William cut across her, laughing. 'I wasn't being serious.'

She exhaled a relieved sigh. 'It's just that Sally told me he called here when we were at the theatre the other night.' Flora studied his face for a reaction. 'Something about needing some papers from your study.'

William's eyes darkened and the corner of the left one twitched. 'Ah, yes. I had completely forgotten.' He scraped back his chair and fiddled with his shirt cuff. 'I'm taking luncheon with Lord Lansdowne, and it's bound to go on all afternoon.'

'Oh? No Prime Minister today? Have you been demoted?'

'Sauce.' He gave a mock-affronted sniff. 'Balfour is busy with domestic problems at the moment, so he tends to leave policy to his Foreign Secretary.'

He consulted his pocket watch, then checked it against the clock. The action so reminiscent of Riordan Maguire, Flora's heart twisted. No matter how hard she tried, she couldn't remove the man who had raised her from the box in her head labelled 'father'.

'We're having problems with foreign agitators starting fights in the East End, so I might be late home again tonight.' William made for the door, his unopened post in his hand. 'Better not keep Gordon waiting, he gets edgy if I spoil his schedule.' He reached for the doorknob, then turned back, his shoulders slumped. 'I feel awful for neglecting you, Flora. Will you be able to amuse yourself again today?'

'I'm sure I'll think of something,' Flora instilled disappointment into her voice, but secretly she relished the time to herself. Especially now she had an interesting case to investigate. 'Please don't worry, it cannot be helped.'

'I'll do my utmost to be back in time for dinner.'

'I'll look forward to it. Now go, Gordon is waiting.' For reasons she couldn't define it came as a relief not to have to exchange pleasantries with William's assistant.

Flora read the article properly this time, which proved unenlightening, the journalist's literary bent having ended with the lurid headline, followed by a brief, uninformative description of the scene and the fact that, so far, no witnesses had come forward.

She laid the paper down again with a sigh. There must be some way she could find out the identity of the woman, which would hopefully prove Evangeline Lange was still alive and well.

Although the prospect didn't appeal, she made the only decision which made sense. She would go to Cannon Row and ask to speak to Inspector Maddox. Not that what she had seen amounted to much, though if the dead woman *was* Evangeline Lange, the police would have somewhere to begin in finding out what had happened to her.

*

'Where are we going today, Miss Flora?' Sally followed her into the lobby, her chin tucked in as she fastened her coat. Sally always called her 'Miss Flora' when angling for something, and 'Missus' when expressing criticism or annoyance.

'I've an errand to run this morning, Sally. Would you ask Mr Dunne to summon a cab?' She folded Bunny's letter and slipped it into her coat pocket, intending to read it on the way to the police station. 'How would you like the morning off? A walk in the park might be pleasant.'

'It's freezing out there, Missus.' Sally's mouth clamped into a thin line. 'You wouldn't want me to go catching a cold and not be able to work.'

'No, we wouldn't want that.' Flora thought quickly as she approached the porter's desk. 'If I let you have some of your wages, you could browse those shops we saw yesterday?'

'Oh well, that's different.' Sally's good humour returned, just as Flora's attention was caught by the sound of brisk footsteps from above as Arthur Crabbe descended the stairs.

'Good morning, Mr Crabbe.' Flora took in his slightly dishevelled appearance which looked as if he had dressed in a hurry. His shirt collar was limp and an angry-looking graze about an inch long sat beside his mouth.

He blinked, startled at first, then as an afterthought raised his hat. 'Mrs Harrington.' He inclined his head, his smile forced as he made his way to the porter's desk. 'I trust you're enjoying your stay?' He collected his post from the piles lined up on the desk, giving each envelope a cursory glance.

'Apart from what happened the other night, I am rather.' Flora nodded towards the newspaper he held in his hand, folded open to the sketch of the murder victim. 'Mr Osborne and I were discussing that same report over breakfast.'

'Ah, yes. Most unfortunate.' Mr Crabbe eyed the door to the apartment she had just left. 'Is Mr Osborne at home? I have something I need to discuss with him.' He nodded to Sally, who bobbed a curtsey though she made no move to leave.

'He's already left for the office with Mr Gordon,' Flora said. 'Is it important?'

'Never mind.' He frowned, confused for a moment as if he hadn't thought of this possibility. 'I shall most likely catch him later.'

'You know,' Flora halted him as he was about to turn away, 'I thought the sketch of the dead woman looked familiar.' She indicated the newspaper. 'In fact, it reminded me of someone I saw leaving the building the other day.'

'What?' The colour left his face as he followed Flora's look. 'I doubt that. This sketch could be of anyone.' He tucked the newspaper beneath his arm so the picture was no longer visible. 'Ah well, I had better get off, I'm running later than I thought.'

Mr Dunne sprang forward and held open the door for him, but Mr Crabbe barely acknowledged him.

'Your motor taxi is waiting outside, Miss.' Dunne released the door that flapped shut and returned to the counter. 'Hope that's all right for you.'

'Oh, yes, I don't mind motor cars.' Flora nodded her thanks. 'My husband is something of an enthusiast.'

'Looked like Mr C had another bad night.'

'Really?' Flora turned to watch Mr Crabb's receding figure as he descended the front steps. 'What do you mean by another one?'

'Insomnia, you know.' He rested an elbow on the counter and leaned conspiratorially towards her. 'Takes himself off for late night walks on occasion. He's out after midnight sometimes.'

'Do you happen to know if he took one of these walks on the evening of the murder?' Flora drifted back to the counter, aware of Sally nearby in full listening pose. Flora contemplated dismissing her but didn't want to distract Mr Dunne from their conversation.

'Let me see now.' He rested a plump finger against his cheek, making a dent in the flesh. 'I was about to go off duty when Mr Crabbe arrived back. It were about the same time those policemen turned up next door.' The reason for her question seemed to hit him in a rush and he blinked. 'What can you be suggesting, Miss?'

'Nothing at all.' Flora broke eye contact and made a show of putting on her gloves. 'You work long hours, Mr Dunne, and have a lot of responsibility. Your employers must think a lot of you?'

'I hope I give satisfaction, Miss.' Dunne straightened, his chest inflating slightly. 'I get three hours off in the afternoons. Anyone who needs me then can ring my doorbell if it's urgent.'

'I'm sure you never neglect your post longer than is required.' Flora inwardly cringed at her own ingratiating tone. 'Were you on duty when Mr Crabbe's visitor arrived that day?'

'I was, Miss, but I had to go and see to Lady Braeburn's squeaky door, so I don't remember no visitors.'

'No matter, I must have been mistaken.' Flora made a show of pulling on her gloves. 'What is Mrs Crabbe like?' She recalled William had mentioned the existence of a wife. 'I cannot recall seeing her.'

'You most likely won't, Miss.' Dunne's voice softened to a whisper. 'She's a lady who enjoys delicate health as they say. She rarely ventures out.' The sound of a buzzer from the desk distracted him. 'Excuse me, Miss, that's Lady Braeburn again. I must see what she wants.'

'I know what you're thinking.' Sally sidled up to her when the porter had disappeared through the office door. 'Just because Mr Crabbe's a poor sleeper don't – I mean doesn't prove he killed anyone.'

'How did you know that's what I was thinking?' Flora narrowed her eyes.

'The kitchen staff at home told me you like to do a bit of sleuthing from time to time.'

'Really?' Flora drew out the word. 'Did you also hear I was quite successful at it?'

'No. Only that you had to be rescued by Mr Bunny. Twice.'

Flora opened her mouth and then closed it again, aware there was no point arguing with Sally. 'What do you think happened?' She glanced through the front door where her taxi idled at the kerb. 'Man with sickly wife has a love affair that goes wrong, so he quietens his rejected amour before she reveals all to his wife?'

'Him?' Sally snorted. 'Not the type, but that don't prove anything either.'

'*Doesn't* prove anything, Sally.'

'That's what I said.' She frowned. 'Are you sure you don't want me to come with you this morning, Miss?'

'Quite sure, and don't worry, it's nowhere you would like to go, I assure you.'

Flora climbed into the waiting taxi, imagining Sally's expression if she said she was on her way to a police station.

Chapter 11

Flora opened Bunny's letter as the motor taxi made its way along Constitution Hill and into the Mall. Savouring the feel of the embossed notepaper, she conjured an image of him seated at his desk beneath the window that overlooked the river. They had not been separated for more than a few hours since their marriage two years before, and she hadn't realized how much she would miss him until now.

He had never had occasion to write to her since their wedding, thus the brevity of the note came as a disappointment. She had hoped for an intimate missive she might have stored away in a scented pasteboard box to mull over at her leisure. Her dismay turned into a warm glow of anticipation when she reached the last sentence, which spoke of his intention to come up to town sometime during the week to have luncheon with her and William.

The taxi swayed sharply as the driver took them past Charing Cross Station, dodging between two horsebuses as it careered into Northumberland Avenue. Flora held her breath, her left hand clenched around the leather strap above her head. Her heart had only just returned to its normal rhythm when the driver brought the motor to a halt on the Victoria Embankment.

Scotland Yard Police Headquarters resembled a French château with elements of a medieval fortress. White stripes of Portland stone contrasted with the red brickwork that formed the two main cubes of brick, with turrets at various corners topped by minarets. Shaw's masterpiece was less than five years old, so showed none of the effects of coal smoke that marred the adjoining buildings.

The driver did not pause on the riverside as Flora expected, instead, he guided the cab round to a back street past an empty lot where workmen crawled over scaffolding, the traffic sounds obliterated by the noise the builders made.

'What will this be when it's finished?' Flora alighted onto the pavement and handed a shilling to the driver.

'Seems that new police building ain't large enough, another one is going up the same size.' He pointed his crop to a stone building on the corner. 'Cannon Row Police Station is on the corner there. I stopped here so you wouldn't have to walk past the building site.'

'I see, thank you.' Flora hitched her skirt and stepped over several discarded scaffolding planks in the road.

'I suggest you walk back to the river if you want a cab back.' He gave a curt nod, and clucked his tongue at the horse, that clopped away back to the main road.

Flora headed for a heavy black street door opening into a dark corridor that smelled strongly of carbolic soap; the walls tiled to half-height in dark blue, topped by shiny yellow paint. With her bag gripped in front of her with both hands, she started straight ahead, her boots making loud clicks across the flagstone floor.

The hallway opened out into a room about fifteen feet square with barred windows at shoulder height. Rows of pew-like benches were set facing a wooden platform at one end, a desk like a pulpit on top where a policeman stood, his head bent over a pile of papers.

A woman in black with a small child occupied one of the benches set halfway along the room, while several rows back, two youngish men sat. One wore workmen's overalls while the other was attired in an expensive suit, an equally well-tailored overcoat draped over one arm. Another middle-aged gentleman sat with his feet spread and a cane propped between his knees, having belligerently refused to remove his top hat.

Flora wondered briefly what had brought each of them there, then decided she didn't want to know.

'Can I help you, Miss?' The policeman behind the desk looked up briefly, his arm protectively covering the ledger in front of him.

'I'd like to speak to Inspector Maddox.' Flora brandished the card she had purloined from William.

'Is he expecting you?' He fingered the card deferentially.

'Er not exactly, however, I spoke to him yesterday about the murder in Old Barrack Yard.' Flora kept her voice low but the room seemed to hold its breath, listening.

'Wait here, Miss.' He slammed the ledger closed, then went left through a door that clanged shut behind him on metal hinges. Inspector Maddox's card still lay on the desk where the policeman had left it. Impulsively, Flora returned it to her bag before taking a seat on the front pew whilst trying not to make eye contact with the other occupants of the room, sneaking looks at them while their attention was elsewhere.

The older gentleman consulted his pocket watch which he then returned to his waistcoat with an impatient tut. A red-headed young man further along the bench in beige workmen's overalls sat twisting his cap in his hands in rhythmic circles but didn't raise his head.

An officer appeared from the side door with a sullen youth in a badly fitting jacket. He paused in front of the woman who sat further along the bench and murmured something. The youth shuffled his feet and stared at the floor. He looked no more than about fourteen or so, with a livid bruise covering one eye and a trickle of blood on the left lapel of his shabby coat.

When the policeman had finished and stepped back, the woman hauled herself to her feet, drew back her arm and cuffed the youth round the head.

The lad ducked away too late as her palm connected squarely with the side of his head. He winced but didn't utter a word, except to scowl at the grinning child on the bench who seemed to enjoy his predicament.

Flora tried not to watch but couldn't help herself as the woman cocked her chin at the youth in the universal gesture that he should follow, and set off along the corridor without a backward look. The smaller child skipped along beside her, the youth trailing behind, his head down as finally, the door slammed shut behind them.

The policeman approached the middle-aged man, who grunted as he rose and followed the officer through the door the small family had disappeared through.

During the altercation with the youth and his angry mother, the red-headed young man had left. Curious, Flora sneaked a look at the only remaining occupant of the room, a young man she judged to be in his twenties. His handsome face looked drawn, and he fidgeted, alternating between running a hand through straight brown hair, and lowering it to rub his neck. His charcoal grey suit and red silk tie spoke of affluence, as did a gold cufflink that winked in the low light each time he lifted his arm. He wore highly polished black shoes which looked barely worn.

Flora was speculating on what had brought him to a police station when the desk sergeant reappeared at the door. 'Inspector Maddox will see you now, Miss.'

Swallowing, Flora rose and followed him into another corridor, identical to the first. The door closed behind her and she gave it a nervous look over one shoulder, hoping it would open as easily when she wished to leave again.

The policeman led her down a narrow corridor past several closed doors. Behind one a voice rose in protest, while from another came a hard thump, then a shout, neither of which appeared to bother her companion.

'Go on in, Miss.' He pointed to a door halfway along the wall that stood ajar.

Flora gripped her leather bag hard between her hands and took a deep breath before she entered the room.

Inspector Maddox sat behind a scarred oak desk in a room with a metal grille on the window behind him. Set too high in the wall to give a view, she wondered briefly if this was designed to keep villains out or the Inspector in. Papers stood in neat piles on a cabinet to one side, though the desk held only a single notebook beside three sharpened pencils laid out in a row.

'Mrs Harrington.' He rose, drawing her name out in surprised enquiry, then motioned her into the wheel back chair opposite. 'This *is* an unexpected pleasure.' Though his tone did not match the compliment. 'What might I do for you?'

Flora swallowed and sat. 'I've come about the body of the woman found in Old Barrack Yard the other night.'

'The one you couldn't possibly know anything about, because you had been in London a mere few hours?' He lifted a sardonic brow as he resumed his chair on the far side of the desk.

'Yes, that one.' Her cheeks warmed. 'I still don't. However, something came to my attention recently which might help you to identify her.'

'And what might that be?' He glanced at the clock over the door then back at his notebook.

'I attended a suffrage meeting in Victoria last evening.' At his bemused look, Flora's cheeks heated but she refused to be rushed.

'Suffrage, eh?' His mouth twitched. 'Does your husband, or indeed your father, permit you to associate with such people?'

Permit her? Flora narrowed her eyes at him, though at the same time it occurred to her that perhaps she was the one who took too much for granted. Even in this new century, women still needed approval for activities far less controversial than a suffrage meeting.

'The world is changing, Inspector.' She forced calm into her voice though tension made her jaw click. 'Women aren't delicate flowers who need telling what to do. Most of us have good minds which are vastly underused.'

'I like flowers, Mrs Harrington,' he said in a calm monotone. 'They serve a predestined purpose, in that they provide beauty and peace. I would hate to see them changed into weapons. Those suffrage women are dangerous.'

Several caustic remarks sprang into Flora's head, none of which she voiced. 'Do you have sisters, Inspector?' she asked instead.

'No, four brothers. All of us raised by a widower father.' He scowled. 'Why? Is that in any way relevant?'

'No reason.' She shrugged, though it explained a great deal about him, whether due to his upbringing or the nature of his job. Still, he appeared to have a poetic side to him for all that. She was about to ask if he was married but changed her mind.

'One of the regular members of the Suffragist group didn't turn up last night, although she was expected.'

'I fail to see what reason you have to connect this woman with the body we found, Mrs Harrington. Though if she was a suffragist, perhaps it explains what she was doing in that area late at night. I've heard they aren't particular as to where they do their recruiting.' He crossed his hands over his flat midriff and tilted his chair away from the desk so it balanced on two legs. 'Unless you have left out a detail of your story?'

'I don't *have* a story. I'm simply here as a concerned citizen.' The flagstones looked cold and hard, and briefly, Flora hoped the detective might overbalance and fall off, but he appeared to have control of the chair. 'I also feel it's unjust of you to imply that ladies who wish to vote are disreputable and deserve any awful fate which befalls them.'

'Mrs Harrington.' He released a world-weary sigh. 'If someone made it a habit to stroll close to the edge of a cliff, why would it surprise me if one day they fell off?'

'That's a somewhat childish analogy, Inspector. But I haven't come here to debate the rights and wrongs of the suffrage movement with you. A woman is dead and I came to help.'

'In which case, I apologize, Mrs Harrington. However, as you can imagine, the police deal with all sorts. As to your question, might there have been any number of reasons for this woman you mention not having attended a meeting? Perhaps a husband or parent might have forbidden her association with such an organization. If I had a daughter, I would—'

'I think I can guess what *you* would do, Inspector,' Flora interrupted. 'However, I was assured that Miss Lange is not so easily dissuaded.'

'Miss Lange, did you say?' He straightened, the chair legs hitting the flagstones with a crack. One eyelid flickered as he picked up a pencil and scribbled on the notepad. 'Do you happen to know this lady's full name?'

'I do. Miss Evangeline Lange.'

His pencil stilled briefly before he continued writing. 'You are acquainted with this Miss...' he squinted at the page, though Flora suspected this was for effect, as his interest had definitely piqued. 'Evangeline Lange?'

'Not exactly. We haven't been introduced, although I saw a lady who might have been her outside Prince Albert Mansions on the night the woman was found in Old Barrack Yard.'

His eyes narrowed. 'You didn't mention that yesterday during our interview.'

'I realize that, and thinking back I should have. I didn't see it as relevant at the time, but when I saw the sketch in the newspaper this morning she struck me as familiar.'

'I see.' He frowned as if confused, which was hardly surprising. Thus far her reasoning wasn't exactly logical. 'And you surmised this – Miss Lange – might be the victim because she didn't attend a suffragist meeting?'

Flora exhaled slowly. 'I can see you find that amusing, Inspector, even feeble. Her friends who were there also expressed concern as to her welfare.'

'Who are these friends?' He drew a circle in the air with his pencil.

'Her fiancé, Mr Harry Flynn. A work colleague.' She was about to mention Evangeline's father had also expressed similar concerns, but she had the impression Inspector Maddox was mocking her. 'No one appeared to know her whereabouts. Her fiancé suggested she might have gone away.'

'And had she?' Inspector Maddox was busy writing. 'Gone away?'

'I don't know. Look,' she kneaded her bag in her lap, frustrated, 'I said from the beginning I'm not sure the victim you found is Miss Lange but it's worth looking into, don't you think?' *If he thought she was wasting his time why did he keep asking her questions?*

'I have a suggestion for you, Mrs Harrington.' He scraped back his chair and rose, skirted the desk and leaned against it. 'That you cease imagining murder victims wherever you look and leave the constabulary to do our job, then everyone will be much happier. Now, is there anything else?'

'Actually, yes.' Flora's jaw clicked with tension and she refused to move. 'If, as I suspect, you have dismissed everything I have just told you, might I suggest you let me see the body? Then I'll be able to tell you for certain if she was the woman I saw outside the apartment.'

'Out of the question.' He pushed away from the desk and strode to the door. 'Even should you recognize this woman as being the one you saw, could you tell me without doubt that she is this Miss Evangeline Lange?'

'Well, no, but—'

'But nothing.' He held open the door and stood beside it, his focus somewhere over her head.

She hesitated, as something which had been nagging at her resurfaced. 'Have you interviewed *all* the occupants of Prince Albert Mansions, Inspector?'

'I believe so, why?' His interest rekindled slightly. 'Did you have anyone in mind?'

'Mr Crabbe. Arthur Crabbe. He lives on the floor above. I doubt he has anything to do with this matter but I-uh heard he had a visitor that evening.'

'I've made a note of your concerns, Mrs Harrington.' Ignoring her question, he flung open the door and took up a position to one side in an invitation for her to leave. 'Now I'll wish you a good day.'

Chapter 12

Following the cabby's advice, Flora strode away from the building site and back to the Embankment, where the Thames lay grey and still beneath a thin layer of yellowish fog that would thicken as the day went on. A light drizzle had begun to fall, filled with tiny black particles that covered the shoulders of her coat in seconds. Still seething, she scanned the road towards Westminster Bridge in search of a cab, then checked the road in the opposite direction towards Charing Cross.

Apart from a horsebus, several carts, and a private motor car or two, there was no sign of a hansom cab. The December chill crept up through the soles of her boots, and she shifted from foot to foot, whilst conjuring choice insults she delivered in her head to the Inspector in respect to his comment about suffragists being dangerous. Did he think that women invited violence simply by being part of a suffrage group? What century did the man live in, to imply murder was justification for anything?

Thus preoccupied, she had not at first noticed the green-painted wooden refreshment hut used by the London cabbies until she smelled fried onions, bacon fat, and tobacco. The end hatch stood open and four cabmen waited outside in an orderly queue, their horse's reins tied to the metal bar that ran along the side of the hut. She crossed the road to the riverside and insinuated herself at the front of the queue.

'Excuse me,' she addressed the man in an apron at the hatch.

'You goin' to join us for a snack, love?' said a driver at the back of the queue, eliciting grins and a ripple of good-natured laughs from the others.

'A kind offer, but I need a cab to take me back to Mayfair. Could anyone help me?'

The man in the apron leaned on the ledge of the open hatch. 'Some of the gents inside have nearly finished their breakfast. I'll ask 'em how long they'll be, Miss.' He disappeared inside the hut, appearing again almost immediately. 'Man 'ere says he'll be two minutes if that's convenient?'

'Thank you, that's much appreciated.' Conscious her nose was reddening in the cold and she could barely feel her feet, she tugged the fur lapels of her coat up to her ears and went to stand at the Embankment wall. Her breath formed a white mist which dissipated rapidly into the fog, which made tug boats and barges that moved downstream look as if they floated on a cushion of steam, obscuring the water. The hairs on her neck prickled and a sudden feeling of being watched crept over her. She swung round and scanned the pavement, but her field of vision extended only twenty or so feet. Two cabmen's horses chewed at a hay bag attached to the side of the hut, but apart from a few hurrying pedestrians on the other side of the road, she was alone. Flora turned back, but the uneasiness persisted. She was about to return to the hut and ask how much longer she would have to wait when a cabman emerged.

'I'll just pull into the road, Miss, and be right with you.' Relieved that finally, she would be out of the freezing air, she took a step forwards, when the creepy feeling came again as she watched the cabby untie his vehicle and climb aboard.

The sound of breathing at her shoulder sent her heart thumping just as the hansom made a neat turn in the road and guided the horse towards her. In seconds, the muzzle loomed above her, just as firm pressure was applied to her shoulder, sending a surge of panic through her. Her stomach lurched and she was convinced she was about to be pushed beneath the animal's hooves. She opened her mouth to call out, but instead of being propelled forward the grip on her arm held her fast.

'Excuse me, Miss,' a soft, yet masculine voice said. 'Might I have a word with you?'

She whipped her head round and came eye to eye with the young man who had been waiting in the police station reception earlier. He wore the tailored coat now, with what looked like a cashmere scarf and top hat.

The shaft of fear that had sent her heart racing died away as the horse came to a gentle standstill beside her. Flora exhaled in a rush and summoned her voice. 'Do you normally greet people by terrifying them half to death?' she said through gritted teeth.

'I'm sorry.' The hand released her, but he made no attempt to move away. 'I didn't mean to alarm you, but it's quite imperative I talk with you.'

Flora's first instinct was to circumvent him and get into the safety of the cab, but his pleading expression turned her alarm into curiosity.

'Where to, luv?' the driver demanded from above, oblivious to her predicament. 'I ain't got all day. I rushed me bacon and eggs fer this!'

'My apologies,' Flora called up to him, then hesitated. Should she get into the cab and send the young man away, or trust him enough to let him speak his piece? Why hadn't she brought Sally with her?

'Perhaps we might talk whilst driving?' he suggested. He opened the front flaps, indicating she climb inside. 'I promise you I'm not a marauding seducer. I really would like to speak with you about Evangeline Lange.'

The name acted on her like a punch, robbing her of whatever resistance remained. Wordlessly, she climbed into the cab and sat, arranging her skirts around her.

'You have five minutes,' she said, attempting to retain command of the situation, her voice made high by nerves. 'I warn you, that if I don't like what you wish to say, I'll ask the driver to stop and ensure you remove yourself.' *Remove yourself! What did she sound like?*

'Understood.' He climbed up beside her and opened the trap in the roof. 'Head towards St James' Park, my man,' he addressed the driver. 'We'll give you a destination presently. And take your time.' He pulled the trap down again, closed the front flaps and relaxed back against the canopy. The cab did another heart-stopping manoeuvre into the middle of the road, narrowly avoiding a horsebus, then immediately turned right at Westminster Bridge.

'I heard you talking to the desk sergeant when you arrived,' the stranger said. 'Which is what told me you were there for the same reason I was.'

Flora eased away from him into the corner of the cab, though he no longer made her uncomfortable, merely curious. 'Do you know Evangeline Lange?'

He nodded, easing his collar away from his neck. 'She is — was my sister.'

'Was?' Flora twisted to face him, her nervousness gone.

'I came to report her missing and was shown into Inspector Maddox's office. He told me they had found the body of a young woman who matched the description I gave him of my sister. I – I was asked to identify the poor creature, but I did not imagine it would be Evangeline.'

'I am so sorry.' Flora exhaled on a sigh. So Evangeline Lange really was dead, and though the finality of this saddened her, she wasn't surprised.

'Thank you. I needed a few minutes alone to compose myself, which is why I was sitting on that bench. I heard you mention Old Barrack Yard to the desk sergeant. That's where they found her, you see. Evangeline.' He slanted a look at her with a shaky smile. 'I was going to approach you when you came out of the police station, but I lost my nerve. I hoped you might know something about what happened to my sister. Again, I'm sorry if I frightened you.'

'I know precious little, I'm afraid.' Flora replied, apologetic. 'I wasn't certain until you told me just now that the woman they found was Evangeline Lange - I mean, your sister. Her description sounded like someone I had seen, but-' Flora gasped, straightening. 'Which means Inspector Maddox already knew her identity when I spoke to him. Then what was that charade he put me through all about? He acted as if I was deluded and wasting his time.'

'I don't know what the Inspector said, but I imagine he was simply being professional.' He fingered his collar again in what she interpreted as a nervous gesture. She might have been dismissed by a pompous bobby, but this man had had to look at the dead body of his sister.

Flora grabbed at the strap on the canopy, the cab swaying on its light suspension as the driver guided them through heavier traffic approaching the park gates.

'I'm sorry to be angry.' Shame made her contrite. 'But Maddox was most unhelpful.'

'The police don't like giving out information on an ongoing investigation if they can help it.'

'Even so, he might have said something.' Flora sniffed. 'Instead, he practically threw me out.' Her anger dissolved as she was being less than sympathetic. 'That must have been terrible for you, identifying your sister's body?'

'I've never seen a body before. I—' He swallowed, his eyes squeezed shut as if he was trying to banish an image that haunted him. 'I tried to ask questions, but my voice wouldn't come. I got out of that mortuary as quickly as I could.'

'Which is quite understandable, but what made you conclude the woman in the alley might be your sister?'

'She hasn't been home in two days, which is so unlike her. I came here hoping to instigate a police search. Not a murder investigation.'

'You didn't think she had gone to Brighton then?'

'Brighton?' His eyes clouded with confusion that struck her as too spontaneous to be contrived.

'Oh, nothing. I must have misunderstood.'

'Father and Evangeline argued about her involvement with those suffragist women the night before last,' he went on. 'They were both still furious when she left the house that evening and didn't come home. We assumed she had gone to stay with a friend to teach us a lesson.' He ran a finger around the inside of his collar again before continuing. 'The second day passed with no word when Father remembered there was a meeting scheduled for last night. He went there to bring her home.'

'You must have been frantic when he returned without her?'

He nodded. 'We sat up all night waiting for her, Mother, Father and me. When I saw the newspaper this morning, I instinctively knew it was her, but didn't tell my parents. I made an excuse about visiting her friends to see if they had seen her, but instead I came straight here.'

'I see.' Flora wondered how a vague drawing in a newspaper made him think of his sister, but perhaps it was a logical step to grasp at any link, however tenuous. Harry Flynn seemed convinced she would go to her godmother's in Brighton. Which of them was misinformed? Or maybe lying?

'How well did you know Evangeline?' he asked. 'Forgive me, but I don't believe we've met. You've never been to the house.'

'I was at the NUWSS Headquarters and spoke to some of her friends.' She answered the question she had been dreading, her answer suitably vague

'That explains it, you're one of her suffrage group.' His face cleared and he nodded slowly. 'Evie never brought any of those people to our home. Father would have had an apoplexy.'

Flora took a deep breath, aware lying to this man was not only unnecessary but might be misconstrued. 'Actually, Mr Lange, I've never met your sister.'

He brought his head up sharply and pinned her with a hard look. 'Never met her? Then how—?'

'It's complicated, but on the night your sister died, I saw a young woman at my father's apartment building, which is close to where she was found. I couldn't be sure she was the same one, which is why I came to see Inspector Maddox this morning.'

'I see.' Disappointment entered his eyes and he stared off. Silence stretched between them, the only sounds of the clop of hooves and the sounds of traffic around them as the driver slowed the horse into a leisurely stroll along Birdcage Walk, then turned right at Buckingham Palace and headed in the direction of The Mall.

'Where is this apartment building you mentioned?' he asked after a pause.

'Prince Albert Mansions. It's in St George's Place in Knightsbridge.'

'And you said you saw Evangeline inside this building?'

'She came out of the building with someone.'

'Then it's possible this person—'

'That's unlikely.' Flora cut him off. 'Evangeline walked off down the road after they spoke and this – person - didn't follow her, so unless they met up later, he didn't kill her. My father knows him and insists he's a respectable man.' The last thing Flora wished to do was set this grieving man off after Mr Crabbe without cause.

'I assume your father is a gentleman, but that's hardly a reason to dismiss this man as a suspect on that premise.'

'Yes, you're quite right,' Flora chose her words carefully. 'I'm sure Inspector Maddox will talk to him if he hasn't already.' She didn't want to contemplate what would happen if Mr Crabbe denied seeing Evangeline after what she had told the Inspector. Whose side would William take if his daughter and colleague gave different stories to the police?

'I'll have to hope this Maddox is good at his job, but I can't sit back and do nothing while whoever killed my sister is still free.' He slumped in his seat, despondent. 'I simply don't know where to begin.'

'Perhaps your first task is to inform your parents of her death,' Flora said. 'They must be frantic by now, and although it's awful for you, they must be told. The news would be better coming from you before the police arrive to question them.'

'The police will come to our home and question, my parents?' His eyes widened in alarm. 'Why would they need to do that?'

'I agree the timing is unfortunate, but it's how they go about things.' Flora eased back in her seat as if to avoid his anger. 'They'll want to know everything about her.'

'Oh, yes. Yes, of course, how stupid of me.' He blinked and ran a hand through his hair. 'I'm not thinking straight. The thought of my poor mother being subjected to such an ordeal on top of everything else. What with the shock of seeing Evie like that, so still and white, I—' he broke off with a shudder. 'How shall I tell them? My father will be devastated. Evangeline was his pride.'

'I'm sure you are too. You'll be his consolation.' Flora's hand hovered above his for a second, but she withdrew hers without making contact.

He flicked a look at her and away again, too fast for her to read anything in it, but she suspected there was a story there. 'My parents always said something like this might happen if Evie insisted on going to that place. And I agreed.'

'What place? Oh, you mean the NUWSS?' At his slow nod, Flora went on. 'What made them think that?'

'Unnatural women putting ideas into her head. And she was right, it ended in tragedy just as Mother said it would.'

'I don't think you could blame—'

'How can you be sure?' His eyes hardened and he dropped his head against one hand. 'These women aren't simply misguided. My father thinks they present a real threat to society and they deserve a good whipping. Perhaps someone decided Evie could act as a warning to others.'

'That sounds a little extreme,' Flora said carefully. Did this man always agree with whatever his parents said? Was

Evangeline the only free-thinker in their family? 'I saw a few odd-looking characters outside the meeting last night, but nothing that would indicate they would want to harm any of the women.'

'You said you were there last night. At the meeting?' Hope entered his eyes as he turned to look at her, or was it suspicion?

'I was.' She contemplated mentioning that she had seen Mr Lange there too but decided against it. 'I spoke to a Miss Grey who said she knew your sister quite well. Lydia Grey. Do you know her?'

He shook his head. 'I told you, Evangeline kept her suffragist activities separate from her family.'

Flora was about to mention they both taught at the same school, but perhaps her family disapproved of her career as a teacher as well. In which case, Evangeline might not have spoken about her work colleagues either.

'Maybe,' he paused, his hand lifted as if an idea had come to him, 'she was distributing those NUWSS leaflets in the public house where she was found and someone took umbrage? They followed her out, got into an argument and killed her?'

'That's pure speculation, Mr Lange. Which, and forgive me for saying this, isn't helpful.' Though she could understand why he might try to come up with a theory, any theory, to explain why his sister was taken from him.

'No, I suppose not.' He slumped back against the seat. 'I have no idea what Evangeline was doing in a public house on her own.'

'The police said she was found outside The Grenadier, but was there any evidence to say she was ever inside? Is it possible she went there to meet someone?'

'That seems most unlikely. Even her fiancé, disreputable lout that he is, wouldn't expect her to go to a public house.'

'Harry Flynn is disreputable?' Flora recalled the charming Mr Flynn. Or was he too charming? Harry had seen Evangeline the day she died, they had met for tea, or was it luncheon? She couldn't quite recall. Was his blithe unconcern for Evangeline's whereabouts been because he had seen her after her parents? 'If so, why would your parents encourage her to marry him?'

'Because he's about to inherit a title and an estate to go with it.' His derisive snort was cut off in response to Flora's hard look. 'Well, perhaps I used the wrong word. A bit of a cad might be more accurate. He's a certainly a ladies' man.'

Flora made no comment, having observed that for herself. 'Did the police have a theory as to who might have hurt Evangeline?' Perhaps Inspector Maddox had been more forthcoming with the victim's brother than he had been with her.

'Only that she most probably didn't know her assailant. That in his opinion, the location of the attack indicated an opportunist thief who strangled her to keep her quiet.' He pounded his clenched fist against the wood flap.

'That would explain the missing brooch, though if that was the case, why didn't the thief simply run away? Why risk killing her?'

'Brooch?' He directed a guarded look on her.

'The one that resembled the Society badge. Lydia told me she had it made specially.'

'Ah, I had forgotten about that. I expect whoever killed her must have stolen it.' He swallowed, his Adam's apple bobbing against his collar. 'I can't think that was the reason she was attacked, that brooch was only worth a few pounds. It probably fell off her coat in the struggle.'

'People get murdered for much less than a few pounds, Mr Lange. Did the police mention that any other jewellery had been taken?' Flora recalled Maddox mentioning only her engagement ring remained on her body.

He shook his head. 'I wouldn't know, but Mother might. I could check with her when I get home to see if anything is missing.' As if mention of his mother made his breath catch in his throat, he looked away.

'I'm sorry, I didn't mean to remind you.'

'No, I'm sorry. This is all still so raw.' He released a breath in a sigh. 'And this is all guesswork in any case and gets us nowhere.'

'I suppose it doesn't.' Flora looked up over the horse's gently swaying rear. As they approached the curved façade of *The Royal Avenue Theatre* beside Charing Cross Station, she realized they had covered a lot of ground. A gentle rain had begun to fall, invisible through the mist but evidenced by a soft drumming on the canopy above them.

'I ought to be getting home or I'll be missed,' Flora said.

'Oh, of course. Prince Albert Mansions, did you say?' He pulled down the trap and gave instructions to the driver. 'I'm sorry, I don't even know your name.'

'It's Flora Harrington.'

'Very pleased to meet you, Miss Harrington, despite the circumstances.' He thrust out a hand, which she took tentatively in hers.

'Actually, It's Mrs Harrington.'

'Ah, just my luck.' He held both hands up in surrender. 'I always seem to meet young ladies at entirely the wrong time. The pretty ones are always betrothed or married.'

'Um-thank you.' Flora retrieved her hand. His rapid change of demeanour from abject dismay to flirtatiousness came as a surprise.

The remainder of the journey passed in silence, and when the cab pulled up outside William's building, Flora felt something like relief. Her emotions swung from awkwardness at arriving home with a strange man, to unease at what to say to him. To express a hope the police would find his sister's killer seemed an inappropriate parting remark.

'Might I ask something of you?'

Flora hesitated. 'Well, it depends what it is. I'm only in London for a few days, but if there's something I can do to help, I would be glad to.'

'I'm afraid I don't have much confidence in that Maddox chap, so if you recall anything else you might have seen, or maybe remember, perhaps you might let me know?'

Flora's more cautious side surfaced, though she was tempted. 'Isn't that a job for the police?'

'Is that what you would do if your sister was brutally murdered? Go home and forget about it, then hope the police do a reasonable job and find the culprit? After all, they never found that Ripper murderer, did they?' His eyes darkened with grief or anger, she wasn't sure which. He had nice eyes, brown and limpid with thick lashes, though despite his apparent distress they remained dry.

'I don't have a sister, but I might feel the same in those circumstances. If I find out anything, I would be happy to pass it on.'

'I appreciate that, Mrs Harrington.' He alighted onto the pavement and helped her down.

Flora fumbled inside her bag, her hat protecting her from the worst of the gritty rain that formed rivulets in the gutter. 'Allow me to pay for the cab, I—'

'Wouldn't hear of it.' Before she could say any more, he leapt back inside the cab and closed the flaps.

Flora's boots splashed through gathering puddles as she hurried inside the building. It was not until Randall had bowed her into the apartment did she realize that Mr Lange had made no mention of where he lived or how she might contact him. The thought gave her pause, added to the fact she knew nothing about him. Then it occurred to her that he might not be Evangeline's Lange's brother all, though what reason could he have for making up such a story?

Chapter 13

'Has Sally returned from her shopping trip?' Flora asked Randall as he relieved her of her wet coat at the door of the apartment.

'She arrived back a few moments before the rain started, Miss. Though I believe she's showing her treasures to the maids in the basement housekeeper's room.' His mouth twitched as he bowed and left, indicating he was peeved that Sally had eschewed his company for that of the downstairs maids.

'Thank you, Randall.' Flora guessed Sally was most likely gossiping about the murder too and resolved to ask her if she had heard anything interesting.

Over her solitary luncheon in the dining room, Flora considered how she might fulfil her promise to Evangeline's brother without treading on the toes of the arrogant Inspector Maddox. Interviewing possible witnesses, like those in the building, would definitely be frowned on, but perhaps there was another way she could discover more about Miss Lange.

'Randall said you wanted to see me, Missus.' Sally's bright announcement broke into Flora's contemplations. Strands of her frizzy brown hair had escaped from the bun on the back of her head, her eyes alight with new enthusiasm.

'You seem to be enjoying your stay here, Sally?' Flora liked to see her happy. She had been a scrawny, pale skinned creature when she first came to Flora. Characteristics which had made her mother-in-law refuse to employ her at first.

'I need someone strong and capable, Flora,' Beatrice had insisted. 'Not a whey-faced mouse with no energy.'

'She'll thrive here, I'm sure.' Flora had stood up for herself at the time, and had been proved right. Sally had filled out in the last few months, with a new spring in her step and she no longer flushed red when anyone looked at her.

'I hear you had a good trip. What did you buy?' Flora enquired.

'Just a few fancies, Oh, and some of those biscuits you liked. Though I didn't pay those Harrods prices. There's a bakers round the corner who make 'em for half the price. They taste as good and you ain't paying for a fancy box.'

'Very enterprising, Sally. Now I wanted to ask you something.' Flora relaxed back in her chair as Sally picked up her teacup, but instead of removing it, she slid it to one side to make room and took the chair next to hers, her arms folded on the table.

'Fire away, Miss.'

'When we were at the suffrage meeting, do you happen to remember the name of the school Miss Grey said she and Miss Lange worked at?'

'How would I know? Sally's eyes rounded. 'I don't listen to your private conversations, do I?'

'I'm not implying you eavesdropped, Sally.' Flora adopted her most ingratiating voice. 'However, while you were in the queue for refreshments, you might have picked up a word or two purely by accident.' If that didn't dilute a possible accusation, then nothing would.

Sally's eyes narrowed. 'Is that what you've been doing this morning, Miss Flora? Poking about in the murder of that woman?'

'Might have been.' She held Sally's gaze for long seconds.

'Well, see'in as you're asking.' She paused, apparently for effect. 'I might have heard something.'

Flora didn't doubt it but waited in silence, rewarded when Sally hunched her shoulders and leaned closer.

'That Miss Grey mentioned Harriett Parker Academy in Lowndes Square. The maids downstairs said it was a school where the gentry sent their daughters. It's only a couple of streets away from here.'

'Ah yes, that was it. I remember now.' Flora wondered if the fact Evangeline worked and was killed within the same neighbourhood was significant. 'I met Miss Lange's brother today, who confirmed it was her. He was very upset.'

'Her brother?' Sally jerked upright. 'How did you happen to meet him then?'

'That's not important.' She decided not to reveal she had got into a hansom with a strange man outside a police station. 'He doesn't think much of Inspector Maddox, so I agreed to let him know if I found out anything.'

'What are you going to do? Visit this school and ask questions?' Sally's eyes sparkled at the notion. 'Like a detective?'

'I'm hardly that, but it's a good place to begin. After all, wouldn't it be kinder to let Miss Lydia know what had happened to her friend before Evangeline's name found its way into the newspapers, along with all the other lurid details which journalists were so fond of?'

'That Inspector bloke won't be too pleased if he finds out.'

'Probably not. But I don't intend to tell him.'

'Shall I come with you to this school?' Sally twisted a strand of hair around her finger, her excitement growing.

'If it's close by, that won't be necessary.'

'This ain't Richmond, Miss Flora. You can't just walk about the streets on your own. What would Mr Bunny say?'

Flora was about to remind her Mr Bunny wasn't there, but there was William to consider. He might not like the idea of her venturing alone in the either. 'Oh, all right. You can come.'

*

According to the *Baedeker's* guide Flora unearthed in William's library, Lowndes Square, was indeed only a short walk along Knightsbridge, with a left turn at William Street which led into the square.

She left the apartment for the second time that day, this time with Sally. The rain had ceased, though the streets were still foggy. Figures loomed out of the mist at the last second and inanimate objects took on a sinister bent, making her glad she had agreed to take Sally with her. The grey pavements glistened and water dripped from the trees in the central railed garden, while the muted sound of unseen traffic reached her from the main road.

Twice on the short walk from the apartment Flora had the feeling someone was walking behind her but when she glanced back, all she could see was a wall of yellowish mist.

'What's wrong, Miss Flora?' Sally asked, peering into the gloom. 'What can you see?'

'Nothing really.' Flora shivered. 'It was a feeling, that's all. I hate this fog, it makes me imagine things.'

The school occupied a smart four-storey townhouse in a terrace of similar properties in the square; the central railed garden exuding a sense of genteel prosperity. Flora conjured a pleasing image of the pupils sitting over their sketch pads or poetry books on summer afternoons. Would they appreciate their privileged youth when they became women and life offered them far weightier concerns? Most likely not, she hitched her skirt and mounted the short flight of steps to where a bell sat beside a brass plaque that read *Harriet Parker Academy For Young Ladies*.

A harsh jangle from inside sent momentary panic through her. What excuse could she give for intruding on Miss Grey's place of work? She hardly knew her, and curiosity apart, she had never met Evangeline. Before Flora could change her mind and retreat, the door was flung open by a uniformed maid.

'I wonder if I might speak to—' but she got no further.

'Do come in, Miss.' She beckoned Flora into a tiled entrance hall that smelled of linseed and lavender. 'I expect it's Miss Lowe you'll be wanting, Miss. The headmistress?' Little more than a schoolgirl, her uniform was bunched loosely around the bodice, her narrow shoulders overwhelmed by voluminous mutton leg sleeves.

'Well, actually no, I wished to—' Flora began, but the maid ushered them inside, still chattering. 'We've had a terrible upset here this afternoon, Miss.' Her mop of curls beneath a frilled cap bobbed as she talked. 'Miss Lowe is in the common room with a police inspector just now, but I'm sure she wouldn't want me to be impolite to a prospective parent.'

'This policeman, his name isn't Maddox by any chance?' Flora asked glancing fearfully at Sally, who shrugged.

'Why yes, Miss.' The girl's eyes widened in admiration. 'How did you know?'

'It's unimportant, though perhaps I should call at another time? I don't want to inconvenience this, er Miss Lowe did you say?'

'Miss Lowe always insists new parents are to be shown into her office straight away. I'll just let her know you're here.'

Flora opened her mouth to object, but the distinctive low tone of Inspector Maddox reached her from a room to her left. 'If either you or any of your staff recall anything which might be relevant, Miss Lowe, you might put in a call to me at Cannon Row.'

Flora calculated that even if she managed to get the front door open again in time, the chances of being seen leaving the building were high. She would never make it to the corner of the square undetected. 'Where is Miss Lowe's office?' she asked the maid in an urgent whisper.

'Upstairs, Miss. This way.' The maid set off towards an inner hall that stretched to the rear of the ground floor. Flora hurried after her, Sally at her heels to where an oak staircase in the style of the previous century curved upwards, ending at the roof where a glass lantern cast weak winter light onto the floors below.

Not daring to look behind her, Flora gained the first landing with Sally close behind. At the sound of voices below, Flora ventured a peek over the balustrade where the top of the inspector's hat was just visible on the floor below. The front door opened, throwing a rectangle of weak daylight onto the tiled floor, then a low female voice said, 'Good day to you, Inspector.'

'If you'll wait in here, Miss.' The maid opened a door at the end of the hall, one hand extended in invitation.

'Oh, yes of course. Thank you.' Gesturing Sally to follow, Flora entered a neat study with floor-to-ceiling bookshelves to two walls. A rectangular oak desk faced a full-height window onto the square, two chairs set on one side and a more imposing one with arms and an upholstered back on the other.

'I'm sure Miss Lowe won't be long.' The maid bobbed a curtsey and left, the door closing with a soft click.

Sally went to the window and twitched the curtain aside, staring down into the street below.

'Come away from there, he'll see you,' Flora whispered, then in a normal voice. 'Has he gone?'

'He's getting into a carriage so he will be in a minute. There's another bloke a bit further down, watching.'

'Watching the Inspector?' Flora's curiosity got the better of her and she joined her at the window.

A man in a charcoal grey overcoat and homburg hat stood half-hidden beneath a low-hanging branch on the other side of the road. The carriage carrying Inspector Maddox pulled away but the man remained where he was. Another policeman, or merely a curious resident?

'He's most likely just waiting for someone.' Flora dismissed him, too relieved the inspector hadn't seen her.

'No he ain't. He doesn't want to be seen. I can tell.'

'*Isn't*,' Flora murmured, not bothering to ask her how she knew. Sally liked to be enigmatic.

Flora strolled the long bookshelf, her neck craned to read the titles on the leather spines of an eclectic collection that ranged from Jane Austen to Dickens. Ancient books with softened covers and faded gilt writing shared space with pristine volumes that might never have been opened. The *Life of Her Majesty, Queen Victoria*, by Millicent Fawcett, jostled with a copy of Arnold Bennett's, *Anna of the Five Towns*, a novel which Bunny had presented to her on her last birthday.

'This looks nice.' Sally plucked a framed photograph from the desk and turned it towards Flora. A square white villa in a Mediterranean style emerged from swathes of tropical flowers.

Despite the sepia tone on the picture, the scene gave sense of endless sunshine beneath a clear sky.

'Don't touch things!' Flora took it from her, her eyes caught by the inscription beneath the image. The words, *Le Palais de Sacchino, Biarritz* in cursive script, together with a scrawled greeting she could not decipher, but which ended with a capital letter 'N'.

Flora indicated a small chair in the corner she hadn't noticed when she entered. 'Sit there, and when the headmistress arrives, you wait outside in the hall.'

'Suits me.' Sally rolled her eyes, just as the door opened with a firm click, revealing a tall lady in a grey gown who strode confidently into the room. Sally flicked a look at Flora, then bobbed a curtsey and eased past her into the hall.

'Good afternoon.' The newcomer's eyes slid to the picture in Flora's hand and back again to her face. 'I'm Miss Helen Lowe. I don't think I've had the pleasure of your acquaintance?'

Flora judged her to be in her mid-thirties, with a wide, smooth brow above clear grey eyes, a straight nose and high cheekbones that were striking rather than pretty. The tight bun pinned to the back of her forehead accentuated the strong cheekbones and a broad forehead.

'Mrs Harrington.' Flora held out her free right hand, while with the other she returned the frame to the desk. 'I couldn't help but admire the house. It's quite beautiful.'

Miss Lowe flicked a glance at the frame, but her expression did not alter as she took Flora's hand, her grip firm but brief, adding softly. 'It is indeed. I spent holidays there when I was younger. Not now, though. Things have changed.' She slid a printed leaflet across the desk towards Flora before taking her seat. 'Have you read the school's prospectus? You'll find we run a comprehensive syllabus here, with emphasis on the arts, although we allocate time to mathematics and some sciences.' She enunciated each word slowly and with careful precision as if English was not her first language.

'I'm afraid there appears to have been a misunderstanding,' Flora interrupted, summoning her most pleasing smile. 'I'm not a parent. Well, not yet.'

'Oh?' Miss Lowe folded her hands on the top of her desk, pinning Flora with a stare. 'I admit you do appear rather young, but I've learned not to make assumptions.' Her handsome face split into a wide smile. 'If you are seeking employment, I'm afraid we have a full complement—'

'Uh no, that isn't why I came. Although I used to be a governess.' She did not add that Miss Lowe's full complement was now minus one, which either had not yet registered or the lady was being tactful. 'Had I not married, I would have welcomed an opportunity to teach at such a prestigious, school as this.'

'Miss Lowe relaxed in her chair, her arms draped on the upholstered arms and regarded Flora levelly. 'How kind.' She spoke the words slowly, with an inclination of her head which implied flattery had no effect. 'If you do not require either employment or enrolment, what can I do for you?'

'I came to-' she broke off as a female cry sounded from the hallway outside, followed by the sounds of distressed weeping and rapid footsteps.

Miss Lowe looked up at the door and back again to Flora. 'I apologize for the disturbance. I'm afraid I've had to announce some distressing news to the pupils and staff.' She made a show of rearranging items on her desk as if playing for time in which to compose herself. 'Now, what were you saying?'

'I think I know what that was, Miss Lowe.' Flora began, wondering how much she should reveal. 'I had a conversation with Inspector Maddox this morning, about Evangeline Lange.' Miss Lowe didn't have to know it had been an entirely unsatisfactory one.

'Ah, I see.' Her slow nod was loaded with speculation. 'You were, a friend of Miss Lange's?' Her words were innocuous but her penetrating grey eyes probed deeper.

'We attended the same branch of the National Union of Women's Suffrage Societies.' It occurred to her Miss Lowe might also be a member and detect the lie, though her expression did not alter.

'I got the impression the police only discovered her identity this morning, Mrs Harrington.' That look again, surprise mixed with a heavy dose of mistrust. This woman wasn't going to be easy to fool.

'Miss Lange did not attend the meeting, at which her friends expressed concern. I found out about her unfortunate death through other channels, and knowing Miss Grey was a friend of hers, I came to inform her before she saw it in the newspapers. However, I appear to be too late.'

'That's very considerate, but I'm afraid the police were no kinder than the newspapers. The poor dear girl is quite distraught. I've left her in the common room with another teacher until she feels a little better.'

'The police implied Miss Lange's death might have had something to do with her suffrage activities. Is that something you agree with?'

'That would be a dreadful indictment of our fellow man, would it not?' Miss Lowe's expression changed from dismay to resignation. 'Although, I've had occasion to reprimand Evangeline for discussing votes for women with the older pupils. I hold similar views on the role of women in society, though I advocate caution as far as my pupils are concerned or risk ostracizing their parents, who wouldn't hesitate in removing them from the school.'

'I quite understand.' Flora smiled, though this sounded more a well-rehearsed speech than a personal opinion. 'I expect Miss Lange's fiancé will be distraught.'

'Ah yes, Mr Flynn.' She drew the words out slowly. 'I haven't met the young man, but as a friend of Evangeline's,' she paused for a heartbeat, her stare unwavering, 'you'll be aware he was the topic of wide speculation when their engagement was announced.'

'Did Evangeline confide in you regarding her engagement?' Flora aimed for nonchalance but doubt she succeeded. Miss Lowe continued to regard her. I heard she was having second thoughts.'

'Not specifically. She did mention that her parents had certain expectations of her which she found burdensome, none of which involved the suffrage movement.' She folded her arms on the desk, her chin jutted towards Flora; a stance she imagined worked well on her pupils. 'I'm sorry, did you say you were a friend of Evangeline's?' Her eyes clouded with suspicion. 'I've just spent a half hour answering similar questions posed by the police.'

'Not as such, but I am curious. You see, Miss Lange was found in an alley quite close to where I am staying. We've had the police crawling over the apartment building asking all sorts of questions. When I discovered who she was, well, as you can imagine, as a member of the NUWSS-' Flora left the rest to Miss Lowe's imagination.

'I see, and maybe you were right about Mr Flynn.' Miss Lowe rose and went to a bell pull beside the fireplace. 'One of the drawbacks of employing young women is that their minds are either clouded with thoughts of a love attachment or crying over the loss of one. In fact I am presently dealing with just such a situation with a member of my staff.'

Seconds after she had resumed her seat, the chirpy maid who had shown Flora in reappeared at the door.

'Ah, Chloe,' Miss Lowe looked up with a smile. 'Would you ask Miss Grey to come to my office? She has a visitor.'

'I don't wish to cause Lydia any further distress.' Flora started to rise.

'Nonsense.' Miss Lowe waved her back into her seat, while at the same time dismissing Chloe. 'The entire school has already been disrupted. Miss Lange was a popular teacher and everyone is too upset to work, so I intend to send the girls home. Lydia needs a sympathetic face at such a time. I'm sure she would be pleased to see you.'

Flora resumed her seat with the strange thought Miss Lowe was teasing her. Then there was the possibility Lydia might not be pleased to see her at all, not after just one meeting.

Seconds passed as they waited, during which Flora searched for a subject which might help dispel the oppressive silence. The framed photograph of the villa caught her eye once more; its impression of blue seas and darkened rooms behind pulled blinds in the midday sunshine appealed.

'You seem quite taken with that photograph, Mrs Harrington.'

'Do I?' Flora fidgeted. 'It is rather beautiful place, and yet not in England, I suspect. Do you know it well?'

'I do.' Miss Lowe's eyes became guarded. 'And indeed, Biarritz is very beautiful. The house belongs to my cousin. She's older than I, but was always generous and invited me there whenever I wished. I have some wonderful memories.'

'Your cousin still lives there?' Flora hoped she was not treading on the lady's sensibilities, or worse, her cousin was dead.

'She does.' Miss Lowe licked her lips slowly. 'Unfortunately, her circumstances have made her a much sadder lady these days.' She broke off as the door opened again to admit Lydia, whose red-rimmed eyes brightened at the sight of Flora.

'Flora!' She strode forward, a handkerchief clutched tightly in one fist. 'What *are* you doing here?' Her bright red-gold curls had been tamed and swept off her heart-shaped face in a smooth style. Her navy-blue mutton sleeved dress with only a touch of white at her neckline and cuffs was a more formal look that made her look younger.

'I heard about Evangeline.' Flora relaxed at Lydia's enthusiasm, grateful she was not about to be denounced. 'I came to say how sorry I am.'

'I can hardly believe she's been killed.' Lydia's face crumpled and she gave a wet sniff. 'And in such an awful, violent way. I knew something was wrong when she didn't come to the meeting, especially when Harry said he expected her too. Then her father marching in like that, demanding-' she broke off to emit another, grief-laden sob.

'I'll leave you two to talk.' Miss Lowe pushed back from the desk, and rose.

Flora reached the door before she had got it fully open. 'Miss Lowe?' Flora lowered her voice. 'Should you have occasion to talk to Inspector Maddox again, might I ask you not to mention my visit today?'

'How interesting.' She slanted Flora a sideways look. 'Is there something you know about Evangeline's death you would like to share?'

'No, well, not yet anyway. I have an idea or two I want to look into, but, well when we spoke this morning, the Inspector was adamant I didn't meddle with his investigation.'

'Does he have reason to think you might?' Her steel grey eyes regarded her steadily.

'Possibly.' Flora bit her bottom lip. 'Thus I would appreciate-'

'Don't worry, Mrs Harrington.' Her lips tilted very slightly, though not enough to be described as a smile. 'I can be suitably vague when I choose.'

Chapter 14

'Poor, poor Evangeline. I keep thinking of her lying on the cold ground all night with no one to help her.' With the departure of Miss Lowe, Lydia had dissolved into fresh sobs. Her chin jerked up and she stared at Flora, her eyes swimming with unshed tears. 'Perhaps she didn't die straight away. Suppose whoever attacked her left her lying there in the cold and she froze to death?'

Flora scraped the second chair on her side of the desk closer, her hand covering Lydia's clasped ones in her lap. 'I doubt that's what happened. Look, why don't you let me take you home?'

'I-I can't. Miss Lowe has asked me to stay behind with the pupils who have to remain until the end of the school day.' She stared round vaguely and kneaded her handkerchief in both hands.

'Don't worry about that. I'm sure if I ask her she'll arrange for one of the other teachers to stay. Now, where's your coat?'

'Well I don't know, I-' Her eyes clouded as she lost focus.

'Never mind.' Flora patted her shoulder. Opening the door to the hallway she gestured to Sally to summon the maid. 'We'll sort that out in a moment.'

The same girl answered the summons, this time she was slightly breathless as if she had been kept busy carrying messages. She listened to Flora's suggestion in silence and agreed to speak to Miss Lowe.

Flora persuaded an unresisting Lydia from her chair and with Sally's help, walked her down the stairs and located her coat and hat.

Out in the street, Flora swapped the smells of linseed oil and soap for sulphur and coal smoke. A swift glance both ways showed no sign of policemen or men in grey coats. 'Sally, would you go to the corner and find us a cab?'

Lydia paused on the top step and pulled on her gloves. 'That won't be necessary.' Her voice stopped Sally mid-stride. 'I live in Kinnerton Street. It's just round the corner.' She pointed the way and Flora fell into step beside her, with Sally a few paces behind.

'You must think I'm a complete ninny falling apart like that.' Lydia tucked her arm through Flora's. 'We hardly know each other, but in some ways, I feel we have met before. In another life perhaps?' Lydia made an obvious effort to compose herself, the colour slowly returning to her cheeks. 'It was so kind of you to come to the school, but I admit it was the last place I expected to see you.'

Flora merely smiled, thus avoiding her scepticism on the subject of reincarnation so as not to offend her. 'I found out this morning that the woman they discovered was Evangeline, and I didn't want you to hear about it from gossip or the newspapers.' They turned into Motcomb Street, a charming street lined on both sides with Georgian shops with bow windows that promised treasures inside. That afternoon, many had their blinds drawn, as if the owners doubted prospective customers would be out in the fog.

'It wouldn't have mattered how I had been told, it was devastating news.' Lydia's breath caught in a distressed sob. She nodded to the corner of the street that loomed out of the fog. 'We don't have far to go now. It's the next turning on our left.' She guided Flora across the road and into Kinnerton Street; a terrace of identical villas, each with neat window boxes on the sills, empty now it was winter. Three storeys high, the facades sported uniform pale grey render, the front doors gleaming with pristine black paint. Narrow steps led down to a basement area, bounded by sets of wrought iron railings.

'I live here with my mother.' Lydia paused before a primrose-painted house three doors from the end, the brass knocker shaped like a fox head.

'It's charming,' Flora said, meaning it. She wondered if Lydia had an admirer, but it seemed inappropriate to ask. She didn't want to add nosiness to her deceit.

'Mother's not in the best of health and relies on me. There are only the two of us,' Lydia said as if reading her thoughts. She fumbled in the small bag at her wrist, withdrawing a brass key. 'Would you like to come in for a cup of tea?'

'I wouldn't wish to intrude,' Flora responded, hoping Lydia would press her. The little house looked delightful and she welcomed the chance to get to know Lydia better. To have a friend in London appealed, and since her marriage, she had had few opportunities to develop a social circle outside that of Bunny and her mother-in-law.

'You aren't, honestly.' She threw a pleading expression over her shoulder as she inserted the key in the lock. 'Mother will be taking her nap at this time. To be truthful, I don't relish being on my own.' She led them into a narrow, tiled hallway, then on into a parlour at the back of the house. Sally followed. A tall, narrow window overlooked a walled yard with terracotta pots arranged against a painted wall. Flora imagined these must add welcome colour in the summer months.

'I'm not usually home this early,' Lydia said, gesturing Flora to remove her coat. 'So Tilly won't have set the fire yet.

I'll send her in to light it for us now, then make us some tea.' At Flora's surprised start, she giggled. 'We aren't impoverished, Flora. Mother and I can afford a maid of all work.' She bent closer, her eyes flashing in mischief, adding, 'We send our laundry out too.'

Suitably chastened, Flora handed her coat to a plump, red-haired maid who appeared at the door.

'Take Mrs Harrington's maid to the kitchen would you, Tilly?' Lydia instructed. After a swift glance at Flora as if for approval, Sally obeyed.

'Tilly would enjoy the company.' Lydia said when they were alone again. 'She cooks for us and looks after Mother while I'm at the school.' She waved Flora into a low armchair beside the fireplace, its upholstery old but well cared for, which proved to be extremely comfortable. 'I must go and check on Mother. I won't be a moment.'

Seconds after Lydia had gone, Tilly returned carrying a coal scuttle and with a perfunctory curtsey, set to building a fire in the iron grate with sticks and newspaper. Flora watched as she coaxed a small yellow flame into a glowing red blaze, curtseyed again and left.

Flora flexed her numb fingers over the flames, and cast an approving eye over the charming room; the sounds of Lydia's tread on the floorboards above adding to the overall cosiness of the house.

The room held one window set on a low sill, from which rust-coloured velvet curtains fell to the floor, pooling on the boards not covered by an orange and blue rug. Apart from a footstool and a glazed corner cabinet, the room held only the two upholstered chairs and a small round table. In some ways it reminded her of the sitting room at Cleeve Abbey she had shared with her father in the attic. Or should she think of him as Maguire now?

A worm of resentment resurfaced that she was expected to submerge her childhood memories since the revelation that William was her real father. Strange, that those who knew her history seemed reluctant to talk about the taciturn Scot who had raised her; as if he no longer mattered.

She was still immersed in nostalgia when Lydia returned and took the second chair set at an angle to the fire, so close their knees almost touched.

'Thank you for indulging me, Flora. I'm sure you must have better things to do with your day than nursemaid me. You must think me selfish after such a short acquaintance.'

'Lydia, I need to tell you something.' Flora worried her bottom lip with her teeth. She might not have chosen the best time for honesty, but Lydia didn't deserve to be deceived. Not if Flora hoped to be considered a friend. 'I have never met Evangeline. I wasn't sure of her name until this morning.'

'But the Society, I thought—' Lydia eyes rounded in confusion.

'I misled you, for which I apologize. I had a vague suspicion, but no proof.'

'Proof of what? And why pretend to be acquainted with her when you weren't?'

Flora took a deep breath. 'This might sound odd, but it began with the brooch.'

'Evangeline's brooch?'

Flora nodded, relieved Lydia seemed more puzzled than angry. 'On the night Evangeline - died, I saw her outside the building where my father lives. She was wearing a brooch that resembled the same emblem on the pamphlet you delivered to the apartments. This was too much of a coincidence to ignore, so I came to the meeting as I hoped Evangeline would be there, thus proving me wrong.' When Lydia did not respond, she added, 'I hope you'll forgive me for lying to you.'

'Of course. In fact I would probably have done the same thing myself.' Lydia blew through pursed lips as if marshalling her thoughts. 'You said you saw her—'

'Outside my building, yes. She was with a man,' Flora interrupted her. 'And they appeared to be arguing.'

'A man?' Lydia's eyes widened. 'Might it have been Harry?'

'No, I'm certain it wasn't him. He, this man, wasn't at all pleased to see her and I got the impression she had sought him out. In fact she threatened him.'

'Threatened? Evangeline?'

'Perhaps that word is too strong. She appeared calm, even confident. I heard her say that if he did not comply with her request, whatever that was, she would be back.'

'Do you get the impression they had met before?' Lydia asked.

'He did use the word harassment, but that doesn't mean much.'

'What did Evangeline want from him?'

'I don't know. It was a brief conversation, and when they parted, Evangeline walked off down the street, which is why I don't think he was the one who killed her.'

'Evangeline saying she would come back sounds ominous, though.' Lydia's brow furrowed in deep thought.

'I agree.' Flora relaxed, grateful Lydia's grief had subsided and that none of it was directed at her. 'Mr Crabbe went back to his apartment after Evangeline left, so there's no reason to suspect he had anything to do with her death.'

Lydia gasped. 'You know him then? This man?'

'He's an associate of my father's.' Flora winced, embarrassed. 'I did tell the police I saw them together, but I'm also guessing they have already spoken to him.' The fact Crabbe had not been carted off in a black maria suggested Maddox had been satisfied with whatever explanation he had given. Or was it too soon to make that assumption?

'Did Evangeline ever mention his name to you?' Flora asked.

'Crabbe?' Lydia shook her head. 'I've never heard of him. Inspector Maddox told us it was most likely a robbery gone wrong, but that doesn't sound right. What was Evie doing outside a public house? She would never venture into a place like that. What about the alley where she was found? Perhaps she was visiting someone there?'

'It's called Old Barrack Yard, but there's nothing down there except a school and a church, neither of which were open at that time of night.'

Lydia eased forward, her arms folded across her middle, shoulders hunched. 'Convince me this man Crabbe didn't kill Evangeline.'

'Truthfully, I cannot know for sure. I have to trust the police to ask the right questions. If he is guilty, they will find out. In the meantime, I want to explore other avenues myself.'

'What avenues?'

'I'm not sure yet, but why would Evangeline leave, then come back and go with him to a public-house down a dark alley? One so close to where he lived, it was bound to make him an obvious suspect?'

'You appear to have made yourself a champion for this man Crabbe.'

'I just don't want to focus on the only possibility we have and ignore any others.'

'Are there others?'

'There's her father. Wasn't he angry about her membership of the NUWSS? Perhaps they argued?'

'Evangeline did clash with him on occasion. He hated her work as a schoolteacher too. When Evangeline first started working at the academy, he tried to talk Miss Lowe into dismissing her.'

'I gather Miss Lowe refused?' Flora could imagine how such a conversation went, with Mr Lange blustering with rage in the face of the headmistress's intransigence.

'She most certainly did.' Lydia snorted. 'Evangeline laughed it off, but Mr Lange never came to the school again, as far as I'm aware. The Langes wanted to get her safely married to Harry because they saw him as capable of safeguarding the family money.'

'What about Harry Flynn?' Flora suggested. 'If Evangeline was having second thoughts about their marriage, he might have tried to persuade her and it ended badly.' A reluctant bride was one thing, a reluctant rich one was worth some persuading.

'Harry isn't the violent sort.' Lydia waved a hand in dismissal. 'And we keep coming back to the question of what was she doing down that alley? Did someone persuade her to go there, or force her?'

A discreet knock at the door heralded Tilly with a tray. She gave Flora a shy smile before placing it on the elbow-height table between the two chairs.

'What about her brother?' Flora asked when the maid withdrew.

'John?' Lydia shrugged. 'I've never met him. Evangeline said very little about him, but what she did say was accompanied by a sigh.' Flora frowned and Lydia added, 'Like when you don't understand someone but accept them for what they are.'

Lydia poured steaming liquid into two blue and white willow patterned cups. 'I do love Earl Grey, it's a weakness of mine. Milk or lemon?'

'Milk please, no sugar.' Flora had thus far only thought of him as Mr Lange, then realized he hadn't actually introduced himself. He had simply said he was Evangeline's brother.

'What was he?' Flora asked, wishing she had been more curious about him.

'No idea, but it seems he agreed with Mr Lange, in that Evie was behaving unreasonably.' She handed Flora a cup, from which a rich smoky fragrance made Flora's mouth water in anticipation.

Delaying her first delicious sip, she blew the wisp of steam gently across the surface and took her first sip.

'What could be better than strong tea in front of a fire on a frigid winter afternoon?' Lydia said, watching her.

'What does Harry Flynn do?' Flora cradled the cup in both hands. 'Or rather what does his family do to make him acceptable to the Langes?'

'Merchant banking,' Lydia replied. 'He's being groomed to take over the business one day.' Her mouth opened in a perfect 'o' and her eyes clouded. 'Someone will tell Harry, won't they? That she's – dead. He thinks Evangeline went to Brighton.'

Flora had not yet decided if Harry had merely speculated or had deliberately misled them about the Brighton idea. Whichever it was, this was not the right time to mention it to Lydia. 'I'm sure her parents will tell him. Harry is wealthy then?' She was blatantly fishing but Lydia gave no sign she minded.

'His family are, but he lives on an allowance at the moment. Evangeline told me he'll inherit from a grandfather when he reaches twenty-five.' She frowned, confused. 'Or was it an uncle. I cannot recall which. Harry is always remarking on the fact his parents enjoy an extravagant lifestyle, so expect him to live on quite a modest allowance.' She lowered her cup and saucer to her lap, the frown reappearing between her brows. 'You don't think Harry could have had anything to do with this, do you?'

'I cannot say. I'm merely running through a list of possibilities.'

'Harry wouldn't hurt Evangeline. I know he wouldn't.' Lydia visibly shuddered. 'Who could be cold enough to murder someone they intended to marry?'

'You'd be surprised,' Flora mused. 'Most murders are committed by people we know.'

'Really?' Lydia's eyes rounded. 'How do you know such a thing?'

'I-um, I have a little experience of these things.'

'I see,' Lydia said, though it was clear she did not, and Flora wasn't about to explain.

'He would have no reason to kill her before the wedding?' Lydia blurted, bringing a hand to her mouth. 'Oh dear, that didn't sound quite so dreadful inside my head. Forget I said it.' She dropped two lumps of sugar into her cup with a pair of tiny silver tongs.

'This is murder, Lydia, so the police will explore all avenues.' Flora slid her cup and saucer onto the table at her elbow and took a biscuit from the plate Lydia held out. 'What other reason would Harry have to kill Evangeline if it wasn't for her money?' Not that Flora had entirely discounted that. She had seen at first-hand what lengths people will go to ensure a comfortable lifestyle. The face of the man who had tried to kill her to get his hands on William's money loomed into her head so she had to suppress a shudder. 'Is it possible he wasn't content with the betrothal? Might he prefer the charms of another lady?'

'You think Harry might have someone else?' Lydia's eyes pinned Flora with a look, which might have been hard had her green-brown eyes not welled with unshed tears. 'Then why press Evie to set a date for the wedding?'

'I had forgotten about that.' Flora bit into a biscuit, allowing it to melt on her tongue, reminding herself they only had Harry's word for that. 'Might another young man have roused *her* interest perhaps?'

'Not-not that I'm aware of.' Lydia's cup rattled as she replaced it on the saucer. 'I don't want to think Evangeline had a secret she was ashamed of. It's disrespectful, especially now she's dead.'

'I'm sorry, I didn't mean to imply anything. I'm simply looking for a reason someone would want to hurt her. Which is why I need your help. You knew Evangeline, whereas I didn't.'

'I don't understand any of this. Miss Lowe said the police think it was a robbery gone wrong.'

'What do you think?'

'Well, it's possible. Perhaps it was a robbery and she unnerved him, so he had no choice but to kill her in order to keep her quiet. Evangeline wasn't the type to freeze in fear.' Her red-rimmed eyes hardened. 'Not like me. She would have screamed and fought.' The handkerchief reappeared from her pocket and she noisily blew her nose.

Flora was tempted to snatch it away and replace it with a freshly laundered one of her own but resisted. Lydia seemed to take comfort from the crumpled square of cotton.

'Did Miss Lowe have an opinion about what Evangeline might be doing at The Grenadier?'

'She was a shocked as anyone. It didn't make sense.'

'Could she have been delivering the NUWSS pamphlets?'

Lydia shook her head, hard enough to dislodge several curly strands from behind her ears. 'She was careful about where she went. Shops, apartments. Hotels sometimes, but not public houses. She would never give her father a reason to accuse her of anything disreputable.'

'Then it's still a mystery.' Flora sighed. *If she discounted Mr Crabbe.* 'It was very considerate of Miss Lowe to let everyone go home,' Flora said, filling the silence.

'That's just like her.' Lydia's handkerchief disappeared into her pocket again. 'She's a delight to work for and so easy to talk to. Evangeline often went to her with her problems. We all did.'

'Miss Lowe has an unusual way of speaking. She's not English is she?'

'Um-no.' Lydia looked confused for a moment. 'She came from Romania originally, or somewhere like that. She thought the English might disapprove of their daughters being taught by a foreigner, so she worked hard to get rid of her accent. That's why her speech is clipped. I find it charming, though, don't you?'

'I do.' Flora returned her cup to the table and rose. 'I should go. I'm really sorry about Evangeline, and even more so at having upset you.'

'Oh, you haven't, truly. None of this is your fault.' Lydia placed a hand on Flora's forearm. 'I just keep thinking about

Evangeline. All that beauty and poise, all her wonderful ideas about how women will take their place in society is gone, and for what? For a promising, meaningful life to end in some filthy alley in front of a public house? It's too tragic.'

'Yes, yes it is.' Whatever Flora said next would be empty platitudes, though the moment called for something apart from silence. 'If there's anything I—'

'— you can do?' Lydia finished for her. She rose and gave a snort the sound more resigned than dismissive. 'Everyone says that when someone dies. But what *can* you do?' She led the way back through the narrow hall to the front door. 'Even if the police do find out who did this, it won't bring her back.' Lydia retrieved Flora's coat.

'No. No, it won't,' Flora murmured, just as Sally emerged from the kitchen.

'You will come again, won't you?' Lydia pleaded as she opened the front door, allowing a blast of chill air and a swirl of leaves across the threshold. 'I feel we would make good friends, and I would like to know if you have found out anything about who might have done this dreadful thing to Evangeline.'

'I should like to call again. I'm here for a few more days yet.' Flora fastened the row of buttons that ran from her shoulder to her hip. 'Though perhaps I should do what Inspector Maddox said and leave this to him. If it was a random robbery, I wouldn't know where to begin.'

'No, I suppose not.' Lydia's shoulders slumped. 'Anyway, Tilly has Saturday afternoons off, so I'll be here with Mother.'

'I'll remember.' Flora gave a parting wave, before she and Sally set off on the short walk back to Prince Albert Mansions. It was not much past four o'clock and yet the streets were gloomy with a combination of the heavy fog and an early falling dusk.

'That Tilly's a talker,' Sally said when they reached the corner. 'Not surprising really when she spends all day with a sick old woman.'

'I gather you told her about the murder?' Flora assumed her reference to 'sick old woman' meant Lydia's mother.

'She knew there had been one, of course, but when I told her who it was, she had something to say.'

Flora only half heard, her focus squarely on listening for the sounds of an engine or a horse in the swirling fog, but the street remained quiet. 'Come on, Sally, cross now, quickly.'

'Don't you want to know what she said?' Sally became slightly breathless as she hurried to keep up.

'Go on then, what did she say?' Flora smiled. Sending Sally into the kitchen hadn't been a deliberate ploy to gain information, but she couldn't ignore the fact servants knew everything about their employers. Who better to wheedle it out of them but another servant?

'Well for one thing, that Mr Flynn is always calling on her. Tilly thinks he's sweet on Miss Lydia.'

'Really?' Flora frowned. Lydia had said Harry wasn't interested in anyone else, but then she would say that in loyalty to her friend. 'They were all members of the NUWSS. It's hardly surprising they spent time together.'

And if Mr Lange disapproved, what better place to discuss women's rights than at Lydia's house? 'I think Tilly might have got the wrong impression.' Lydia didn't strike her as they type to betray her friend, or perhaps Lydia wasn't aware Harry was fond of her?

'Tilly's no fool, Missus. That Miss Lydia might look as if butter wouldn't melt, but she's had other admirers. She's sharper than she looks.'

'Did Tilly mention whether or not Mr Flynn has called recently?'

'He brought Miss Lydia home from that meeting last night. Stayed an hour she said.'

'Perhaps they discussed where Evangeline was. They were both worried about her.' Harry couldn't have called to make a condolence call, because Lydia hadn't known Evangeline was dead until two hours ago.

Flora lowered her head against a fine drizzle that deposited moisture on her scarf, while she resumed her speculation as to where the search for Evangeline's killer would go if Harry Flynn and Arthur Crabbe were eliminated, which they must be if the police were right about a random killer. Into the stews of London's underworld, she supposed, and the police informers and pawnbrokers with whom such secrets resided.

'I thought you'd be pleased.' Sally's snort of derision indicated she felt wholly unappreciated.

'I'm sorry, I was just thinking. You did well, Sally, thank you.'

The corner of Prince Albert Mansions loomed out of the mist and Flora hastened her steps, drawn by the thought of a hot drink and a warm fire. Distracted, she almost collided with a man wearing a long grey overcoat. Flora turned her head to apologize, but he merely grunted, pulled his hat down further and hurried past her and was immediately swallowed up in the murk.

'Nobody has any manners in this fog,' Sally tutted in disgust. 'Everyone's too busy trying to see where they are going.'

Flora agreed but did not respond, still distracted. If Harry preferred Lydia to Evangeline, wouldn't he have simply called off the wedding? Why kill his fiancée? Was Harry's insistence he had pressed Evangeline to name a date, genuine affection or subterfuge?

By the time she entered the lobby of the apartment building, Flora decided that perhaps she should leave this case to the police after all. A decision which would undoubtedly please Inspector Maddox.

Chapter 15

William released a sigh, lowering himself into a chair by the fire, an air of weariness to the set of his shoulders. Purple marks sat like bruises beneath eyes clouded with fatigue, lacking their habitual gleam of amusement.

'Weren't you hungry this evening?' Flora asked, pouring coffee for both of them from the arrangement on the sideboard. 'You barely touched your dinner.'

'Not very,' William replied. 'Which will put Randall into a fever adjusting his menus. He always reacts badly when I don't eat his food. I don't mean to be poor company, Flora, but I've a lot on my mind just now.' He had brought his unfinished drink with him from the dining table and now fingered the stem of his glass absently, the weight of whatever was bothering him clear in the set of his shoulders.

'You seem distracted tonight.' She attempted to instigate conversation, or they risked sitting in complete silence for the remainder of the evening.

'I'm sorry, Flora. It's just that the Government is in a mess with this Serbian business.' William rubbed his forehead with his free hand. 'What with these endless debates on whether or not we should recognize the new regime or boycott them. It's quite worrying.'

'Will ending diplomatic relations produce the result the government wants?' Flora settled on the opposite sofa with her coffee. 'Surely Serbia's too far away to have repercussions here?'

'For us to maintain cordial relations with the Austro-Hungarian Empire is important, their powers stretch a long way. Balfour hopes to force them to arrest King Alexander's assassins.'

'Will King Peter comply do you think?'

'He daren't upset the nationalist faction who put him in power in the first place.' William's half-hearted smile reflected his troubled state of mind. 'Then there are those in the Cabinet who think as you do, that Serbia is of little consequence.'

'It does matter though, doesn't it? I can see by your face.'

'Political factions who employ assassination as opposed to the ballot box cannot be trusted. There is usually another militant group waiting for a chance to overthrow them.'

'Ah, I see. Only those of strong moral character should be heads of state?' She slanted a sideways look at him as she placed the coffee at his elbow, smiling when his lips twitched. At least he hadn't completely lost his sense of humour.

'Perhaps I shouldn't be telling you this, Flora, but it appears Serbian spies are operating in the city.' Ignoring the coffee, he took another swig from his glass.

'Spies? In London?' Flora halted her cup in maid air.

'I'm afraid so. A gang were discovered recently in some lodgings near the city docks. Among their belongings was a list of the addresses of other Serbians living here.' At her shocked stare, he held up a hand. 'Most are non-political, though some are royalist sympathizers of the former Queen Nathalie.'

'Nathalie? I thought the queen was called Draga. And isn't she dead?'

'Not her. Her mother-in-law. She was very popular in her day before King Milan, Alexander's father, divorced her. She went to live in the south of France.'

'I see.' Something she had heard recently drifted into her consciousness but proved too elusive to pin down. 'What are these nationalist spies planning to do to the royalists?'

'Nothing good.' William sniffed. 'They've instigated fights among the Serbian community as a warning to supporters of Nathalie. Thus far we've managed to keep it out of the newspapers. Publicity is like food to them, credits them with too much importance and frightens the populace. Before you know it we'll have Londoners attacking Serbians for no reason.'

'Talking of publicity,' Flora began, keen to get away from such depressing talk. 'The police have identified the dead woman they found outside The Grenadier.'

'I heard.' William slid his glass onto the table. 'A young lady called Lange, I believe. Her father's well known in the city.'

'You already knew?' Flora stared at him, surprised. 'Why didn't you mention it before?'

'Before what?' William peered over the rim of his cup. 'I haven't seen you since breakfast.'

'Well no, but—' Flora shrugged her resentment away as unreasonable. 'You might have said something at dinner.'

'Sorry, slipped my mind.' His voice sounded perfectly calm but the way he held his shoulders told her he kept something back.

'Evangeline Lange was also a member of the NUWSS. I met some of her friends last night.'

'Is that why you went? To poke about and ask questions?'

Avoiding his eye, she retrieved a plate of Randall's almond biscuits from the tray and held it out. 'How could I not be interested in a murder that happened on our own doorstep?'

'Interested is one thing, but you shouldn't get in the way of the police.' He declined the biscuits with an upraised hand. 'I'm sure Inspector Maddox has his own methods of wheedling the truth from suspects. You risk contaminating his investigation if you've already spoken to witnesses.'

'I doubt anything *I* could do would scupper a police investigation.' She looked up and met his eyes as a thought struck her. 'When exactly did you speak to Inspector Maddox? I thought Mr Gordon had taken your dictated statement to the police station?'

'Er, that's not relevant, Flora. I'm talking about your actions now. I know what you're like when you discover a trail worth following.' William shot her a look, then away again, too fast for her to read anything in it.

'Don't you wish to know how I found out who the woman was?'

'Didn't I?' He brushed a hand down his thigh as if dislodging dust. 'I assumed word had got round the building via the staff.'

'I went to see Maddox at Cannon Row this morning.' Flora waited, while the feeling persisted that she was not telling him anything he didn't already know.

'I cannot think why. We were at the theatre when that woman was killed. What information could you possibly have that might be pertinent to his investigation?'

'I mentioned the other night I had seen Mr Crabbe outside the apartment building. Well the young woman who was with him was Evangeline Lange.'

William placed his wine glass on the table at his elbow and leaned towards her, his weary disinterest changing to keen attention. 'What do you mean leaving with her? You never mentioned he was with anyone.'

'He was rather harsh with her,' Flora said, ignoring his question. 'I heard him order her not to bother him again.'

'You're confusing me, Flora. How did you know this was the same woman who was found in the alley?'

'I didn't. Not at the time.' Flora buried her nose in her coffee cup, suspecting she had approached this the wrong way. William had been ambivalent a minute ago and yet now glared at her. 'She wore this unusual brooch which resembled the National Union of Women's Suffrage Society emblem.'

'Wait a moment. That was before you went to the meeting. Which means you went there primarily to find out about this woman?'

'I did.' She swallowed. Now he was beginning to sound like a father. 'All right. I saw Mr Crabbe with a woman whom he called Miss Lange. I didn't say anything at the time because you told me Mr Crabbe was married.'

'I see. But if Crabbe and Miss Lange parted company on the street hours before, then he cannot have been involved in her murder.'

'Which is exactly what I told Inspector Maddox. However, Mr Crabbe still might know something.' She still had her doubts about their nondescript neighbour and his alleged insomnia, but she didn't want to accuse him. Not without firmer evidence. 'He was likely the last person to see Evangeline alive.' At William's hard look she added, 'Apart from her killer that is.'

'I know for a fact Crabbe mentioned their encounter to the police when they questioned him. If they think he has something to add to his original story, I'm sure they'll speak to him again.'

'What about Mrs Crabbe?'

William's head jerked up. 'What about her?'

171

'I assume she'll confirm he was with her all that evening?' Flora recalled Dunne's story about Crabbe's late night walk.

'I'm sure she did. Besides, Maddox is convinced it was an attack by a random thief.' He moved to the sideboard and held the coffee pot in mid-air. 'More coffee?' The subject of their enigmatic neighbour evidently at an end.

'No thank you, I'll not sleep tonight if I drink any more. It appears my contribution wasn't needed. Evangeline's brother reported her missing. He identified her, poor man.'

'Inspector Maddox told you that?' William abandoned his cup on the sideboard and returned to his chair where he perched on the edge of the squab, his hands held loosely between his knees.

'Well, no.' She winced, recalling she had intended to keep that part back, but it was too late now. 'He introduced himself to me under the impression I was a friend of Evangeline's.' She decided not to add that he had accosted her on the Embankment and practically forced her to take a tour of the London parks.

'You *have* been busy.' William resumed his seat, his coffee cup dwarfed in his hands.

'Inspector Maddox seems to think Evangeline's association with the suffragist movement might have contributed to her fate.'

'Is that what he said?'

'Well, no, not exactly. Though perhaps that theory isn't so outrageous. Suppose someone disagreed with her politics? Confronted her, even challenged her, but she refused to be swayed?'

'That doesn't sound like a credible motive for murder, Flora.'

'Perhaps they argued and things got out of hand? He didn't intend to kill her, but—'

'Enough!' He laughed; the first time she had heard the sound that evening. 'You're letting your imagination run wild. The poor woman was attacked and robbed by some ne'er-do-well because she was in the wrong place at the wrong time. Without witnesses, the police might never discover who it was. No amount of theorizing on your part will make any difference.' Stifling a yawn, he eased back and stretched his legs toward the fire. 'How did young Sally feel about being dragged along to a police station? From what I know of East Enders, they tend to give the constabulary a very wide berth.' He tugged his collar away from his neck, reminding Flora that Mr Lange had exhibited that same habit. Perhaps they shared a laundry which was too liberal with the starch?

'Actually, I didn't take her with me.' Flora avoided his eye but his frustrated sigh was enough to tell her he disapproved. 'I took a cab to Cannon Row,' she added by way of mitigation. 'London is full of young women walking around on their own and no one turns a hair. Besides, Sally gets restless and huffs and puffs beside me. I would gain more co-operation if I were walking a dog.' She broke off, aware she was gabbling, a habit of hers when she knew she was in the wrong.

William watched her with a sardonic lift of his left brow. 'Maybe so, but while you are here, I insist you take Sally with you whenever you go out. Would you do that? If only to please me?'

'How old-fashioned you are.' Flora attempted a laugh, but it fell flat in the face of his uncompromising glare. He was in a strange mood this evening, and just when she thought she was beginning to understand his mercurial character.

'I'm serious, Flora. A young woman from a notable family close to your own age was strangled not fifty yards from this door. We don't know by whom or why, so until the killer is found, you should take more care.'

'I'm sorry, I should have thought of that.' A shudder ran through her at the notion she wasn't entirely impervious to danger.

'I know you consider yourself a modern young woman, but this isn't Surrey. London is a dangerous city with crime and corruption on every street corner.'

'You make it sound like Babylon.' Despite his insistence, she did not intend to surrender her interest in the case entirely. Evangeline Lange deserved more than to be consigned to the victim of an unknown assailant.

William's jaw hardened. 'I'm aware I have only recently stepped into my role as your father, but I assure you I take the responsibility quite seriously.'

Flora was about to remind him that as her husband, Bunny, had taken over that duty, but offered a conciliatory smile instead. 'I'm sorry, I'll be more careful in future.' It was an easy promise to make, though the prospect of having to endure Sally's constant grumbling made her regret the impulse.

'Then we'll say no more about it.' William retrieved his coffee, which Flora suspected was lukewarm by now.

The ticking of the mantle clock and crackle of the fire were the only sounds the break a companionable silence that followed. William opened a newspaper while Flora read an instalment of the latest Conan Doyle story in Strand Magazine, but couldn't concentrate.

What had sent Evangeline Lange to Mr Crabbe's apartment that night? Her words, 'Unless I get what I want, you may well see me again,' had certainly sounded like a threat. Was it one their neighbour shrugged off or had he felt the need to prevent her carrying it out? And why was William so adamant the man couldn't have had anything to do with it?

'So tell me, Flora,' William asked, turning a page of the broadsheet. 'What did you do with the rest of your day?'

'Well…' Flora hesitated. She had annoyed him enough for one evening and had no wish to compound her error, but there seemed no reason to be secretive now. 'I went to see Miss Grey to tell her about Evangeline. They were friends and colleagues, so I wanted to spare her hearing her friend was dead from an unsympathetic source, like the police. I was too late as it happened, for they were already there.' She held up the silver coffee pot. 'Would you like some more?'

'Not for me, thank you. Already where? At this Miss Grey's house?'

'No, sorry, didn't I say?' She threw him a distracted smile. 'I went to see her where she worked, at the Harriet Parker Academy. It's in Lowndes Square.'

William's cup hit his saucer with a harsh clunk which sloshed coffee onto the rug.

'Oh dear.' She stared at a teardrop-shaped brown stain in dismay. 'Will you tell Randall or shall I?'

Ignoring her, he leapt to his feet and made for the door.

'Where are you going?' Flora asked.

'Sorry, I er-forgot I need to see to something. Shan't be long.'

'William, it's after ten. Can't it wait until morning? Surely whatever it is cannot be that im—' She broke off as she realized she addressed an empty room.

*

175

Flora rose the next morning with her head full of questions, a situation Sally appeared to share as she chattered all the way through the dressing ritual, although she had no more to add to what Flora already knew. Her thoughts drifted back to William's dash from the apartment the night before. She had lain awake for a while, but he must not have returned until after she had fallen asleep. If he had returned at all.

Once Sally had rushed off to the basement housekeeping room in search of more gossip, Flora went along to the dining room and poured a cup of coffee, just as the click of the front door opening sounded and she heard William's voice from the hall. 'We need to find out what connection this woman had with our man, if any.'

'You're certain it's not simply a coincidence?' Mr Crabbe responded.

'I very much doubt it. There have been too many of those lately.' A muffled cough and a shuffling noise followed.

Cup in hand, Flora crept to the half-open door, where William's head appeared around the jamb, startling her. 'Ah, there you are, Flora.' The cup and saucer tilted, spilling hot coffee onto her fingers. 'I shan't be joining you for breakfast. Crabbe and I need to go, but Randall will prepare anything you like.'

'I'll see you this evening then.' Flora flexed her wet, stinging fingers, aware of her cheeks burning at the possibility she had been caught listening.

He gave a mock salute and started to back away.

'William,' Flora halted him, 'is everything all right? You seem, well brittle and worried this morning.'

'Perfectly!' His over-bright response was unconvincing, but before she could challenge him, he rapped the door frame with his fingertips. 'Must go. Crabbe's waiting outside in the taxi.'

'No Mr Gordon this morning?' Flora said in an attempt to delay him. Despite his warning on their first night, and her assurances she had kept busy, Flora couldn't help being frustrated by the fact he always seemed to be rushing off when the purpose of her visit had been to get to know one another better.

'Ah, no.' He glanced towards the window, beyond which the hansom patiently waited. 'I've dispensed with his services as a nursemaid. He cast a swift glance at the window, beyond which the cab waited. 'I'm quite capable of getting myself to the office without his assistance, so I have instructed him to meet me there in future. It's not as if there isn't enough paperwork to keep him occupied.'

'I see, well have a good day then, and is there anything special you would like for dinner?'

'You're supposed to be having a holiday from domestic duties, Flora. Leave all that to Randall. Take Sally with you to visit the shops and maybe take a walk in Hyde Park. Anything to distract you from thinking about murderers.' He gave a half-hearted wave and pulled the door to, his voice mingling with Randall's in the hall as he left.

Flora couldn't have felt less rejected had he patted her on the head, but with no one to complain to, she went back to the table and replenished her coffee cup.

Her breakfast arrived, but she barely touched it, occupied by questions which crowded her head; the main one being that William seemed to know far more about Evangeline Lange's murder than he admitted to. Gordon was too efficient not to have taken William's statement to the police station, so when had Inspector Maddox informed William they had identified the body? And why?

The rhythmic click of silver against china as she stirred her coffee mingled with distant traffic sounds on the road outside. What had William meant when he referred to 'our man?' and what were these coincidences he talked about?' It was all very puzzling.

On the one hand, her regard for William prevented her dismissing his wishes, but her more determined side refused to allow a murder to go unsolved. The image of Evangeline lying on the ground on a frosty night, cold, alone and dead, plagued her. It brought to mind thoughts of Flora's own mother, whom everyone believed had been murdered when she was a child. The fact her mother's body had never been found, or that there was no grave she could visit contributed to Flora's determination to secure justice for Evangeline. Justice her own mother would never have.

At that moment Randall appeared.

'Randall?' Her question made him pause. 'Has Inspector Maddox called here in the last day or so?'

'Not that I am aware, Miss Flora.' He regarded her with his habitual bland expression before his gaze shifted pointedly to the tray in his hands.

'I see. Thank you,' she murmured, dismissing him with a sigh. If William had instructed him not to mention the policeman's visit, she wouldn't learn of it from his manservant.

Chapter 16

Flora *had* felt hungry while she waited for her breakfast, but when it arrived, the food had tasted odd, so she abandoned it half-eaten.

'Is something wrong with the food, Miss Flora?' Randall eyed her plate, his expression anxious. 'If it's not satisfactory, I could get you something else?'

'Please don't worry, Randall. There's nothing wrong. I'm simply not hungry.' As she rose from her chair, the room spun around her. She staggered, braced both hands against the table to stop herself falling, and waited for a stomach churning nausea to abate.

'Well, if you're sure, Miss Flora.' Randall cast her a worried look before removing her plate to the sideboard.

Not trusting herself to speak, she forced a smile until finally, he bowed and left the room at which she exhaled in a rush and slumped back onto her seat. She dropped her head in her hands, her breathing fast and shallow as bile rose in her throat.

When the queasiness finally passed, she rose unsteadily to her feet and made her way slowly to her room. The corridor seemed endless as the nausea threatened to return, until at last she closed her bedroom door and leaned against it.

'Are you going out this morning, Miss Flora?' Sally looked up briefly from sorting a pile of linens, halting with a petticoat hanging from one hand. 'Are you all right, Miss? You do look awful pale.'

'Maybe, only I need to lie down for a few moments.' She crawled onto the bed and pulled the coverlet over herself, registering Sally's disgruntled look that told her she had just straightened it.

'I didn't sleep well last night,' Flora lied. If she told Sally breakfast had made her ill, her maid would take her complaint straight to Randall, which was the last thing she wanted. Flora had more than a vague notion what was wrong with her and it was nothing to do with bad eggs.

'I could ask Randall to get you some dry biscuits.' Abandoning the linens, Sally gave her a knowing look she was unable to interpret. 'They sometimes help with – well you know.'

'Help with what? And please don't mention food.' Flora's stomach clenched and a sour taste flooded her mouth. She threw off the coverlet and bolted from the room, saw she had gone the wrong way but it was too late to correct. Instead, she made for the tiny guest cloakroom, pushing past an astonished Randall in the corridor. With no time to explain, she burst inside the tiny closet-sized room just in time to empty her stomach into the washbasin.

Sally followed her in and secured the lock, most likely to keep out an inquisitive Randall.

'Why is this called a cloakroom when there aren't any coats in it?' she asked.

The horrible process repeated itself and Flora grabbed a small hand towel from a pile and wiped her mouth while Sally rubbed Flora's back in firm rhythmic circles. 'It-it's for the use of guests.' Flora took a deep breath to steady her rapid heartbeat and waited for the awful feeling to settle.

'Much better than an outside privy.' Sally leaned nonchalantly against the wall and stared round, one hand still kneading Flora's back.

Flora dragged in another lungful of air, her eyes squeezed shut. 'Sally, is that pounding you're giving my back supposed to help?'

'Yes, Miss, why?'

'Because it isn't. At all. Do you mind—' she broke off as another surge of sickness overwhelmed her, and lurched for the washbasin again. Her stomach clenched and her throat went into spasm and her heaving turned to dry retching.

Sally pressed a cold, damp towel against Flora's brow, which brought some relief, but in seconds, she was retching again. The spasms continued, and Flora's knees started to shake. She crumpled to the tiled floor, her forehead pressed against the brass frame that supported the washbasin.

'What's that?' Sally opened the door a crack and peered into the hall.

'What's what?' Flora groaned, too miserable to care.

'Listen!'

Flora ignored her. Her head spun so badly she didn't dare move, much less show an interest in what was happening outside the room.

'Oh, lord, Randall's let someone in.' Sally shut the door, then shook Flora by the arm, though there was barely room for the two of them in the tiny room. 'Miss Flora, you must get up.'

'Why?' Flora pressed her forehead to the cold porcelain of the washbasin, both arms wound around the brass pole.

'You have to, Miss!' At any other time, her maid's tone would have acted as a warning, but Flora's head felt as if it were full of cotton wool and her throat was sore from all the retching.

'Miss Flora is, er, indisposed, sir.' Randall's distinctive voice came from immediately outside the door.

'What is that supposed to mean?' Bunny's voice penetrated the fuzziness that crowded Flora's head. 'I insist you allow me to see her.'

She was hearing things now. Surely Bunny was still in Richmond? 'Sally, send whoever it is away. I want to be left alone.'

'Wish I could, Missus, but I've this horrible thought—' Whatever the thought was, Sally didn't finish it, as suddenly the door was thrust open, shoving Sally hard into the corner behind it.

'My darling, whatever is wrong?' Bunny's voice penetrated Flora's fogged thoughts, but she couldn't summon the energy to move. Was it was really him?

'Sally,' Bunny snapped. 'Come out from behind the door. Your mistress needs some air.'

'I can't sir, you've trapped me behind it. I can't move.'

'For heaven's sake.' Bunny growled. He circled Flora's waist with one arm, flung her other one over his shoulder and hauled her upright. 'Randall, direct me to Miss Flora's room. And where is Mr Osborne?'

'Down that way, sir,' Randall said. 'And my master has gone to his office, sir. I could call him if you think it is necessary?'

'No, I'll do that myself. Firstly, I want to know what's wrong with my wife.'

Flora offered no resistance as she was half-dragged, half-carried along the hallway to her room. Bunny manoeuvred her through the door and laid her on the bed, still rumpled from when she had left it. She groaned again at the notion of Bunny finding her sprawled on the floor with her head pressed against the washstand support.

'Bunny?' Flora mumbled, finding her voice at last, though her words came out slurred. 'What are you doing here? I didn't expect you for another day or so.' All she wanted to do just then was lie down so her head would stop spinning.

'Have you summoned a doctor, Sally?' Bunny demanded, covering Flora with the heavy coverlet. 'If not, then perhaps someone ought to do so now?'

Flora smiled as his cool hand brushed her hair away from her forehead.

The thick mattress and soft pillows felt wonderful but a voice inside Flora's head told her she had to stop him. She opened her mouth to speak but nothing came out.

'No, sir,' Sally answered Bunny's stern question. 'She doesn't need no doctor.'

'What are you talking about?' Bunny pushed a hand into his hair and kept it there. 'Look at her, she's in a faint. And why was she so sick? Have you considered she might have food poisoning?'

'Certainly not from my cooking, sir!' Randall protested from the door frame, apparently reluctant to come inside. 'I'm very careful about cleanliness in my kitchen.'

'Bunny, it's all right, really.' Flora's head began to clear and she summoned strength enough to grip his arm. 'I don't have food poisoning and I've already seen a doctor.'

'When? Since you arrived here? How long have you been ill?' Bunny lowered himself onto the side of the bed, his face a mask of concern. 'What did he say?'

From the corner of her eye, Flora saw Sally propel an indignant Randall out of sight. They could say what they liked about Sally, her discretion couldn't be faulted when she chose.

'Listen to me.' She tugged Bunny onto the mattress beside her so she didn't have to shout. 'I saw the doctor two weeks ago before I came here.'

'I had no idea you weren't well.' His eyes widened behind his spectacles. 'I would never have let you come if I had known. It isn't serious is it?' He rose to his feet again and stared around, frantic. 'Why didn't William call me?'

'Bunny, please sit down.'

He complied, if reluctantly, grasped her hand in both of his and patted it ineffectually.

Flora wanted to pull it away but resisted, despite the rhythm was grating on her nerves. She pulled herself into a sitting position. Her head had stopped swimming and she felt reasonably sure she wasn't going to be sick again. 'There was nothing you could have done which would have made any difference.' His face fell and panic entered his eyes which told her she had said it all wrong. 'No, I didn't mean—' She tried again. 'The doctor said—' She broke off as bile rose in her throat again and she had to concentrate on fighting the mounting nausea.

'Sally,' Bunny shouted. 'Get a bowl – quick!'

Sally reappeared from wherever she had been hiding, dumped the pitcher on the dresser and held the bowl beneath Flora's chin. Her vision trained on the pattern of apricot peonies on the edge but nothing happened. Sighing, Flora relaxed back against the pillows again.

'Darling, you aren't making sense.' Bunny gestured to Sally, who obligingly removed the bowl and disappeared again. 'If you aren't ill, then why are you so pale?' He bit his lip, his brows drawn together. 'You're still shaking and your eyes are clouded. In my book, those are all signs of—'

'Pregnancy.'

'Pardon?' He blinked, his lips parted as he digested the word. 'You mean you're—'

'Going to have a baby. Yes. The sickness is quite normal, though had I known it was this awful I—' Her last few words were lost in the thick folds of his woollen jacket as he pulled her towards him and held her tight.

'Flora, that's wonderful. I never thought—'

'It would happen? – no, nor did I.'

'That wasn't what I was going to say.' Though the look in his eyes told her otherwise.

'I hoped to have told you in a more romantic setting. One which did not have me sprawled on a bathroom floor with my head over the sink.' She released a tiny burp, muttered an apology and covered her mouth with a hand.

'Oh, heavens, I don't care about that.' He hugged her tighter. 'It frightened me to see you like that is all. My poor darling, I had heard of ladies who experience such symptoms but I had no idea it was so – well violent. Are you feeling better now?' He released her and peered into her face, handing her a handkerchief from his pocket.

'A little.' She dabbed at her mouth, waiting for the nausea to begin again, but nothing happened. 'Could you pass me that glass of water?'

'Oh, yes, yes of course.' He pressed the glass into her free hand.

'You didn't answer my question. I expected you to luncheon later in the week. Although I'm really thrilled to see you. It's been strange waking up without you in the mornings.'

'I'll say.' He scooted further onto the bed so they were side by side, sliding an arm around her shoulders. 'I had to come into town for a meeting today, so thought I would take an earlier train and pay you a visit. I'm sorry if I spoiled your surprise, but at least I've seen one of the worst aspects of what you are going through.' He smoothed the wayward curls that had sprung from their pins away from her forehead. 'I'll do my best to be both sympathetic and understanding.'

The mixture of worry and happiness in his eyes made Flora want to cry and laugh at the same time. 'Whatever makes you think this is the worst of it?'

She liked this sentimental side of him, especially on a subject in which gentleman weren't supposed to show an interest until there was a final product to feel proud about.

Flora took a few sips of the water, which helped banish the soreness in her throat. 'However, as a man, you'll be spared the very worst part altogether.'

'Ah yes, I see what you mean.' He flushed and looked sheepish, but in seconds was smiling again. 'Although it's rather exciting. In a few months, there will be three of us?' He hunched his shoulders like a boy and hugged her tighter.

'Four, there's still your mother, don't forget.'

'You know what I mean.' He pressed a kiss to her temple then lowered his voice. She thought she heard him mumble something about it being time to make changes, but wasn't sure what he meant, then louder, 'Did the doctor tell you when it's due?'

'The end of May, or maybe the beginning of June.' A shiver ran through her as the inevitability of what those few months would bring occurred to her. 'Everything will be all right, won't it? I mean, most women have babies quite successfully.'

'I'll employ all the best medical people to ensure everything goes smoothly.' He nuzzled his chin into her hair. 'It might be better if you came home to Richmond with me and rest properly. I'll ask Sally to pack your things and Randall can let William know. I'm sure he'll understand.'

'No!' Bunny's chin jerked back at her vehemence. 'What I mean is, there really is no need. The sickness isn't any worse just because I'm here, and I have plenty of time to rest as William is busy.'

'Does he know about the baby?'

'No, of course not.' She frowned, dismayed. 'No one knew. Though Sally guessed.'

How could she explain that she wanted to keep their baby safe, but also that she was making progress in another murder investigation. She had no wish to sit at home with her feet on a stool with Beatrice telling her she was doing everything wrong. There would be plenty of time for that, not to mention when there was a grandchild for her to fuss over.

'Bunny,' she softened her voice, 'I'm glad you know, but now that you do, I would like to stay and tell William myself. I don't want to put it in a note or rush away without an explanation. He might think I feel awkward being here and we are just starting to get to know one another.'

'I should have thought of that. It was selfish of me wanting to keep you to myself.'

'I'm the selfish one,' she said and meant it. 'But I will take care. I promise.'

The tiny ormolu clock on the mantel struck ten and Bunny gasped. 'So much for my vision of a romantic breakfast with my wife. At this rate, I'll be late for my meeting.' He released her, rose and went into the hall. 'Randall? Would you call me a cab?'

Flora heard a faint 'Certainly, sir' from the depths of the apartment and her stomach knotted, in sadness that he was leaving so soon.

'Although—' Bunny hesitated, his eyes clouded with concern. 'Perhaps I should stay here with you after all. I hate to see you so frail-looking.'

'There's nothing you can do and, as I said, I'm not ill. This meeting's important, isn't it?'

'Well yes, but not as important as you.'

'Rubbish. You must go, but you're still coming to luncheon as we arranged, aren't you?'

'Naturally. Now you must promise to rest for a while this morning. You're still very pale.'

'That won't be too hard. I do feel a bit shaky still and William is out all day, so I'll do nothing more strenuous than a bit of light reading.'

Sally gave an exaggerated cough from the doorway which Flora ignored.

'See that you do.' Bunny kissed her cheek just as Randall arrived to say the cab was waiting outside. 'I'll telephone William later to check you have been following instructions. And, Sally,' he turned a steady stare on the maid that made her blush. 'Take care of your mistress.'

'Of course, sir.' Sally clasped both hands behind her back, her head bowed as he threw a final kiss at Flora and left.

As his footsteps receded down the hallway, Flora relaxed against the pillows again, sure she heard Sally heave a gentle sigh.

*

Flora must have drifted off to sleep because the next thing she knew the shadows in the room had shifted. Sally stood with her back to her, bent over a drawer into which she placed clean shifts and petticoats. She must have sensed Flora was awake and turned round, wariness in her half-smile.

'How do you feel now, Miss Flora?' Her eyes darkened with concern.

Flora eased up onto an elbow, taking inventory of her head and stomach, both of which had settled with no residual dizziness. 'Almost normal.'

'You did look poorly. Mr Bunny got himself into a right tizz.'

'The next time he sees me, I hope I won't be crouched over on a bathroom floor or pale and sick in bed.' She peered myopically at the clock but the figures were blurred. 'How long did I sleep?'

'Just under two hours.' Sally slid the drawer shut and came to her side of the bed.

'How did you know, Sally? About the baby?'

'I can count, Missus, and there's been no sign of your flowers for over two months. Don't take a scholar to know what *that* means.'

'I suppose it was naïve of me to keep it secret from you.' Flora swung her legs over the side of the bed onto the floor. 'To be honest, I've been pushing the fact to the back of my mind because I don't quite believe it myself yet.'

'You've been to see a doctor, though, haven't you? Like you told Mr Bunny?'

'For all the good it did me. I didn't know what questions to ask him.' She was relieved to be talking about it at last. It had been like a secret between her and her body, one she could neither prove nor feel. 'He seemed to think I would know what to expect, and when I asked, he reeled off a whole list of symptoms I might experience. I was getting worried because until this morning, I haven't had any of them.'

'That's as maybe, Miss Flora, but the only thing I can say to that is bacon.'

'I beg your pardon, Sally?' Was this a Whitechapel insult she had never heard of?

'It's been weeks since you've been able to look a rasher in the eye. And you complain when I tie your corset too tight when you never said a word before.'

'I suppose that's settles it then, I *am* having symptoms.' She brought a hand to her hair that lay in an untidy knot of curls on her neck. 'Which comes as something of a relief. I think.'

'Why didn't you tell Mr Bunny before now?' Sally demanded.

Flora hesitated. 'I don't know. Apart from the bacon thing, I don't look or feel any different.' She rubbed her belly as nausea threatened. 'Isn't the morning sickness supposed to wear off after the first few weeks?'

'Not always.' Sally giggled knowingly. 'My sister lost her dinner every day for months when she was expecting.'

'Oh, dear, that's not very reassuring.' Flora planted her feet on the floor and pushed herself upright. 'I certainly don't intend to lie here all day either.'

'You're not still going to try and find out who killed that poor girl are you?'

'I'm not sure what direction to take next, but I don't see why not.' Avoiding Sally's eye, Flora bent to her reflection in the dresser mirror, where she tweaked stray hairs into place. 'Asking a few questions hardly comes under the banner of not looking after myself. I thought I would begin in Old Barrack Yard as it's practically next door.'

'There won't be anything to see down there now.' Sally sniffed. 'Coppers will have tramped about the place in their size twelves since they found her.'

'Maybe, but it wouldn't hurt to take a look.' She slid onto the stool in front of the dresser. 'Now, see if you can do something with my hair. This awful fog makes it frizz horribly.'

Chapter 17

Although it was mid-morning when Flora ventured out, the skeletal trees in Hyde Park were frost-rimed and the pavements still slippery; the air filled with a pungent combination of fresh manure mingled with smoke and sulphurous fog, thankfully, dampened down by the cold.

Flora entered Old Barrack Yard from the street crowded with purposeful walkers, while motor cars, carts, and horse-drawn hansoms moved along Knightsbridge like snails in the gathering fog. The clamour of the main road receded as she ventured between the high buildings on either side which loomed above her.

'Do you think we should go down here, Missus?' Sally plucked at Flora's sleeve. 'I'm sure Mr William wouldn't like it. You never know, the bloke who done that woman in might still be hanging about?'

'I doubt that, and Mr William is too busy to worry about me at the moment.' Flora reached a hand to the brick wall beside her that leached damp cold through her glove. If Sally's warning was meant to discourage her, it did the exact opposite. 'Go home if you like, but I'm going to take a look. You never know, the police might have missed something.'

The alley forked to the right, where it opened out into another, wider road lined with one-story buildings, each with wooden coach doors which told of their former life as an army barracks. Scarred and with peeling paint, one hung drunkenly to one side, revealing a pile of crates stacked on clumps of dirty hay where cavalry horses were once stabled.

In the shadow of a gothic church that loomed to her right at the end of the row, a neat squat building no bigger than a small family house stood, with three sash windows in a façade slightly above street level, a short flight of stone steps bounded by black railings leading up to a front door. A hanging sign above sported a soldier in Regency uniform and the words The Grenadier in black lettering.

'Is it true this place is haunted, Miss Flora?' Sally hung back.

'I didn't think you believed in ghosts.' Flora shook her head as she caught Sally's wide-eyed look. 'It's a building made of bricks and mortar, that's all. Nothing to be afraid of.'

'It's not that, but ladies don't go into public houses by themselves. It's not done.'

'I appreciate the lesson in social acceptance, but I'm here pursuant to an enquiry. Besides, there's no one here.'

The street lay empty, the only occupant a girl who swept the steps of the public house, a black wooden gate to one side led into a small yard in which wooden barrels had been stacked.

'Come ta see where that woman was killed, have ya?' The girl paused in her sweeping. She wore a faded green apron over a patched woollen dress, her arms bare to her elbows. Flora doubted the dress gave her much protection from the cold as goose bumps stood out on her white skin.

'We were just passing,' Flora said, realizing too late the alley was a dead end where a sturdy fence separated it from the next street.

'You ain't the only ones interested.' The girl planted both feet apart and tucked the broom into her side, one hand draped over the top. 'We've 'ad no end of nosey parkers coming round since it happened. Hobbes says it's been good

193

fer business, so he ain't complainin'.' Her voice contained a hard, cracked quality as if she were accustomed to shouting.

'Hobbes?' Flora enquired. 'Is that the landlord?'

'Nay, he's the manager, and a grasping sod he is an' all.' The girl wiped her free hand down her grubby apron. 'Wouldn't surprise me if he didn't start charging for the privilege. Joe Fulcher's the landlord, but there's no harm in him. Close as ye can get ter a gentleman, he is.'

'Did you see anything that night? Was the dead woman with anyone? A man maybe?' Flora crept closer. The girl was younger than she first thought, made world-weary by a sullen expression.

'Miss Flora,' Sally warned, giving the street a worried glance, but Flora ignored her.

'I couldn't say.' The girl shrugged. 'We was crammed to the rafters that night. Even the card room downstairs was full.'

'What about the other staff?' Flora persisted. 'Someone must have seen something. The woman's body was found not far from your front door.'

'I told yer, I didn't see nothing.' She swiped an arm beneath her nose, looking from Sally's plain brown coat to Flora's expensive cornflower blue one with its frogged fastenings.

'I don't mean to harass you,' Flora pressed her. 'I live nearby, you see and when I heard about that poor woman…' Flora shrugged. 'As you can imagine it was quite a shock.'

The girl eyed her as if this concept was beyond her understanding. 'We've 'ad lots of new customers since it 'appened. Seems murder's good for business. I heard she turned out to be a lady, do yer think that's true?'

'I believe so, yes.'

Panic flashed into the girl's eyes but was gone in an instant. 'Anyway, I didn't see nothing and now if you'll 'scuse me, I've work to do.' She swung the broom in a wide arc, catching the end smartly with her other hand, turned and disappeared through the black gate that clicked shut behind her.

'Well, that didn't get us anywhere,' Flora muttered.

'Course not, Missus.' Sally rolled her eyes. 'Girl like that ain't going to say anything to a toff, even if she does know something.' Wordlessly, Sally eyed Flora's cashmere coat and fox fur muff, ending with another dismissive tut when she reached the matching hat.

'I'm not a toff.' Flora's cheeks burned, partly because she acknowledged that she had changed since her days as an upper servant, but to be referred to thus sounded like an insult.

'We may as well go.' Flora started to leave. 'I doubt the landlord would be any more cooperative, even if I went inside, which I won't.' Loitering outside a licensed premises was one thing, but Sally was right, only women of a certain type would dare venture inside a bar alone.

'There are ways.' Sally placed a restraining hand on her arm. 'I've got an idea. Got any money?'

'I beg your pardon?'

'Lucre, coppers. You know, for a bribe?' She stuck out her gloved hand. 'Look, if you ain't going to listen to me or Mr William, I might as well see what I can find out.'

'I hope you know what you're doing,' Flora muttered, delving into her bag for her purse. 'Is that enough?' She handed over four half-crowns.

'Depends who I offer it to.' Sally's cheeky grin lit up her face.

'Depends to whom you offer it,' Flora corrected her.

Sally rolled her eyes. 'You wait here and I'll be back in a jiffy.' Before Flora could question her further, she had disappeared through the side gate.

Alone in the cold alley, the light muted by a layer of fog, Flora fidgeted, her discomfort worsening when two men in workmen's clothes and battered bowlers emerged from the public house; loud laughter drifted from the open door behind them. The younger of the two raked her with a half-amused, almost insulting glance as he passed. She could have sworn the other one winked at her.

The two disappeared into the mist, only to be replaced by a shadowed figure moving toward her. A well-dressed man in a black overcoat appeared from the corner, cane swinging as he walked. She narrowed her eyes but could not make out any individual features. Unwilling to be subjected to speculation she looked around in panic, then her alarm dissolved at the sight of a familiar face.

'Mr Lange?' Her uncertainty dissolved as he drew nearer. 'It is you.'

'Mrs Harrington?' His cane halted in mid-swing, his eyes wary. 'What are *you* doing here?'

'I assume that like me, you are curious about where your sister was murdered.' A shadow crossed his features and she winced. 'I'm sorry, that sounded awful, didn't it? I'll try again. I felt there may have been something the police missed and, as I live close by, I came to take a look.'

'Strangely you are right, in that I have come on a similar mission.' He relaxed his shoulders and leaned on the cane. 'I too harboured a desire to see where my sister spent her last hour. Does that seem morbid to you?'

'Not at all. You lost someone close to you in shocking circumstances. It's natural to seek answers as to why it happened.'

'It's such a nondescript place, almost shabby.' His eyes swept the front of the public house, its less attractive features blurred by the mist. 'I cannot imagine what she was doing here.'

'Not that uninteresting, apparently the place is haunted by the spirit of a subaltern who was murdered by his colleagues because—' she broke off as his face drained of colour. 'It's not important. Just something I heard.'

'In which case, Evie might have some company.' A smile pulled at the corner of his mouth, reminding Flora that he was an attractive man, though his features were marred once again by melancholy. 'I thought I might find some answers here, but all I have are more questions.'

'What kind of questions?'

'That she might have been—' he hesitated before continuing. 'Perhaps her attack was of a more – intimate nature?'

'Oh, I see.' His words struck her like a blow. This was something that had not occurred to her before. 'Inspector Maddox didn't intimate that it was that sort of attack. Did he do so to you?'

'He did not, but then why would he? I doubt he would take my feelings into account.' He sounded almost bitter, but then was that surprising?

'The police don't normally keep that sort of detail secret. Not from relatives.' *Unless they feel it might help trap a murderer.*

'I suppose I ought to take comfort in that.' He gave the alley another sweeping glance. 'I still cannot fathom why Evie would come here.'

'Nor can I. If she had an assignation with someone, why not choose the lounge of the Alexandra Hotel round the corner? It's more respectable than here.'

'I see you have given the matter some thought, Mrs Harrington.' He shifted his cane from one hand to the other. 'But then I seem to recall you said that you saw Evangeline the night she died.'

'I did yes, but she walked off in the opposite direction, so it seems odd she would come back here later in the evening.'

'Yes, yes that does seem odd.'

'Is it possible Evangeline's fiancé brought her here?' Flora blurted, mainly to stop him bringing up the fact Evangeline had last been seen with Mr Crabbe. There was still something about that man William was keeping to himself.

'Harry Flynn?' He spat the words as if they tasted bitter. 'It's possible, I suppose. Maybe he wanted to shock Evangeline by showing her a darker side of life. If so, his plan went wrong.'

Flora didn't respond. It would have had to go *very wrong* for Evangeline to end up dead. Though somehow Flora doubted that was what happened. What intrigued her more was the reason for Mr Lange's low opinion of his sister's fiancée? 'Did you disapprove of their engagement?'

'I'm in no position to approve or disapprove.' He sniffed, but his feelings were clear. 'Harry Flynn is a type, if you understand what I mean.'

'Not really, but if you're about to be indiscreet, I assure you it will go no further. I won't be shocked either. I'm a married woman, don't forget.'

'A fact you have reminded me of at least twice to my recollection.' He smiled, propped his walking cane between his splayed feet and rested both hands on the top. 'Mr Flynn has a certain – reputation. I suspect he is one of those men who feel a chap should be free to conduct liaisons with women whether married or not. It wouldn't surprise me to hear he frequents places like this.' He cocked his chin at The Grenadier behind him.

'Would Evangeline have agreed to come here if Harry had asked her?' Flora had her own opinions of men who treated marriage as an inconvenience, but this was not the time to voice them.

'Had he lured her with promises of enlisting others to the suffragist cause do you mean?' He cocked a satirical eyebrow. 'I doubt she would have found many recruits here. As you see it's not a place for women.' His eyes widened as if something had occurred to him. 'Of course, I had forgotten. Flynn is a convert isn't he?' He wrinkled his nose in distaste. 'In which case, I've no doubt Evangeline would have marched straight into Hell itself to bring more followers into the fold.'

'You think they *could* have been here together that night?'

'Every chance I would think. Inspector Maddox won't reveal anything about his investigation, despite that my father pesters the man daily for news. He's still adhering to the belief she was killed in a random robbery.'

'I'm not convinced of that theory either. Strangling is too direct, too personal.'

'She knew her killer do you mean?' He slanted a downward glance at her she couldn't interpret? Whatever had gone through his mind he kept to himself.

With still no sign of Sally, an idea came to her. 'We could talk to the landlord. Maybe he remembers seeing Evangeline with someone that night'

'I-I uh don't know if that's wise.' He tugged his collar away from his throat with one hand and swallowed. 'I'm sure the police must have already questioned him.'

'What harm could it do to simply ask? It won't take long, and after all, why did you come here if not to discover something?'

'You're willing to enter a public house?'

'I'll come into the saloon bar with you,' Flora said carefully. 'Even I'm not brave enough to enter the public one.' His reticence seemed odd, but the fact he was there at all showed he was tortured by what had happened to his sister.

The low-ceilinged saloon bar was deserted but for a lone drinker nursing a glass of unidentifiable dark liquid at a corner table. A blast of cold air accompanied them inside, quickly dispelled by a roaring fire that crackled and spat in a room no larger than a domestic parlour. The smell of fresh sawdust mingled with stale beer and a faint odour of male sweat made Flora take shallow breaths.

'What would you like to drink?' her companion asked as they approached the counter.

Flora hesitated, eyeing the row of wooden casks arranged on the back bar. Each one displayed the contents, among which was light ale, brandy, and Old Tom, which she knew to be sweet gin, but she had never tried it before and doubted this was a suitable time to begin.

'Er, I have no idea. What do you suggest?'

'I cannot see you trying the ale, but most pubs keep ginger beer on draught.' He raised his arm and summoned a man in a leather apron and striped shirt who slowly wiped a glass with a linen cloth. His sleeves were rolled back to his elbows and secured with black bands.

'A half and half for me and a ginger beer for the lady.'

At the word "lady", the barman gave Flora what Riordan Maguire would have called an old-fashioned look. His wary glare through black pebble eyes told her this was likely the man, Hobbes, the skivvy outside had spoken about. Without taking his eyes off her, Hobbes retrieved two glasses from the shelf above their heads, half-filled one glass with ale from a cask then topped it up from a bottle of porter. He inserted a second glass beneath a spout into which cloudy amber liquid frothed and set this one in front of Flora.

'Have one yourself,' Mr Lange said brightly, adding a shilling to the pile of coins he pushed across the counter. 'Keep the change.'

'That's most agreeable of you, sir.' Hobbes' expression cleared in delighted surprise, the money disappearing with lightning speed.

'Heard you had some nasty business here the other night?' Mr Lange said, taking a mouthful of his drink.

'Nasty indeed.' He pulled a pint for himself. 'Not had anything like that happen around here before. Even had a couple of reporters nosing about last coupla days.'

'Did you know the lady?' Flora cradled her glass in her gloved hands and took a sip, finding the contents delicious, if slightly tart. She scuffed her feet on the sawdust-covered floor, hoping none would stick to her boots, relaxed now he had stopped glaring at her.

'She weren't no lady.' He leaned one elbow on the bar, his chin jutted forward. 'Not if she was hanging about outside. But as I told that policeman who was in here asking questions, that woman was never inside this bar.'

'Are you sure?' Flora asked.

'Positive. My staff would have asked her to leave if she had been.' His eyes shifted towards Flora, then narrowed. 'I don't allow *that* sort inside my pub.'

'Which sort are you referring to?' Flora demanded, incensed by the innuendo.

'Women who go about town alone late at night, when it ain't respectable.' He wiped his hands on the same linen towel, then slung it over one shoulder.

'How do you know if she didn't come inside?' Flora asked, no longer shy. 'And this gentleman is Mr Lange, who happens to be her brother.'

'Didn't mean to give offence, sir.' The hostility faded from the barman's eyes and he tucked in his chin. 'I run a tidy house here. And er-my condolences, sir.' His eyes lingered on Flora's companion as if he was trying to place Mr Lange, but failed as his eyes slid away, displaying no recognition.

'I'm sure the lady didn't mean to imply otherwise.' Lange cleared his throat and turned aside quickly, a hand to his face as if he were embarrassed. He nudged Flora's arm as he did so, spilling ginger beer onto the countertop.

The barman tutted, but before he could apply a cloth to the spill, a man at the corner table loudly demanded a refill. With a curt nod and another mumbled platitude about death and loss, he excused himself.

'I apologise for his disrespect.' Mr Lange eased his arm away from the spill on the counter. 'However, I wish you hadn't said that. Whatever gossip is circulating, my presence here will now be added to it.'

'I'm sorry, but the man was offensive. I was only defending your sister's reputation.' Aware her own appeared to have received a battering in the last few minutes.

'I doubt we'll get any more out of him. Not that there is anything to learn if he didn't see Evangeline.' Lange retrieved his cane and extended his arm to indicate they leave.

Flora set her half-full glass on the counter and preceded him outside where she was greeted by a blast of frigid air.

'Might I escort you somewhere, Mrs Harrington?' he asked as they gained the alley. 'I would rather not leave you here on your own.'

'I was here when you arrived, Mr Lange.' A smile twitched at her mouth as she caught sight of Sally, who waited by the gate.

'Then I'll bid you good day.' He tipped his hat and, cane swinging, strode away towards the gate that led to Wilton Place.

'What's wrong wiv 'im?' Sally joined her when he was out or earshot, her chin cocked at Mr Lange's receding back.

'I think I spoke out of turn – again.' Flora couldn't help feeling his annoyance was out of proportion to her faux pas. Why didn't he want the barman to know the dead woman was his sister? And if not, why come to The Grenadier at all?

'Do you think you should be encouraging strangers, Missus?'

'Not a stranger, we're already acquainted. He's Evangeline Lange's brother. He wanted to see where she died, though I don't think he was comfortable about it. I pushed him into talking to the barman, who said Evangeline was never inside his bar.'

'Or he doesn't want her to have been. Might be bad for business.'

'You could be right about that.' Flora couldn't help a smile in grudging respect for this wisp of a girl who knew so much about the less agreeable aspects of life. 'Anyway, you were gone a long time. What have you been doing?'

'That girl with the broom, whose name's Meg, by the way. She showed me the cellar, which is used as a card room and there's money pinned to the ceiling. Paper money. She said it was to pay Cedric's debt or something. Very odd she was, maybe she's a bit soft in the 'ead?'

'Ah, I think I know what that's about. That ghost Mr Dunne mentioned the other day. And don't look at me like that, I know you were listening. Did Meg happen to see Miss Lange?'

'I did better than that.' Sally reached into her coat and withdrew a square tapestry bag the size of a small book with a gilt catch. 'This belonged to that Evangeline woman.'

'Where did you get that?' Flora reached out a hand, but Sally was quicker and whipped it out of sight under her coat.

'Not here.' She made a 'follow me' gesture and set off back the way they had come.

'You're being very mysterious.' Flora hurried to keep up with her as Sally sped back along the alley, turned right into Knightsbridge and headed for Prince Albert Mansions.

'I don't want anyone to know we've got it,' Sally whispered as the door flapped shut behind them, muffling the traffic sounds from the street. 'I promised she wouldn't get into trouble.'

The lobby was empty but for the porter, Dunne, who stood behind his desk, a heavily veiled woman on the other side stood with her back turned to them. She didn't turn around when Flora greeted Dunne with a smile and a nod, though even had she done so, her veil was so thick, Flora would still not have known who she was.

'Come into my room,' Flora said once inside. 'Randall won't bother us in there.'

'How can you know this is Evangeline's?' Flora watched as Sally upended the bag onto the bed.

An expensive item, the bag was hand-stitched with a floral tapestry design on one side and good quality russet velvet on the other; the clasp made of heavy brass. Flora examined the jumbled contents on the counterpane, amongst which were an enamelled mirror, an empty change purse, and a tortoiseshell comb, together with a tiny cone of twisted paper which contained liquorice comfits.

'This might convince you.' Sally held up a lace handkerchief with the initials "EL" embroidered in one corner.

'I see, yes, that makes it more likely. But why don't the police have this? Or at the very least the landlord of The Grenadier.'

'From what Meg said about him, no one would have seen it again, not least the coppers. Besides, Meg's a barmaid, and a "lush toucher".'

'I beg your pardon?' The soft material of the bag crackled beneath Flora's fingers. Frowning, she delved inside.

'Someone who robs people when they've had too much to drink. Spotted it the minute I saw her.'

'Which begs the question as to how this Meg stole Evangeline's bag if she wasn't inside The Grenadier?'

'I'll tell yer if you don't go repeating it to that police inspector.'

'Why wouldn't I mention— Oh, never mind, what did she say?' Flora decided to exercise a healthy dose of scepticism to whatever the girl might have said, but she might as well hear it.

'She came into the yard to throw out some rubbish and spotted what she thought was some drunk fallen over in the alley, but when she went to take a look, she saw it was a woman and she was dead.'

'Didn't she go and fetch someone to help?'

'I ain't finished.' Sally silenced her with a hard look. 'She said she was about to, but spotted the bag tucked under the body. She bent to pick it up, which was when some punters

205

came out the front door of the pub and spotted the body. It was them who alerted the landlord.'

'So this Meg just took the bag and didn't tell anyone?' Flora frowned at Sally's blithe acceptance of the barmaid's behaviour. 'She robbed a dead woman?'

'Don't look so shocked, Missus.' Sally hunched her shoulders though she couldn't meet Flora's eyes. 'It's not so easy to do the right thing all the time. Meg felt bad about the bag or she wouldn't have come clean would she?'

'And why exactly did she "come clean", as you put it?' Flora rummaged in the silk lining.

'Simple.' Sally shrugged, apparently pleased with herself. 'I gave her five bob and said she could keep whatever was in the purse.' She held up the coin purse and shook it. 'I doubt Miss Evangeline Lange walked about with an empty coin purse, but I didn't ask how much she took. Getting the bag was the important thing.'

'Good work, Sally. I suppose.' Though Flora wasn't entirely happy about how the bag was obtained. It would have to be handed over to Inspector Maddox at some stage, but she would think about that later. 'There's something else here.' Her fingers closed on a folded slip of paper that she brought into the light and opened it out. 'It's some sort of receipt.'

'What's it for?' Sally peered over her shoulder.

'A box number at Boltons Library. That's a few doors down in Knightsbridge.'

'What would this Miss Lange want to buy a box for?' Sally asked.

'She didn't *buy* a box, Sally, it's a mail receiving service. You pay a rental and have correspondence delivered to their address.'

'But it says it's a library.'

'They lend out books as well. We've walked past it on our way to Harrods. Have you not noticed it?'

'Don't go in much for books.' Sally shrugged. 'Why would she want one of those?'

'I have no idea, but I'm going to find out.' Flora refolded the receipt and climbed off the bed.

Why would Evangeline need to have her letters sent anywhere but her home? What kind of people was she writing to? Another part of the puzzle that made up the enigmatic Miss Lange. Flora scooped up the items back into the bag and glanced at the ormolu clock on the mantle whose hands stood at twenty minutes to one o'clock. 'Come on. We might make it before they close for luncheon.'

'First put me coat on, then take it off, now you want it back on again,' Sally mumbled, following her out. 'I'll catch pneumonia at this rate.'

'Stop complaining, girl, you haven't had so much fun in months.'

Chapter 18

Flora pushed through the main door of Prince Albert Mansions but was forced to a halt when she almost collided with a woman who was on her way in. Flora backed away, murmuring her apologies.

'It is of no consequence,' the stranger muttered through a heavy black veil as she swept past Flora and up the stairs, a hint of a floral perfume trailing behind her.

'Good afternoon, Miss,' Dunne said, distracting Flora. 'Damp out today. That fog's nasty stuff. You're soaked afore you knows it.'

'Uh, yes indeed.' Flora turned towards him with a polite smile, then glanced up at the landing, which stood empty. 'Who was that lady who came in just now? You were talking to her when I arrived earlier.'

'That would be Mrs Crabbe.' He stroked his chin with one hand. 'Can't say I was talking to her exactly. She tends not to engage in conversation with the likes of me, if you see what I mean.'

'I think I do, Mr Dunne.' Flora smiled as an image of her mother-in-law floated into her head. 'Didn't you say she doesn't go out much?'

The porter's brows rose into his hairline. 'Come to think of it I did, and she doesn't. That's the first time I've seen her all week.'

'I see, well thank you, Mr Dunne.' Flora ushered Sally outside into a light drizzle, glad she didn't have to go far as drops of moisture gathered on strands of hair that escaped her hat. The road was less crowded now it was nearer the luncheon hour. Apart from the horse buses and carts that whooshed through gathering puddles, the only pedestrians were a nanny who manhandled a bulky, coach-built pram through the narrow Hyde Park gate and a man in a grey overcoat with his hat pulled down who strode along on the park side of the road.

The shop window of Boltons Library was partly obscured by handwritten cards of all shapes and sizes, some pristine and new, others faded by the sun. Most of the messages they contained offered handyman services or appealed for lady's maids, butlers and domestic staff. Each displayed an accompanying number in a corner to which the applicant could apply, thus keeping the employer's identity a secret, which reiterated to Flora that Miss Evangeline Lange had a desire for secrecy.

The heavy glazed door resisted Flora's gentle push, opening just enough to give her a reflected view of the road behind her. The man in grey had halted opposite, his attention focused in her direction. His face struck her as familiar, but she couldn't remember where, or even if, she had seen him before. Pausing, she turned back to get a clearer look, but a horse-drawn bus blocked her view, disgorging a stream of passengers onto the pavement. When it pulled away again, the man was no longer there. *Really, Flora, you are imagining things.*

'What's wrong, Missus?' Sally stared up at her.

'I thought— Oh, it was nothing. This constant fog makes me see shadows everywhere.' She straightened her shoulders and gave the door a firm shove. 'Wait for me inside the door would you, Sally, while I go to the counter.'

Set to one side behind a stout counter stood a wooden cabinet similar to the one at Prince Albert Mansions into which Mr Dunne placed the residents' mail. Rows of doors were stacked six high, each about nine inches square with a brass plaque below a number.

Gas lamps hissed from the walls, throwing a sulphurous glow onto rows of bookshelves that clung to the walls up to ceiling height on all sides. Assistants slid ladders attached to poles across the front of the shelves, their intermittent clicks the only sound except for hushed whispers.

'May I help you?' An unsmiling woman alerted Flora to the fact she had reached the head of the line. Her mousy hair was pulled back from her face in a severe bun, her dress a black bombazine garment with mutton-leg sleeves making her shoulders so wide, her top half looked triangular.

'I hope so.' Flora scrabbled for the speech she had prepared on her way there. 'I wanted to enquire about the box number service you offer, what do—'

'Sixpence a week for each box, payable in advance,' the woman recited in a bored voice.

'Ah, well I didn't exactly want to rent one, I wished to know whether or not any correspondence had been put into a specific box over the last few days. I have the number here.' She withdrew the receipt from her pocket and held it out, though the woman didn't glance at it.

'Is the box in your name?'

'No. My cousin hired it,' Flora said without so much as a blink, though she hoped the lie wouldn't come back to haunt her.

'Details of who hires the boxes and the nature of their contents at any time is the property of the person who signs the hire agreement,' she recited in the same irritating monotone, her attention focused on a point above Flora's head.

Flora inhaled slowly as she summoned patience. 'I understand that however, the person – my cousin – who hired this particular box is now dead.'

'In that case, your cousin won't be needing it anymore will she?'

Flora gaped, though in the next breath, she had to agree the woman had a point. Annoyed with herself at not having thought this through, she hesitated, then jumped at the sound of a man's voice.

'The library is about to close. If you don't mind.' A man in an old-fashioned stove pipe hat held in both hands pushed past her to the counter.

'I do apologize.' She stepped aside and re-joined Sally.

'No luck?'

Flora shook her head. 'Now, what do we do?' While she contemplated her next move, a fair-haired young man emerged from a hansom that had drawn up at the kerb and entered the library.

He glanced up and his eyes met Flora's. 'Mrs Harrington?' He paused with his hand on the brass handle in the act of closing it. 'It is Mrs Harrington, isn't it? Harry Flynn. We met at the NUWSS meeting.'

'Yes, of course. Mr Flynn.' She accepted his outstretched hand. 'What a coincidence. I had no idea you used this library.' Perhaps it wasn't pure chance which brought him here. Could he be following her?

'There's no reason why you should,' he replied reasonably. He glanced up at the counter, then back at Flora. 'Look, they are about to close, so let me get my letters before we continue this conversation. What do you say?'

'Well - Yes, if you would like to, I—'

'Excellent. Wait there, I won't be a moment.'

The sour-faced woman behind the counter had her coat on and looked about to leave, but on seeing Harry, her face broke into a parody of a girlish smile and she rushed forward to offer assistance with a flirtatious tilt of her head.

Flora watched with amused resignation as she leapt to retrieve his letters, handing them to him with a caressing touch of her hand.

'Some people are just too bleeding obvious,' Sally said at her shoulder.

'Hush,' Flora whispered as Harry strode back and guided her onto the street where oppressive slate grey clouds hung overhead which augured more later.

'You were about to tell me what brought you here,' Harry said.

'Actually, I don't think I was.' Flora pushed her hands into her muff, having hoped she would do the questioning. 'I'm staying a few doors away at my father's apartment. I thought I might investigate how to join the library while I'm here. I'm fond of reading.'

'Never did get along much with books.' He offered her his arm. 'I'm more of an outdoor sports enthusiast. However the library also runs a mail service, which I use on occasion.'

'I see.' She checked behind her to ensure Sally followed, while wondering why a young man of evident means would have his mail sent to a box number.

He must have seen the confusion on her face and laughed. 'I can see you are dying to ask, though the explanation is uninteresting. I have a flat around the corner in Lowndes Square, but there's no porter. The mail tends to be left in the hall. A few items have gone astray in the past, so this way I can be sure nothing goes missing.'

'Your family don't reside in the city?' She cast him a slow, sideways look as they walked. He lived almost next door to the Harriet Parker Academy, though she wasn't sure if this was significant or not.

'Heavens no. they prefer the quiet countryside of Berkshire.' He laughed a rich, deep laugh which did not sit well on a man who was supposedly grieving the death of a fiancée. As if he guessed her thoughts, his smile faded. 'Sorry, I don't mean to be flippant. It's only that at times I completely forget Evangeline is gone. Then it hits me when I least expect it and – well, I'm sure I don't have to explain.'

'I quite understand. Losing someone forever takes some getting used to and you must still feel raw.'

Their slow walk had brought them to the Alexandra Hotel, where his steps slowed as he stared at the entrance to Old Barrack Yard.

'I wondered.' A nerve twitched beside his mouth, rapidly suppressed. 'Would you care to join me for a cup of coffee?' He indicated the door to the hotel. 'It's bitter out here and we could take advantage of their lounge fire.' He shuddered in comical emphasis. 'And no one could regard my invitation as improper if your maid is here?'

Flora hesitated, then glanced back to Sally, who nodded in encouragement before pretending to examine one of the statues that flanked the hotel entrance.

'I should be delighted to join you for coffee, Mr Flynn,' Flora said. Why not? After all they were in a public place and as he pointed out, Sally was with them.

The doorman bowed them into a lobby dominated by a curved wrought-iron staircase that twisted above to an upper landing, its fine detailing picked out in gold. A reception counter took up the entire side of the room, beside which stood a cluster of immaculate bellboys in blue uniforms.

In response to a silent gesture from Flora, Sally took a bench seat beside the main door, where a doorman relieved them of their coats.

'We could go upstairs if you wish by means of the ascending room?' Harry suggested.

'I beg your pardon?' Flora halted beneath the entrance canopy and stared at him. Had she misjudged him completely and his invitation was anything but innocent?

'Forgive me, I expressed myself badly.' He flushed, and coughed discreetly into a fist. 'This is one of the few hotels with an elevator. There is also a rather grand coffee room on the first floor, but perhaps you're right and the lounge will do.'

Flora couldn't help but smile at his obvious discomfort, as still blushing, he extended his arm to indicate she precede him into the lounge, while Sally's snort of amused laughter followed.

Ignoring her, Flora took in her surroundings, where she noted walls covered in flock wallpaper and hangings in womb-like red, lifted by reflected light from a chandelier several feet wide that hung inches above their heads. Typical of a hotel popular during the last half of the previous century; all sombre colours and heavy fabrics, giving a feeling of warm intimacy.

'Madam.' A waiter showed them to a pair of high-backed chairs set in a bay window. 'Coffee for two is it, sir?'

'If you please and ask what the lady in the corner would like.'

The waiter snapped a brief salute, departing with the words, 'And it's nice to see you again, sir.'

'Oh, er, and you.' Harry gave him a vague look as he backed away.

'Is this place a favourite haunt of yours?' Flora stared around at the opulent gilt and glass that shimmered in the light.

'Not really, and now I come to think of it, I haven't been here for some time. Not since last Easter. I'm surprised the chap remembered me. Oh, well, I must have one of those faces.'

'Yes, you must. And you were right about the fire, it's lovely.' Flora eased closer to the wide Adam-style hearth where orange flames crackled and spat. 'This was a good idea. And it was nice of you to order a drink for my maid.'

'Well, I could hardly invite myself to your father's apartment,' Harry said. 'That would have been most improper.'

'Almost as improper as inviting me to go upstairs with you.' Flora slowly removed her gloves.

'I hoped I had adequately apologized for that.' Harry tugged his trousers above the knees and lowered himself into a chair at right angles to hers. 'I intended no offence.' His tone softening into persuasion, something Flora imagined he used often. 'Lydia told me you brought the dreadful news about Evangeline to her at the school. It was kind that you tried not to let her hear it from the police. Though that doesn't answer the question as to where your interest lies in the affair.'

'Perhaps I do owe you some sort of an explanation.' The warmth of his charm reassured her, which she hoped she would not come to regret. She had trusted handsome and plausible young men before who had turned out to be murderers. Two of them in fact. 'By coincidence, I happened to see Evangeline outside my father's apartment building on the night she died.'

'Lydia told me that curiosity brought you to the suffragist meeting, but I'm still not sure what that has to do with anything.' He arranged his jacket as he spoke and buffed one shoe tip with a hand so she could not see the expression in his eyes.

Flora licked her lips, suddenly nervous, the fact she had been economical with the truth came back to her in a rush. 'I'm sorry if you think I deceived both you and Lydia, but it was more than curiosity. I had hoped the lady I saw wasn't Evangeline, but as it turned out my suspicions were correct. Do you always share close confidences with Miss Grey?'

'There was nothing untoward, I assure you. I've known Lydia for a while, and losing Evangeline was devastating for us both.'

'I'm sorry I didn't mean to imply anything.' Or did she? Didn't Lydia say Harry liked the society of free-thinking young women prepared to defy their families and move about town unchaperoned? Then there was what Tilly had said about Harry's frequent visits to Lydia.

'You're forgiven, though am I to assume that your visit to Boltons Library was not a coincidence either?'

'Not exactly,' she said carefully, his directness taking her by surprise.

The waiter returned with the coffee, though as he bent to place a cup before Flora his glasses slipped from his nose and bounced off the surface of the table.

'I'm, exceedingly sorry, Madam.' He retrieved them clumsily. 'Small accident in the kitchens earlier which resulted in the breakage of my best pair. These are my spare and don't fit so well.' He backed away, red-cheeked.

'Not a problem at all,' Harry waved him away with an amiable smile then leaned forward to whisper, 'I shan't allow that to affect his tip.'

Flora studied him covertly, wondering if a man concerned about not disappointing a waiter could murder his own fiancée in cold blood. If it was cold. For all she knew they could have had a passionate row in that alley, and Harry had strangled her in a sudden moment of uncontrolled rage.

'I hope you don't take this as an insult, Mrs Harrington.' Harry returned his coffee cup to its saucer, and leaned closer. 'But you are quite easy to read. Your startling eyes give so much away.'

'Really?' Flora raised one brow at him in an attempt to be enigmatic, but it only served to make him laugh.

'You want to know if I'm the type of man who could strangle someone I profess to care for.'

'I wasn't thinking any such thing.' Flustered, she buried her nose in her own cup but knew she did not fool him.

'For your information, I had a pet rabbit when I was a child and it broke its leg. My father told me to put it out of its misery, but I couldn't bring myself to do it. Pater wasn't at all impressed.'

'What happened to the rabbit?'

'My mother killed it. Quite efficiently too. I, however, lost the respect of both of them. I blame that incident for their abandoning me to make my own way after university. I feel sure they would have cancelled my inheritance if they could, but my wealth comes from my grandfather so they cannot do much about it. And in answer to your next question, I inherit the lot when I reach twenty-five. Therefore I didn't need Evangeline's fortune.'

'I promise you I wasn't going to ask such a question, but I will admit the strangling part intrigues me.'

'I asked Inspector Maddox about that too.' He eased forward on his seat, both forearms balanced on his thighs. 'Do you know it would take thirty seconds of steady pressure as a minimum to strangle someone of Evie's physical make-up and strength. Thirty seconds is a long time to watch the life leave someone, don't you think?'

'Indeed, yes.' Flora replaced the shortbread biscuit she was about to bite into onto her plate, no longer hungry. 'It would take a callous person to do such a thing, and a strong one.' She changed the subject. 'I was unaware you lived nearby, Mr Flynn. Or that you used the library.'

'I haven't been following you if that's what you think.' He replenished their cups with a steady hand. 'Though I'm glad of the chance to talk to you.'

'Oh, and why is that?' A whiff of steam rose from the cup he handed her, from which an enticing aroma filled her senses without a repeat of her earlier nausea.

'Lydia seemed to think you might know something about who killed my Evie.'

His possessiveness was so unlike his casual attitude toward Evangeline's whereabouts at the suffrage meeting, Flora looked up in surprise. *But then he didn't know Evangeline was dead at the time. Or did he?*

'My connection with her is no more than you already know, in that she met her death a few yards from my front door. Or rather my father's. As I said before, I hoped it wasn't her, but hoping doesn't change anything, does it?'

'No, it doesn't.' He relaxed back into his chair. 'Might I ask why you thought the woman you saw was Evie?'

'It was the brooch. The one shaped like the NUWSS society badge which prompted me to attend the meeting. I met Lydia there and, well, you know the rest.' Flora cradled her coffee cup. 'How did you learn of her death? Did Lydia tell you?' Evangeline's name hadn't been released to the newspapers as yet, but Harry Flynn seemed to know what had happened.

'Inspector Maddox subjected me to some rather impertinent questioning last night,' he replied, ignoring her reference to Lydia. 'He said I had been implicated by her brother, John Lange.' He fidgeted and adjusted his tie. 'Not that I was very surprised. The man has never liked me.'

'Having become recently acquainted with the Inspector, I sympathize.' She was about to mention an even more recent acquaintance with Evangeline's brother but decided it might be counterproductive when she had not yet made up her mind about either of them. It occurred to her then that Harry and John Lange were not physically dissimilar, with the same height and build, though Harry's hair was lighter and he was not quite so handsome. Strange how a heavy lower lip marred otherwise perfect features.

'I wrote a letter to Evie the other night,' Harry said, bringing her thoughts back to the present. 'The same night she died as it turned out. In it, I apologized for upsetting her. Told her if she wished to wait longer for the wedding I would understand and accede to her wishes.' He fiddled with his shirt cuff. 'The marriage was our parents' wish, you know, but I simply thought that as she had accepted the idea, what was the point of waiting?'

Flora nodded, though his directness surprised her. Or was he trying to divert her suspicions by being the concerned fiancée?

'When her father turned up at the suffrage meeting,' he went on, 'I really did think she had gone to Brighton to teach us both a lesson. Me for being insufferable and her father for his continued scenes about her activities with the NUWSS. He's one of those men who thinks slavery should never have been abolished.' He gave a laugh that was more a snort. 'I didn't send it of course. The letter, I mean. It's still in the bureau in my flat.' He caught the eye of a passing waiter and requested a refill of their coffee pot, giving Flora time to conduct an internal debate.

His controlled tone struck her as more exasperated than heartbroken, whereas John Lange's emotions had affected his composure. But then when she had first met him, John had only just learned of Evie's death, whereas Harry had had the luxury of a few hours to grow accustomed to it. Was there a cracked mirror or a smashed vase brushed into a corner somewhere in Harry's apartment to attest to how he first reacted?

Both Lydia and Miss Lowe had suggested Evangeline was unhappy about their engagement or was the only doubt on Evangeline's side? Couples married for many different reasons, especially those given guardianship of money. To preserve bloodlines was one, but sometimes for security also, neither of which Flora would have entertained as a reason to spend one's life with someone. She counted herself fortunate to have found Bunny.

'Unlike her father, you didn't disapprove of Evangeline's enthusiasm for the NUWSS, Mr Flynn?' She had to raise her voice slightly as the reception area had grown noisier as it filled with people arriving for luncheon.

'Me?' His brows pulled together in an enquiring look. 'Ah, did you think I joined the movement to please Evie, or perhaps because I sought the company of free-thinking young women?'

'I didn't mean to imply anything like that,' she lied, uncomfortable with his powers of perception.

'I'm a great admirer of Mrs Fawcett as it happens. She's worked tirelessly for years trying to change the government's view of women's role in society. I only hope this new order led by the Pankhurst woman doesn't ruin what she has thus far achieved. Howard Lange's objections were purely selfish. He thought Evie's involvement might affect his career, but then he said that about most of her views on life. Her being a teacher was also a bone of contention between them. They thought she was lowering herself.'

'You agree then, that women should have a place in the running of the country?'

'Actually, I do.' He raised his chin and smiled as if congratulating himself. 'Evie's father had given her some shares in his company when she reached her eighteenth birthday. Shares on which she was expected to pay tax, but she wasn't allowed to vote for the government which collected those taxes. They had some heated debates about it on occasion. Evie was always so enthusiastic about the future that we never ran out of things to talk about.' His eyes dulled suddenly, surprising Flora yet again with the depth of his feelings. He didn't strike her as a man who treated women lightly. Was John Lange wrong in his assessment of his sister's fiancé, or prejudiced against Harry Flynn for other reasons?

'You still haven't told me what you were doing at Boltons Library,' Harry asked suddenly.

Flora considered her response as he thanked the waiter who replaced the empty coffee pot with a full, steaming one.

'I think I did. As I said, I enjoy reading.' She wasn't ready to tell this man everything. After all, he could simply be an excellent actor.

'I see. You're sticking to that story, eh?' He chuckled but didn't appear angry, simply resigned. 'Inspector Maddox did give me a few details, which I assume he expected me to contradict and thus incriminate myself.'

'I can imagine him doing that.' Flora smiled.

'He said Evangeline's brooch was missing. Well, those weren't his exact words. He said she wasn't wearing any jewellery other than her engagement ring.' A shadow crossed his features and he stared off across the room. 'It's a family piece, the ring. The police seem to think it will come back to me when all this is over, but I don't care if I never see it again. When I mentioned the brooch he seemed to know nothing about it.'

'Which wasn't true as I had already mentioned I saw her wearing it that night,' Flora said. 'It's a horrible thought. To be killed for a piece of jewellery worth no more than a few shillings. Strange that her attacker left the engagement ring. If it was a robbery as Maddox believes.'

'A few shillings?' Harry scoffed. 'I should think not. Those were rubies and some rather fine emeralds. Evangeline had the brooch made to her specifications and was very proud of it. I often warned her to be careful where she wore the thing, but she took no notice.'

Flora frowned. John Lange had told her the brooch was made of semi-precious stones. He hadn't seemed very concerned to hear it was missing. Perhaps she was wrong. Or maybe Evangeline had misled John on purpose? It wouldn't be the first time a young woman was economic with the truth where her spending was concerned.

Chapter 19

Flora declined Harry's offer to walk her back to the apartment with the excuse her father's building was in sight of the hotel. They parted outside the main door, when, too late, she realized Harry now knew where she lived; which she found worrying, with him still high on the suspect list.

A sudden, heavy cloudburst sent her through the entrance doors at a run with Sally close behind her, the pair exploding into the lobby laughing hysterically and shaking raindrops off their coats and hats.

'I'll go and get the fire started, Miss Flora,' Sally called as she disappeared into the apartment.

Dunne noticed Flora's dismayed look at the double trail of wet footprints that now marred the pristine floor. 'Don't worry about that, Miss. I'll call someone from the housekeeping staff to see to it.' He approached a table, from which he swept a thin pile of newspapers and added them to a larger pile on the counter.

'That's quite a collection you have there, Dunne.' Flora nodded to the neat piles as she tweaked a damp curl off her forehead.

'Aye. I store them for the maids to light the fires in the mornings.'

Flora halted on her way to the apartment as a thought struck her and she returned to the desk. 'Mr Dunne, how far back do those papers go?'

''Bout four months or so.' He shuffled the pile and withdrew one from near the bottom. 'This pile here is from June. Why, Miss?'

'Might I borrow them for a few hours?' She summoned her most winning smile. 'I'll bring them back when I've finished with them.'

'Don't see why not.' The furrows in his forehead deepened. 'Though why you would want old copies of *The Times* is beyond me.'

'Thank you, Mr Dunne, you'll have them back as soon as I've finished with them.' She smiled again and hefted the pile into her arms.

'What have you got there, Missus?' Sally stared as Flora hurried past her.

'Come with me, I've got an idea.' She headed for the dining room, stopping short when she caught sight of the single place for luncheon set at the end of the oval table. 'Mr William isn't coming back for luncheon, I assume?'

'Er, he left a message with Randall.' Sally bit her bottom lip. 'He's eating out and is going straight to some meeting this afternoon.' She smoothed her apron and planted herself in front of Flora, obviously in an attempt to distract her. 'What's this idea you had then?'

'What? Oh, yes.' Swallowing her disappointment, Flora dumped the pile of newspapers on the sideboard. 'I was trying to work out why Evangeline would need that mailbox she had hired. I assume she was receiving correspondence via the box and not to her home, in which case, who would it be from?'

'It don't make sense to me.'

'It's quite logical really.' Flora arranged the papers in neat piles at the end of the table. 'How did whoever was writing to Evangeline know to contact her using the mailbox?'

'Because she told them?' Sally's upper lip curled in obvious confusion.

'That wouldn't make any sense would it? No, what if she wanted to hear from people she didn't know?'

'You've lost me, Missus. Why would she want letters from people she didn't know?'

Flora propped her hands on her hips and exhaled noisily. 'This made more sense inside my head, but I still think there's something to it. Suppose Evangeline was appealing to young women like herself who wanted to be suffragists but didn't know how because their families wouldn't allow it?'

'Go on, I'm following so far.' Sally narrowed her eyes. 'I think.'

'Consider this. To help young women who wanted to join the NUWSS without their parent's knowledge, Evangeline put an advertisement in the newspapers inviting correspondence. For instance, something like: "Do you want to know more about women's suffrage in confidence?"' Excitement mounted as she sifted through the papers, laying them in date order on the polished table. 'Lydia said Evangeline was an eager recruiter for the NUWSS. Perhaps she used that mailbox to attract new members without the correspondence being delivered to her home address where her parents would surely have disapproved.'

'But what's that got to do with her death?'

'That's the flaw in my theory, but it's worth pursuing. It's also the only lead we have. These papers might be able to tell us who was writing to Evangeline.'

'The classifieds you mean?' Sally asked, brightening.

'Exactly. We need to search for one which refers to Boltons Library and has the same number of the mailbox which is on the receipt.' Flora withdrew the slip of paper from her pocket and peered at it. 'Number 32. And while I'm doing this, would you finish lighting the fire, Sally? It's freezing in here.'

Sally hefted the coal scuttle into both hands with a grunt and crouched at the grate.

Randall appeared just as Flora finished sorting the papers into piles in date order, a plate covered by a metal dome held in both hands as if he carried the crown jewels.

'Your luncheon, Miss Flora.' His glance slid to the pile of newspapers, then to Sally, who bent to the hearth brushing coal dust into a shovel. 'Yours is in the kitchen, Miss Pond.'

Sally grunted and heaved to her feet, swiped a hand over her forehead leaving a soot mark. 'Would you serve it in here? Miss Flora and I has things to do.'

He gave a start, and with a muttered, 'As you wish,' backed out of the room.

'You shouldn't goad him, Sally.' Flora bit her lip to prevent a smile. 'He's not used to having someone like you disrupt his routine.'

'Aw, he's not as bad as he seems, Miss Flora. He's just a bit proud, like and not used to sharing his kitchen.' She slapped her hands together to remove the coal dust. 'I'll make him some tea this afternoon and tell him what I heard about that Lady Braeburn on the top floor. That'll bring him around.'

Flora smiled to herself as she picked up one of the papers from a pile on the dining table, admiring of her maid's ability to turn hostile characters to her advantage. Sally's sterling efforts with the barmaid, Meg had shown that.

*

The clock on the dining room mantle struck three and as the last melodious chime faded away, Sally yawned, her back arched against her chair. 'We've been at this over two hours, Missus, can we please stop. I'm getting the cramp in me back.'

'Not yet, we're only halfway through these.' Flora added the paper she was looking at to the pile on her left, then plucked another from the diminishing stack beside her.

'Staring at all those small letters is making my head hurt.' Sally picked up another one with obvious reluctance.

'Which is it, Sally, your back or your eyes? Choose an ailment and stick to it or no one will take your complaints seriously.'

'If I'm tired, Missus, I can't imagine why you aren't.'

'I'm on a quest and thus energized. Besides, why should I be?' Flora examined a list of requests for ladies' maids, valets, and private tutors. 'Goodness, there's a man here looking for his third wife.'

'How did he manage to lose her in the first place?' Sally grunted.

'Don't be facetious, Sally. He wishes to marry again and appears to think the classified section of a national newspaper will be the easiest course. I don't know whether to admire his confidence or condemn him for laziness.'

'Depends what he did with the previous two.' She slapped a hand on the paper in front of her. 'Are you sure you ain't tired? Ladies in your condition need to sleep a lot in the first weeks.'

'Please stop talking about it.' Flora lowered the paper and simultaneously cast a swift glance at the closed door. 'It's relatively early days and sometimes, well, these things don't work out the way we hope.'

'You don't have to tell *me*. Me eldest sister lost three before she had her boy. 'Is it 'cos you don't want the old Missus to know yet?'

'I simply wish to choose my own time to let people know the news.' Flora refrained from reminding Sally not to use that epithet in front of Beatrice Harrington. Sally was not stupid.

'I'll tell you now,' Sally snorted, 'if that woman don't know already, she'll sniff it out before long. Can't keep anything from her for long.'

'I'm aware of that.'

A month after she and Bunny married, Beatrice Harrington had dropped loaded hints which indicated the entire process was in Flora's control, and therefore her fault it had not happened sooner. She had made it clear that Flora had not benefitted from the correct upbringing in order to prepare her for the privilege of being married to her son, therefore producing the next in line was bound to be deemed too much for her to cope with without her mother-in-law's superior knowledge.

Then, of course, the entire experience would become a whole lot worse when the child arrived.

'Well you've got Mr Bunny,' Sally said as if she had read Flora's thoughts. 'He's such a lovely man and will make a wonderful father.'

'Thank you, Sally. I think so too.' She placed a hand on her lower belly, but it felt as flat as ever. 'I wish I could be so confident I'll make a good mother.'

That her own mother had disappeared when she was six re-emerged with all its accompanying doubts. No one knew what had actually happened, or claimed not to know, but Flora could not help wondering if the task of motherhood had proved too much for Lily Maguire, and she had sought escape?

Everyone who had known her mother said she never would have left of her own accord, but the truth remained unknown. Perhaps her mother *had* left her.

'You'll be all right, Miss Flora. Everyone will take good care of you and make sure nothing goes wrong.' Sally had apparently misinterpreted Flora's silence. 'Me second oldest sister got into the family way when she was in service. Wouldn't tell us who the dad was.' She folded and refolded the corner of the newspaper she was studying. 'She had to foster the baby out to a couple in the country or she would have lost her job.'

'That must have been very difficult for her.' Flora briefly forgot her own problems at the sadness in Sally's voice. 'Does she manage to see the child?'

'She used to. Every week on her day off.' Sally shrugged, her fingers stained by the ink from the page screwed in her hand. 'The woman who took her wrote and told us the baby died of diphtheria when she was ten months old. We found out later it was one of those baby farms. We'll never know if the little mite died, or was sold to a family somewhere. Me sister's married now and got another little girl, so perhaps she's better off not knowing the truth of it.'

'I'm so sorry.' Flora shuddered for the tiny life inside her that had barely begun. She went back to the newspaper, though the words blurred through sudden, inexplicable tears. She pushed thoughts of babies to the back of her mind and ran a finger down the page. A phrase scraped at her brain and she went back to read it again. 'I think I've found something,' Flora murmured, then louder. 'It's got nothing to do with suffragists, though. Listen to this, Sally.'

Miss EL seeks ladies who have endured ungentlemanly conduct from a man named 'Victor', reputed to be in his late twenties, of medium height with dark hair, a swarthy complexion and what have been described as 'hypnotic eyes'. To discuss your experiences with a view to restitution for grievances, reply to Miss E L Box No 32, Boltons Library, Knightsbridge. All information will be treated with sympathy and strict confidentiality.

'Do you think that's the one?' Sally's tone sounded doubtful. 'The number's right but there's no mention of Miss Lange or those suffragist women.'

'Miss EL?' Flora enunciated slowly, but Sally still looked sceptical. 'Forget the suffragists, I must have been wrong about that. It appears Evangeline was looking for someone named Victor, but the advertisement gives no more details or a surname.'

'Why would she be looking for him, Miss Flora?'

'I get the impression he has wronged someone and Evangeline is willing to help put that right.' *What had this man Victor done? And why was Evangeline taking it upon herself to do something about it? Was this Victor the reason she was reluctant to marry Harry Flynn?*

'Seems a bit convoluted to me.' Sally sniffed. 'Are you sure you ain't making something out of nothing?'

'*Are not*, Sally,' Flora corrected her without thinking, a finger pointed at the black framed advertisement. 'It's dated a week before Evangeline was killed.'

'Do you think this bloke found out she was asking about him and strangled her for it?'

'It's possible, though maybe this Victor is in trouble, and Evangeline was killed to stop her warning him. What we don't know is if she received any replies to this advertisement. It won't be easy finding out either.'

She recalled the stone-faced assistant at Boltons Library and chewed her bottom lip as she pondered what to do next. The part about restitution of grievances had struck her as particularly ominous.

The sound of William's voice in the hall as he greeted Randall brought Flora to her feet. She put the paper containing the advertisement to one side and gathered the others into an untidy pile.

'I'll keep him occupied while you return the rest of these papers to Dunne.' She slid her chair back neatly beneath the table. 'Go on, Sally.' She flapped an impatient hand when Sally did not move.

'I'm going.' Sally gathered the pile into her arms. 'Though I dunno what's so secret about a load of old newspapers.'

'He's bound to ask what this is all about and, again, I want to explain things in my own time.' She slid the remaining paper beneath one arm and emerged from the dining room in time to see William approaching the sitting room.

'I do apologize for missing yet another meal, Flora,' he said when she reached him. He gestured her to enter the room ahead of him, and followed her in, setting his briefcase down on a sofa. 'Work, you know. Although I would have much preferred your company to Crabbe's.' He opened his briefcase and rifled through the contents, removing a thick yellow covered folder.

'I quite understand. You're busy doing important government work. Did you have a good luncheon?'

'We had Simpsons' Original Fish Dinner. I would have asked you to join us, but I'm afraid they don't allow women in their dining room.' He exchanged one folder for another as he talked. 'Did you know, that they've served the same meal since 1757?'

'I expect it must smell rather by now,' Flora muttered under her breath.

'I beg your pardon?' William looked up from the folder which seemed to command all of his attention.

She shook her head, smiling at his obvious confusion. 'William, there's something I would like to—'

'Actually, I've pretty much finished for the day.' He consulted his half-hunter he took from a waistcoat pocket. 'How about I take you out to tea? As a sort of apology for having neglected you lately?'

'What, now?'

'Yes, why not?' He dropped the folder back into his briefcase, clicking the catches shut.

'That-that sounds lovely, thank you.' She fingered the paper in her hand, dismissing the speech she had prepared. Perhaps her revelation could wait.

'Is that today's newspaper? I haven't had a chance to read it yet.' He held out a hand.

'Er, no. Randall has left today's *Times* on your desk.' Flora took a deep breath, tucked the paper further beneath her arm and made for the door. 'I'll get my coat and hat.'

When she entered the street on William's arm, he made no attempt to hail a cab. Instead, he guided her to the left along the Knightsbridge Road.

'Where are we going?' Her breath formed a mist in front of her face, mingling with the fog as an early dusk descended on the city, infused with a sulphur yellow glow from the windows of the shops they passed.

'You'll see. It's only a ten-minute walk.'

Flora hurried to keep pace with William's long stride as they left the main thoroughfare of Knightsbridge, with its blare of traffic and discordant clop of horses, and turned into Hill Street.

'It just on the right here.' He drew her to a halt before a long building with a glass roof, the front façade decorated with stone dressings and ball finials. A sign on a parapet proclaimed it Prince's Skating Rink. 'This used to be a floorcloth factory, but was converted into a skating rink a few years ago.'

'Are we going inside?' Flora asked, hoping he wasn't about to initiate her into the sport at that moment. 'I've never been ice skating.'

'Don't worry, I don't expect you to venture onto the ice on your first visit. I saw an ice hockey match here last month, a sport which is becoming quite the thing.'

'I thought they played mostly in Canada? They get a lot more ice and snow than we do.'

'That's true, but it's growing in popularity here. I blame the Rhodes Scholarship, which has brought many Canadians and Newfoundlanders here to study. They have even formed a team called the London Canadians to play against Cambridge University, right here at The Prince's Sports Club.' He gave her a gentle tug through the double doors of the main entrance. 'The club also serves afternoon tea, which is why I brought you here. I thought you might like to watch the skaters.' He drew her into a main arena beneath an iron and glass roof that rose into a vast arch similar to a station, thus proclaiming its former use as a factory. Tables and chairs were set on a raised platform on all sides of a railed skating rink. A waiter who stood sentry at the door led the way to an empty table set for two in a row beside the rink, while others balanced tea trays and eased expertly between the tables, delivering tea, cakes, and sandwiches to those who watched skaters whizz or stagger by on the ice.

'Is it real ice?' Flora asked, charmed by William's thoughtful attempt to show her something new and interesting.

'Real ice, artificially manufactured. Clever isn't it?' He took the chair opposite, his lips twitching into a smile.

Children scooted fearlessly on the other side of the fenced area, swerving between ladies in long skirts who wobbled and swayed, their faces set in expressions of fierce concentration. Couples danced, their arms round each other's waists, moving with as much skill as if they were in a ballroom. The constant slice and whoosh of their feet as they glided over the ice echoed into the high roof.

'What an amazing place. Who owns it?' Flora stared round at the glass roof and the icing rink.

The waiter returned with a tray which he set down before them, complete with finger sandwiches and tiny iced cakes that made Flora's mouth water. Sally was right, if the sudden, overpowering need for food was one of them, she was indeed having symptoms.

'Actually, that's an interesting story.' William dismissed the waiter and poured for them both. 'When the old flooring factory was put up for sale, Mary Russell, the Duchess of Bedford, bought it and turned it into this skating rink. She's a keen skater, and here's a coincidence for you, she went to Cheltenham Ladies College.' He held out a plate of sandwiches towards her.

'I wasn't educated there.' Flora took a smoked salmon one. 'You're confusing me with your nieces. I was the home-schooled governess, remember.'

'Oh, yes of course. How silly of me.' He frowned and smiled at the same time. 'I always think of you four girls as a unit and I forget – well never mind. Now the interesting part is that the Duchess has vehemently refused to pay the required business taxes due on the club.'

'Vehemently?' Flora frowned at him over the rim of her cup and waited for him to go on.

'Indeed. As a protest against the way, women are treated by the government. She is not permitted to have a vote and yet is expected to pay tax on this place as a business. She wrote to the government suggesting they send their tax demand to the Duke, her husband.'

'Now *that* is the sort of active protest women should make, especially those with influence.' Flora beamed. 'What better way of concentrating the government's minds than depriving them of their precious taxes.'

'I thought you would approve,' William said, laughing. 'Her Grace's protest has caused quite a stir, especially as she's determined to hold out against them and create as much adverse publicity for the government as she can.'

'You speak as if you know her well.'

'We've met on several occasions,' he said carefully. 'She's quite a daredevil. Runs about in motor cars, shoots like a marksman and rides like a hoyden. I'm afraid she'll break her neck taking a fence or I'll read in the newspaper she's gone off on an adventure and disappeared.'

'Or maybe she'll simply die the way she lived, doing exactly what she loved.'

'That's an interesting philosophy.' William's eyes settled on her face as if he were looking at her properly for the first time. 'Now, tell me what's so fascinating in that newspaper you've been clutching in your hand all the way here?' He nodded to the offending item that sat neatly folded beside Flora's plate.

'I was waiting for the right moment to show it to you.' She slowly lowered her cup, reached for the paper and opened it at the appropriate page. 'Miss Evangeline Lange rented a mailbox at Boltons Library.'

'The woman who was found in Old Barrack Yard?' At Flora's nod, William frowned. 'Do I wish to know how you discovered this?'

'Most probably not.' She cleared her throat. 'The important thing is she put an advertisement in this paper soliciting replies to that box number.'

William returned his own cup to his saucer and sat back. 'Flora, why have you been digging into this woman's murder? You didn't even know her.'

'I'm aware of that. And please don't look at me like I'm a naughty schoolgirl, I've been discreet.' Discreet in mentioning neither John Lange, her visit to The Grenadier nor Harry Flynn. 'At first, I thought Evangeline had done so to keep her suffragist correspondence separate from her family.'

'Sounds reasonable.' William made no move to pick up the paper, instead, he spread strawberry jam on half a scone with a knife. 'It's not remarkable for bored heiresses to join the suffragists to fill in their time between society lunches.'

'Well take a look at this.' She was about to push the paper towards him but halted at what he had just said. 'William? How did you know Evangeline Lange was an heiress? It wasn't in the newspaper report of her murder.'

He hesitated for a heartbeat before answering. 'I must have read it a news report somewhere. Her father is quite an important man, so word gets around. Go on then, let me have a look.' He took the paper from her in his free hand, the full

236

teacup held aloft in the other. 'Is it this black outlined one just here?' At her nod, he took a sip of tea as he read. His air of bored disinterest changed to shock and he lowered his cup rapidly, spilling tea on the pristine cloth. 'Good grief, what was the woman up to?' His face had suffused with red and his eyes flashed with anger. He crumpled the page in his hands and gave the room a swift piercing look. 'Well, this has made the entire affair more complicated.'

'What affair?' Flora popped the remains of an iced fancy in her mouth and chewed. 'The murder, or afternoon tea at a skating rink?'

'This isn't a game, Flora.' William's warning tone made her sit up straighter. He refolded the paper and left it on the table.

'What isn't? I don't understand, why are you so angry?' Only the fact his ire wasn't directed at her gave her the courage to question him.

He scraped back his chair and stood. 'I cannot explain right now, that is, not unless you're prepared to sign the Official Secrets Act.'

'What? And where are you going?' Flora paused in the act of reaching for another cake.

'The office. You stay here and finish your tea.' He pushed the chair back beneath the table. 'Watch the skaters for a while. I'll ask the manager to order a cab to take you home.'

'But what about your tea?'

'I'm sorry, Flora, it's unavoidable, but I have to go.' He tossed a pound note onto the table, replaced his hat on his head, and left.

'William!' Stunned, Flora watched him stride toward the exit, her mouth open.

What was going on?

The waiter eased to her side, head bowed and his hands clasped in front of him. 'Would you like anything else, Miss?'

'Nothing more, thank you. Oh yes there is. Could you order me a taxi in about fifteen minutes?' She plucked the pink iced cake from the plate with one hand, the note with the other. 'I have somewhere to go to. But I'm going to finish my tea first.'

Chapter 20

Flora alighted from the taxi outside Prince Albert Mansions. Having asked the driver to wait, she rushed inside the apartment and went in search of Sally, whom she ushered back out again before the girl could fasten her coat.

'Where are we going, Miss Flora?' Sally struggled with the flying end of her scarf as she was bundled unceremoniously into the taxi, her hat askew.

'I'll tell you in a minute. Now get in.' Flora climbed in beside her and rapped on the glass partition. 'Connaught Square, please driver, as quick as you can.'

'What's in Connaught Square?' Sally adjusted her hat, though it remained lopsided.

'We're going to make a call on the Lange residence. I want to speak to John about this Victor character. I've brought Evangeline's bag with me as I feel guilty at not having turned it over to the police. I should have done so already now we know what the Boltons Library receipt was for. I only hope Inspector Maddox won't be angry with me for withholding evidence.' She reached for the grab handle as their enthusiastic driver took a sharp turn round Hyde Park Corner and into Park Lane.

'How did you know where the Lange's live?' Sally righted herself on the seat.

'I looked them up in William's copy of *Who's Who* he keeps in his study. I assume Mr Lange lives at home, but if not, I can always enquire after him there.' She wiped condensation from the window with her gloved hand and peered outside, but it was already dark and the fog obscured everything the night did not.

The driver must have taken her plea for urgency to heart, for in a shorter time than Flora imagined possible, they rolled to a gentle halt before a short flight of steps that led to a black painted front door, only the top half visible from an overhead light.

Flora alighted onto the mist-shrouded pavement and climbed the steps up to a stone portico supported by two white pillars.

'That was a scary ride.' Sally stared after the motor taxi as it chuntered away.

'It was indeed.' Flora narrowed her eyes at the departing taxi. 'Perhaps we'll stick to a hansom on the return journey.' She gestured the bell pull on Sally's side of the door. 'Now, ring the bell for me, would you?'

'Are you sure Mr William would approve of this?' Sally moved to obey. 'He won't like you going about questioning strangers about the murder.'

'When Mr William stops keeping so many secrets, I might take his concerns into consideration. Anyway, this is a condolence visit and nothing to do with any investigation.' No one had come to the door so Flora leaned across Sally and gave the bell pull a sharp tug.

Finally, the door was unhurriedly eased open by an emaciated butler with a thin layer of grey hair combed over his bald pate.

'Is the master expecting you?' he asked when Flora had stated her business.

'I expect so, I did mention I would call,' Flora lied. 'Though if Mr Lange is otherwise engaged, I could return at another time. Perhaps you would enquire of your employer as to when would be convenient?'

'Mr John Lange is not at home, Miss. However Mrs Lange is here, but I doubt she will receive visitors.' He indicated the black ribbon tied to the bell pull. 'This is a house of mourning.'

'Which is precisely why I have come.' Flora returned his look steadily.

He raised his thick, scruffy eyebrows, gave a resigned sigh and stepped aside, allowing them entry into a black and white tiled hall. 'If you'll wait here a moment, Miss.' He gave an acquiescent nod, before disappearing into a room off to one side.

'You're getting better at this, Missus,' Sally whispered.

'Being a detective do you mean?' Flora tugged off her gloves while gazing around the sumptuously appointed hall.

'No. Lying.'

Flora opened her mouth to protest, but just then the butler reappeared.

He tilted forward onto his toes with his hands behind his back. 'Mrs Lange asks if you would join her in the sitting room.'

'Thank you.' She took a step towards the room he indicated, then turned back at the last second. 'Oh, would you mind directing my maid to the kitchens? She can wait for me there.'

'The kitchens?' Sally muttered. 'Couldn't I wait on this posh velvet seat here just as well? More comfortable anyway.'

'I have my reasons,' Flora whispered through the corner of her mouth. 'I want you to discover what you can from the staff. Be friendly but polite. Can you do that?'

Sally's eyes gleamed with new-found enthusiasm. 'Ah, well that's more like it. I'll see what I can do.'

The butler sniffed, cocked his chin at Sally and muttered, 'The kitchen is that way. Turn left at the end of the corridor.'

Sally threw a conspiratorial look over her shoulder before disappearing into the inner recesses of the house, whose burgundy and navy wallpaper and dark paint resembled a cave.

The butler showed Flora into a sitting room, where a woman who looked to be in her forties rose unsteadily from her chair, her fair hair bundled into a pile of untidy curls on her head. In a plain black gown that did not suit her pale colouring, the lady's large eyes were overly bright, the pupils dilated, obscuring their colour. The decorations were sombre, a combination of purple and black, the curtains partly drawn and a black cloth was draped over the mirror above the fireplace in keeping with a house of mourning.

'How nice of you to call,' her hostess said in a high-pitched voice. 'John will be here presently, but in the meantime, do join me for some tea.' She gestured Flora into one of an assortment of upholstered chairs arranged round the hearth, each in differing styles and flowered fabrics.

'I rarely meet John's friends,' she said in her high, affected voice. 'Thus I do appreciate you coming to visit. I gather you heard about our darling Evangeline? This has been such a dreadful time for all of us.'

'Yes indeed. I hope you don't think it improper of me, a virtual stranger, calling to offer my condolences for your—'

'Not at all, it's very kind,' Mrs Lange cut her off. 'Do tell me how you met John?'

A small fire burned in an iron grate, not large enough to banish the chill of the air that smelled of dust and lavender as if the room wasn't used often.

Seated, Mrs Lange didn't look at all comfortable perched a few inches from the edge, her hands laced together in a vice-like grip on her lap. Hands with protruding knuckles and raised veins scattered with age spots told Flora she was older than she first appeared.

Flora opened her mouth and closed it again. John hadn't told her? Apparently not, or why would she assume they were friends?

'Um, our acquaintance is quite recent actually.' She sidestepped that it had happened at a police station. Then inspiration struck at the sight of an NUWSS leaflet on a table at her elbow. 'I'm an acquaintance of Lydia Grey.'

Her hostess's face showed no recognition at the name, only confusion. 'She was a work colleague of your daughter's, at the Harriet Parker Academy'

'Ah yes.' Mrs Lange gave a grimace of distaste. 'The establishment run by that foreign woman. Why Evangeline felt she needed to work was quite ridiculous. We provided her with all she could possibly need.' She twisted her hands with increasing agitation as she spoke. 'Anyway, she would have had to give it up when she and Harry Flynn married, so I chose not to make as much fuss about it as my husband.' She broke off as a maid entered the room with a tea tray. 'Ah, thank you, Jane. Put it on the table beside me. And when Mr John returns, would someone inform him that his friend is here?' She waved a vague hand in Flora's direction. 'What was your name again, my dear?'

'I didn't give it, but it's Flora, Flora Harrington.' Her gaze strayed again to the NUWSS pamphlet lying on top of a pile of magazines.

'I meant to throw that awful pamphlet out.' Mrs Lange followed Flora's look. 'Another of Evangeline's causes. I wouldn't be surprised to learn her involvement with those people was what got her killed.'

Was the woman's distracted manner part of her grief, or anger with Evangeline for making her own choices? As if she couldn't resist the self-righteous triumph of having her predictions proving true.

'How is your husband coping with the tragedy, Mrs Lange?' Flora asked, taking a sip of the too weak tea. She began to feel awkward and wished John would arrive.

'He's devastated, poor man.' She released a long sigh. 'Evangeline was his joy. However, he isn't one to mope about the house. He goes to the police station every day in order to ensure that detective person is doing his job.'

The click of the door announced the arrival of John. 'Jenks informed me I have a guest, but I wasn't expecting anyone – oh!' His face paled at the sight of Flora, then his eyes shifted nervously to his mother.

'John, darling, there you are.' Mrs Lange's face creased into a beatific smile more appropriate for a lover. 'Why haven't you mentioned this charming young woman to me before now?'

'Haven't I? How remiss of me.' His chin hardened as if he gritted his teeth, giving the impression he had hoped not to have to explain.

'Good afternoon, Mr Lange.' Flora set down her cup and saucer. 'I apologize for arriving unannounced, but I came to offer my condolences.' She split a look between him and his mother. 'To both of you.'

'That's most – kind.' He rushed to his mother's side and eased her out of her chair, despite her mild protests. 'Thank you for looking after her, Mother. Mrs Harrington and I have something important to discuss, so I'll take over now. Perhaps you could go and lie down for a while?'

'*Mrs* Harrington?' Mrs Lange levelled a withering glare at Flora. 'You might have mentioned that small detail, my dear.'

Flora's lips parted in sudden shock, but her hurried apology dissolved on her tongue as John shoved his mother bodily into the hall. He muttered something Flora couldn't make out before the door closed behind him with a loud click.

*

'I'm sorry, that must have appeared rude of me.' John reappeared and took the chair his mother had vacated. 'Mother is still very distressed about Evangeline. I thought it best we discuss anything pertaining to the – attack alone.'

'I take it your mother is keen to see you settled?' Flora ventured, though it seemed a poor excuse for the way he practically threw the poor woman out of the room.

'Indeed. I'm afraid she tends to view every young lady of our acquaintance as a possible wife for me, which can be very tiresome. Also, I haven't told her how you and I met; I feared she might consider our unorthodox introduction improper.'

'I suppose it *was* unconventional.' Flora conjured the scene on the Embankment when she was convinced John was about to push her beneath the hooves of a carriage horse. 'Your mother seems angry about your sister's death as well as distressed. It must be so very hard on her.'

'She isn't handling Evangeline's death well.' His eyes fluttered closed briefly. 'Our doctor makes frequent visits to calm her, for at times she forgets Evie isn't coming home and rails at her as if she were in the room.'

'How awful for her.' Flora's sympathy rose, recalling how losing Riordan Maguire had left her numb and exhausted. John's mention of the doctor also explained Mrs Lange's enlarged pupils and disorientation, most likely due to laudanum as distress.

'Now.' John clapped his hands together as if banishing the heavy mood he had himself introduced. 'What brings you to Connaught Square?'

'Well, after you left me the other day, my maid and I located Evangeline's bag.'

'Her bag, where?' His eyes widened and he rubbed his neck with one hand. 'Inspector Maddox said it wasn't with her... body. Thus the assumption she had been killed during a robbery. Where *did* you find it?'

'It's complicated.' Flora had no intention of explaining the exact circumstances. 'Someone found it before the police arrived. It contained something which might—'

'Do you have it with you?' he interrupted her.

'Er-yes.' Flora withdrew the small bag from inside her own larger one and handed it to him. 'I wanted you to see it first out of courtesy, but my next stop should be to the police.'

'Why, is there something in here which might help?' His hand trembled as he took it from her, the silk cord hanging free.

'Well, not as such, but-'

'Then I shall return it where it belongs,' he interrupted her. 'Amongst the rest of Evie's possessions.'

'But what about the police?'

'I-I suppose you're right.' He flicked a sharp look at her and away again. 'However, if you don't mind, might *I* be the one to take it to them?'

'Of course, if you prefer. Although,' she hesitated. 'I realize you must find this difficult, but there was something inside which might be pertinent to their inquiry.'

Frowning, John sorted through the meagre contents. 'There's nothing here as far as I can tell. Just a few personal items. 'He held up the empty coin purse. 'I assume whoever attacked her stole whatever was inside this?'

Flora merely smiled, refusing to make the matter any more complicated than it was. Paying off Meg might be seen as interfering with police matters and the last thing she wanted was to incur Inspector Maddox's bad temper.

'I don't suppose it matters now anyway.' He clicked the clasp shut and placed the bag on a table.

'Your sister rented a mailbox at Boltons Library.' She withdrew the receipt and the square of paper she had cut from the newspaper from her bag and handed them to him, adding, 'The second one is an advertisement she placed in the classified section of *The Times*.'

'I-I had no idea.' He scanned the cutting, his eyes shadowed. 'Who's this chap Victor, and why did Evangeline want to speak to anyone who knew him? Are you quite certain these are hers?'

'Certain? I hoped you could tell me that.'

'The name means nothing, but it occurs to me that without a surname it's a pseudonym. The only person I can think of is Harry Flynn.' He eased his collar again in a gesture he had made his own and laid the cutting and the receipt beside the bag.

'I doubt it. Harry is not swarthy nor does he possess dark hair and hypnotic eyes.' In response to John's casual shrug, she added, 'Do you genuinely suspect Harry, or is that your personal prejudice talking?'

'Maybe the latter. But then do you expect a chap to hand over his beloved younger sister to any plausible young man who asks for her hand?'

'Harry doesn't strike me as just any young man,' Flora said, confused as to why she was defending him. Harry was just as likely a suspect as anyone. 'Your parents were satisfied Mr Flynn was a suitable match for Evangeline, weren't they?'

He snorted. 'Our fathers attended the same public school if you feel that qualifies as suitability.'

He cupped the back of his neck in one hand and rotated it in a half-turn, his features slightly contorted. Briefly, Flora wondered if he was in pain.

'I'll go and see Inspector Maddox and show these things to him. Perhaps it wasn't a random robbery after all.' His eyes brightened as if the thought had that moment occurred to him. 'Or this Victor person discovered Evangeline was looking for him and killed her to keep her quiet.'

'That was my first thought too. But what was it she could have found out that would make someone kill to keep it quiet?'

'That's the police's job, though I'm afraid I have low expectations of Inspector Maddox if he relies on young women with a heightened curiosity to do his job for him.' He held up the two pieces of paper in emphasis.

'I don't think he'll see it quite that way. Thus I would appreciate it if you would not mention how you came by the bag. The barmaid at The Grenadier er-came upon it in actual fact.'

'I'll be happy to keep your name out of it.'

'I'd better go. I only came to show you those.' She turned towards the door, but his hand shot out and grabbed her upper arm.

'Please don't go, you've only just got here. Stay and take another cup of tea with me. You can tell me more about Evie's friends at the NUWSS. I never did pay much attention at the time. And now, well, it's too late.'

Flora eased her arm from his hold, surprised at the strength of his grip.

He released her, both hands held out open palmed. 'I apologize, I didn't mean to be so insistent. It's simply that – well a house of mourning can be a gloomy place.'

'I understand, but I'm expected at home, so I really should go.' Although not unsympathetic, she found his mercurial moods unsettling; stricken with grief one moment, then without warning, he became angry, which turned in a heartbeat to flirtatiousness. 'Do thank your mother for me, won't you?'

'I will. I expect she's sleeping now.' He summoned the butler and asked him to find Sally.

Once settled in the hansom on her way back to the apartment, Flora decided she was being too harsh toward Mr Lange and that grief affected people in different ways. She also hoped he would keep his promise and not tell Inspector Maddox how he came by Evangeline's bag.

*

Flora pulled up her collar against a grit-laden wind as the driver guided the horse into the Bayswater Road. Perhaps

249

motor taxis did have their advantages. At least they were warm.

'What have you got there?' Flora asked when Sally's head remained buried in a copy of *The Woman at Home* dated several weeks before.

'The housemaid gave it to me.' Sally beamed. 'Mrs Lange lets her have it when she's finished with it, and she gave me this one. It's full of articles and pictures about female beauty and fashion. Have you ever had a gown made for you by a court dressmaker, Miss Flora?'

'Hardly. I find my mother-in-law's seamstress in Kingston more than adequate.'

'Mrs Lange does, according to the housekeeper. She likes her clothes and spends a fortune on them.'

'That's all very fascinating, but not quite what I sent you to find out.'

'Your dresses are smart enough,' Sally continued as if she hadn't heard her. 'But think what it would be like to go to a real dressmaker who makes clothes for the cream of society?'

'I'm not likely to be presented to Queen Alexandra, Sally. That sort of thing is a little beyond my circle.' *Not to mention her purse.*

'You don't have to have a debut or mix with toffs to go to a court dressmaker. This one is in Dover Street which is less than a mile from Master William's apartment.' She shoved the magazine under Flora's nose. 'Madam Kate Reily's establishment is visited by ladies just like you. It says so right here.'

'I'm sure she's excellent, but I won't be able to fit into my existing clothes in another few weeks, let alone an expensive new gown.' Sally's shoulders slumped and Flora gave her an awkward pat in consolation. 'Perhaps I'll save up and try Miss

Reily's when the baby comes. Now that's enough about clothes. How did you get on in the Langes' kitchen?'

'Well, the cook and housemaid are mother and daughter.' Sally laid the magazine in her lap and tucked the blanket provided by the driver around their knees. 'Not very grateful for their jobs either, if you see what I mean.'

'Not really.' Flora was prepared to wait for an explanation, glad Sally had returned to the subject in hand.

'Well.' Sally wiggled her hips further into the seat. 'I hadn't even begun my cup of tea before they gave up the goods on their mistress. The cook said Mrs Lange is a bit of an odd one, but her daughter was quick to call her a very rude name. Began with a b and ended with a 'haich''

'I wouldn't know how she treats her servants, but she was distracted rather than odd.' She recalled Mrs Lange's sharp disappointment when she found out Flora was already married. 'Not that I can condemn her under these circumstances. To have lost a daughter in such a way must have been dreadful.' If Mrs Lange used medication, or even the brandy bottle to help her through life, Flora had no right to judge her.

'She didn't,' Sally announced with more than a little triumph. 'Evangeline's mother died in childbirth. Camille Lange is her stepmother.'

'Really?' Flora's eyes widened and she drew the word out slowly. 'Now I wonder why John Lange hadn't mentioned that?'

'Mr Lange married her exactly one year after his first wife died. Evangeline was still a nipper. No more'n four or five.'

'In which case, Camille would have been instrumental in raising Evangeline. Bonds would have been formed even if she wasn't her own child.'

'Not according to the maid.' Sally cast a glance at the box above and then lowered her voice. 'She said Mrs Lange hated Evangeline.'

'*Hated*? She used that word?'

Sally nodded. 'By all accounts Evangeline was strong-minded and she clashed with her stepmother over all sorts of things. The suffrage thing for one, and her working at the school.'

'Maybe they simply didn't get on.' Flora cut off the thread as she had heard all this before. 'And as I heard it, Mr Lange didn't approve of her independent ways either. That doesn't mean much, Sally.'

'Just telling you what was said.' Sally picked at a corner of the magazine with a fingernail. 'Lots of shouting and slamming of doors according to the housekeeper, Mrs Hicks.'

'Between Mrs Lange and Evangeline?'

'Mr Lange too. Mrs Hicks said when he bellows, the whole house shakes. Thinks them suffrage women are – what was the word – con-ten-tious.'

'And John? Did they have an opinion of his attitude to Evangeline? As he's obviously older than Evangeline I assume he's Mrs Lange's child but Mr Lange's stepson?'

'He was about ten at the time, Mrs Hicks said. Quiet boy always, but he always supports his sister, and the housemaid seems to be a bit sweet on him.'

'I see.' Which pretty much fitted with what Flora had learned herself. 'You did an excellent job, Sally. Thank you.'

'I haven't finished.' Sally tutted. 'The night Miss Evangeline died, she had an argument with. She was all dressed to go out, but he didn't want her to go and tried to persuade her to stay at home.'

'A pity then that he didn't succeed. She might still be alive. Did she hear anything more specific?' *Like actual words.*

'Not really. Mrs Hicks kept saying as how Miss Evangeline was a wilful miss and should have been more mindful of the gentleman's wishes. Then the housemaid chimed in saying she was being old-fashioned. They was going it at it like knives when that creaky old butler turned up and said you were about to leave.'

'Even so, you did well, Sally.' Flora rather liked the idea of having a willing accomplice, a role Sally seemed to have adopted easily. 'What do you say we walk the rest of the way home? We can go through Hyde Park and we'll make it before it gets dark.' A layer of fog shimmered above the browned grass and obscured the upper half of the trees. 'I need some time to think and the walk will do us both good.'

'As long as there's a pot of tea at the end of it,' Sally muttered, tugging her scarf higher.

Flora pulled down the trap and told the driver to stop. She paid him and then stepped down from the cab. Sally followed her onto the pavement.

They fell into a companionable silence as they followed one of the pathways between the trees, while Flora's thoughts swirled and collided in her head.

Why did Evangeline visit Mr Crabbe that night? Was it something to do with this Victor person she was so keen to find? Did Mr Crabbe know who Victor was?

And why did John make no comment about the fact Evangeline's brooch wasn't in the bag. Even if it wasn't worth much, was he not sad that an item which meant so much to his sister was lost or stolen? Or perhaps the brooch was of little interest if he believed it was paste jewellery?

Chapter 21

'Well, can you see anything?' Flora said in a fierce whisper. She pressed herself against the wall of the building next to Boltons Library, careful she couldn't be seen by anyone inside.

'That sourpuss you spoke to last time isn't there.' Sally stood with one hand shielding her eyes and her nose pressed to the glass.

'Perhaps she's in the back. Give it a moment and see if she appears. I'm not going in if she's there. She might recognize me.'

Sally pulled her head back. 'I was with you that time, she might remember me as well.'

'Not likely.' Flora waved her back to the window. 'Go on, take another look. Is she there?'

'There's one young man on his own. Now, what are you going to do?'

'Not sure yet. Stay here. I'll be back in a while.' *A very short while if this doesn't go well.*

Flora pushed open the door of the library, giving the long room a swift glance to make sure the young man behind the counter was the only member of staff on duty. 'Good morning,' she addressed the man, whom she could now see was little more than a youth.

'Good morning, Madam. 'Ow might I 'elp you?' His expression was eager, but he had a little trouble with his aitches.

'I was here yesterday and hoped to speak to the lady who helped me on that occasion. Is she here?'

'I'm sorry, Madam. Today is 'er day off. Might I be of assistance?'

'Oh dear, and she was so helpful too.' Flora released a long, exaggerated sigh and did her best to look distracted. 'She was dealing with my sister's mailbox and she said she would make arrangements for me.'

'If it's something to do with the rented boxes I'm sure I can 'elp.'

'Well, the lady said,' Flora halted, grimacing. 'Oh, dear, I cannot remember her name.'

'Gladys Holt,' the young man replied, with barely restrained dislike.

'Of course, I remember now.' She gave him her most charming smile. 'My sister rented a mailbox here, but…' Flora heaved an exaggerated sigh. 'She died you see, quite recently. Miss Hold was making the required arrangements to let me have the contents of her mailbox.'

'Miss Holt,' he corrected her. 'She'll be back tomorrow, Madam. I could ask 'er then.'

'Yes of course. Miss Holt. Oh, dear.' Flora brought a crumpled handkerchief to her nose and blew into it noisily. 'It's the funeral tomorrow and I – oh this is so hard for me.'

'I do understand, Madam, and allow me to offer my condolences on the loss of your sister.'

'Thank you.' Flora sighed again. 'You're so kind. I don't suppose—' She directed a look at him filled with appeal. 'No, I cannot ask that of you. After all, you're only a junior member of staff. I imagine they don't let you do anything around here but sweep the floor and make the tea without having to ask permission first?'

He drew himself up to his full height. 'I assure you, Madam, I'm a respected member of the staff with every authority to offer a full service to the public.' He flicked open a wooden box filled with keys attached to brown cardboard labels. 'Which number was your sister's box?'

'Number thirty-two. Oh, I'm so grateful. And if my sister were here, I'm sure she would be too.' *Don't overdo it, Flora.*

He rifled through the box, withdrew a small key with a large black number on it and approached the bank of doors behind him, counting along the row as he went. 'Ah, 'ere it is.' He opened the door with the key and withdrew two slim envelopes. 'This is all that was in it, Miss Lange.' He gave the envelopes a cursory look before handing them to Flora.

She tucked them into her bag before he changed his mind and took a step back. 'I shall be sure to let your employers know how efficient and helpful you were.'

'But—' the young man held up a hand. 'You'll need to sign the waiver.'

Pretending she hadn't heard, Flora backed away from the counter, just as a portly gentleman barged past her and commanded the young man's attention in brusque angry tones.

'Did you get it?' Sally asked out on the pavement.

'Hush!' Flora looked both ways before hurrying her back in the direction of Prince Albert Mansions. 'There were only two letters in the box. I just hope it was worth that excellent performance. Perhaps I should go on stage.'

'I thought you laid it on a bit thick, myself.' When Flora glared at her, Sally shrugged. 'I could see you from outside. All that handkerchief waving and limpid looks. Goodness knows what he thought.'

'Oh, do be quiet. I got the letters didn't I?'

The first envelope had the Boltons Library address written in neat cursive script on thick, lilac-coloured bond, while the other was an untidy scrawl on thinner, white paper that looked as if it had been torn from a notebook.

Both said virtually the same thing but with different syntax. 'This Victor appears to have struck up an acquaintance with both women, then dropped them equally as suddenly and with no explanation.'

'What are you going to do with the letters?' Sally asked. 'Give them to the police?'

'How can I, unless I tell them about the bag as well. I'll have to be sure John Lange has given it to them or we'll both be in trouble.' She cast a swift glance back at the library. 'They are bound to discover this place, and I might even have committed some sort of crime by lying to that chap behind the counter. Besides,' she gestured to the pages in her hand, 'Inspector Maddox might dismiss them as unimportant.'

'Isn't that up to them?'

Flora bridled. 'Sally, when did you become my conscience? Look, when I've discovered what these women know about this Victor, I'll give them to the police.' She tapped the lilac sheet of paper with a forefinger. 'Starting with this one.'

*

The following morning, Flora took Sally with her to Lennox Gardens, which was the address quoted on the lilac-coloured letter.

'Sally, please don't look so furtive. What are you staring at anyway?'

'Not sure, Missus. But that bloke over there looks like someone I saw yesterday when we was at the library.'

'Who?' Flora gave the street a sweeping glance. The day's fog had not yet thickened to invisibility, but a thin white mist obscured anything more than twenty feet away, throwing more shadows in the garden square behind them than people.

'Grey coat, hat pulled over his face. He's over there by the lamp post.'

'Sally that *is* a lamp post.' She turned swiftly back to the door which was being opened slowly. A plump, soft-faced lady stood on the threshold, a mild look of enquiry on her face.

'Oh, I'm sorry. I didn't mean to be rude,' Flora said when she caught herself staring. 'I was expecting a butler.'

'It's his day off,' the woman said, her voice matched her face. Kindly and soft. 'In fact, it's everyone's day off. The Mistress has gone to the country for Christmas and taken most of the staff with her.'

'I see, and Miss Moffatt?' Unsure as to Cecily's role in the household, Flora hoped the housekeeper would enlighten her.

'Cecily?' The woman's face softened further. 'Oh, she's still here. You were lucky to catch her. She'll be escorting Madam's luggage on the train tomorrow. Are you friends of hers?'

Ah, so Cecily was a servant, and if she was entrusted with her mistress's luggage, maybe she was a lady's maid.

'Not exactly. Look, this may sound unorthodox, Mrs—'

'Atkins,' the lady supplied.

'Mrs Atkins. I wanted to ask Miss Moffatt about someone she may or may not have known recently. A young man.'

'If you mean that Victor, I doubt she'll want to discuss him with anyone.' Mrs Atkins raised one bushy eyebrow, her hands crossed over an ample belly she used as a shelf.

The use of the name made Flora hope she wouldn't be turned away. 'I don't wish to upset her, but if she could spare me a moment or two, I would be very grateful.'

Mrs Atkins gave Flora a slow, appraising look, then opened the door fully. 'All right then, but don't you go upsetting her.' She led them along the lower hall to a door at the back. 'Dreadful how that rogue treated her,' she muttered, throwing the door open that led into a small parlour at the back of the house. 'Most of the downstairs rooms have dustsheets over the furniture, so you'll have to talk in here. The Master and Mistress are never back until mid-January.'

'That's perfectly all right, it's kind of you to let us see Miss Moffatt at all.' Flora hoped the girl in question would feel the same.

'Yes, well, heed me mind.' The woman issued her warning and withdrew.

'Interesting that the housekeeper knows who this Victor is,' Flora mused as she wandered to the window that overlooked a neat courtyard garden.'

'Miss Flora,' Sally began.

'She appears to be quite fond of Cecily to warn us like that,' Flora continued, ignoring her. 'I—'

'Miss Flora.' Sally nudged her in the ribs, causing Flora to swing around sharply, poised to reprimand her.

Sally stood with her eyes rounded, a finger pointed to an oil painting of a distinguished looking man with silver hair that hung over the fireplace. Dressed in the fashion of some twenty years before, a stand-up collar and cravat tied loosely at his throat and a superior expression.

'Must be the master of the house,' Flora said. 'He looks very proud, but quite handsome. For an older gentleman.'

Sally tutted, and snapped. 'Never mind that. Look at the label.'

Flora stepped closer and peered at the engraved gilt plaque. 'Jervis Stanton Hanson, Secretary of the Foreign Office.' Flora gasped. 'Oh, my goodness, he's William's boss!'

'Perhaps we should slip out before the housekeeper gets back?' Sally whispered.

'Didn't Mrs Atkins say he was in the country? We mustn't lose our nerve, Sally. This investigation is about to become interesting if it wasn't already.'

The door clicked open, admitting an attractive girl in her early twenties with almond-shaped blue eyes. 'Mrs Atkins said you wished to speak to me?' She looked from Flora to Sally and back again, but did not invite them to sit.

'I appreciate your agreeing to see me, Miss Moffatt,' Flora began. 'This might seem an odd question, but are you acquainted with a Miss Evangeline Lange?'

'The woman who was found dead in Knightsbridge?' Her eyes flew open in shock. 'I read about it in the newspapers. No, no I didn't know her at all.'

Flora withdrew the advertisement she had cut out of the newspaper from her bag, together with Cecily's letter. 'You replied to this advertisement, with this letter.'

Cecily read the newspaper clipping quickly but did not touch the letter, handing both back with a brief nod. 'I did, yes. I sent it as instructed to the postbox.'

'And you weren't aware that box belonged to Miss Lange?'

The colour left Cecily's face and she staggered slightly, a hand reaching for something to hold onto. For a moment, Flora thought she was going to faint and leapt forward to help her into a chair. Her breathing grew shallow, her hands pressed to her middle.

'Shall I send for the housekeeper?' Flora whispered, awkwardly patting her hand.

'No, please – I'll be quite all right in a moment.' Cecily took several short breaths and then longer ones. Her colour evened out but her lip still trembled. 'Was it my fault?'

'Was what your fault?' Sally removed a white handkerchief from her bag and held it by two corners and rapidly flapped it in front of Cecily's face.

'Sally, will you stop that, you're causing a draught!' Flora snapped.

'Sorry, just trying to help.' Sally hunched her shoulders and backed away.

'Miss Moffatt,' Flora urged. 'You were telling us something might have been your fault.'

'Is-is Miss Lange dead because I wrote that letter?'

'Why would you think that?' Flora's voice rose and she reminded herself not to alarm this girl more than she already was.

'Because – because of *him*?'

'You mean Victor? The man she asked about in the advertisement?'

Cecily nodded, her tears, like transparent pearls clung to her cheeks.

'Miss Lange never saw your letter, Cecily. It was still in the mailbox after Evangeline was killed.'

'Then what are you doing here?' Her perfectly arched brows lowered over a pair of vivid blue eyes.

'I hoped you would tell me what you knew of this man Victor.'

Cecily gasped and rose, backing toward the door. 'You came from him?'

'You misunderstand.' Flora grasped her hand and drew her back towards the chair, taking the one opposite. 'Please, calm yourself. I haven't come to cause trouble, or embarrass you.

However, your letter to Miss Lange written in response to this advertisement says you were acquainted with him. That's the only reason I'm here. I'm trying to find out who killed her.'

'You think Victor might have hurt Miss Lange?'

'I don't know. That's why I need you to tell me what you know about him. Evangeline was obviously interested in him – but why?'

'Excuse me!' Sally interrupted. 'Is this your employer?' She cocked her head at the portrait of the grey-haired man.

'My employer's husband, yes.' Cecily left her chair and came to stand before the painting. 'He's an important man in the government.'

Heat flooded Flora's cheeks, but she remained silent.

'He's in the country,' Sally said. 'That's right, ain't it?'

'Mrs Hanson is. She's gone to their estate in Sussex for the festive season. Mr Hanson will follow in a few days. There's some crisis as the Foreign Office he has to sort out first. Why do you ask?'

'Oh, nothing,' Sally widened her eyes at Flora. 'Just interested. Wouldn't want him walking in, would we?'

'Cecily.' Flora cleared her throat, more eager than ever to end the interview and leave before Mr Hanson returned. 'Was Victor your young man?'

'I thought he was.' Cecily's pretty eyes welled with tears.

That was all she needed, vagueness. 'Well, how did you meet him?'

'Victor always seemed to be in the vicinity whenever I left the house. I didn't think anything of it at first, seeing him in the street, the park and browsing through the shops I frequented. After a few weeks, he approached me and struck up a conversation in the way any young man does when he wishes to become acquainted with a lady.'

'You accepted his attentions?'

She nodded. 'I was flattered and he was very attentive. We went for talks, visited tea shops. He took me to a concert once. I didn't see any harm in it. However, after a while, I came to trust him and I-I let down my guard. He was so – passionate. We became close, too close.' She released a sob. 'I thought he liked me.'

'He most probably did. You're a very pretty girl, Cecily, any man would be flattered to have your affection. I gather things didn't go well between you?'

She shook her head and stared at her lap. 'I let him take – liberties.'

'Oh lord,' Sally snorted. Flora gestured her into silence.

Cecily's head jerked up and she glared at Sally. 'Not *those* sort of liberties.'

'I'm sorry, my maid didn't mean anything.' She widened her eyes at Sally, who retreated. 'What do you mean, Cecily?'

'When the Hansons were at church, I allowed him into the house sometimes. To take tea and read poetry, that sort of thing. He had such a lovely speaking voice and always recited from memory. I never saw him use a book.'

'Please go on, Miss Moffatt.' Flora frowned as a memory surfaced. She had heard something similar recently but couldn't quite grasp where.

'Once,' Cecily swallowed before continuing, 'I found him in the master's study. He told me he had got lost, so I thought nothing of it, but when I checked, I saw the top drawer of his desk wasn't quite closed. The master never leaves his desk like that. I didn't say anything that time, but when it happened again, I told him to leave and never come back. That I could lose my position if the master ever found out.' Her mouth twisted but not enough to spoil her delicate looks. 'I really need this position.'

'Was anything missing?' Flora asked.

'I couldn't very well ask him, could I?' Cecily's penetrating gaze made Flora feel she was being stupid. 'The master hasn't said anything, so I assume not.

'I don't suppose you had any idea as to what he was looking for?' Flora asked.

Cecily shrugged. 'I imagined he had befriended me so he might steal from the house.'

'But he only ever searched the study? And nothing went missing?'

'It does seem odd, I agree. I caught him on those two occasions, but how do I know he hadn't been elsewhere when my back was turned?' Her eyes, still tear-filled, glistened.

Flora nodded. *This girl was brighter than she looked.*

'It wasn't until afterward,' she went on, 'did I realize I don't even know where he lived or what he did for a living. How could I have been so stupid?'

'Did you tell anyone about Victor?'

'No!' Cecily looked up, her nose red, but still annoyingly pretty. 'That letter to Miss Lange was the only time I have ever admitted I knew him.' Cecily released a half sob. 'If Mrs Hanson knew I had brought a strange man back to the house, she would dismiss me with no references.' She accepted Flora's proffered handkerchief and sniffled into it. 'I addressed it to Miss EL, just as the advertisement said.' She blinked. 'Are you sure she was this Miss Lange?'

'I'm afraid so,' Flora replied aware there was nothing more this girl could tell her.

'What will happen to me now?' Cecily asked, the tears flowing freely now. 'If Victor killed this woman the police will want to talk to me, won't they? Then Mr Hanson will have to be told.'

'As I see it,' Flora spoke carefully, aware she was about to make a promise she might not be able to keep, 'I have no reason to tell anyone about your relationship with Victor.'

'Do you mean it?' Cecily pleaded, hope in her face.

'I certainly shan't be the one to mention you to the police.' The fact that someone would, whether it was via the woman at Boltons Library, or William when his boss found out, was something Flora chose not to think about.

William! The thought occurred to her that his reaction to Evangeline's advertisement meant he knew far more about the murder victim than he had admitted to. Did he also know why she had visited Mr Crabbe the night she died? Was she looking in the wrong direction, and the answers to this case were much closer to home?

'Mrs—' Cecily dried her tears and blew her nose noisily. 'I'm sorry, but I don't even know your name.'

'I didn't give it, and hopefully we shan't have to repeat this conversation.' Flora rose and gestured to Sally that they were leaving. 'Best we forget it altogether.'

'Thank you for being so discreet.' Cecily showed them out, the handkerchief still clutched in her delicate hand. She was still thanking them when Flora was fifty yards down the road.

*

'Are you thinking what I am, Missus?' Sally asked once they were back at the apartment. 'That this Victor did a similar thing to the nurse who wrote the other letter?'

'We cannot be sure, but it sounds very much like it. We have no proof he actually stole anything from the Hansons. If he had, surely someone would have noticed, and Cecily seemed quite convinced nothing was missing.' Or perhaps Mr Hanson did notice and reported it to a higher authority?

'In my experience, the servants are always questioned first when anything goes missing.'

'Apparently not in this case. Thus if anything *was* taken, it wasn't something a servant would want.'

'So what was he looking for?' Sally asked.

'There's no way we'll know, Sally. Cecily was certainly enamoured of him until he betrayed her trust. She's an unusually attractive girl, so he's most probably a handsome man.'

'How do you make that out?'

'Pretty women are rarely attracted to homely-looking men, Sally. Like goes for like.'

'Handsome or not, that Cecily got shot of him quick enough.'

'Yes, she did, though she still felt aggrieved enough to answer Evangeline's advertisement. Also, if Victor courted her in order to gain access to her employer, it's doubtful he would have used his real name.'

'That means we know even less than when we went in,' Sally groaned.

Flora considered for a moment. 'The advertisement particularly mentioned Victor's eyes. Which makes me feel he shouldn't be too hard to recognize.'

Sally released an exasperated sigh. 'Well, it's something. 'She said he liked poetry too.'

'Doesn't make him sound very dangerous, does it? Nosey maybe, and a possible thief, but a murderer who reads poetry? That doesn't sound likely.'

'What about this nurse who wrote the second letter?'

Flora retrieved it from her bag and opened it out, while Sally read over her shoulder.

The writing was looped and slightly uneven on a thin sheet of poor quality white paper. 'It's from a Molly Bell who's a nurse at St George's Hospital.' She tapped the page against her bottom lip. 'What could a lady's maid to the wife of a government official and a nurse have in common?'

'Perhaps he just likes women' Sally shrugged. 'Don't matter who they are or where they came from.'

'I doubt it's that simple.' The Foreign Office connection was too much of a coincidence for Flora. 'We need to speak to this Miss Bell. I have a feeling her story will be infinitely more interesting than Cecily's.'

'We, Miss Flora? Can I come too?' Sally visibly brightened.

'You might as well. You've come this far.' Flora pushed aside her misgivings as to what William would have to say about it if he knew what she was doing. She refolded the letter and returned it to the envelope. 'I doubt we can simply charge into a public hospital and drag a nurse away from her work.' Flora recalled her days as a governess when her time was not her own and personal plans were always a rare luxury that had to fit around the demands of her employer. 'I'll write a note for you to take to the hospital to ask if she would be willing to meet me, possibly at a tea shop close to the hospital. The one near Marble Arch might suit. She probably works on a shift basis, so we'll arrange it for one of her breaks.'

'Suppose she doesn't want to see us?' Sally asked.

'You're the one who is good at persuading people, Sally. And aren't nurses very poorly paid?' She jiggled her bag up and down making the coins inside jingle.

'Good point, Miss Flora.' Sally grinned.

Chapter 22

When Flora arrived at the tea shop near Marble Arch the following morning, apart from Sally, the only other customer was a man in a brown suit who did not look up from his newspaper when she entered. She removed her gloves and waylaid a waitress in a monochrome parlour maid's uniform, requesting her to bring a pot of tea. She doubted her delicate stomach could stand coffee. 'And another portion of whatever my maid is eating.'

'Thanks, Missus,' Sally said when the waitress had left. 'I do like those milly foil things. I could eat them all day.'

'*Millefeuille*, Sally.' Flora smiled. 'They are nice, aren't they? If a bit rich for me at the moment. What time did Miss Bell agree to be here?'

'Stop fretting, she'll get here. The porter at the lodge wasn't at all helpful, but one of your half-crowns bought me ten minutes in the nurse's home.' She took another bite of her cake, leaving a line of cream and crumbs around her mouth. 'Did Mr William come home before you went to bed last night?'

'No, he didn't, and after I waited up until midnight.' Flora had resolved to tell him about Evangeline's bag and the letters before he discovered their visit to Mr Hanson's house. She had decided not to wait until he heard about her investigations from elsewhere and confronted her. Besides, it was easier to seek forgiveness than permission.

Her evening of tense indecision had been considerably lightened by a telephone call from Bunny, who confirmed that

269

he would be coming to luncheon the following day as planned. The only glitch in the conversation being when Flora had to admit that she had not yet told William about the baby. 'Maybe we could tell him together?'

'That wasn't the plan, Flora. But I suppose it's better than turning up on his doorstep with a screaming bundle.'

'Our child won't scream,' Flora had insisted.

The jangle of the shop doorbell banished all thoughts of Bunny, bringing Flora's head up to a slab-faced girl in an ill-fitting olive-coloured coat that had seen better days, who hovered on the threshold.

'That's her.' Sally nudged Flora.

'How many half-crowns did it take to persuade her to come?' Flora whispered.

'Half-crowns didn't do it.' Sally's expression turned sheepish. 'She wants a fiver.'

'A what?' Flora stared at Sally, aghast. 'And you agreed? That's three months wages for a nurse.'

Sally shrugged. 'You want her to talk, don't you? Now hush, she's on her way over.'

Flora gritted her teeth and indicated to the newcomer she join them at the table; but the gesture was apparently too subtle, for the girl still hovered uncertainly in the doorway. The tearoom had filled up since Flora's arrival, but at a wave from Sally, she finally made a beeline for their window table.

'It is extremely kind of you to agree to this meeting, Miss Bell.' Flora indicated the empty chair next to hers. 'Do take a seat.'

'Can't stay long, my shift starts in half an hour.' Her brown felt hat sported a bedraggled feather hanging limply above one eye. She slapped her bag on the tabletop and plonked herself down on the chair.

'Haven't you recently finished a night shift?' Flora asked.

'I need the money, so the extra shifts come in handy.' She made a gesture of dismissal with her hand. 'Are you the woman who put that advert in the paper?' she asked, forestalling Flora's attempt at an introduction. She directed a nod at Sally. '*She* said it was someone called Miss Lange.'

'Not exactly.' Flora debated whether to admit the truth or keep silent in case the girl clammed up once murder was mentioned; though her expression showed more belligerence than nerves.

'My sister inserted the advertisement,' Flora said, compounding the lie she had told at Boltons Library. 'In your letter, you said you were acquainted with this man, Victor.'

'Where is she then?' Ignoring the question, she gave the tea shop a swift, searching look. 'This sister of yours.'

'Ah, no, Miss Lange couldn't be here this morning,' Flora said. 'I understand if it's a delicate situation, I shall be most discreet.'

'There wasn't anything delicate about it.' Miss Bell helped herself to a Chelsea bun from the plate the waitress slid onto the table. 'Victor and I weren't involved in *that* way. I only wrote that letter hoping there might be something in it for me.' She took a generous bite of the bun and chewed noisily.

'Is nursing not as lucrative as you hoped?' Flora masked the irony behind an obsequious smile.

'Huh!' She swallowed and licked sugar from her fingers. 'I thought I'd hand out pills, place cold cloths on hot foreheads, or read books to those too weak to sit up. The truth is I clean up blood, shit, piss and God knows what else for ten hours a day.' She caught Flora's grimace, adding. 'Pardon me, Miss. I'm a straight talker, always have been.'

'Don't apologize on my account, Miss Bell,' Flora said, bemused. 'It's er – refreshing. Which in some ways makes this interview much easier.' She withdrew a white five-pound note from an inside pocket, folded it into a palm-sized square and pressed it into the girl's hand.

'Well, there's a turn-up.' Miss Bell stared at it for a second, then tucked it into a shabby black purse that hung from her forearm, patting it with satisfaction. 'Didn't expect anything that quick. You can call me Molly. And just so's we're clear, I know about Miss Lange. I saw the report in the paper.'

'Then why did you ask if I was her?' Flora asked, mildly irritated.

'Thought *he* might be a copper.' She cocked her chin at the man who sat huddled in the corner. 'I don't need me collar felt if that's what you had planned.'

'I've no idea who that man is, but I doubt he's a policeman and he's definitely not with us.' She turned to Sally for confirmation, who nodded.

'That's all right then.' Molly signalled to a waitress from whom she ordered a Chelsea bun and pot of tea. 'Can't abide coffee,' she said in answer to a question no one asked.

'Miss Bell, Molly,' Flora said carefully, annoyed the nurse appeared to have taken the upper hand. 'If you knew Miss Lange had been killed, why didn't you go to the police yourself?'

'What for?' A brow twitched above one expressionless brown eye. 'Didn't have anything to do with me, did it?'

'Not even if this Victor might have been responsible for her death?' Flora persisted.

'Why would I think that?' Molly took a sip of her tea which was more like a loud slurp. 'I never met Miss Lange and I haven't seen Victor for weeks.' Her plain face remained bland, making Flora wonder if she knew more than she was saying; or perhaps the girl possessed no sense of civic duty, let alone compassion for others.

'Would you mind telling me under what circumstances you met this man Victor?' Flora nibbled at a sugar biscuit, hoping the nausea that had visited her that morning would not return.

'It was one Sunday last June.' Molly lifted the top of the teapot the waitress brought, dunked in a spoon and gave the contents a vigorous stir. 'It was the day of a riot at Speakers' Corner. About a dozen casualties were brought to the hospital that afternoon. Bloodied heads and broken noses mostly. I wasn't sure what he was doing there at first. He wasn't bleeding and didn't seem to be one of them.'

'Victor, you mean?' Flora asked.

She nodded. 'Then someone knocked into him. He went white and grabbed at his arm, clearly in pain. I offered to get him a doctor, but he refused.' She tilted the pot and poured golden brown tea into her cup from which a wisp of steam rose.

'Was Victor involved in the fighting?' In response to Molly's gesture, Flora passed her the sugar bowl.

'I don't think so.' Molly tipped three lumps into her cup and stirred, the metal clink against china unnaturally loud.

'If he didn't want to see a doctor, why did he come to the hospital?' Flora clenched her hands in her lap wishing Molly would get on with it.

The nurse gave her a 'who's telling this story?' look. 'He'd put his shoulder out, but said he didn't want to take up the doctor's time with something so trivial.' She snorted. 'He must have taken me for a fool because I could see him eyeing the coppers who came to question the other injured. Anyway, I let him sit in the nurses' room until everyone left, then I put his shoulder back in.' She mimed a twisting movement accompanied by a cluck of her tongue.

A sudden wave of nausea made Flora squeeze her eyes shut and hold her breath until it passed. When she opened them again Sally was staring at her from across the table.

'You, all right? You look a bit poorly.' Molly frowned, her fork held aloft covered in whipped cream.

Flora nodded. 'Manipulating a dislocated shoulder is indeed a skill, Miss Bell.' This blatant flattery was greeted with a self-conscious blush, instead of the scorn Flora had expected.

'Yes, well, I've done it enough times, so I've got the knack.' She smiled, revealing even white teeth marred by one crooked canine. 'Anyway, that's when we got to talking. It was late by then and only a skeleton staff was on. He didn't seem in any hurry to leave so I made him a cup of tea.'

'I'll bet he wasn't.' Flora's nerves stretched at the harsh jangle of the shop doorbell as the gentleman in the corner left. 'I gather Victor wanted something more than the enjoyment of your excellent company?' She didn't bother to mask her sarcasm, aware she was in a tetchy mood but without knowing why.

'Yes, well. Took me about a while to twig, didn't it?' Molly blushed furiously as if she were ashamed to admit she had fallen victim to Victor's charms when she should have known better.

'What did he want from you?' Flora asked, growing impatient.

'Their names and addresses. He said that some of the men injured in the riot would need help as they couldn't work. That he managed a relief fund for an organization that supported foreigners living in London.'

'That sounds unlikely,' Flora said, sceptical. 'Did you believe him?'

Molly shrugged, took a large bite of her half-eaten bun, and chewed. 'I didn't see the harm. I mean it's not as if he was asking me to raid the drugs cupboard for laudanum or anything like that. All he wanted was their names and addresses.'

'All? That's quite a lot to ask of you. Aren't patient details kept private?' Flora broke off at Sally's scowl, aware her temper was growing increasingly short. Nausea still threatened and she wanted to get this meeting over with quickly in case she embarrassed herself. 'Can you remember any of these names?'

Molly's vigorous shake of her head set her felt hat into a wobble that threatened to dislodge the precarious feather altogether. 'I couldn't pronounce them, let alone remember. They were all foreign. We have plenty of Frenchies and Italians where I live in Kings Cross, but they didn't sound anything like them. One of the coppers said something about, "Ruddy Balkans", but I'm not sure where Balkan is.'

Balkans. Flora straightened, her tone sharpening. 'Did Victor tell you anything else?'

'Only that he was in Hyde Park by accident and was passing the riot when someone threw him to the ground. That his shoulder was an old weakness and didn't take much to put it out. He took me for a drink afterward as a thank you. Not that it was a romantic meeting if you see what I mean.' Molly flushed a deep red as if aware she was unlikely to be singled out for such attention by a man like Victor. 'All he did was ask questions about the men brought in.' She stared into her teacup, held in hands that sported short fingernails and roughened skin which had evidently spent a lot of time in hot water. 'Y'know, thinking about it, he could have been one of them Balkans himself. He had the look of a foreigner, although he spoke English really well, and without an accent.'

'Did you give him the names and addresses?' Flora asked gently.

'Might have done.' Molly shrugged and picked at the cake crumbs on her plate. 'Those who gave their names anyway.'

'Did you meet Victor on any other occasion?'

'He said he would meet me at the cafe near the Serpentine the next Sunday afternoon but he didn't turn up.' She shrugged again. 'Haven't seen him since.'

'And on the strength of this one meeting, you decided to answer the advertisement?'

Her cup clattered noisily into the saucer. 'If Miss Lange was keen enough to put an advert in a newspaper, she might pay me for what I knew.' She glanced at the clock on the wall, murmured something indistinct and scrambled to her feet. 'I must go. I've been late on shift twice this week.' She upended the untouched plate of biscuits into her bag, clicked the metal clasp and patted it with a pleased smile. Aiming a swift nod in Sally's direction, she strode outside, the tea shop door shuddering on its hinges as she left.

'What are you thinking?' Sally asked when they were alone again.

'Several things.' Flora played for time as she tried to reach a decision about what she should do next. 'What did you think about Molly's story?'

'Well.' Sally eased backward to make room for the waitress who had come to remove their empty plates, waiting until she was out of earshot before answering. 'Somehow, Evangeline found out about Cecily and Molly and she threatened to expose Victor, which is why he killed her.'

'That sounds a little extreme. After all, approaching women is hardly a crime.' Flora recalled she had heard something similar quite recently. But where?

'Maybe he's married and didn't want his wife knowing that he was loitering outside houses waiting for pretty lady's maids to appear.'

'That theory works where Cecily is concerned, but Victor wanted information from Molly.' *Information she didn't seem reluctant to give.*

'Yes, all that talk of Balkans did seem odd.'

'He said I would have to sign the Official Secrets Act,' Flora murmured as something William said came back to her. She cradled her teacup in both hands, staring thoughtfully into the inch of muddy liquid at the bottom as a conviction formed, making her head spin, though this time not with nausea. She replaced her cup without finishing it.

What William had told her about Serbians came back to her in a rush. Both Cecily and Molly believed Victor was foreign, so either he was Serbian too or sympathized with them. Was he involved in these riots which William said had taken place recently? If so, he was either a supporter of the deposed pro-Austrian Obrenović dynasty, or the faction who put King Peter on the throne?

He had befriended Cecily to gain access to her employer's study, and Molly so he could find out where the Serbians in London were. Whether to recruit them or intimidate them, either way that still made him a spy. No wonder William reacted the way he did when he saw the advertisement.

She would have to tell the police about Evangeline's advertisement, though how Inspector Maddox would react to that sent a shiver through her. Didn't female prisoners at

Newgate in previous centuries plead their bellies to avoid hanging? Flora snorted at the thought.

'What are you thinking, Miss Flora?'

'Whatever it was, I have changed my mind after this morning.' She nodded at Sally to indicate it was time to leave. Until that morning, she had fully intended to show the letters to John, but now it made more sense to give them to William. Something told her he already had a head start on finding Victor.

Chapter 23

It was already eleven thirty by the time Flora and Sally left the tea shop, giving scant time to return to the apartment and change her clothes before Bunny's expected arrival at noon. Not that he would care what she wore, but she wanted to show off a new dress she had bought during her visit to Harvey Nichols.

She stood with Sally at the kerb opposite Prince Albert Mansions, shifting her cold feet as she waited for a break in the traffic when a motor taxi slowed to a stop outside the apartment building. The door to the lobby swung open and Dunne hurried forward to a tall woman in purple, wearing an enormous matching hat. She gave the porter a cursory glance followed by a regal bow of her head before she swept into the building, her chin in the air.

'Lawks, it's the old Missus,' Sally gasped, voicing Flora's own panicked thought. 'What's *she* doing here?'

'Sally!' Flora feigned shock as she asked herself the same question. 'Don't call her that. One day it will slip out in her hearing and she'll dismiss you on the spot.'

But what *was* her mother-in-law doing here? Bunny didn't mention he was bringing her on his visit. Then the thought struck her that something might be wrong. She silently railed at the stream of traffic between her and the taxi, until Bunny emerged from the cab.

Flora's heart quickened with pride at the sight of her husband's tall, athletic figure and fair hair in need of a cut. Bunny wore his favourite wire-rimmed spectacles, which on some men might detract from their looks, but made his blue eyes sparkle.

He paused to exchange a greeting with Dunne before disappearing inside the building in his mother's wake.

Finally, a break came in the traffic and, with Sally at her heels, Flora darted across the road. She shouldered through the main door, only for Sally to collide with her, so together they exploded into the lobby.

Her husband and mother-in-law swivelled slowly towards them; one with disdain and the other barely concealed amusement. William broke off from shaking hands with Bunny to regard her with wide smile.

'Ah, here's Flora now. I was just saying I expected you at any moment, Flora. Your guests have arrived.' Did she imagine it or was there special emphasis on the plural?

'Good morning, mother-in-law, and to you, dearest.' Flora tucked a wayward strand of hair that sat against her cheek back beneath its pins. 'You're early.'

'We caught the earlier train,' Beatrice gave Flora a slow, top to toe glance, her dismay almost palpable. Flora's one saving grace was Sally's presence, which Beatrice ignored, but at least she couldn't criticize Flora for gallivanting all over London alone. Fortunately she could have no idea what she had been doing and if Flora had anything to do with it, neither would she.

Bunny extended his arms in welcome and all thoughts of decorum faded as Flora launched herself into her husband's arms. He smelled of laundry starch and the citrus cologne which always conjured memories of dark, warm nights alone. She blinked tears away and snuggled into his shoulder, not caring what her audience thought.

'Flora, dear,' Beatrice drew out the word like an insult, her head dwarfed beneath the oversized hat. 'Why weren't you here to greet us? Instead, you left your poor father to introduce himself to perfect strangers.'

Flora returned her stare. 'William is well acquainted with Bunny, as I am sure you are aware.'

'Hmm.' Beatrice scrutinized Flora's dress with a raised eyebrow that made her think her skirt must be stained, or she had smuts on her face.

'Sorry,' Bunny whispered beside her ear, folding her into a hug. 'I had no choice, Mother insisted. But I'll make it up to you, I promise.'

'Yes, you will.' She planted a firm kiss on his mouth and stepped back in time to see Bunny's eyes widen and hear Beatrice issue a sharp gasp.

'Let's not hover here on the doorstep.' William clapped his hands together. 'Please, do go inside.' He led the way into the apartment where Randall stood guard at the door; another witness to Flora's embarrassment.

The butler's lips moved as he did a rapid headcount, and she imagined he made plans to rush away at the first opportunity to set a fourth place at the table. As they passed him at the door, he clamped his lips in a firm line, his back stiff, which told Flora she might have gained an ally in her feud with Beatrice.

'I've wanted to meet you for such an age, Mr Osborne.' Beatrice leaned against William's arm, simpering like a girl. 'Had I waited for an invitation from Flora, I would still be at home. Whenever I asked, she always had some excuse.' Her blue eyes beneath beetling fair brows narrowed into icy slits levelled on Flora as if daring contradiction. Bunny possessed those same eyes, but on him, they were heavily fringed and sensual, whereas his mother used them as weapons to convey disapproval or anger, both to startling effect.

Flora gripped her bottom lip with her teeth, hard enough to cause pain. Beatrice was right in that Flora had deliberately kept the two spheres of her life separate while she came to terms with her new relationship with William.

'Well, you are here now, Mother-in-law.' Flora followed her into the apartment on Bunny's arm past the ornate gilt mirror, resisting the urge to make adjustments to her hair, keenly aware of the knot of curls that sat heavily on her collar.

She still missed Riordan Maguire and still found herself seeking him in crowds, though he had been dead over a year. A grief that if ever expressed, was greeted with the reminder from her mother-in-law that her father was still alive, so her continued mourning was inappropriate. William's new status was one thing, feeling a daughter's respect for him, even love, was another.

Bunny's arms encircled Flora's waist, his fingers laced behind her back. 'These last few days have dragged interminably. Remind me not to let you go away on your own again.'

The sight of Flora in her son's arms was apparently too much for her mother-in-law, who turned away with an impatient tut. 'Really, dear. Married couples don't parade their affection in such a way.'

'On the contrary, Mama,' Bunny said, his words clipped. 'My wife's affectionate nature is a delight to me. Much better than carping about every person one sees, don't you agree, William?'

'I-er, I trust you had a comfortable journey from Richmond?' William offered her his arm, on which Beatrice delicately balanced the splayed fingers of her hand. 'And please, do call me William. After all, we are family now.'

'I wasn't carping, Ptolemy,' Beatrice's habit of using Bunny's given name made him wince. 'That guard was impudent, and the hansom driver no less so. Naturally, I had to reprimand them for disrespect. I might even write a letter of complaint to the railway company.'

'Was your journey not comfortable, Mother-in-law?' Flora asked, not much caring one way or the other.

'Adequate I would say rather than comfortable.' The look she gave her son indicated she would not forget his disloyalty. 'I'll never get used to those motor taxis. They travel much too fast and the way they swerve and dive through the traffic disrupts my nerves.'

At one time, Flora would have a sharp rejoinder for her mother-in-law's sarcasm, but these days she largely ignored it. Not because she had stopped noticing, but because it was simply too much effort to no effect.

Seeing William's reaction to Beatrice's acid tongue brought back Flora's own feelings of shocked inadequacy she had experienced during the early days of her marriage. When had she become so passive? For Bunny's sake, or because she felt she deserved the woman's criticism?

Beatrice disappeared into the sitting room, her cries of delight at the stylish furnishings echoing back into the hall. William's low, cultured voice drifted along in response to something Beatrice said, making Flora proud of the effort he was making and resolved to make a point of thanking him later.

Bunny was about to follow them in, but at the last second, Flora tugged him back to her side. 'What possessed you to agree to bring her?' she demanded under her breath. 'I had

283

hoped we would have some time alone this afternoon.' She batted a stray curl away that had fallen over her eyes.

'I am so-oo sorry, my love.' Bunny grimaced. 'I tried to dissuade her, but you know what she's like.' He fiddled with one arm of his spectacles, which he always did when embarrassed. 'I must say William didn't bat an eyelid when he saw her. The man's solid as a rock.'

'Now she'll monopolize William and tell him about all the women you should have married instead of me.'

'If she does, I'll insult every single one of them to show her I am happy with my choice.' He pulled her back into his arms, his chin tucked in as he looked down at her. 'And I doubt you need to worry about William, he's encountered far worse in Africa. They have lions there you know. Besides, you know very well why Mother behaves like this. She still hasn't made the adjustment to having to share me with you.'

'That's what you always say.' Flora adjusted his tie, though the knot was immaculate. 'I know you do your best to stand up for me, but I suspect that deep down you love having two women competing for your affections.'

'Mother's sharp tongue is a part of her character, not an impediment to domestic bliss between us.' Flora narrowed her eyes at him and he winced. 'I know, it's not charming at all and I too wish she would stop. But she's jealous, Flora, surely you know that?' He twisted a finger into a curl and tucked it behind her ear. 'You occupy all of my heart now and she knows that's the way it will be. I firmly believe she's hurt.'

'It doesn't make things easier.' She snuggled closer. 'Besides, I shouldn't be upset now. Not in my condition.'

His face blanched and he swallowed. 'I didn't think of that. I'm so sorry, my love. I'll have another word with her.'

'Not yet. Wait until we have told her our news – together.' Perhaps it was her own fault for not making more of a fuss, but as a former governess, confrontation had never been her strong suit. 'I'm sorry I was late, but I didn't expect you so soon. I bought a new dress just for you, but didn't have time to change into it.'

'I'll look forward to seeing it when you get home.' He planted a kiss on her forehead.

'Hmm, if I can still get into it by then. I think I'm getting bigger by the day. Incidentally,' Flora asked, as they lingered the hall, in no hurry to reach the sitting room, 'what was your father like? You never talk about him.'

'He was quiet, reserved, but had a wicked sense of humour. If I told you Mother always called him Dr Harrington, even in private, would that explain her attitude more clearly?'

'To some extent, yes it does. Was that at his insistence, or hers?'

'I have no idea, but I never saw them so much as touch each other either. Not once.'

'I find that quite sad, though I refuse to accept it as an excuse. I did not have a mother, and yet affection is not alien to me. Even my father was—' she broke off as she realized what she had said. 'Sorry, I forgot for a moment.'

'I know.' Bunny tightened his arm in acknowledgement of her slip. 'How are things going between you and William?'

'We're attempting to transform a polite, respectful acquaintance into a parent and child relationship, each in our own way.' She halted just short of the sitting room door, keeping her voice down. 'It isn't easy. He's in the Foreign Office now, and since the May Coup, there's been some major crisis on which takes up his time.'

'Something to do with Serbian nationalists causing riots in the city isn't it? Sounds like serious stuff.'

'I believe so, though I don't know the details. He's being very secretive and hasn't been here much since I arrived. When he is, we get to a certain point, then he shuts down and will go no further.'

'I suspect he's trying to protect you. Especially if your inquisitive nature encroaches on his work.'

'What makes you think I'm interfering in William's work? Has he said anything to you?'

Bunny's eyes darted to the sitting room door and away again, his arm tightening around her waist. 'What opportunity has he had to do that? Come on, let's join them. I could do with a sherry. Mother turned a relatively short journey from Surrey into a major expedition. I doubt the train guard will ever be the same again.'

'Serves you right,' Flora teased.

*

Luncheon was every bit as awkward as Flora imagined, the atmosphere lifted only by the excellence of Randall's cooking. Beatrice made a valiant attempt not to enjoy it by questioning every ingredient and where it was purchased; then supplemented every answer with how superior foodstuffs could be found in Surrey, despite which, she managed to clear her plate at every course.

Having subjected William to a long interrogation of his colourful life spent in America, Australia, and South Africa, she proceeded to make shuddering insults at those who chose to subject themselves to such primitive environments.

'America is every bit as civilized as England, Mother-in-law, and most of the houses in New York have both electric light and indoor plumbing,' Flora reminded her, forgetting her resolve to stick to non-contentious answers.

'Ah yes, I had forgotten you travelled to the colonies in your post as governess for the Vaughns,' Beatrice said.

'They haven't been colonies for some time, Mother,' Bunny reminded her but was waved away with an impatient tut.

Randall stepped forward to remove Flora's plate, and as she turned her head to thank him, the sympathy in his eyes warmed her.

'Ptolemy, did I mention Jessica Weatherby, who is Jessica Ashton now, of course, has just had her third child? They even sent me an announcement, which was extremely thoughtful.'

'I believe you did mention it, Mama, twice on the train in fact.' He turned to Flora. 'The Wetherbys were friends of Mother's when I was at school.'

'I had such hopes for you and Jessica. Such a truly lovely girl.' Beatrice sighed.

'With a beauty undimmed by a wall-eye and freckles certainly,' Bunny said, making Flora almost choke on her dessert.

Beatrice sniffed, her eyes narrowed. 'Physical perfection isn't important. Jessica is from an impeccable family line.'

'She pushed me into our garden pond when I was ten.' Bunny dabbed his lips with a napkin. 'I've always seen her as more tormentor than prospective wife.'

'Oh, Ptolemy, don't be ridiculous,' Beatrice snapped. 'I do believe you're mocking me.'

Flora couldn't contain her laughter, which proved so infectious William joined in. He caught Beatrice's pursed lips and broke off, noisily clearing his throat as a prelude to rising.

'Might I suggest we take a postprandial walk in Hyde Park?' he crumpled his napkin onto the table. 'The fog isn't so intrusive there. Instead of coffee, I know of an excellent little kiosk beside the Serpentine where they serve the most delicious hot chocolate. What do you say?'

'What an excellent idea,' Beatrice said with enthusiasm, the seduction of hot, sweet beverages overruling her aversion to the weather, despite it being less than half an hour since she had devoured a winter fruit compote. 'Flora, make sure you're well wrapped up. You're looking decidedly peaky at the moment.'

The corner of Bunny's mouth twitched and he grabbed Flora's hand, squeezing it in acknowledgement of their secret.

Flora wished it could remain that way, but she would have to share not only the news but, in a few months, the baby too.

'I thought perhaps we might make it just the two of us, Beatrice?' William interrupted. 'Let Flora and Bunny have some time alone.'

'Whatever for?' Beatrice frowned, her lips puckered into invisibility, then in the face of William's smile, she visibly softened. 'Oh, well, if you really think it's necessary.'

Coats and hats were retrieved and after a protracted leave-taking, Flora stood at the sitting room window while Bunny hugged her from behind, his chin resting on her shoulder.

'She seems to like him,' Bunny said, his breath warm on her cheek.

They watched as William held open the gate of the park opposite to allow Beatrice to pass in front of him, performed with an elaborate flapping of hands and a flirtatious gesture of her head.

'She resembles a tall, fussy chicken strutting along beside a panther,' Flora said.

'Never mind Mother, now I've got you to myself for a while.' Bunny twisted her around to face him, head bent so their foreheads touched. 'I've been longing to ask you since we got here, though I didn't dare with Mother present. What did William say?'

'Say about what?' At his sudden start she recalled what he meant. 'Um – I haven't actually found the right moment. Not yet.'

'Flora!' He slid his hands down her arms, took a step back but did not release her hands. 'You promised you would tell him. How much time does one need to tell a man he's about to be a grandfather?'

'I know but – look, this may sound odd, but to be quite honest, I don't feel as if I'm going to have a child. Not yet.'

'But you told me the doctor said—'

'I know what he said, and it's not that I don't believe him.' She looked down at her flat belly and shrugged. 'It doesn't seem real to me. No more real than William being my father in some ways.'

'It's early days yet.'

'Exactly. I need to come to terms with what's happening to me.' The bewilderment in his face both annoyed and dismayed her. 'Before I can tell William, I have to feel it myself.' She removed one hand from his grasp and pressed it to her lower belly. 'Real in here, as well as in my head. That might sound strange, but it's the only explanation I can give.'

'I would have thought that bout of sickness I witnessed would have convinced you.'

'I haven't felt that bad since, so I've not thought about it too much.' Flora had always imagined giving such news to Riordan Maguire. That she would never see the pleasure on his face made the situation as sad as it was happy. For her at least.

'It's complicated.' She laced her fingers with his and tightened her grip, willing him to make allowances. 'William has been so distracted, what with all this panic about Serbian spies, the one time I did try to tell him we were interrupted.'

'I see,' he murmured, though Flora doubted that he did.

'I went to an NUWSS suffragist meeting and met a lovely young schoolteacher called Lydia Grey, and-'

'Flora.' His voice held a warning. 'You haven't been getting involved in the Lange murder, have you?'

'Ah, you heard about that?' Her stomach knotted and she braced herself for a lecture.

'Of course, I have. It was reported in *The Times* under the heading, "Knightsbridge Murder". I'm not likely to have overlooked it. Please tell me you haven't been nosing into something that doesn't concern you? Especially now?'

'When have I ever done that?' Flora winced in response to his slowly raised, perfectly arched eyebrow. 'Well, yes, I suppose I have. The death of Mr Van Elder on the steamship was nothing to do with me, but my father's murder, I mean Riordan's, was very much my concern.'

She entwined her arms around his neck and leaned into him in the way he always found difficult to resist, knowing she would get her way.

'Really Flora.' He released a long-suffering sigh that was beginning to be a common theme of their marriage. 'This was supposed to be a pleasant visit with your father. A little shopping, a few quiet suppers and maybe a museum visit. Not a murder enquiry.'

'I couldn't help it.' She experienced a small satisfaction that her ploy worked and he nuzzled her cheek. 'I observed the victim talking to William's colleague, who happens to live right here in this building with his wife. Then hours later she was dead.'

'The wife?'

'No.' She pulled back slightly, aiming a gentle slap at his chest. 'Evangeline Lange.'

'You think the neighbour killed her?'

Flora shrugged. 'Maybe at first. But there is no evidence, let alone a motive. Then William told me the two of them are working on something connected with this Serbian situation. He won't explain, but I'm sure he knows far more about Evangeline Lange than he'll admit. Oh, don't look at me like that. You know I hate mysteries and this is a complicated one.' She recalled the two occasions when William had rushed from the apartment after something she had said, only to behave afterward as if it had never happened.

'Does William know what you have been up to?'

'Partly. Although he made it clear he wants me to stay out of it.'

'Good. I hope you'll listen for once. I don't want you upset. You should be resting as much as possible.'

'I'm not tired. Although I have developed an aversion to bacon, and a liking for cake. Lots of cake. Besides, when did puzzle-solving upset me? You could at least listen to what I've found out before you make any snap judgements.'

'Go on then.' He drew her down beside him on the sofa in front of a crackling fire Randall had prepared in advance. 'I can see you won't be content until you've told me the entire story.'

'Really?' She tucked in her chin bringing his face into focus. Such a rapid capitulation wasn't like him and she had been prepared to evade the subject altogether. 'Well, all right then.'

Weak winter light seeped through the long windows and accompanied by the soft tick of the clock on the mantel, Flora told him about her meeting with Lydia Grey and Harry Flynn, the Harriet Parker Academy, her unsatisfactory encounter with Inspector Maddox at Cannon Row and finding Evangeline's bag with the letters held for her in Boltons Library and what Cecily and Molly had to say about Victor.

'Goodness, Flora,' Bunny said exasperated when she had finished. 'You'll be joining the police force next.' He slanted a downwards look at her. 'I may as well have saved my breath, although the Victor part is mysterious enough to be interesting.'

'I thought so too.' She pounced on his interest with enthusiasm. 'Once I began, one thing led to another. Cecily Moffatt works for the head of the Foreign Office and she knew this Victor person.'

'Or she says she did. You have no evidence they were acquainted.'

'That's true, I hadn't thought of that.' She nodded slowly. 'I doubt it's a coincidence that Evangeline was seen coming out of this very building the night she died.' She pushed herself upright and twisted on the seat so their faces were on the same level. 'I think Victor is using women to gain information about his fellow countrymen, either because he's staging these riots, or maybe they are against his cause and he wants to intimidate them. William says the British government won't acknowledge the new king. They suspect one faction of Serbians are plotting to put King Alexander's mother, Queen Nathalie, back on the throne.'

'Which cause is Victor working for do you think? The new King Peter or the murdered king Alexander's mother?'

'That's the problem, I don't know.' She tilted her head with a frown. 'You seem to know rather a lot about it.'

'I read the newspapers.' Bunny fiddled with one arm of his spectacles. 'It's important to keep up with current politics.'

'I see, all right then.' A worm of suspicion insinuated into her head, but she was too busy with her account to pay too much attention. 'William's believes these Serbians are active in London. Or maybe the men Victor wanted to know about at the hospital are his enemies and he's reporting back to his own government?' Bunny opened his mouth to respond but she forestalled him. 'William won't discuss it with me because of something called the Official Secrets Act.'

'Which comes as a relief, though I must say you put a good case.' Bunny leaned both forearms on his knees. 'I'm still not clear what the connection is between Victor and Miss Lange. Unless you think a girls' school is a hotbed of Balkan spies?'

'There's no evidence Evangeline was aware he was involved in spying. Perhaps she needed to find him because he had treated her as casually as he had Cecily and Molly. Thus the advertisement. What Evangeline didn't bargain for was Victor seeing it, and when he did, he must have suspected she was getting close to his activities, so he killed her.'

'It all sounds very involved, not to mention dangerous. And a matter I trust you'll leave the police to follow?' He slanted another downwards look at her, which made her cheeks grow hot. If he knew exactly what she had been doing he would take her home with him that very afternoon.

'Believe me, I don't want to get involved with spy rings and violent men who kill royals.' She wasn't sure if she sounded convincing enough but Bunny made no comment so she relaxed again. 'Somehow this all goes back to the assassination of King Alexander and Queen Draga in Belgrade?'

Bunny looked about to say something, but voices from the hallway alerted them to the return of William and Beatrice, breaking the mood.

'I promise I'll tell William about the baby before I leave,' she whispered, giving him a final, desperate hug.

She had just that second managed to create a space between them on the sofa and patted her messed up hair back into place when the door opened on a beaming Beatrice and a somewhat subdued-looking William, his nose bright red from the cold.

Chapter 24

Despite Beatrice's insistence that it was entirely unnecessary, Flora prevailed in her plea to accompany Bunny to Waterloo Station where they were to catch the six-twenty train that evening. Beatrice managed to exert her authority into the arrangement by dismissing the motor taxi Dunne had summoned and insisted on a hansom instead.

'I don't know why there's all this fuss about these ridiculous contraptions.' Beatrice tutted as she arranged the blanket provided by the hackney company over her knees against the frigid December wind. 'Hansoms are a far superior mode of travel.'

'Tell that to the horses,' Bunny said, attracting Flora's admiration. 'Their lives are hard and short in London. Motor taxis are more efficient and the horses can return to the fields where they belong.'

'Horses, indeed.' Beatrice turned her head, causing Flora to press back against the seat to avoid being assaulted by her hat.

'I know Richmond isn't far,' Flora squeezed in between them, 'but I always think there's something romantic about waving you off on a train.'

At Waterloo, their driver joined the end of a winding queue in front of the station and at Beatrice's insistence, left his perch and helped her down.

'If you could wait here,' Bunny instructed the driver, at the same time pressing a generous tip into the man's hand. 'My wife shall be returning to Knightsbridge momentarily.' He turned to help Flora down the step, where she tucked her hand beneath his elbow and squeezed his arm against her side as they stepped onto the platform.

'Do enjoy the rest of your stay, Flora.' Beatrice offered a powdered cheek in a rare gesture of affection. 'I trust you not to do anything rash during your remaining holiday.' Her instruction delivered, she accosted a passing porter. 'My seat must face the engine and be located out of the way of any coal smoke,' she declared, then glided through the crowds that streamed from a newly arrived express, the unfortunate porter dancing at her side.

'What have you told her?' Flora whispered as Bunny guided her toward the platforms.

'Nothing about the murder enquiry,' Bunny replied through gritted teeth. 'And I don't intend to. However, she has a point. My instinct is to demand you come home with me right now, but how would you explain cutting your visit short to William? Besides, you have yet to tell him our news.'

'I shall, of course.'

'As long as you don't join that new suffragist group while you are here. The NUWSS is moderately acceptable, but Mother would have a fit if I told her what those WPSU women are planning.'

'The civil disobedience? I'm not sure I could go along with that either. Smashing windows and disrupting meetings in the Commons strikes me as somewhat extreme. And you?' Flora looked up at him. 'How would you feel about my campaigning for the women's vote?'

Bunny stooped to retrieve a cream kid glove a woman dropped at their feet, returning it to her with a slight bow. 'Put it this way.' He accepted the stranger's grateful thanks with a smile. 'Mrs Fawcett's patient lobbying for women to have a stronger role in politics is admirable. Mrs Pankhurst, however, is another breed altogether and she's too radical for my taste.' A teasing smile appeared. 'Perhaps she needs a good whipping?'

'Taking your quotes from the late Queen Victoria?' Flora viewed him askance. 'I believe she once used those exact words.' She pressed closer to Bunny as a man in a homburg and long overcoat pushed past her and demanded the porter hold the train about to leave from the opposite platform.

'But if I don't go right now, that will be me.' Bunny brushed his lips against her cheek as he nodded to the man, now engaged in a tussle with the porter who had firmly closed the gate and refused to open it again.

A guard's whistle broke the brief silence, just as a plume of white steam erupted from the engine, followed by the screech of a train hooter, all of which combined to make Flora wish she was going home with Bunny right now.

Beatrice appeared at the door of a first-class carriage. 'Ptolemy, do come along. Or the train will leave without you.'

'If only I could be that fortunate.' Bunny climbed into the carriage, pulled down the window and stuck his head out.

'You could have stayed with me at William's. He invited you.' Flora propped her chin on her gloved hands on the window ledge.

'I know, but I'm working long hours at the moment and couldn't spare the time. I hope my efforts will come to fruition soon. I may even have a surprise for you before long.'

'Surprise for me? What sort of surprise?' The sudden, harsh screech of the whistle sounded again and the train began to move slowly.

'If I told you, it wouldn't be a surprise, would it?' Bunny raised his voice above the chug of the engines.

Flora kept pace for a carriage length as the train gathered speed. She released her hold at the last moment, staring after the window behind which Bunny waved as the train disappeared along the track like a massive snake. When all she could see of him was his hand, she returned to the obligingly waiting taxi.

Flora propped her chin on her hand as the hansom crossed Waterloo Bridge, the grey ribbon of the Thames flowed beneath them and Somerset House sat straight ahead, warmed by thought that she and Bunny would be together again in Richmond by the end of the week. With this though uppermost, she was determined to find out who killed Evangeline by the time that happened, determined to finish what she had begun.

It wasn't until the cab pulled up outside Prince Albert Mansions, did it strike her that Bunny had been strangely accepting of her enquiries into the murder. He had listened to her story in silence but had issued none of the furious rebukes and husbandly edicts she had expected. Perhaps he was growing used to her penchant for solving puzzles and had decided to let her alone? Or was there something else?

*

Flora felt her separation from Bunny more keenly after their short reconciliation, making supper that evening a subdued affair. Between courses, she decided she owed it to William to keep him informed as to what she had discovered about Evangeline Lange. Having rejected several accounts as being too apologetic or detailed, she settled on the simple, unvarnished truth. She waited until Randall had banked up the sitting room fire and set the coffee tray before she began.

'William.' She kept her back to him as she poured his coffee. 'I need to talk to you about the Lange murder.' Turning, she handed him a full cup, his favourite Florentine biscuit tucked into the saucer. 'Would you like a brandy to go with that?'

His perplexed smile turned to delighted surprise and a firm nod. 'I could do with one after the day I've had.'

'My mother-in-law can be difficult at times, but you managed her perfectly. Your suggestion about the hot chocolate was a master stroke. It was kind of you to make it possible for Bunny and me to be alone for a while. Our meeting the other day was a little fraught as I had my head over a bowl for most of it.'

'He told me. Food poisoning can be most unpleasant. I hope you are quite recovered now.'

Flora merely smiled, hoping there would be no repeat performance over the next few days. She had explained away the first with a story about Fullers serving day old fish, but that wouldn't convince him a second time. She had a small speech prepared and wanted to tell him about the coming baby in her own way. Hopefully, after she had broached the subject of Evangeline Lange's murderer.

'Actually,' he went on, 'I found Beatrice Harrington quite charming in fact, despite her sharp tongue, which I suspect conceals an even sharper intellect.'

'Really?' Flora gave this some thought as she returned to the sideboard, reassessing her own opinion of Beatrice. Perhaps he was right and her mother-in-law's obsession with social climbing was merely a façade, cultivated so she might appear less intelligent? Beatrice wouldn't be the only woman brought up to believe men did not like clever women. Perhaps she should make more of an effort to know her better as a person and not simply as a rival for Bunny's affections.

'Did you wish to say something to me, Flora?' William asked, interrupting her thoughts.

'I did, actually, I—'

'By the way,' William interrupted her, 'I had a talk with your Inspector Maddox this morning.'

The solid crystal decanter came up heavier in Flora's hand than she had anticipated and almost slipped from her grasp. 'He's not *my* Inspector Maddox. He's entirely the property of the Metropolitan Police Force.' Why did mention of the man raise her hackles? She shifted her grip on the crystal and set it back onto the tray.

'I stand corrected.' William chuckled as he took the balloon glass from her and cradled it in his hand, his free elbow propped on the mantel. 'Anyway, he told me that on the night she died, Miss Lange was seen at the Alexandra Hotel with a man at around nine-thirty.'

'Really?' Flora swung to face him, the milk jug now in one hand. 'Do they know who he was?' She whitened her coffee which she carried back to the sofa and sat.

He shook his head. 'The staff claim not to remember them well enough to give a description. The only thing they all remember was a piece of costume jewellery she wore. A brooch, wasn't it?'

'A brooch, yes, but I'm not sure the one I saw was what they are talking about. Both Lydia and her brother said it wasn't valuable, but Harry Flynn seemed to think it was made of rubies and emeralds.' She took a tentative sip from her cup, savouring her first taste, relieved her sickness was confined to mornings. Randall made it just the way she liked it. Strong and hot.

William's brows lifted. 'Well, that changes things somewhat, in that rubies and emeralds are enough motive for any thief.'

'Do you really think Evangeline was killed by an opportunist thief?' She was about to ask him why he had rushed away from the ice rink after seeing Evangeline's advertisement, but changed her mind in case he clammed up completely – or rushed out again. She had rejected the robbery theory almost from the start, and wasn't prepared to change her mind now.

'I cannot say, and as yet no one knows what happened.' He stood with his back to the fire and swirled the dark amber liquid in the bottom of his glass.

'What about Mr Crabbe?' Flora caught his sharp look, adding, 'I know he's not a suspect, but he took a late night walk at about the time Evangeline was killed. He might have seen her with this man?'

'You can forget Crabbe altogether, Flora. He *was* out for a walk, though I won't ask you how you knew that. However, he insists he was nowhere near the alley or the hotel.'

'If you say so, in which case I won't mention him again.'

'Something is obviously on your mind, Flora. Would you care to share whatever it is?'

'I went to Old Barrack Yard the other day to see where Evangeline died.' She ran her tongue over lips suddenly dry. William looked about to speak but she held up a hand. 'No, don't interrupt, I need to tell you everything before you start asking questions. Or lecturing me.'

'I'm listening.' He took a sip from his glass.

Flora repeated what she had told Bunny that afternoon, even the part about Evangeline's bag and John's reluctance to trust the police to find his sister's murderer.

'Not everyone has faith in the police,' he said when she had finished. He pushed away from the mantelpiece and strolled to the tray where he refilled his brandy glass. He was calm, almost detached as if nothing she had told him was news to him. 'May I see these letters?' He set his glass down on the low table and waited.

Flora retrieved them from the bureau beside the window and handed them to him. She returned to her seat where she sat in tense silence waiting for him to finish reading them.

'And this Cecily allowed Victor inside the home of the Secretary of the Foreign Office?' he said when he had finished.

'Not allowed. He slipped away from her when she wasn't looking. She would never have given him permission and she threw him out when she discovered what he had done.'

William pursed his lips, tapping the letter against his other hand. 'I apologize, Flora. You do indeed have something here.'

'I do?' Blood rushed through her thighs and up into her chest in sudden excitement. 'You aren't angry with me for poking my nose into things which don't concern me?'

'No.' He frowned. 'Why would I be? I just want you to stay safe that's all; I wish I had such a resourceful investigator as you. Crabbe will be most annoyed when he finds out you have trumped him.' He chuckled.

'Mr Crabbe is your investigator?' Flora asked as realization dawned.

William had the grace to blush. 'He's not experienced, but he has his uses,' he said, neatly avoiding any explanation as to what he was investigating, and whom. 'I'll take charge of these if you don't object.' He gathered the letters together and tucked them into an inside pocket. 'I'll put them safe in my desk tonight, but first thing tomorrow I'll take them to Cannon Row as proof my Serbian spy is indeed linked with his murder.' He retrieved his brandy glass and swirled the brown liquid lazily. 'I blame myself for having neglected you since you arrived. I should have known you wouldn't be content sitting in the apartment reading Tennyson or out shopping for trinkets at Mr Harrod's store. You forget, I watched you grow up at Cleeve Abbey, witness to all the scrapes you got yourself into. The tree climbing and scaling of hay bales in the barn in your best clothes.' He waved the glass in her direction. 'Do you recall that summer you and Jocasta built a raft to cross the stream?'

'It fell apart midstream and we got drenched.' Flora smiled at the memory, which returned with all the laughter and incipient fear of getting both her and Jocasta into trouble.

'My sister made the most dreadful scene when you both came running back over the lawn in just your petticoats in front of a whole garden full of guests.' William laughed.

'Our dresses soaked up all the water and dragged us under. We had to take them off.' Flora recalled with a pang Lady Vaughn's horror when she saw them from the terrace. Flora had assumed she would be blamed for that escapade at the time, but due to William's intervention that did not happen. If only she had known then why he was so ready to jump to her defence, perhaps things might have been different. But then her childhood had hardly been unhappy, so knowing William was her father might have simply made things more confusing. For the first time, she began to see William's dilemma and entertain the thought that maybe his frequent visits to Cleeve Abbey might have had something to do with her.

'Since I discovered who you were, I always thought nothing could have affected my feelings for Riordan Maguire. That his place in my heart was fixed, and yet now—' She fought sudden tears as unresolved feelings for the man who had raised her vied with what was happening between herself and William.

'I never sought to supplant him, Flora. I could see how much he loved you, and despite my jealousy at the fact he was raising you when I was denied that privilege, I would not have spoiled that for you.'

'Don't you see it *is* spoiled in a way? He lied about Mother. He told me she was dead, when all along he wasn't sure if she ran away or was taken from us.'

'He was trying to protect you. What *could* he say? That she had left and he didn't know why? What would a young girl make of that? You would have blamed yourself as much as he did.'

'I never thought of it that way.' Flora frowned. 'He lied to me about you too.'

'I know, but for a very good reason. I also think he truly believed Lily was dead, so felt it unfair to give you false hope that she might return.'

'In the back of my mind, I always knew there was something missing. Not just the fact Mother didn't have a grave, but he would never discuss her. He refused to, no matter how many times I asked. I thought it was because he couldn't bear to. Now I'm not so sure.'

'Don't cast Riordan as being at fault. He did what he thought was right, and you were happy being his child, weren't you?'

'Of course I was, but I thought we had no secrets. Yet now, when I am in no position to demand an explanation, I discover he kept the most important one from me.'

'You're still angry with him? Even after all these months?'

'Yes, yes I am, and there's no way to put it right.' She swiped the tears from her cheek. 'Why didn't he tell me when I was old enough to understand?'

'Maybe he didn't want to take the chance that knowledge might change the way you saw him? For not being honest about Lily as well as the fact he had married her partly for your sake?' He took a sip from his glass, swallowed. 'While it was all happening, and Lily and I vacillated, blaming each other and being weak, Riordan took charge and acted in all our interests.'

'What about you? Did you ever wonder how the truth would finally affect me? Or did it suit you to ignore your indiscretion.' He winced and she instantly regretted her harshness. 'I'm sorry, that was cruel, and when you are trying your best to make up for it all now.'

'Was it – difficult for you?' she asked when he stayed silent. 'Knowing about me, I mean, and yet having to treat me like Riordan Maguire's child?'

'How could it not have been?' His eyes clouded with remembered pain. 'When you turned eighteen and became Eddie's governess, I went to Riordan and asked him if we could tell you the truth, together.' He raised the brandy glass to lips but moved it away again without taking a sip. 'He refused.'

'I'm sorry.'

'Don't be.' He sauntered back to his chair, leather creaking as he settled into the cushions. 'I understood he wanted to keep you to himself. He loved you very much.'

His words hung in the air as silence grew heavy between them. William stared off through the window towards Hyde Park, his eyes suddenly dark, which made her hope he recalled the happier moments of his life rather than what he didn't have.

Flora blew her nose and wiped away the remnants of tears. Though not all that sat between them was resolved, she felt better about things and more prepared to bring the subject up again at another time. One day she might even feel comfortable with calling him, Father.

'Now.' William stood and placed his unfinished glass on the mantel and huffed a breath. 'As you've been honest with me about what you have been doing these last few days, I think you should know that we are aware of Victor's relationship with this Miss Cecily Moffatt. Although we did not have a name.'

'By we,' she began, 'do you mean you and Mr Crabbe, or your superiors at the Foreign Office?'

'The latter, although we're an exclusive circle. Do you imagine much happens in Lennox Gardens without someone reporting it back to us? We deal with some sensitive information, so have informants everywhere.'

'Mr Hanson reported to us that his study had been disturbed, so I put a man to watch his house. The man saw Victor just the once and then not clearly, and as you know he broke off with Miss Moffatt soon after that. By the time we realized, we still had no idea who he was.'

Flora relaxed slightly, relieved. She had begun to feel guilty about the Boltons Library masquerade. Not to mention what she would say if Inspector Maddox had discovered she had spoken to Cecily and Molly.

'Cecily won't get into trouble will she?' Flora edged forward on her chair. 'As soon as she discovered Victor in the study she made him leave.'

'The man's an expert spy and an innocent lady's maid stood little chance. I expect all she'll receive is a reprimand. As for Miss Lange, I doubt she knew anything about spies. In fact her involvement was an inconvenient coincidence which we haven't quite worked out yet.' Retrieving his glass, William warmed his brandy with both hands round the bowl, his attention leaving her as he looked to be deep in thought. Did this mean Mr Crabbe was exonerated too? 'This man Harry Flynn,' William forestalled her question about Crabbe, 'he seems to pop up all over the place. Are you sure he doesn't know more then he pretends to?'

'I've wondered that myself. The truth is, I cannot be sure, though Harry doesn't seem the type to strangle a woman.'

'Any man might be, given the right circumstances.'

'I suppose so. He admits to having an argument with Evangeline about when they should be married, though as far as I know she didn't call off the wedding. I also recognized genuine grief in him. I don't think he would have hurt her.'

'You're still young, Flora.' He released a world-weary sigh. 'You see attractive young men as being largely honourable and the world as a kind place.'

'Isn't your world kind?' She searched his face which, apart from a cynical lift of an eyebrow, revealed nothing. He was the handsome, carefree man she had always known, and one who had led a life of comfort and privilege. Or perhaps those things didn't matter when he had been forced to live without the woman he loved most in the world? One thing which had struck her forcibly was William's insistence that he had truly loved Lily. He had tried more than once to convince her to elope with him, but she had refused. When she disappeared, he had been distraught.

'Don't listen to me.' William placed his glass on the table between them with a tiny click. 'Middle age and dealing with politicians is making me taciturn.'

Flora refrained from stating the obvious, that he neither looked nor acted middle-aged. 'What about Victor? Do you think he could have killed Miss Lange?'

'It's beginning to look that way.' He pressed the tips of his fingers together and rested them against his upper lip. 'However, ideas aren't proof. We need to find out who he's working for, as well as the names of his co-conspirators.'

'He could be a murderer too?'

'Indeed he could.' He shifted in his seat, his expression softening. 'Now, enough of unpleasantness. You seemed very happy to see Bunny this afternoon. I hope I'm not keeping you from him?'

'Not at all.' She recalled her promise, and taking deep breath she said, 'William, there's something else I need to— She broke off as the door opened to reveal Randall, who skirted a small bow, but before he could speak, Arthur Crabbe barged into the room, a waft of freezing fog clinging to his overcoat.

'Never mind that, man, I don't need announcing.' He nudged Randall out of the way, then addressed William, hesitating when he caught sight of Flora.

'Don't worry, Crabbe. Flora and I have just enjoyed an enlightening conversation about Balkan spies. You may speak freely in front of her.'

Crabbe actually smiled, which made his normal taciturn looks soften into near handsomeness. 'Well, sir, I'm sorry to interrupt your evening, but our man has been seen again.'

'Where?' William rose, his fists clenched as if prepared for flight.

'At a public-house in Tottenham Court Road. The landlord rented an upper room to a group of foreigners who claimed to need somewhere to hold a prayer meeting. Then some others, also foreigners, turned up.'

'I take it there wasn't much praying going on?' William asked as he checked his half-hunter.

Crabbe shook his head. 'The landlord said things began to get out of hand, so he sent for the constabulary. I've called Inspector Maddox, who'll meet us there.' He aimed an apologetic nod in Flora's direction. 'Pardon me, Mrs Harrington, but we must be off or it will all be over before we get there.' Crabbe took off along the corridor and William followed, making a brief stop at his study to put the letters Flora had given him into his desk drawer.

Flora followed them into the hall, where the front door stood ajar.

'I'm sorry, Flora,' William said as he shrugged into his overcoat. 'We'll have to continue our talk at another time.'

She nodded. Maybe this wasn't the right time to tell William about the baby after all. Not when this spy business occupied him. 'Who does Mr Crabbe mean by "our man"? Did he mean Victor or someone else?'

'We aren't sure, as yet.' William pinched the bridge of his nose between thumb and forefinger. 'There are some aspects of this case which only came to our attention recently. This Evangeline Lange business, for instance. It was totally unexpected, although I'm not dismissing your part. What you have found out is significant.'

'I gather there is a "but" coming?' Flora said, resigned.

'You must let me handle this from now on. I hope you understand.'

'You could at least tell me whom you suspect for Evangeline's murder? Is it anyone we've talked about?' She did understand, but that didn't mean she was willing to capitulate so easily.

'Not now.' He slung his scarf over one arm, retrieved his hat and put it on. 'I'll explain everything when I know more.' Giving her a brief, farewell nod, he jammed his hat onto his head and strode across the tiled hall and onto the street, the glazed front door flapping behind him.

Chapter 25

Flora woke with a start, bolting upright, then shivered as the chill night air slid across her bare arms. She tugged the heavy satin coverlet around her shoulders, certain that what had woken her had no place among the usual night-time noises of the apartment.

She groped for the light switch and blinked as a yellow glare flooded the room, blinding her. Would she ever grow accustomed to these electric lights? Though at the same time she had to admit they were easier than having to fumble in the dark with matches and a taper.

When the spots in front of her eyes cleared, a glance at the clock told her it was almost midnight. Seconds passed and nothing stirred, though she grew increasingly uneasy. Had she overreacted, and it was only William returning?

Going back to sleep became impossible, so she slipped from the bed, and drew on her dressing gown, her fingers fumbling with the slippery cord. She opened the door a crack onto a shadowed hall, lit only by a shaft of winter moonlight from the window at one end.

She froze, listening, but apart from the distant chime of the clock in the sitting room heard nothing. Her rapid heartbeat slowed a little, and reassured, she was about to return to bed when a sound from behind the door of William's study brought her alert again.

William wouldn't walk around in the dark, and both Sally and Randall had retired at the same time she had. Someone else was in the apartment.

Flora flicked off the light switch, plunging the room in deeper black than before, while she debated whether or not to press the bell for Randall, then decided against it. It would take too long by the time he responded and she had explained; as would attempting to wake Sally, whose heavy slumber was a permanent joke at home.

She crept along the hall to where the door to William's study stood firmly closed, but as she stared at it, a ribbon of light swept across the gap between it and the floor.

'Step away, Miss.' Flora jumped at the fierce whisper, her heart thumping, and bounced on her toes in preparation for flight, only to exhale again in relief. Randall stood beside her in a checked woollen dressing gown and slippers, the colours reduced to various shades of sludge-grey in the low light. He held an oil lamp at shoulder height in one hand, and what looked to be a yard long window pole in the other.

'There's someone in the study!' She gestured with a hand, her voice lowered and her breathing shallow.

'I know.' Randall placed the lamp on the floor, held the pole up and pushed the door open. 'Stand still whoever you are,' he yelled. 'I have a weapon!'

Flora pressed herself against the wall, and waited, unconvinced a burglar would be intimidated by a window pole. She held her breath, but nothing happened. No startled gasp or the sound of footsteps. Only silence.

Randall stepped into the room and lowered the pole, his face reappearing at the door seconds later. 'I think he's gone.'

Flora picked up the lamp and followed him inside, where chaos reigned in William's normally immaculate study. Every drawer and cupboard had been thrown wide, the desk almost invisible under a mountain of jumbled papers. More papers spilled out of the drawers and onto the floor.

'How did he get out when we were standing in the hall?' Flora asked.

Randall lifted the lamp, which revealed the jagged gash of a broken window. 'He might still be on the grounds. You stay here, Miss Flora, I might be able to—'

'No.' Flora laid a restraining hand on his forearm. 'Master William wouldn't want you to put yourself in peril. If this man is whom we suspect, he has already murdered one person, he won't baulk at another. He can only hang once.'

She tugged her dressing-gown around her and shivered again, hoping the intruder was streets away by now. Then a thought occurred to her and she skirted the desk set in the middle of the room and threw open a bottom drawer where William had put Evangeline's letters before Crabbe had called him away. The drawer was empty. 'Randall, you may as well telephone the police, and wake Dunne and tell him what has happened.'

By the time Randall returned, Flora was ensconced on the sofa in the sitting room, her feet tucked beneath her. Her toes were bone-white from the cold and virtually numb, but she was reluctant to pass William's study to retrieve her slippers.

'Neither Dunne nor the night porter heard anything.' Randall bent to set the fire as he talked. 'There are no signs other apartments have been broken into, but he's reluctant to wake anyone in order to ask them. He'll enquire in the morning.'

Flora was about to ask if Mr Crabbe's apartment had been disturbed but thought better of it. She would find out soon enough.

'The gate to the rear yard bears marks from what looks to be a crowbar,' Randall went on as flame caught the crumpled newspaper that flared into life. 'There's broken glass in the flower bed outside Master William's study.'

She was about to ask how long the police would be when the rattle of the front door opening was followed by the arrival of William.

'Goodness it's freezing outside, and not much warmer in here.' He flung his hat onto the chair beside him. 'What are you both doing still up?' His puzzled look went to her then the butler and back again.

'I take it you didn't catch your Serbian spy?' Flora asked, confident she already knew the answer.

'No, we didn't. The police had halted the meeting and brought them all in for questioning, but we couldn't arrest any of them as they weren't doing anything which could be described as illegal. If Victor was among them, he was careful not to give himself away. It will take weeks to check all their names and addresses.'

'I might be able to save you a job there. Victor wasn't at the public house. He was here.'

'What?' William froze. 'What are you talking about?'

'We had some excitement of our own while you were out.' Flora held her hand out to the meagre flames that licked around the pile of coal and spread, driving warmth slowly into the room.

'What sort of excitement?' William perched on the chair arm, his knees splayed, though did not remove his overcoat. 'And why do you think Victor was here?'

'Because he used the meeting as a distraction to break into your study about half an hour ago.'

'What?' William leapt to his feet and headed back along the corridor, flicking light switches on as he went. The sound of a door opening and a muffled 'Good God' floated back to her.

She eased her stiff muscles and rose, reluctantly leaving the fire, and followed. She leaned against the study door frame, shivering in the cold blast that sliced through her thin nightclothes from the ruined window.

Randall crouched amongst the mess, gathering papers from the floor he attempted to arrange in neat piles on the desk.

'Never mind that.' William gently waved him away. 'It can wait until the morning.'

'It is morning, sir,' Randall said, one brow arched. 'Mr Dunne will be here soon to make some basic repairs to the window. Shall I make some cocoa?'

'What?' William said again, then frowned in confusion, taking a moment to collect himself. 'Oh, oh, yes, Randall, that's a capital idea.'

'He took the letters,' Flora said when the butler had gone. 'I cannot tell if there's anything else missing.'

'Damn the letters, Flora! Are *you* all right? You didn't come face to face with this intruder did you?'

'I didn't even see him.' Flora moved to his side, a hand on his arm to calm his agitation. 'He must have heard Randall and me in the hall outside your study so he broke through the window.'

'Well that's something. It's annoying about the letters, but not the end of the world.' He stared at the papers in one hand, then at those he held in the other, dropping them both onto the desk with a sigh.

'I don't imagine he did all this to cover up the theft of those letters.' Flora surveyed the mess with dismay. 'Those weren't what he came for.'

'I think you're right, though it will take a while to discern what exactly is missing.'

'Cecily and Molly,' Flora murmured as something occurred to her. 'When he reads them, he'll know both women were about to expose him. Do you think they are in danger?'

'Good point.' William propped his hands on his hips, thinking. 'I'll make sure the police are aware. They don't have the resources to protect them, but they can make their presence known in the area. Fortunately, I've had most of my more sensitive papers taken to my office, and there wasn't much of interest in those letters was there?'

'No, only some vague quasi-romantic nonsense.' *And not enough to get Evangeline killed.*

'What was Victor looking for if those letters were merely a bonus?'

'My guess is, papers containing the names of Serbian nationals, or any document that referred to Balfour's decision about King Peter's government. Either that or he couldn't find what he wanted and became desperate.' He released a breath in a long sigh as he surveyed the devastation again. 'I'm sorry, Flora this shouldn't have happened.'

'It's not your fault.' She sniffed, her nose made runny by the cold, the moment seemed right to venture something which had been bothering her lately. 'William? I wasn't going to mention this, but I've had a strange feeling this last few days. I think someone has been following me. I've spotted him a few times. He wears a grey overcoat with his hat pulled down low so I cannot see his face properly. Do you think he might be this Victor?'

'Ah.' William shoved a pile of papers to one side and perched on the corner of his desk, arms folded. 'I'm afraid I'm responsible for that. Since the body of that young woman was found, I've had one of my men keep an eye on you.'

'Whatever for?' She stared up at him as a mixture of relief and anger surged through her.

'Your own safety, that's what for. I knew it would be useless to order you not to poke about in the Evangeline Lange business, but we didn't know how to dissuade you. Not in a way you would pay any attention to.'

'We? We who?'

'Me and Arthur Crabbe. Oh, and Bunny, naturally.'

'What do you mean, Bunny naturally?' She tugged her robe tighter, her arms crossed beneath her breasts. 'Have you and my husband been conspiring against me?'

'Conspiring? That's somewhat melodramatic.' He winked, which only made her angrier. 'When the woman you saw with Crabbe was found dead, I knew you simply wouldn't leave it at that. Other than sending you home again with no explanation, I didn't know what to do. So I called Bunny. He agreed with me. He said packing you off home a day after you got here would only make you more suspicious. That I couldn't stop you asking questions, but he approved of my idea to employ someone to ensure you weren't in any danger.'

'You and Bunny discussed what to do with me?' That's why he arrived unexpectedly that day and had been so sanguine about her discovery of a murder? William had been keeping him informed. At the time she had attributed his detailed questions to admiration for her detective skills, though it appeared his concern was more for herself than justice for Evangeline. The idea rankled somehow. Then she imagined the frantic telephone calls he must have exchanged with William and acknowledged she was being unreasonable. Naturally, Bunny would be worried.

'Once or twice.' William remained infuriatingly vague. 'He told me you might be able to discover things I couldn't. He was right, as it happened. The police talked to all the same people you have, at the school and The Grenadier, but you learned far more than they did.'

'I didn't find out that much, and most people would happily chat to me rather than answering a policeman's questions.' Met with what amounted to a compliment her anger didn't last, then something else occurred to her. 'Does Inspector Maddox know I've been talking to his witnesses?'

'Hmmm.' He waggled his hand from side to side, palm downwards. 'He's not exactly relaxed about your getting in the way of his investigation. It was only when I said his own enquiries had stalled that he agreed to allow you to continue. After all, no one had linked Evangeline Lange to Victor until you did.'

Flora smiled, wondering what it had cost Maddox to admit to that. 'We still don't know exactly what connects them. Evangeline certainly knew of Victor, but we have no idea whether or not they had actually met.'

'That's a good point, but right now, he's still the main suspect. No one we know of had a reason to kill her. Maddox is still working on the robbery theory.'

'I wish you had told me I was being, kept an eye on, as you put it.' She wanted to stay angry, but was too relieved that the man she had seen was not a threat, and that hopefully Victor wasn't even aware of her existence.

'I apologize. Maybe keeping it a secret wasn't the best idea. Bunny said you wouldn't like it.'

'He's right. I don't.' Parental and husbandly affections aside, she didn't appreciate being treated like a wayward child.

'Am I forgiven?' William wrapped an arm around her, giving her shoulders a brisk rub.

'Maybe.' She slanted him an oblique look, just as the rattle of a tray announced Randall's passage along the hall.

'I'll have to ask Inspector Maddox if he can spare a man to keep an eye on the apartment in case Victor comes back.'

'Why would he?' Flora frowned. 'By the looks of your study he got what he came for.'

'Even so, he is a murderer don't forget. However while we await his arrival, and as no one seems inclined for bed, let's warm ourselves with some cocoa.' He gave the hallway a vague look. 'Has young Sally missed all the fuss?'

'It would take a full-blown police raid to wake her.' Flora skirted Randall and made for the door. 'I'll look in on her before I have that cocoa, just in case.

She padded down the hall and peered around Sally's door, smiling at the rhythmic snore that came from the bed.

The ring of the doorbell followed by muted male voices told her the police had arrived at last. She waited until she spotted William leading two uniformed officers into the study, then crept out again and made her way down the hall.

Shivering, she pulled her dressing gown round her and quickened her steps toward the sitting room in anticipation of some hot cocoa. Then she recalled that on their first evening, William had told her working at home was one of the attractions of the job. And yet by the look on his face when he'd walked in, he certainly hadn't expected someone to break into his home. So why had he moved all his papers to his office?

Chapter 26

Despite her disturbed sleep, due to the fact the police didn't leave until after two in the morning, Flora rose at her usual time and after breakfast, she gave her telephone number to the operator at the exchange and waited for the call to be put through. The butler who answered at the Richmond house informed her in imperious tones that, 'Mrs Harrington is not at home, Madam.'

'No, Frederick, *I* am Mrs Harrington. I want to speak to Master Harrington. Is he there?' For some inexplicable reason, the Harrington butler was always referred to by his first name. Flora had once asked why this was and was told it was to differentiate him from his father who, though now retired, had also worked for the family in the past.

The sound of stentorian breathing continued down the line as the elderly butler at the other end processed her request, then went silent again for a full two minutes, before Bunny finally came onto the line.

'Good morning, my darling, and how is your visit going? You've only just caught me actually, I was about to leave for the office.'

'I was enjoying myself immensely until I became convinced I was being followed around the streets of Knightsbridge by a dangerous spy.' Instead of an explosion of shocked surprise, an ominous silence echoed down the line. 'I can hear your brain working from here,' Flora went on before he answered. 'There's no use you denying it, either. William told me that you contrived together to have me followed.'

'Ah, I see, well. Perhaps that wasn't the best decision.' Bunny's sigh was clearly audible over a background hum. 'His purpose was to keep you out of harm's way since I couldn't be there to do so myself. If you recall I also tried to bring you home, but you resisted that as well, so this was the only solution we could come up with.'

'Very noble, but have you any idea how frightened I was?' Flora vastly exaggerated her distress, but Bunny wasn't to know that. 'Especially in my condition.' She had lowered her voice, though she doubted she would be overheard. The chilly hallway wasn't somewhere anyone would linger from choice.

'I am so sorry, my darling. Obviously, we should have told you. However, to be honest, we never imagined you would spot him.'

'I don't think you should use the word honest too freely right now. It wasn't very straightforward of you to have discussed this with William and leave me out. Perhaps I shouldn't have mentioned the Evangeline Lange business to you at all.'

'It wasn't just the murder William was worried about. At the moment he's involved in something pertinent to the country he considers dangerous.'

'Yes, I know, Serbian spies, which might have nothing to do with Miss Lange's murder.' Though after the previous night, she didn't believe that.

'You were caught in the middle, Flora, and had I instructed you to return home immediately, what would you have done?' His voice kept drifting in and out, interspersed with crackling so she had to concentrate hard to hear him.

'Well, I—' Flora blustered. He knew her too well.

'Exactly. When you sniff out a mystery you'll keep poking at it until you root out the answers.'

'I thought you liked that about me.' Despite herself, Flora's lip trembled. Why was she so emotional these days?

'I do, of course I do.' His voice softened and she blinked back tears. 'Though you must admit you can be stubborn too and – look, Flora. I really have to go or I shall be late for the office.'

'I haven't finished!' She still had her carefully prepared lecture about deception, lack of trust and downright subterfuge to deliver.

'I know, but I must go, I'm in court this morning. But I promise we'll talk about this more fully when I come to fetch you in a day or so.'

'Bunny, there was a—'

'Now take care of yourself,' he cut across her. 'If you must look for some adventure, join that Women's Suffrage organization you went to the other night. I would much prefer that to hearing you have annoyed high-ranking policemen by asking awkward questions.'

'I'll think about it.' She decided that to mention the break-in now would guarantee his insistence she come home, and she had no intention of abandoning her hunt now. 'I miss you,' she whispered into the silent mouthpiece in her hand.

Sighing, she returned it to the hook, just as Randall let Inspector Maddox into the apartment. On seeing her, he inclined his head in a polite nod and murmured, 'Mrs Harrington.'

'Good morning, Inspector. Was there something you forgot to ask me last night?' Shortly after the police arrived the previous night, Maddox had stumbled into the chaos, rumpled from his own disturbed sleep and in a belligerent mood that did not appear to have improved.

'I have an unrelated matter to discuss with Mr Osborne.' He looked past her along the hall as if he had already forgotten her. 'Please don't let me detain you.'

Flora bridled at his brusque dismissal. 'You won't. And had I known you would be back to see us so soon, I would have asked Randall to lay a place for you at breakfast.'

He looked about to deliver a suitable rejoinder when William emerged from the study and greeted him like a long-lost friend. 'Ah, Inspector, there you are. I apologize for summoning you back, however there has been a development.'

Flora lingered in the hope she might learn more, when Sally appeared at the kitchen door and gestured with a series of hisses and elaborate hand signals. When the study door had closed on William and the policeman, she obeyed Sally's summons.

'I didn't want to say anything in front of that copper.' She drew Flora into the kitchen, then checked the hallway again before closing the door.

'What is it, Sally? Surely you aren't afraid of Inspector Maddox? He's not as scary as he looks.'

'Not me, Missus – her.' Sally stood aside, revealing the hunched figure of a young woman who sat at the kitchen table, her arms folded in front of her and her head down. 'It's Meg.'

Flora recognized the barmaid from The Grenadier, though her presence in William's kitchen remained a mystery. She gave the kitchen a brief look, but there was no sign of Randall.

'He says he wants nothing to do with this.' Sally interpreted her look. 'Says he'll come back when she's gone.'

'I see.' Flora turned back to the girl. 'Well, Meg and what can we—' she broke off with a gasp when Meg raised her chin and pinned Flora with one, wide blue eye. The other was an angry red, swollen almost closed, and a blackened scab had begun to form on her split lower lip.

'Who did this to you?' Flora asked, horrified.

*

Meg hunched her shoulders and stared at the oversized mug of stewed tea that sat on the table in front of her, but made no attempt to explain.

'Well go on then,' Sally prompted. 'Tell Miss Flora what you told me.'

Flora's brief head to toe glance revealed a pair of thin shoes which had begun to crack, a shabby, patched skirt and a blouse which showed shadows of old stains, much washed and which had probably never seen a flat iron. Her frizzy, brittle hair and the pallor of her skin indicated a poor diet in a life which must be a constant fight for survival.

Finally, Meg inhaled a noisy breath and fingered her cut lip with the bitten-down nails on one hand. She took a sip of her tea, swallowed and released a sigh. 'I was leaving the pub last night and I got jumped by some bloke.'

'Jumped? You mean you were attacked? By whom?'

'Dunno, do I?' Meg's scathing look told Flora she was being naïve. 'He came at me, from be'ind.' She seemed reluctant to meet Flora's eye and continued to stare at the mug she cradled in both hands. 'I-I didn't tell your maid everything the other day.' She flicked a look at Sally and away again. 'But when I first saw that woman, there was a man bent over her.'

'You saw who strangled Miss Lange?' Flora gasped.

'Not exactly.' Meg hunched her shoulders in a deprecating gesture which revealed her shame. 'He was standing over her when she was on the ground, holding her hand, looked like, but I couldn't see clearly. I was in the pub yard and saw him through the gate.'

'Could you describe him?' Flora's heartbeat quickened, but only for an instant as Meg shook her head.

'No. I must have cried out, for as soon as he saw me, he took off. It's dark in that alley and I couldn't see him properly. He wore an overcoat and a cap pulled down, but he wasn't old as he moved pretty quick.'

'Are you saying he returned to The Grenadier and beat you because of what you saw? To make sure you stayed silent?' At Meg's nod, Flora went on, 'Did he say anything to you?'

'Only that he knew it was me who took the bag. Said he saw me the other night.'

Flora took the wheelback chair opposite and dragged it closer to the table, then sat. 'Did you tell anyone about the bag?'

Meg glared at Sally as if she held her responsible. 'I didn't tell no one 'cept you.'

Flora ran through the names of those who had been told about the bag since that night. Apart from herself, Sally and John Lange, it included William and possibly Arthur Crabbe.

'You're sure it was the same man who did this to you?'

'Must have been. I tol' you, I didn't see his face that time either, but who else could it be?'

'If he attacked you from behind, how did your eye get injured like that?' Flora asked. 'You should report him to the police.'

Meg started to rise as panic entered her one good eye. 'Now look, I don't want no trouble.'

Flora waved her back down again. 'I'm sorry, it's your choice of course.'

Meg sank back down onto the chair. 'I didn't see's face 'cause I didn't want to. I kept me eyes and me mouth shut.'

'What did he want, Meg?' Flora asked.

'The brooch.' Meg slumped further in her chair.

'What brooch?' A rush of excitement sharpened Flora's voice. Meg flinched and fingered her eye, either from pain or guilt Flora couldn't tell. 'Is that why he came back?'

Sally uttered a derisive snort as if that conclusion was obvious. Flora gestured her to be silent as she waited for Meg to answer.

'The brooch weren't in the bag,' Meg said after a moment. She lifted the mug of tea again but found it empty and set it down again. 'It was on the ground near her. I said the police had found it when they came for the body, but he didn't believe me. That's when he punched me in the mouth.'

'You said you gave me everything you found apart from the money.' Sally strode forward and pointed a finger at Meg's chest, then jerked her chin at Flora. 'A guinea and two half-crowns she told me.'

'That's irrelevant now, Sally.' Flora leaned closer to Meg, keenly aware of the smells of mildew and sweat that emanated from her drab clothes. 'What did you do with the brooch?'

'After this?' Meg's eyes flashed and she pointed to her face, where the beginning of ugly purple bruises had started to erupt. 'I gave it to him didn't I?'

'That eye looks painful, Meg. Have you seen a doctor?' Flora drummed her fingers on the tabletop, her thoughts whirling.

'Don't have no money fer doctors,' she murmured, though her defensive manner dissolved and she looked no longer poised for flight; which Flora imagined would change if she knew Inspector Maddox stood a few feet away. She also chose not to remind Meg that she kept the money in Evangeline's purse, plus what Sally had given her. 'It's your decision of course, but you should tell the police what you saw the night Miss Lange was killed.'

'What for?' Meg's left eye widened, though the right remained no more than a slit, which probably meant her attacker was right-handed. Not that it meant anything; most people were. 'I can't tell them anything, so what's the point? I didn't see the bloke's face. Not then or last night. I only came here this morning to well, let you know that he came back.'

'Huh! Hoping for another reward, more like,' Sally muttered.

Flora rolled her eyes at the maid's cynicism. She could not find it in herself to blame Meg. Even the sparse kitchen where they sat with its clinical walls and plain furniture must seem comfortable compared to wherever this girl laid her head every night.

The concept of doing the right thing or a sense of public duty were principals other people lived by. That Meg might face punishment for taking Evangeline's bag was also a reality; the police were not known for their compassion.

'I ain't going to the police,' Meg muttered under breath to anyone who might be listening.

'I understand.' Flora was tempted to remind her that had she told the police in the first place, the beating might not have happened, but it was too late for that. 'See she has something to eat, Sally.' Then lowered her voice, 'And give her something for her trouble, but don't let her leave until you are sure Inspector Maddox is off the premises.'

'I'll see what I can do about those bruises first,' Sally halted her with a hand on her arm. 'That was kind of you not to grass on her to the flatfoots. She's a sorry-looking scrap, but there's no real harm in her.'

'I know.' She squeezed the maid's hand, partly in acknowledgement that Meg and her maid had come from a similar background. 'And when Master William's visitor has left, would you tell him I went for a walk and I'll see him tonight?'

'Would you need me with you, Miss Flora?' Sally asked, though the glance she gave Meg told her she did so reluctantly.

Flora shook her head. 'I'm only going into the park. I need some air and some time alone to think.'

Chapter 27

Hyde Park was considered one of the more healthy areas of the city where St James' and Green Parks provided what constituted a barrier against the more industrial riverfront with its tanneries and factories that churned out sooty smoke into the atmosphere.

Flora liked the mornings before the worst of the London fog obscured the buildings and muted the daylight. The sky above the park was almost clear apart from a blanket of white mist that hovered at the tree line. She walked the entire length of Rotten Row with its constant parade of horses and riders out to see and be seen, just as they had done for hundreds of years.

Pausing at the Serpentine bridge, she leaned against the wide stone balustrade to stare at the water, her thoughts on Meg and her strange story.

Why had the killer returned to Old Barrack Yard at all? For the brooch, or the bag? And if so, why, when there was nothing in it. Unless he knew about the mailbox receipt and didn't want anyone to know Evangeline had been searching for Victor. Which made sense if Victor was the killer.

Meg *had* told her attacker who had the bag, that's why he had broken into the apartment the night before. A surge of anger against Meg rose but died in an instant. Who wouldn't reveal everything in the face of such a violent assault?

She hoped Sally didn't give her more than a half-crown this time.

The killer wasn't to know Flora had given the bag to John, but why was it so important. Or was it? Had the robbery, if that's what it was, been about the brooch all along? Was Lydia's conviction that Evangeline might have fought her attacker accurate? That in the struggle, the brooch was ripped from her coat and lost in the dark alley, and the killer fled when Meg saw him.

But then why would an opportunist thief risk coming back to the scene to retrieve the brooch?

Flora expelled her breath in a rush as the thought came her to her in a flash.

He would have – if he knew for sure it was valuable.

A group of black-garbed nannies in uniforms and pert hats came into view on the edge of the Serpentine, distracting her from these and other questions that had drummed inside her head but were no closer to answers. Flora smiled, watching their respective charges squeal and throw bread at a flock of enthusiastic ducks who crowded round them in hope of a few crumbs. One child panicked and with a high-pitched scream, abandoned her handfuls of bread and ran to seek shelter behind her nanny's skirt.

Flora pushed away from the balustrade, tucking back a loose strand of hair the wind had pulled from her hairpins. As she flicked it back, she caught sight of the man in the grey overcoat beside a tree at the far end of the bridge. When he saw her looking at him, he turned away and studied a flower bed with fierce intensity, while she resisted a mischievous impulse to wave at him.

William had apologized again at breakfast for having her followed, his touching plea that he only sought to keep her safe overriding all her objections. Bunny's complicity, however, was another matter, but she would deal with him later. The thought she would see him again soon put a spring into her stride as she approached a line of benches set beside the glistening grey water which swept through the centre of the park in a sinuous curve. A line of willow trees enclosed the lake, their heads dipped to the water, while pigeons bobbed and strutted close by in search of crumbs the ducks had missed.

A little boy of about four years old ran full pelt into the heaving mass of grey bodies, scattering them into alarmed flight. As they flapped into the air and soared away towards the Bayswater Road, his lower lip trembled. Before it could develop into a full-throated wail, one of the nannies gathered him up and comforted him with the offer of a sweet from a cone of paper.

Flora smiled. One hand crept across her middle in an unconscious acknowledgement to the tiny life that grew there. There would be a time quite soon when she might well stroll this same spot with her own child, warning him or her not to stand too close to the water, or explaining patiently that the ducks didn't like being chased or trodden on.

Thus preoccupied, she didn't notice the young woman join her on the seat until she spoke.

'Good morning, Flora.'

Flora spun round, then relaxed with a smile as she recognized Lydia. 'Sorry, I was miles away.'

'I know. I waved from the bridge but you didn't see me.'

'It's nice to see you. No school today?'

'No. Miss Lowe has arranged for the younger girls to visit the British Museum, so I have the morning off. I went to your building first, but that nice porter said he saw you enter the park, so I followed. I hope you don't mind?'

'Of course not. I meant to call on you again but I've been busy lately. How have you been?'

'I think about Evangeline a great deal.' Lydia's eyes welled. 'I still cannot quite accept she's gone.'

'That's understandable.' Flora contemplated how much she should share of what she had learned about Evangeline and Victor. If anything.

'I don't know whether or not you wish to attend her funeral,' Lydia said. 'The service is at St John's the day after tomorrow. She's to be buried in the Lange family vault at the Brompton Cemetery.'

Flora nodded, not sure if she would be welcome or not. She was a stranger to Evangeline after all. But then funerals were for the living, to close a final chapter. She would have to think about it. 'Was that why you sought me out at the apartment? To tell me about Evangeline's funeral?'

'Not exactly, though I did come here in order to speak to you. About Evangeline.'

Flora stared out at the water, waiting, conscious that Lydia struggled with what she wanted to say as her eyes kept darting from treeline to the lake but did not settle on anything.

'I wish you had known her.' Lydia closed her eyes as if she were summoning Evangeline into her head. 'She had charm, beauty and determination to live her life and not simply endure it. She was also convinced that one day, women would be treated the same as men.'

'You're right. I would have liked her.'

'You remind me of her in many ways.' Lydia's eyes welled with unshed tears, at odds with her sweet smile.

'Do you know her family?'

'Not really. I met her father once, but he didn't have much to say to me. You must remember him, from the meeting the other night.'

'I do indeed.' Flora recalled an angular man with piercing eyes who towered over those around him, his face set in obdurate anger. Was his disapproval of his daughter's principles enough to drive him to murder? 'You said you had never met her brother, John.'

Lydia blinked as if surprised Flora should mention him. 'No, though he came to the school a few times, mostly with some complaint or other I assume began with their father. He was bad tempered, even bullying toward Evangeline. She was always generous about him too, which I found odd, making allowances when he agreed with her father. As if she were compensating for something.'

'Really? From what I saw he was devoted to his sister.' Flora recalled the cautious young man who had approached her outside Cannon Row. 'He's grief-stricken and determined to discover who was responsible for her death.'

'Brothers and sisters don't always get on. That's natural, isn't it? It doesn't mean they aren't distraught if one of them dies. Not that I know, as I have no siblings.'

'Neither do I,' Flora drew the words out, remembering the constant teasing and squabbles among the Vaughn sisters, but who were all devoted to one another. 'I don't understand how those relationships work either.'

'Do the police have any idea yet as to who might have killed her?' Lydia asked.

Flora hesitated. Not that Lydia could possibly be a suspect. 'Since you ask…'

She gave Lydia a brief account of the sequence of events which had led to their having found the receipt for Boltons

Library, the letters, now stolen, and her encounters with Molly Bell and Cecily Moffatt. She kept to salient details, which did not include a reference to either William or the Serbians. 'It's possible this man Victor, whoever he is, might have killed Evangeline to prevent her ruining his reputation. That might seem like a weak reason but murders have been committed for far less, and—'

'She was doing it for me,' Lydia's low whisper halted Flora's chatter.

'I beg your pardon?' Flora frowned, unsure if she had heard her correctly. 'Who did what for you?'

'That's what I came to talk to you about this morning. Evangeline was killed because of me.' Lydia twisted the end of the ribbon that fell from her hat in her gloved fingers.

'I don't understand.' Flora inhaled sharply as the only explanation that made sense hit her. '*You* knew Victor?'

Lydia nodded, dislodging fat tears from her lower lashes and slid down her cheeks.

Flora twisted to face her, making their conversation more intimate. 'Tell me everything.'

Lydia inhaled slowly, then started to speak, though she kept her eyes straight ahead, the conversation obviously difficult for her. 'I was coming out of the school one afternoon after the pupils had gone home and he was sitting on the wall of the house next door. I asked him if he was waiting for someone.' Lydia swiped her face with a gloved hand. 'He smiled at me, and said he had seen me go into the school several times and asked if I worked there.' Her hands stopped twisting and she tugged at a button on her glove that had begun to loosen. 'I know I should have rebuffed him because we hadn't been properly introduced, but it was like being hit in the chest. I could hardly speak. I just wanted him to go on smiling at me.'

'I understand.' Flora smiled. Had she not experienced the same thing with Bunny?

'He apologized for his forwardness and invited me to take a walk in the park. This park actually.' She stared around for a moment with a wistful expression as if she recalled happier times. 'We would meet here after the school day and when the holidays started I-I invited him back to the house after Mother had gone to bed.'

'Why did you feel you had to keep him a secret?'

'Because he insisted.' Her eyes rounded in surprise. 'He said his family back in Belgrade would disapprove if they knew about us. That we would tell everyone later- when—'

Belgrade!

'You're sure that's what he said, Belgrade?' Flora snapped.

Lydia blinked. 'Yes, why?'

Nothing. Just something - then what happened?'

'I never found out.' Lydia's attempt at a laugh was more like a sob. 'He didn't keep our last appointment. I waited over an hour but he didn't come. I haven't heard from him since.' She tugged at the same button on her glove. 'I thought something might have happened to him. That was when I realized I hardly knew him. Not his address, or even his full name. Just Victor. I didn't know whom to ask.' She rummaged in a pocket of her coat and brought out a folded handkerchief she held to her nose. 'I know it wasn't respectable of me to keep him a secret, but he was so persuasive.'

'How long did this liaison last?'

'Seven weeks and two days.' She gave a strange little shrug as if embarrassed she had kept count.

'When was the last time you saw him?'

'The last week of August. By the time the autumn term began, I hadn't seen him for a month.'

'And you told no one about him?' Flora looked up, distracted briefly by the same young boy who now chased a mallard along the shoreline, his nanny in pursuit.

'I told Evangeline. She found me crying in the common room one afternoon. I made an excuse but she prised it out of me. I was upset because I had seen him that morning at the school and he had ignored me.'

'Go on.' The button on Lydia's glove took some more punishment until Flora was convinced it would part company with the material.

'At first, I thought he had come to see me, but then the maid showed him into Miss Lowe's office. He walked straight past me on the stairs and didn't even appear to see me.'

'Victor went to see Miss Lowe? Are you sure about that?'

'Definitely.' Her hazel eyes widened in mild reproof at being doubted. 'I had to go and take my next lesson, and by the time it finished, the maid said he had just that moment gone.'

'Do you know what he wanted to see the headmistress about?'

Lydia shook her head. 'I told you. He left without speaking to me. Evangeline said she would see that he faced the consequences of his actions.'

'What did she mean by that?'

'I had no idea, not then. But when you mentioned the advertisement and those letters, I realized what must have happened. You see, Evangeline admired Mrs Fawcett and longed to emulate her.'

'I'm sorry, Lydia, I don't understand.' Flora massaged her forehead as she tried to make sense of Lydia's confused ramblings. 'What does Millicent Fawcett have to do with Evangeline and Victor?'

Lydia clamped her lips together before she began speaking again. 'Mrs Fawcett invited a few of us from the Society to her house in Gower Street for tea on one occasion. She told Evangeline and me that some fifteen years ago, a servant of a friend of hers was pestered by an army colonel. Mrs Fawcett had been incensed, but society never blamed men who behaved in that way. She and a friend decided to shame him by throwing flour over him in the street.'

'She did that?' Despite the seriousness of their talk, Flora couldn't help but laugh. She could imagine the diminutive, gentle but forceful Mrs Fawcett acting in such a way.

'I know, I could hardly think she would do such a thing either,' Lydia said. 'She treated us to a wonderful description of how the flour stuck to his waxed moustache, got into his eyes and down the back of his neck. Then the ladies pinned a paper on his back saying, this man is a cad or something like that.'

'Did it have the desired effect?' Flora asked, wiping tears from the corner of her eyes.

'Apparently so, as he was turned out of a gentleman's club, and cut by his lady friends. He became a laughing stock and his fiancée was so humiliated, she ended their engagement. Mrs Fawcett said she had no pity for the odious creature and would have had him cashiered if she could. Evangeline laughed so much, and from that moment, she almost worshipped Mrs Fawcett.'

'I'll have to become better acquainted with Mrs Garrett Fawcett. She sounds like an admirable woman.'

'Oh, she is. She's done so much for the suffrage movement over the years. I think it's dreadful the way Mrs Pankhurst has broken away to form her militant group. Mrs Fawcett is convinced it will set the cause back years.'

Flora silently agreed, but was eager to get back to the subject of Evangeline. 'Then you believe that advertisement in the paper was part of Evangeline's scheme to embarrass Victor?'

'Don't you?' Lydia's eyes widened. 'Evangeline loved to take up causes. She saw herself as a pioneer for women. I can imagine her confronting a rake in public to make him look foolish. That's what she called Victor, a rake.'

'Did Evangeline ever meet Victor?'

'Not meet exactly.' Lydia crumpled her handkerchief in one hand. 'One afternoon about three weeks ago, I was with Evangeline outside Harrods when I spotted him with another man. I must have looked shocked because Evangeline knew immediately something was wrong. I pointed him out to her and she marched right up to him.'

'She did?' Flora gasped. 'What happened?'

'Victor said she must have mistaken him for someone else. That she had accused him unjustly.' A deep crease appeared at the bridge of her nose. 'But he lied. It was him, I know it was. He was embarrassed to see me and brushed us aside.'

'What about the man who was with him? Did he have anything to contribute?'

'Nothing, as far as I know. Victor told Evangeline she had no right to accost him in front of his employer.'

'He said that this man was his employer?'

'That's what she said,' Lydia snapped, as if annoyed Flora kept echoing what she said. 'Evangeline was furious and insisted we follow them, though I knew it wouldn't do any good.'

'Where did they go?' Did Victor see this confrontation as threat enough to silence Evangeline?

Lydia flapped a hand as if this were irrelevant. 'I've no idea. They walked off in the direction of Hyde Park. Evangeline followed them, but I couldn't bear to be near him anymore, so I went into the store and walked around.' Lydia sniffed into the handkerchief. 'When she came back she took me out to tea. She was sweet and kind and understood how awful I felt.'

'How long was she gone?' Flora asked as something occurred to her which was no more than an unformed idea.

'What? Oh about twenty minutes, maybe a little longer. Why?'

'It's nothing.' Harrods was a ten-minute walk from Prince Albert Mansions. Was Victor's employer someone who lived in her building? Was that why Evangeline visited Arthur Crabbe the night she died? Suddenly Flora felt guilty about not telling Inspector Maddox everything.

Restless, she patted Lydia's hand and rose. 'I think we both deserve a cup of hot chocolate.'

'That would be very welcome. It's quite cold here.'

The children and their nannies had gone, the queue for the kiosk short when they arrived at the tiny wooden hut. The cheerful kiosk owner kept up a constant stream of chatter as he presided over copper urns of steaming tea and hot milk, the latter whipped expertly into a rich, purple-brown liquid topped with a layer of creamy froth.

'Does this mean you'll have to mention me to the police?' Lydia took the cup Flora held out.

'Haven't they already interviewed you?'

'About my friendship with Evangeline, yes.' Lydia blew the thick froth to one side before taking a sip. 'I'm afraid I didn't mention Victor at all.'

Flora took a sip from her own cup as she pondered, the hot, sweet mixture warming her stomach, reminding her she had not eaten much that morning.

'I'm not sure if they need to know, I'll have to take advice about it.' Though with whom she would discuss Lydia's dilemma was also subject to debate.

'I knew the moment I heard Evangeline was dead that I would have to tell them about Victor at some time.' Lydia's drink left a line of froth on her upper lip which she didn't appear to notice. 'Some people think her connection with the NUWSS was the reason she was murdered, but I'm sure they are wrong.'

'I think so too.' Flora took her own handkerchief from her pocket and used it to wipe Lydia's lip. 'It will give me some satisfaction to see Inspector Maddox's face when he realizes that.' Though her theory about Arthur Crabbe still did not fit. Why would an officer of the Foreign Office kill Evangeline because she had recognized Victor? And who *was* Victor? A Serbian diplomat the government wished to protect, or maybe one of William's spies? Was Arthur Crabbe working with the Serbians? William's reaction at seeing the advertisement came back to her. Did William have any idea of what was going on?

'Are you all right, Flora?' Lydia's breathless voice interrupted her thoughts. 'You've gone quiet.'

'I was just thinking.' Flora drained her cup, the liquid having cooled quickly in the sharp cold. She took Lydia's empty one from her hand and wandered over to the kiosk, handing both cups back to the stallholder, who wished them a cheery good morning.

She tucked her arm through Lydia's, and together they strolled back across the bridge and along the path towards the

Knightsbridge Road, their ponderous walk taken in virtual silence while questions lined up in Flora's head.

Victor's visit to Miss Lowe kept nagging at her. Was the headmistress in some way connected to William's spies, or was she another of Victor's conquests? It was unlikely to have had anything to do with Lydia as he had abandoned their relationship before then.

'Did Victor ever question you when you first met, Lydia?'

'What about?'

'I don't know. The school, Miss Lowe?'

'Well, actually yes he did.' Lydia's steps slowed. 'He asked me what I knew about her. How long she had lived in London. Things I couldn't really tell him.'

'But what you could tell him was of interest?'

'I suppose so.' She thought for a moment. 'I didn't know anything about her life before she came to the school, but I did mention the villa in Biarritz. Oh, what was it called now?' She thought for a moment, her lips moving as she searched her memory. 'Palais de something. It began with an 's' but I cannot remember exactly.'

'Le Palais de Sacchino,' Flora murmured.

'What was that?'

'Never mind, Lydia, it's probably not important. I don't suppose you would know why Evangeline would visit Arthur Crabbe's apartment on the night she died?'

'I didn't know she had. Who is Arthur Crabbe?'

'Ignore me, I'm just trying to put together loose ends, but they keep eluding me.' She set off again, pulling Lydia with her toward the gate which lay opposite Prince Albert Mansions. Morning traffic had become a steady stream in both directions so they had to shout about the noise of hooves and engines.

'I know I shouldn't have been so secretive.' Lydia paused at the kerb. 'I didn't want Mother to find out I had been, well, indiscreet.'

'That's understandable. But I don't think you should punish yourself, in fact—' Flora broke off, aware Lydia was no longer listening, her attention on something past Flora's shoulder.

'Who is that woman, Flora?' Lydia asked.

Flora waited for a motor bus to pass, then scanned the façade of Prince Albert Mansions.

A woman in a black coat, her hat and face covered by a thick black veil had emerged from a hansom opposite.

'That's Mrs Crabbe,' Flora replied. 'She wore that veil the last time I saw her. I wonder if she has some facial disfigurement she doesn't want anyone to see?'

'Are you sure?'

'Sure about what, her name or the disfigurement?'

Lydia continued to stare as Dunne came bustling from the building and helped the woman down from the cab.

'Her name. I cannot see her face but her gait is similar; the way she pokes her head forward when she walks. The pupils always joke about it at school.' Lydia glanced at the clock above a shopfront opposite and released a gasp. 'Oh, look at the time. I must get back to Mother. I gave Tilly the day off, and Mother gets out of sorts if her medication is late. Thank you so much for listening to me, Flora, although I don't know if it will help find out who killed Evangeline.'

'You have no idea,' Flora mused to herself, still watching the woman being shown into the building.

'Flora.' Lydia's hesitant tone brought her attention back to her. 'You won't say anything about – well you know?'

'Not if I don't have to.' Flora hoped she could keep her promise, though, at the same time, she was aware the police would have to decide whether Lydia's secret was relevant or not.

Chapter 28

Fuming with impatience, Flora waited for a line of motor buses and cars to stream past her in the road as the woman disappeared inside the building. A gap finally appeared in the stream of traffic and Flora hurried across the road and up the front step.

'Did you enjoy your walk, Mrs Harrington?' Dunne asked, holding open the door.

'Um-yes, thank you.' She climbed the stairs to the first landing, conscious of the porter's confused stare following her as she paused outside the door of Arthur Crabbe's flat. Before she could think better of it, she pressed her finger to the brass doorbell. A tinny tone sounded from inside, and for a long second while the door stayed closed, she almost changed her mind. She could be quite wrong in her sudden suspicion about Mrs Crabbe. If so, she could always invite her to afternoon tea. An innocuous enough suggestion to make to a neighbour.

The woman who opened the door still wore the thick veil, from behind which she regarded Flora in silence.

'Good morning,' Flora said with false brightness. 'I'm staying with my father in the apartment below and, thought I would come up and introduce myself.'

The fact she couldn't see the woman's face properly unnerved her. What expression sat behind that thick gauze? Surprise? Pleasure? Anger?

'That is kind of you, but quite unnecessary.' The woman's careful enunciation and slow speech banished Flora's reticence, certain she had heard it before. The woman made to close the door, but before the lock caught, Flora shoved against it.

'I couldn't possibly leave without making some effort to be cordial.'

'In which case, you had better come in.' A sound came from behind the veil which could have been a sigh of either disappointment or frustration. 'I seldom encourage visitors as a rule.'

Ignoring this obvious snub, Flora stood her ground until the woman released the door and stepped back, allowing Flora into an apartment smaller than William's; the entrance hall was shorter and contained fewer doors.

Flora tried to think of a way to get her hostess to remove the veil, but short of ripping the thing from the woman's head she was at a loss.

The woman gestured her into a room on Flora's right, where the door stood a few inches ajar and a man's lace-up shoe visible at the end of a black trouser leg.

Flora hesitated at the thought they were not alone, but with a strength that took her by surprise, the woman gripped her arm and bodily shoved her through the door, where Flora found herself face to face with Mr Gordon.

His black eyes widened when he saw her, then narrowed. 'What's *she* doing here?'

'Good morning, Mr Gordon.' The sight of him confirmed all Flora's suspicions, which she was still unsure of up until a few moments before. 'And to you too, Miss Lowe.'

Sighing, Helen Lowe flung the veil aside, but remained with her back to the now closed door, her face impassive and cold. Her eyes, which had danced with animation at their first meeting at the Harriet Parker Academy, were empty and soulless.

However, it wasn't her changed demeanour that sent a frisson of alarm through Flora as much as the small black revolver she held levelled at Flora's waist.

'What exactly *are* you doing here, Mrs Harrington?' Miss Lowe's voice was slow and menacing.

'I-er I was in the park when I saw you come into the building.' She was unable to drag her eyes away from the tiny hole at the end of the gun barrel. 'I thought you were Mrs Crabbe.'

'Don't lie to me.' She tossed the veil onto a nearby chair without looking to see where it landed. 'I saw you from the hansom with Miss Grey. It was she who recognized me, wasn't it?'

There was little point in contradicting her, but Flora still didn't know what these two were doing in Mr Crabbe's apartment? Whatever it was, she doubted it was Foreign Office business. Her instinct was to warn William – but how?

'What gave me away?' Gordon asked, his eyes as cold as Miss Lowe's.

'Does it matter now, Petar?' Miss Lowe snapped.

'It does to me!' Gordon advanced on her, his face grim. 'I want to know how she found out after all my hard work.'

'Actually, it was the poetry,' Flora said, halting him when he was still several feet away. 'My father said you have an excellent memory, Mr Gordon. Cecily Moffatt said the same thing. That you recited poetry to her without referring to a book.'

'That's all?' He slammed a hand against the door making Flora jump. '*That's* how you identified me?'

'It's always the little things which give us away, Petar,' Miss Lowe gestured him away with her free hand, a wry smile curving her thin mouth. 'Now go and lick your wounds somewhere else, I have work to do.'

'What work?' Gordon frowned, then his eyes cleared and he gasped. 'Elena, what in God's name are you doing? Don't you know who her father is?'

'I cannot help that.' She looked from Flora to Gordon and back again. 'Anyway, this is all your fault! I told you not to mess with that Grey girl? She was never part of our scheme.'

'What can I say?' Gordon smiled, sheepish but triumphant despite his nervousness. 'She's an attractive girl, I couldn't resist. Besides, she led me to you, so you should be grateful.'

'I don't wish to hear your excuses.'

The gun in the woman's hand shook, creating a light-headedness Flora found difficult to fight. She wanted to ask if she might sit down before she fainted, but didn't dare. What had possessed her to barge into the apartment without knowing the dangers?

'You aren't thinking straight, Elena.' Gordon paced the floor, both arms flailing. 'You'll bring the entire might of the government down on us. We need to get out of here. Her father is due back with Crabbe any moment.'

That Crabbe wasn't part of whatever was going on, reassured Flora, though Miss Lowe's implied intention made her mouth go dry. She prayed Gordon could talk her out of it as he seemed the most squeamish of the two.

'Go and keep an eye out for them then!' Emotion chased across the woman's face as she considered what Gordon had said. 'I need time to decide what to do with her. Keep them talking if you have to but don't let them come up here!' Her grip on the gun changed when she brought the other hand up to steady it.

Flora swallowed. Dare she hope the woman was inexperienced with firearms and was thus a poor shot? But then if so, it could go off by accident.

Growing panic made Flora's breathing fast and shallow, combined with a small triumph that she had been right about Gordon, or Petar, if that was what his name was. He had not reacted as he should have when he caught her eavesdropping.

If these two were the Serbian spies William had been so worried about, they didn't seem very experienced. What had they been doing? Agitating activists in London? Arranging riots? Either or both seemed too trivial to necessitate killing Evangeline. Though maybe not if she had discovered their activities. Flora pushed all questions aside and tried to concentrate on the, more pressing need of finding a way out of there in one piece. She still felt faint, and conscious of the sofa behind her, bent at the waist, intending to sit.

'Don't move!' Miss Lowe's shout brought Flora upright again, making her feel dizzy.

'Elena, think.' Gordon stopped his pacing. 'Mrs Harrington seeing us here together is proof of nothing.'

'Just go, Petar,' Miss Lowe said without looking at him.

Gordon threw Flora a look filled with regret before he made for the door, a path which took him between her and Miss Lowe, a pause during which Flora debated whether she could duck behind him when he reached her; an idea she rejected at once as being too risky. The room was too close to the front door and precious seconds would be lost opening it. Even if she managed to use Gordon as a shield, bullets could penetrate two bodies close together.

A voice inside Flora's head screamed that she must do something, but her body remained paralyzed. The dull click as Gordon closed the door sent dread flooding through her. He might have been persuaded to mercy but the dull-eyed woman in front of her was quite ruthless.

'Sit down!' Miss Lowe flicked the gun toward the sofa she had denied her a moment ago.

Flora didn't hesitate. Her head swam and she felt nauseous.

'Now.' The woman took a straight-backed chair opposite, the look she directed at Flora of pure contempt. The vulnerable, almost ingratiating demeanour she had exhibited at their first meeting was entirely absent. 'What *are* we going to do about you?' She stroked the gun with her other hand as if it were a pet. A particularly dangerous one.

Flora was about to say she thought she had already decided, but there was no point in goading her. 'Miss Lowe, Elena or whatever your name is. It's not as if I could tell anyone anything. I have no idea what you and Mr Gordon are up to.' Her gaze strayed back to the gun and she swallowed, wishing the woman wouldn't keep it pointed at her like that.

'Then why did you come to see me at the school?' Her eyes narrowed giving her face a more pronounced Slavic quality

'To see Miss Grey. Your maid jumped to the wrong conclusion and took me to your office. I wanted to tell Lydia about Evangeline Lange before the police did.'

'You have a certain innocence about you that I find quite intriguing, Mrs Harrington, though you should know I'm not fooled by it.'

A rush of fury drove away Flora's panic and anger took over. 'Look, Miss Lowe. Whatever association you have with Mr Gordon is none of my concern. I'm prepared to overlook your pointing that gun at me. Now if you don't mind, I'll be going now.' Flora started to rise, but the room tilted around her and she collapsed onto the sofa again. 'Perhaps not.'

'You aren't leaving until you tell me what William Osborne told you.' Her mouth twisted into a cruel smile. 'And maybe not even then.'

'Why would he?' Perhaps this woman wasn't as clever as she thought? 'My father is bound by the Official Secrets Act. He isn't allowed to tell me anything. Besides, I wasn't aware you and Gordon knew each other until I walked in here.' Flora closed her eyes at a sudden wave of giddiness accompanied by a sense of the ridiculous. She talked like one of those villains from the cheap novelettes her mother-in-law read. All black cloaked men with long noses and wide eyed heroine's. Who did this woman think she was keeping her here? Was the gun even loaded?

Could she keep her talking until help arrived? *If help arrived.* No one knew she was there except maybe Dunne who might have seen her go up the stairs. Would he mention it to anyone, or simply wait until she was missed?

'True.' Miss Lowe's lips pursed as she considered Flora's response. 'Perhaps. However, you are an inquisitive young woman, or you wouldn't be here.'

'I told you, I don't know anything!' Flora snapped, the notion she might die for what she didn't know struck her as ironic.

This couldn't be happening. Where was this bodyguard William had engaged to look after her? She would have his job if this woman shot her; a thought so ridiculous, she giggled.

'You think this situation amusing?' Miss Lowe sneered.

'Not really.' She fought down hysteria and tried to keep her voice calm. 'I'm impressed you managed to get a spy into the Foreign Office though. My father will be most disappointed.'

'Ah yes, Petar. Not the most intelligent of men, but he proved useful.'

'Useful for what? Seducing young women then abandoning them?' Lydia's tear-stained face came into her head, followed closely by Miss Moffat's. Is that how spies behaved?

'That and other things. Surely you must know by now, Mrs Harrington, that your government has thus far refused to acknowledge our king?'

'Probably because of what you did to the last one,' Flora said without thinking. Then a thought struck her. 'Was Gordon involved in the assassination of the Royal family in Belgrade?'

'Gordon isn't a killer.' Elena snorted. 'He's simply a hired thug. Don't let his good looks fool you, Mrs Harrington. He's a primitive with an ingrained penchant for violence. It wasn't difficult to make him believe I share his hatred of the pro-Austrians.' She gave a small sigh of satisfaction. 'It's a long and complicated story, but I should enjoy telling it. After all, it's only fair that you should know why you are about to die?'

'Oh yes, that's going to make all the difference,' Flora murmured beneath her breath. She knew she should stop talking, but couldn't help herself. Though how much more trouble could she get into?

'We had nothing to do with the assassination of King Alexander, or his wife's family, though that doesn't mean I'm not delighted that the odious brute and that awful woman are gone. However, when I heard of the plan to reinstate the late king's mother, Queen Nathalie, I knew I could not let that happen.'

'May I ask why?' Not that Flora was particularly interested, but the woman was obviously a fanatic. She seemed a little calmer now she had an audience for her story, though her grip on the gun hadn't changed.

'Gordon is of Magyar extraction,' Miss Lowe went on. 'His people suffered under King Alexander, who favoured the Austrians. My reasons are far more prosaic, in that I have a personal hatred for Queen Nathalie and would like nothing more than to see her dead.'

'That's a strong emotion to feel for a virtual stranger, unless...' An image of Miss Lowe's desk at the Harriet Parker Academy sprang into Flora's head. 'The photograph. The one of the house in Biarritz that belongs to your cousin. *She's* Queen Nathalie?'

Miss Lowe inclined her head. 'Very astute, my dear. My mother was Nathalie's maternal aunt, and when she lost her parents, she came to live with my family. From the day she arrived I was pushed aside. Ignored, neglected. Treated like little more than a servant to the oh-so-perfect Princess Nathalie.' She spat the words out like grape pips. 'She was seven years older than me, and very beautiful, even as a child. She dominated my mother's every thought.'

'That must have been very difficult for you.'

'You cannot imagine.' Her eyes darkened with old and bitter memories. 'I became someone of no importance, no more thought of than my mother's maid. When the servants saw what was happening, they too treated me with disdain. I did not deserve that.' Pride showed through at the calm toss of her head. 'When she married Milan, that monster, she was sixteen, which is when I thought I was rid of her, but I was wrong. I fell in love with an army officer, but my family refused us permission to marry because he wasn't good enough for the cousin of the great Queen Nathalie.' She poked her own chest with a finger of her gun free hand. '*My* happiness meant nothing to them, only appearances.'

'Didn't Queen Nathalie divorce King Milan?' Flora recalled what she had learned about the Serbian royal family from her recent talk with William. 'It was in the newspapers. How did that affect you?'

'Because, my mother sent me to live in Biarritz with Nathalie. To keep her family close, and make me forever subservient to that...' She trailed off as if she couldn't think of a suitable epithet. The veins on her neck stood proud and her eyes burned with hatred. She raised the gun in line with Flora's face. 'What about *my* life?'

'You seem to have solved that problem by coming here,' Flora said reasonably.

'I had to sell all my jewels to do so. I changed my name to one the English would accept and got rid of my accent so the governors of the school would let me teach their spoiled daughters.'

'And made a success of your life at the Academy.' Flora shrugged, not comprehending her motives. 'What changed?'

'Petar Gordon did. Or Victor as he called himself. He knew of my connection to the former queen and invited me to join him in his plans to destroy the Obrenovich dynasty for good.' Miss Lowe relaxed back in her chair with a self-satisfied smile. 'Then the world will be rid of them all forever. It's exactly what she deserves. Not least for spawning that odious son of hers. Alexander was a monster too you know.'

'So you intend to assassinate Queen Nathalie?' Had jealousy turned this woman's mind or was she coldly, horribly sane? Neither prospect said much for Flora's life expectancy.

'How else to rid the world of her kind?'

'And Mr Gordon? What was his role?' Flora listened for any sound outside the room, but there was only silence beyond the walls.

'Revolutions require money. Lots of it. Petar has raised funds among the Serbians who live here. Not all of them sympathetic to us but he has his ways of persuading them.'

'Will you return to Serbia when you have disposed of the queen?' What *was* she saying? The conversation had become so unreal, they might have been discussing a shopping trip.

'Whatever for? I am someone who matters here. I like your country. I will stay and teach young women how to fight their oppressors.'

'Oppressors? Flora's sense of justice overwhelmed her fear at the thought of the young minds this woman could influence if she went free. 'Their father's, or do you mean their husbands?'

'Their rulers.' Her eyes flashed again with a dangerous fervour. 'I shall make rebels of them.'

'I agree young women should think for themselves and fight for their rightful place in society. But I don't think that's what you mean is it? Serbia's fight, or even Romania's, isn't theirs.'

'Women in every country have a right to respect, Mrs Harrington. And besides, what makes you think my pupils are all English? This city heaves with Slavs, Russian Serbians, Albanians, Romanians, even Austrians.'

Flora hadn't considered that, but it made sense that the wealthier Eastern Europeans could afford to send their daughters to the academy.

'You managed to fool Mr Crabbe as well then? Or why would he let you use his apartment?' Flora experienced sympathy for the poor man. Would his job be safe if William found out he had been duped? Or had William been taken in as well? The urge to find and warn them looked large but for that gun. If she had a weapon, or could distract her, she might stand a chance. But that gun was impossible to fight.

'I convinced your gullible Mr Crabbe that I was being threatened by activists. He offered to protect me in exchange for my co-operation.' She smiled again. 'Though he made it clear my co-operation in providing information about Queen Nathalie was required in exchange for my right to remain in this country. I blame your father for that.'

'My father threatened to deport you if you didn't spy for the British government?' The fact she intended to kill Queen Nathalie seemed to have been overlooked.

'Don't look so horrified, my dear. Your government is no less ruthless in its dealings than Serbia's. Nothing is too brutal if done in the name of a country's security.'

'I see, so in exchange for your spurious information, Mr Crabbe tells everyone you are his wife so you may hide here in safety?'

'A simple subterfuge. Who would suspect the reclusive Mrs Crabbe brings messages for your government? False ones of course.'

Flora nodded. Now it was beginning to make sense. 'You told Mr Crabbe about the meeting in the public house last night to distract him while Gordon broke into my father's study.'

'Innocent, but shrewd too. You would make a good spy, Mrs Harrington.'

'Thank you, but I have other plans for my life.' Flora wrapped a protective arm across her abdomen, one which Miss Lowe did not appear to notice.

'Then I am sorry that they will never come to fruition.' She raised the gun again and the tiny black hole took on monumental proportions.

'Wait!' Flora held up her hand as if she could deflect a bullet with fingers of flesh and bone. 'You aren't a murderer yet. Your life could still continue here.' It was all nonsense, but the only way she could think of to delay the inevitable.

'I won't have to worry about that. Crabbe will return sometime this afternoon and find you here. I will be long gone, but this,' She lifted the gun a little higher, 'will be found beside you. It's Gordon's gun.'

'You'd let your accomplice hang for murder?'

'Why not? He's already being hunted for killing Miss Lange. Whereas *I* have co-operated with your government from the beginning. Mr Crabbe will attest to that. Whatever Gordon claims will be disregarded.'

Flora's breath left her in a rush as she recalled Evangeline's words that night. If she didn't get what she wanted she would be back. Was that why Evangeline Lange went to see Mr Crabbe? To tell him Petar or Victor was a spy?

'But he didn't believe her did he?' Flora said aloud. 'Crabbe didn't believe her and it got her killed.'

'I don't know what you're talking about.' Miss Lowe's eyes held irritation not triumph. 'Where is Petar? He should have returned by now.' The gun waved dangerously in her hand as if she had forgotten it was there.

Flora's stomach tightened in fear. What if it went off by accident? With nowhere to run she hunched on the sofa in an effort to make herself as small as she could, while at the same time became vaguely aware of a sound coming from outside, like a scuffling but was too far off to make out. Flora tensed as a shout followed, then a loud bang that she hoped was someone breaking in the door.

Suddenly the door flew open and the room was full of dark, shadowy figures.

Miss Lowe inhaled sharply, her eyes widened and she raised her arm and spat out a word Flora didn't understand. A sharp crack sounded close to Flora's head, who ducked as painful pressure in her ears was followed by a heavy silence that reverberated inside her head.

Inspector Maddox' face appeared amongst the crowd, but he moved in slow motion, and though his mouth was open, no sound came out.

The last thought that went through her mind before everything went dark, was that Bunny would be furious with her.

Chapter 29

'Flora!' The loud male voice in her ear made her flinch. She hunched her shoulders and groaned in protest, a hand raised in the general direction of the noise to make it go away.

The voice came again, this time louder, and though familiar, didn't match the images that crowded her head. She rolled her shoulder to remove the firm grip, but the voice persisted. 'Flora, wake up!'

'What? What is it?' She blinked against a harsh light that stung her eyes, then raised herself onto one elbow, blinking as she tried to focus on the room.

It took a moment to absorb that the roughness against her cheek was the tweed of a man's jacket. For a fleeting second she imagined it might be Bunny's, but when she raised her head she found herself staring into William's concerned face.

'Where did you come from?' Her head still spun a little, then sharp reality intruded and she grabbed his sleeve. 'Miss Lowe! She's got a gun, she—'

'We know. But it's all right, we got here just in time.' William gathered her into his arms again and rocked her gently. 'You aren't hurt are you?'

'No, I don't think so.' Flora eased away from him and performed a rapid inventory of each of her limbs. One hand drifted to her stomach, relieved that she felt no internal pain.

A brief glance around told her she lay on the sofa in Arthur Crabbe's sitting room. 'I think I just fainted. What happened?' She swung her legs onto the floor and sat up, making room for William to ease more fully into the space beside her.

'As you said, you fainted just as we burst through the door. Miss Lowe fired the gun, but Maddox knocked her off her feet and the shot went wild.'

'Wild, as in the bullet went right through my Charles Korschann,' Arthur Crabbe said from somewhere over her shoulder.

Frowning, Flora turned her head to where Crabbe stood silhouetted by the window. He stared at a small bronze statuette of a wistful-eyed woman he held in one hand, a thumb-sized chunk missing from the lady's hip.

With a long sigh, he replaced it on the polished surface, thrust his hands in his pockets and rocked on his heels. 'What made you take her on?' he asked, obviously impressed.

'I didn't take anyone on, as you put it.' Flora massaged her forehead and released a nervous laugh. 'I had no idea what I was walking into.' An image of the revolver returned and she hoped it was somewhere where it could do no harm. 'Where is she now? Miss Lowe?'

'We have her safely in custody.' Inspector Maddox handed her a glass of water. She glanced at him briefly, but he didn't appear angry. Instead a wry smile curved his mouth as he looked at her. Perhaps he was saving a lecture for later?

'Did Dunne tell you I was here?' Her hand shook as she gulped the cool water greedily.

'He did in actual fact.' William chuckled. 'When Crabbe and I returned from luncheon, I saw Neale outside.' He indicated a man in a grey overcoat by the door, his hands clasped in front of him like a soldier on guard.

Flora recognized him as her recent shadow and gave him a tiny nod, which he returned.

'He said he had followed you out of the park, but assumed you had come home. When I realized you weren't there, we knew something was wrong and that's when Dunne said he had seen you come up here. Then Gordon appeared and tried to distract us with some nonsense about you leaving with a strange man, but he was very nervous, so we knew he was up to something. I was going to come up here straight away, but Crabbe insisted we call Maddox first.' He rubbed his hand up and down Flora's back in agitation. 'It was the longest twenty minutes of my life, I can tell you.'

'We couldn't take any chances, sir.' Inspector Maddox said from the door. 'Had you been shot, Mr Osborne, I would have been held responsible.'

'I appreciate that, Inspector,' Flora began. 'I know it was my fault, I shouldn't have been so foolhardy, but when I saw Miss Lowe enter the building, I followed her without thinking.' She giggled with a mixture of relief and what was probably delayed shock. 'I was convinced she was going to recite her entire life history while I waited for someone to appreciate what was going on.' She paused and steadied her breathing, telling herself she was safe, though there was an odd echo inside her head, and voices seemed to come from a distance. 'You didn't let Gordon get away did you?'

'Certainly not.' Crabbe interrupted the policeman's response. 'Dunne has him under lock and key in the porter's room. We've been keeping him under surveillance since Randall said he had turned up here that night you and Mr Osborne were at the theatre.'

A young policeman whispered something to Maddox, who nodded, then followed him out of the room. The sound of authoritative voices reached her from the landing, followed by the indignant ones of residents demanding to know what was going on.

'He shouldn't have been anywhere near so the surveillance was a precaution,' William took up the story. 'Until then we didn't suspect him at all.'

'Did you suspect Miss Lowe?' Flora took another sip of water, vaguely aware the room had cleared leaving only the three of them. Even Neale had slunk away when she wasn't looking.

'Maddox searched her office at the Harriet Parker Academy this morning where he found the plans of Queen Nathalie's house in Biarritz.'

'We knew her real name was Elena Leskovac.' Crabbe rocked back and forth on the balls of his feet. 'She isn't political, but has some personal grudge against the former queen Nathalie. What did she tell you?'

'That she had deceived you into thinking she was working for you.'

'Maybe at first,' Crabbe looked affronted. 'But we discovered early on she was giving us duff information, so we let her carry on to find out what she was really doing. It seems she and Gordon persuaded a group of his countrymen living here to carry out the assassination, then return to London before the authorities knew what had happened.'

'Don't they have enough assassins of their own in Serbia without sending them here?' Flora placed the glass on a nearby table, though didn't expect an answer. She craved something stronger than water, like sherry or maybe Madeira, then remembered she needed to take care of herself. She wasn't the only one she had to think about now.

'What was he looking for in your study?' Flora felt calmer now, even a little proud of herself. Funny how near death experiences conjured a sort of euphoria.

'Lists of London-based Serbians, I expect,' William answered. 'Most likely they intended to either recruit or intimidate.'

'I knew that was Gordon at the theatre that night,' Flora said. 'He left during the interval so had plenty of time to come back here and kill Evangeline. I should have paid more attention to Sally's misgivings that first day at Waterloo.'

'We had no idea what he was up to at that stage.' William exchanged a loaded look with Crabbe. 'We knew a spy existed, but we had no name or even a description. It was when you found that advertisement of Evangeline Lange's looking for Victor, we made the connection with the Harriet Parker Academy and Miss Lowe.'

'Has he admitted to killing Evangeline?' Flora looked from Crabbe to William and back again.

'As well as burglary, false imprisonment, and attempted murder.' Crabbe went back to the examination of at his ruined statuette. 'No doubt we have enough evidence to lock them both up. I'm confident we'll get confessions out of them both for everything.'

'I don't think I wish to know how that might be achieved,' Flora murmured, aware he had used the word 'we' not the police. Perhaps Miss Lowe was right about the British government being ruthless?

'Why did Evangeline come and see you the night she died?' Flora studied the younger man more closely, surprised at how attractive he was now he was neither angry nor worried. He had also said more in the last ten minutes than he had since they had met. Maybe he was feeling a bit euphoric too?

'Evangeline came to tell me I had employed a man called Victor who was seducing respectable young women and insisted he be sacked.' He replaced the statuette, dragged a stool up beside the sofa and perched on it. 'I didn't know who she meant because we didn't have anyone called Victor on staff. I had no idea why she connected me to him.'

'She saw you in the street with him. She and Lydia Grey.'

'Oh, I see. Well that explains it.'

'It doesn't explain why you dismissed Evangeline. Or don't you believe breaking young women's hearts is a sacking offence?' Flora took a small triumph in the deep flush that rushed to his cheeks. 'Anyway, Mr Dunne thought Miss Lowe was your wife.'

'Ah, that was my idea.' Crabbe sported a boyish grin at this remark which she did not associate with the serious-minded clerk. 'She said she needed somewhere safe when she thought she was being followed. Not that she was, but – well you know what I mean.'

'There isn't a Mrs Crabbe, is there?' Flora said.

'I regret, no.' Crabbe's sigh indicated this fact was a source of disappointment.

'It was only after Miss Lange's death that things began falling into place.' William had stopped rubbing Flora's back and relaxed on the sofa, though he held onto her hand. 'We've been watching Gordon for the last week, but he distracted us with the riot the other night. Had I thought it through, I would have known he was playing with us, but I acted on impulse.'

'Beats me how we came to engage the fellow in the first place.' Crabbe ran a hand through his sandy hair, making it stand up on end. 'He was vouched for by a high-ranking Foreign Office employee.'

'Would that be Cecily Moffatt's employer by any chance?' Flora ducked her head and slanted a look at William through her lashes.

'How did—' Crabbe groaned. 'Of course.' He clicked his fingers in the air. 'That's why he befriended Cecily Moffatt. To gain access into Mr Jervis Hanson's study to steal some of his embossed notepaper. Gordon's credentials are forgeries.'

Flora stayed silent, allowing the details to sink in. She might have misjudged the situation, death threats notwithstanding, but she found it exhilarating to have discovered aspects of this case that had eluded the so-called experts.

'I'm glad you didn't turn out to be a spy or a murderer, Mr Crabbe,' Flora said. 'I'm also sorry about your statue. Was it valuable?'

'I hoped it would be someday.' He huffed a breath. Ah, well never mind. All's well that ends well and all that. Though no one has cast me in the role of a dangerous killer before.'

'Not to mention a wife beater.' Crabbe looked up sharply as she added, 'I assumed Miss Lowe wore that veil to hide the bruises.'

'Oh, I say, that's rather unnecessary!'

'She's joking, Crabbe!' William gave him a mock scowl, then turned relieved eyes on Flora. 'At least I hope she is.'

*

Weak beams of winter light poked through the gap in the curtains while Flora lay in the soft bed, her arm behind her head as she sifted through the events of the previous day. After an emotional but short journey back to William's apartment, Inspector Maddox had taken everyone's statements, while Sally fortified several members of the Cannon Row constabulary in the kitchens with copious cups of tea.

Sally fussed over her in half sympathetic but mostly annoyed tones as if the entire debacle was her own fault. Even Randall appeared unusually ruffled and kept offering to bring her restorative drinks, blankets and even smelling salts.

Flora finally managed to cut through their solicitous attentions, reassuring everyone that she was quite unhurt but wouldn't mind a nap.

Before going to her room, she telephoned Bunny and informed him the spies had been apprehended, but left out all the details of her near brush with death. She knew William would most likely put him straight at their next meeting but she would deal with that when it happened.

'I'm coming to town tomorrow to bring you straight home,' Bunny had insisted, despite her protests that it wasn't necessary. 'It's unimportant that you weren't hurt. You might have been and I cannot have you upset at such a time. No, don't argue,' he interrupted when she tried to protest. 'I need to be sure you are all right. I'm sure William will understand.'

'I know he will. And so do I. The thought of home sounds wonderful. I've missed you more than I believed I would.' She ended the call with another rush of tearful endearments and a feeling of happiness that not only did she have a husband who cared so much for her welfare, but she had helped track down a murderer too. It wouldn't help Evangeline, but perhaps John would be happy to know his sister's killer would not escape justice.

Flora had slept since then and woken the next morning refreshed, looking forward to Bunny's arrival, though there was one more thing she had to do before she went home.

Sally arrived in response to her ring, a cup of tea in one hand and wiping what looked to be toast crumbs from her skirt with the other, Flora's summons having interrupted her maid's breakfast.

'Are you feeling better this morning, Miss Flora?' She handed Flora her tea and gathered Flora's discarded linens from the floor where they had fallen the night before.

'I was fine last night, just exhausted.' Flora yawned. 'I still can't believe Mr Gordon is a spy.'

'I can.' Sally grunted as she plumped up the pillows and straightened the coverlet 'I said he was foreign, didn't I? He could have murdered us all and we'd never have known.'

'You could be right,' Flora replied, not wishing to pursue that particular train of thought. She shrugged away a shiver at an unbidden image of Miss Lowe, or Elena Leskovac or whatever her name was, pointing that gun at her. 'Could you run a bath for me, Sally?' She handed the maid her empty cup and saucer. 'Might as well take advantage of the luxury of a private bathroom.'

'Don't have ter lug buckets up three flights from the kitchens here, Miss Flora.' Sally deposited the china on the dresser. 'All you have to do is turn a couple of taps. Any fool could do it.'

Flora chose not to remind her that they had indoor plumbing at Richmond. Noisy, inefficient and erratic, but still better than pumps and outdoor privies.

'I'm going out this morning, Sally,' she informed her when the hot, fragrant water had done their work on her muscles. 'I'll wear the sapphire blue skirt with one of my white lawn blouses. Oh, and don't overtighten my corset. I might not be showing yet, but this bodice feels snug across my chest.'

'Are you sure you want to be going out, Miss?' Sally's head jerked up and met Flora's reflection in the cheval glass. 'Master

William said you should rest today, what with you being almost killed yesterday.'

'*Almost* doesn't count,' Flora said with a smile. 'Then I suggest you don't mention it to him.

'Which won't be difficult, Miss, as you haven't yet told me where we're going.' She knelt to retrieve Flora's slippers from under the bed. ''Sides, Master William went to see that Inspector Maddox first thing. Something about witness statements and such.'

'Good. He'll be gone for a while then. Could you ask Dunne to hail me a cab for after breakfast?' She looked up at her maid's reflection in the mirror in time to see her pull a face behind Flora's back on her way out. 'I saw that, Sally. And don't slam the door.'

Flora smiled to herself. Either pregnancy made her lazy or having Sally exclusively at her disposal contributed to her lethargy. Whichever it was, Flora quite liked the freedom it gave her. She had served her time being at the beck and call of others, so could quite easily get used to it.

Chapter 30

Flora stepped from the taxi onto a pavement slippery with frost outside the Lange residence. The wreath of white camellias intertwined with evergreen and black ribbon that hung from the brass knocker had wilted, giving the house a neglected appearance.

She waited at the gate while Sally paid off their driver, frowning when he made some comment about his tip being derisory.

Reluctantly, Sally dropped another coin into his palm, at which the man gave her a grudging nod, then flicked the reins and the cab pulled away.

'I gave you an extra sixpence for the driver,' Flora said as she pushed open the black wrought iron gate and negotiated the monochrome tiled path to the front door.

'Din't think he deserved it.' Sally avoided her eye as she drew up beside her on the top step. 'I gather you want me to get the servants to talk again?'

'That won't be necessary, Sally. With Mr Gordon and Miss Lowe safely locked away in Cannon Row Police Station, I doubt there's anything new to learn.'

The jangle of the doorbell had barely faded away when the butler pulled the door open a bare four inches and informed them in sombre tones that Master John was not at home. He started to shut the door again when Mrs Lange's face appeared at his shoulder.

'Let Mrs Harrington in, Jenks. I haven't had a visitor for days.'

Jenks inclined his head and, resigned, stepped aside to allow Flora and Sally into the hall.

Camille Lange stood with one hand braced against the sitting room door frame, a small glass in the other which held a trace of some brown liquid. Her mourning black made her look shrivelled and pallid, though her eyes were overly bright, her angular cheekbones tinged pink.

'How are you, Mrs Lange?' Flora waited while the butler helped her off with her coat. 'And Mr Lange?' she added as an afterthought.

'I'm the same as ever, my dear.' She appeared to have forgiven Flora for being married, though slurred her words even more than last time. 'Jenks, take Mrs Harrington's maid to the kitchens, would you?'

The butler bowed again and strode away, Flora's coat slung over one arm, leaving Sally to hurry after him.

The familiar sitting room was still gloomy in the half-light, the curtains drawn and with the mirror above the mantle covered with black cloth.

'My husband is devastated, poor man.' Her hostess indicated a hard, upright sofa with a shaking hand and bade Flora sit. 'Evangeline was his joy. He's out at the moment, though I have no idea where.' She refilled the glass from a decanter on a low table then lowered herself into the chair beside it, but misjudged the distance. Falling the last few inches, she landed with a bump on the upholstery, spilling stray drops onto her skirt, which she didn't seem to notice. 'He's most likely haranguing that detective person as to how far he has got in the investigation.'

'This must be a difficult time for you all.'

'Indeed. Evangeline's funeral is tomorrow and the entire affair has been impossibly fraught.' She took a sip from the glass and then set it down carefully beside the decanter.

'Are you all right, Mrs Lange?' Flora asked.

'Of course.' Her head wobbled on her neck, her eyes unfocussed. She planted her clasped hands in her lap and fixed Flora with an amiable, if shaky smile. 'Now, what shall we talk about? I haven't had a decent conversation since this whole thing began.'

'That's really why I came.' Flora concealed her revulsion for this self-absorbed woman and summoned a smile. 'To let you know that a man has been charged with Evangeline's murder.'

'When? When did this happen?' Mrs Lange stiffened and blinked rapidly as if this information confused her.

'Last night. Inspector Maddox took him to Cannon Row Police station.' She did not mention whether or not he had yet confessed, but everyone seemed to regard that as formality.

'You cannot know how relieved I am to hear that.' Mrs Lange pressed a hand to her bodice, exhaling slowly. 'Howard will be too when he gets home.' She jumped up again and plucked another glass from the tray and waved it in the air. 'I think this is cause for celebration, don't you? Might I offer you a glass of Madeira?'

'Not for me, thank you.' Flora held up her hand. From the looks of it, her hostess had already consumed several glasses. But then who was she to judge? Grief took many forms. 'Mrs Lange, you haven't asked me who the man was.'

'What?' Her hostess blinked again, her eyes suddenly vague and unfocused. 'Oh yes, yes of course.' Then a thought seemed to strike her and she lifted a finger to her cheek. 'It wasn't Harry Flynn was it, or someone Evangeline knew?'

Flora shook her head. 'The killer was a stranger to you, and in fact to Evangeline as well. He was a Serbian.' Flora stopped talking, information about spies and government officials would be far beyond the woman's comprehension in her current state. 'Suffice it to say he will stand trial.'

'I see.' Mrs Lange broke off to take a large gulp from her glass of Madeira. 'But why are *you* here? Why not the police?'

'I was present when the - assailant was apprehended.' Her connection to Mr Gordon was bound to come out later. 'I thought you'd like to hear the news from a friendly face. I'm sure Inspector Maddox will call at some stage to explain.'

Mrs Lange merely hiccoughed loudly, a strange smile on her face as she resumed her seat, her glass now cradled in both hands as if it were precious.

'I can see I've called at a difficult time.' Flora gathered her bag and placed the condolence card she had brought with her on a side table, giving it a small pat. 'Perhaps I should return when either John or your husband are at home?'

'Oh, please don't go yet.' Her features twisted in childish disappointment. 'We haven't had a proper chat and I hardly see anyone these days.'

The door opened a crack and Sally's face appeared round the jamb, beckoning with a finger. Flora looked from her maid's eager expression to Mrs Lange, who seemed unaware of the interruption.

'Would you excuse me for a moment?' Flora asked, but not waiting for an answer, rose and stepped into the hall. 'What is it, Sally?'

'You were wrong, Missus.' She cast a swift glance through the half-open door to where Mrs Lange sat smiling to herself. 'There's more going on here than you thought.'

'What do you mean?' Flora lowered her voice.

'The maid complained to the housekeeper just now about Master John's laundry. He's taken to changing his collar several times a day.'

'Really, Sally.' Flora tutted in frustration. 'And you decided to mention that to me now?' She looked back at her hostess, who hummed between taking sips from the glass. 'I'll make my excuses in a moment and we'll go. You can tell me all about it in the taxi home.'

'I haven't finished.' Sally pouted. 'The housemaid said Master John has hurt-his-neck.' She enunciated the words slowly as if explaining to someone half-witted. 'His collars have had blood and puss on them every day for a week. It's got no better and now the collars are disgusting.'

'Sounds to me like he has a wound that has become infected.' Flora grimaced. The hall seemed to tilt, then recede and a rush of ice ran through her veins. She grabbed Sally's hand. 'Get our coats, we have to go. Right now!'

'Why, Missus? I can find out more if you-'

'No time. Quickly. Get our coats.'

Flora's panic seemed to transfer to Sally. She nodded, then scampered back along the hall and disappeared through the green baize door into the kitchens.

Flora smoothed down her skirt and prepared to return to the sitting room when the front door opened. Her stomach tightened at the sight of John Lange.

'Good morning, Mrs Harrington.' His smile was wide and genuine as he slowly removed his coat. 'I didn't expect to see you today.' He slung the coat over a hook, his gaze never leaving her face, closed the door and leaned against it, his smile fading. 'Is something wrong? You look nervous.'

'Good morning, Mr Lange.' Flora licked her dry lips and summoned a smile. 'I-I called to see your mother, but she seems distraught. I don't think she's very well, so perhaps I ought to go.'

'So soon? We've hardly exchanged more than a few words.' He planted his feet apart, his arms folded across his chest effectively blocking her way. 'You know I always enjoy your company, Flora.' He raised one sardonic eyebrow, his unblinking stare strangely unnerving.

Flora's nerves prickled at his use of her name, something he had never done before. 'Inspector Maddox has apprehended the man who killed your sister. That's what I came to tell you.'

'Step-sister,' he growled. 'Then why rush away?' His voice turned silky, ingratiating, and entirely at odds with the hard expression in his eyes.

Flora thought quickly. 'Your mother was talking to me just now when she became disoriented and unsteady on her feet. I thought she might be unwell and I wasn't sure what to do.' She extended a hand to where Sally had gone. 'I was about to summon your butler.'

John pushed open the door to the sitting room. 'Mother, what have you been saying to our guest?' he demanded in a brusque, cold tone, very different to the reticent, almost shy young man she had met on the Embankment.

Flora's gaze snagged on a thin, but ugly-looking scratch just below his ear; red and swollen it had left a yellowish mark on the edge of his collar. She stiffened and looked away quickly, but it was too late. His eyes glinted and he tugged up his collar to cover the wound.

Mrs Lange stumbled into the hallway, her glass still in her hand, the other braced against the wall to keep herself upright. 'There you are, John, darling. Flora came to tell us that they've arrested someone for killing Evangeline. Isn't that simply marvellous?'

'You promised me you wouldn't take any more laudanum today.' John hissed and he snatched the glass from her hand.

'I don't care anymore.' Mrs Lange swayed against the doorframe, her shoulders slumped 'This has all been such a strain. But it's over now, don't you see?'

Flora eyed the front door which bore not only a cumbersome lock, but a bolt that had been drawn across. She would never get it open quickly enough before John stopped her.

'I asked you,' John slammed the glass on a small table beneath the hall mirror, 'what have you been saying to Mrs Harrington?' He grabbed his mother's upper arms with both hands and shoved her roughly onto the chair beside the hall table. The movement dislodged the sheet of black serge that covered the mirror, but no one appeared to notice except Flora. Her own face in the glass looked white and scared. No wonder John had guessed what was in her head.

'Nothing,' his mother whined, eying the glass greedily. 'You know I wouldn't do that, John. We agreed.' She made a childish mewling noise and rubbed her arms with both hands where he had gripped them.

'Don't blame her.' Flora made to step between them, but John's fierce expression sent her backward. 'She didn't say anything. I put the details together myself. You killed Evangeline,' she blurted, unable to stop herself.

'Straight to the point as usual.' John's face darkened with anger. 'You're quite good at this detective stuff, aren't you?'

'I like to think so.' He didn't have to know she had completely misjudged everyone so far, except Lydia. And even she had harboured a secret in the end. 'That is how you hurt your neck. Evangeline did that to you while you were strangling her.'

His hand drifted to his collar. 'She caught me off guard with that blasted brooch of hers. Not that it did her any good.' The ghost of a smile tugged at his mouth but was gone again in an instant.

'Why did you kill her?' Flora felt suddenly cold. She didn't want to hear his reasons. The man disgusted her, but she had to keep him talking.

'Why?' he repeated. 'I should have done it before. You have no idea what it was like living under this roof with that indulged brat and my Machiavellian stepfather?' His eyes narrowed to slits as he spat the words which must have repeated in his head often. 'For me anyway. Things weren't quite so fraught for you, were they, Mother?'

'I did my *best* to make him like you.' Mrs Lange's childlike whine grated on Flora's nerves. 'You simply didn't try hard enough to endear yourself to him.'

'He always resented me,' John sneered. 'My presence was a constant reminder that Mother had a son when he didn't.'

Ignoring him, Flora addressed Mrs Lange. Surely one of them had a conscience. 'You raised Evangeline. She was your child in everything but her birth.' She knew better than most that blood wasn't everything. Riordan Maguire had been devoted to her and, as it turned out, they weren't related at all.

'She was never my child!' Her vehemence sent Flora back a step. 'She was always Howard's.' Mrs Lange rocked back and forth on the chair, both hands gripped tight to the squab on either side of her knees. 'The child of a dead saint and the only one he had time for. John and I might have been servants for all the care he took of us. I – we could never compete.'

'She was a child.' Flora slid a foot closer to the door, which neither appeared to notice.

'Exactly!' Mrs Lange's eyes flashed as if her real personality was trying to break through. 'A child, who should never have owned his heart the way she did. I was his wife.' In an instant she had become vague again, an unsteady hand reaching for the glass.

Is that what had driven these two? Jealousy? Or was it avarice? Probably both.

Without warning, John's hand shot out and grabbed Flora's upper arm, his fingernails digging painfully through the fabric of her blouse.

'We learned to live with his neglect, even expected it,' he snarled in her ear as he pulled her roughly along the gloomy hallway towards the staircase. 'What we hadn't anticipated, was his leaving everything to his precious daughter. When he dies, which won't come soon enough for me, Mother and I would have been forced to live on Evangeline's charity for the rest of our lives. Then she would have married that upstart Flynn, and between them, they would have made our lives miserable.' He twisted her roughly towards him, his face an inch away from Flora's, his eyes dark and menacing but tinged with what could have been regret. 'Why did you have to meddle?'

'If you recall, Mr Lange,' Flora said through gritted teeth. 'At our first meeting, you asked for *my* help.'

'That was *my* mistake.' His face loomed inches from hers. 'Being so good at it was yours.'

Chapter 31

Flora's boots slid easily across the slick tiles as he dragged her along the hallway toward a flight of stairs that curved sharply to an unseen upper floor, rendering her efforts to resist useless. As the gap closed, she gauged the sturdiness of the rail which was highly polished and likely slippery, but the rails might prove easier to hold onto. Dismay sharpened her fear when he ignored the staircase, and instead, hauled her toward a door in an alcove to one side of the newel. Slightly smaller than the others, this one had a wooden knob instead of a brass handle.

The cellar.

She gritted her teeth, but refused to react to the pain in her arm, determined not to give him the satisfaction he was hurting her.

The door grew large in her vision as he pulled her closer, while panic built inside her chest. Where were the servants? There was Jenks and the two maids from the kitchen. Had they no idea what was happening? And Sally? Where was she?

'I need to know how you did it.' Flora shifted her weight onto her left foot, forcing him to a near halt, gambling on the fact he wouldn't be able to resist boasting how clever he had been. 'Tell me, John. How did you lure Evangeline into that alley?'

He turned towards her, a cruel smile twisting his features, his grip on her arm loosening, but not enough for her to extricate herself. She would be bruised in the morning.

'Evangeline couldn't resist sharing her scheme to unmask a seducer of women. I followed her that night and saw her go into the same building where you are staying. I've no idea who the man was whom she went to see, but assumed he must have been this Victor.'

'He wasn't.' Flora couldn't let him think he had been too clever. 'Victor was someone else entirely.

He gave a bored shrug as if this detail was irrelevant. 'I waited in the Alexandra Hotel until I saw her leave the building. I caught up with her in the street and pretended to be in a panic. That Mother had found an obliging establishment willing to provide her with brandy and I needed her help.' He issued a low, evil-sounding laugh which did nothing for Flora's fears. 'I said Mother was in The Grenadier, drinking. That we had to get her home before Father discovered her gone. He disapproves you see, as he does most things.' He gave a self-satisfied snort. 'Evie didn't suspect a thing, nor did she hesitate to accompany me. We must keep up appearances, you see?'

'How could you strangle your own sister?' Flora had almost forgotten she was there under duress, apart from his painful grip on her arm. She listened for voices or approaching footsteps but nothing interrupted the silence.

'Step-sister! It was easier than I imagined. She was so shocked she didn't react at first. When she realized what was happening, she ripped that damned brooch from her coat and jammed it into my neck.' He winced, rubbing his neck with his free hand, his lips twisted in fury.

Flora's stomach churned at the thought that while she and William were at the theatre, John had taken Evangeline to her death.

She turned her head to where Mrs Lange still sat, but the woman remained in the chair where John had put her, examining her empty glass with open disappointment.

'When I heard you asking about Evangeline that day.' John shook her to make her look at him again. 'I knew I had to watch my step. Then you brought me that cursed bag.' His superior smile returned. 'Which, by the way, I left beside her body deliberately. I knew about the library receipt.'

'You wanted the police to find it?'

'Naturally, in order to lead them to this Victor person. You almost spoiled everything. Almost' He gave her arm another rough shake which made her teeth click together painfully.

Flora's thoughts raced.

It was the brooch that had convinced Flora he had killed Evangeline. The brooch he was so keen to make her believe was virtually worthless. It would be the one thing which could seal his fate. If she lived long enough to tell the world. This fact struck her as ironic and she almost laughed. How could she have allowed herself to get into two life-threatening situations in two days? This wasn't happening.

'Was Evangeline's brooch that valuable you had to beat a barmaid to get it?'

His grating laugh sent a wave of fear through her veins. 'Have you any idea what that brooch is worth? I had intended getting that ring Flynn gave her as well, but I was still struggling with her glove when that slut from The Grenadier saw me. I had to abandon them both and get out of that alley before she raised the alarm.'

'You would let an innocent man be hanged for a crime you committed?' The second the words were out she regretted her naivety. Just like Elena Lowe, this man too was a monster and wouldn't hesitate. She cast a fearful glance at the green baize door, willing it to open, but then changed her mind. Sally might still remain undetected, and if so, there was a chance she could find help. The desperation she had felt the day before in

Crabbe's sitting room returned in full force, despite the absence of a gun.

'Why not? The police don't suspect me.' He slammed her up against the wall beside the cellar door and reached for the key that sat in the lock. 'And they won't, because I don't intend to risk you telling anyone.'

'I have no proof you murdered her.' Flora managed to keep her voice steady. The brooch might be evidence enough but she didn't have that either.

'It's too dangerous.' He shook his head, frowning, almost as if he was talking to himself. 'Not when I've gone to so much trouble.'

He fumbled with the key one-handed, the lock stiff and difficult to manipulate, his vice-like grip on her arm still firm. The lock finally gave and frantic, Flora aimed a boot at his shin, but it connected weakly, eliciting nothing from him but an angry grunt. He was far stronger than she had imagined, evidenced by his swift kick to the door that flew inwards, revealing the top of a steep wooden staircase that dropped into what looked like a black, bottomless hole.

Flora glanced behind her where the butler Jenks had appeared silently from the servant's door. A rush of hope made her flail her free arm. 'Mr Jenks. Help me please, I-' she broke off at the sight of his flat colourless eyes and the fact his face had not changed expression. He would be no more help than Mrs Lange. What kind of house was this? Though if they were all terrified of John, she had even more to worry about.

Flora gripped the doorframe with one hand, and with the other clawed at John's fingers that dug into her arm. A fingernail broke but she felt no pain, only the satisfaction of hearing him grunt again, then utter a curse as the broken edge scored his skin.

A hard push to the middle of her back sent her over the threshold. Her stomach lurched as her foot trod thin air and with a startled cry, she flailed her arms. Her left hand struck a rail and she grabbed it and hung on, landing hard on a wooden step which wobbled alarmingly beneath her weight, but held.

The door closed behind her with a bang and the key turned in the lock with a dull, ominous click.

*

Flora hung onto the wooden handrail with both hands. Disoriented and light-headed, she waited for her frantic breathing to settle into a normal rhythm. Slowly, the dizziness receded and she stood still. Darkness pressed against her so she had no idea how steep the staircase was or how high the treads, but at least she hadn't fallen the rest of the way. Apart from the darkness, her overriding impression was frigid, numbing cold, the air laden with a damp, musty smell of old furniture, rotting vegetables and something else she dare not think about.

The steps were rickety but held as she felt each step with the toe of her shoe and slowly descended to a packed earth floor. Maybe John hadn't intended for her to break her neck, but she doubted he had her health in mind.

The air was even colder at the bottom, with the mustiness of all unheated spaces that made her want to cough. Unable to see where she trod, she banged her shin on something hard that shook. Glass rattled and something fell and hit the floor. A tentative hand-over-hand examination told her it was a set of shelves stacked with glass jars, some tools and packets of something she would rather not think about. Rat poison probably, which meant there was likely vermin down there.

She shivered and remembered with longing her thick wool coat that hung on the stand upstairs. Her eyes adjusted slowly, until the darkness shifted, lightening into varying shades of black and grey, with darker areas that indicated solid objects. A weak rectangle of light came from a tiny window little bigger than a house brick set above head height; the room itself barely eight feet square and mostly empty apart from the set of shelves and one or two packing cases set in the far corner. More a lower ground floor than a true cellar, though that made little difference when a locked door stood between her and the house.

Where had Sally got to? She was no fool, and surely by now had guessed something was happening when Flora had disappeared without explanation. Or had John found her too and she was now locked up in some storeroom in the servants' quarters?

Goosebumps erupted on her skin and her breath left her lips in a white cloud. Shivering, and with tentative patting of her hands, she searched the shelves for an item she could use to relieve the cold which bit into her fingers and made her nose run. Her fingers closed on something soft, which felt like fabric. Not sacking, but too silky to be a blanket. She hauled it from the shelf, sending a cloud of choking dust into the air that made her cough. It was heavy, the silky side was some sort of lining with velvet on the other side. Maybe the Lange's had stored an old pair of curtains down there?

With no idea how long it had been there, or what might have crawled on it, she gave it a wary sniff. It didn't smell damp, so she dragged it across her shoulders where it pooled onto the floor. Better a few crawlies than freezing to death.

She paced the floor a few times, then frustration drove her back to the stairs, where she crouched on the bottom step and chewed at a fingernail, the length of cloth rucked in folds around her shoulders.

What had she done?

She hadn't even told William where she was going this morning, so no one knew she was there – except Sally. Miss Lowe threatening her with a pistol was bad enough, but what had John planned for her when he had proved himself a cold-blooded killer? Then there was Bunny, who would be furious and likely never to let her out of his sight again. If she got out of there alive? Not that any of this was her fault, not really. Inspector Maddox had some explaining to do as well. If he had done his job properly he would have known John was the killer and not Victor. If she hadn't accepted without question that he would get Gordon to confess, she wouldn't be in this mess. Each scenario was followed by another until her mind screamed with frustration and panic. Oh, why had she come here? To boast how clever she had been? Probably. Definitely.

Now she had to find a way to get out of this cellar before John came back and – and what?

The sound of a bolt being shot sent a ripple of fear through her and she bolted from the step into the darkness. She felt her way, hand over hand, to the far end of the set of shelves, her curtain cloak swishing across the flagstone floor. She froze, her heart thumping against her corset, her breathing shallow and fast.

Was it John coming to finish what he had started?

The shelves offered little protection, but at least she would see him before he saw her. For the first few seconds or so anyway. Now if only she could find a weapon.

The door creaked open, throwing a beam of light onto the wooden steps that penetrated the slats. A scuffle of feet, followed by an angry, colourful oath. A man's voice. John's? Then the door slammed shut again, followed by the slam of the bolt and the cellar was thrown into darkness again.

Silence.

'Miss Flora?' a whispered voice called.

'Sally?'

'Where are you, Missus? I can't see.'

Flora emerged from behind the shelves and traced a path back to the bottom of the steps. 'Give it a moment for your eyes to adjust, but be careful of the steps. There are six.' She found she was whispering, but somehow the occasion warranted low voices. Flora slumped onto the bottom step with a deep sigh and slid to one side to make room for her. Her last hope that Sally had managed to summon help slipped away when she heard her maid's voice.

'Where are you, Miss Flora?' A tentative creak was followed by another.

'Directly below you, and don't tread on my curtain.'

'Curtain? What curtain?' Sally crouched beside her on the bottom step making it creak.

'This one.' Flora tugged the material out from beneath Sally's foot. 'What happened up there?'

'I came back with our coats and found the hall empty but for Mr John who was locking the cellar door. Mrs Lange was off with the fairies and he said you'd taken ill and gone home and I was to follow. Well, I knew you wouldn't go without me, and I had your coat, so I pretended I was leaving, then crept back round the side of the house and hid.'

'I don't suppose you happen to know what John was doing?' Flora asked.

'I sneaked through the scullery and saw him take his dotty mother back into the sitting room. When he came out again, he went into the garden with that Jenks. It was when I crept closer to try and hear what they were saying that they caught me. They dragged me back in and shoved me down here.'

'We can forget asking for help from the butler, he's obviously under John's control.'

'He's got some dodgy business going on with the tradesman, the maid said.' Sally pulled up her sleeve and grimaced. 'And he ought to cut 'is fingernails, my wrists are bleeding.' She rubbed her upper arms and drummed her heels on the wooden step. 'Blimey, it's brass monkeys down here.'

'Here, you can share my curtain.' Flora didn't bother correcting her slang, but simply wrapped her end of the heavy, lined fabric around Sally's shoulders.

'Is that what this is?' Sally huddled beneath the soft material, giving it a tentative sniff Flora didn't see but clearly heard. 'It smells funny.'

'Don't think about it. I hope it's just damp, but I didn't like to consider the alternatives.' Flora turned to look at her, though she was little more than a black shape in a dark grey room. 'I'm sorry about this, Sally, but in my defence, I had no idea John Lange had done anything wrong.'

'Too busy with spies weren't you?' Sally gave a snort. 'You and Mr William.'

Flora refused to rise to the bait. 'Did you say John was in the garden?' She felt rather than saw Sally's heavy nod. 'What were they doing? Did you see?'

When Sally didn't answer, Flora nudged her. 'Sally?'

'They was digging.'

'Digging?' Flora's stomach tightened. 'They intend burying us in the garden? Well that's a ridiculous idea. It's the first place the police would look.' She inhaled sharply. 'Gracious, listen to me, what am I saying?' Suddenly Flora couldn't breathe. The air around her seemed to drop several degrees and she couldn't get her ribs to work. Her breaths came shallow and sharp and she began to feel dizzy. At least she was sitting down.

'Don't you go having hysterics on me, Missus,' Sally scolded giving her a hard shake.

The rough contact seemed to do the trick and Flora sucked in cold, mildew-laden air.

'There *must* be a way out of here, Sally?' She stared around, but could hardly make out where the walls ended and the ceiling began, let alone pick out objects. 'What about a coal hole?'

'I wouldn't know where to start, and I ain't scrabbling around on the floor in this murk looking for one neither.'

'I see what you mean.' Flora continued to take slow even breaths, forcing herself not to become hysterical. 'There could be anything down here. Blades, knives, even arsenic.' She shivered again and wrapped the length of material tighter around them both. 'He can't keep us down here forever. He has to get us out before—' She couldn't bear to think of what would happen next. How long did it take to dig a grave? Two graves? Or one large, all-purpose one? At the thought, she released a harsh, choking laugh that dissolved into a sob.

'Stop that, Miss Flora,' Sally snapped. 'He won't get me into that garden without a fight, that's for sure. He'll have more than a sore neck when I've finished with him an' all.'

'This is all my fault. I'm so sorry.' Flora huffed her breath in a white mist and teeth started to chatter. Shivering, she rocked back and forth as the damp of the freezing cellar seeped through her clothes. Despite the heavy material draped over her, she could barely feel her feet and kept sniffing as her nose ran.

'I know it's your fault, but don't fret it now.' Sally hunkered down into the folds of the curtain.

'When shall I fret it then?' Flora laughed again. Or was Sally right and she was hysterical? A thought crept into her head that at least her baby was safe and warm inside her. For now.

Sally muttered something under her breath Flora didn't catch.

'What was that?'

'I said, how long have we been down here?' Sally's diction had vastly improved, maybe through fear.

'About fifteen minutes, but it seems longer.' Flora cupped her numb fingers and blew into them. 'How long do you think it will be before John and that treacherous butler come and get us, Sally? Or do they intend to let us freeze to death first?'

'We'll get out of here, don't you worry yourself, Miss Flora. The fates won't be that unkind.'

'I admire your optimism, but we might have to face the fact there *is* no way out. Not unless we find something with which to knock that monster up there senseless when he comes to get us.' Flora straightened. 'Actually, that's not a bad idea. Come on, we'll search these shelves again for something heavy. It mustn't be too cumbersome or I won't be able to put any force behind it when I swing it at John's murdering skull.' She scrambled to her feet, her blood surging again as a satisfactory image played in her head. She hitched the curtain higher to prevent her tripping over it as she felt her way along the shelves. 'A plank of wood, maybe, or a good sized pot.'

'I thought you had already looked, Miss Flora? You didn't find anything before.'

'No, but—' A floorboard creaked overhead and Flora froze, staring upwards, though she couldn't see the ceiling, only blackness.

The sound stopped and the cellar door stayed firmly closed. Flora strained her ears for any ominous noises from the other side but there was nothing. After a moment she started moving again, carefully placing hand over hand along the shelf while trying not to think about what she might be touching. 'Don't be defeatist, Sally. Get off your backside and come and help me.'

'No thanks. I'll think I'll wait for the police.'

'I hate to say this, but I doubt they'll be coming.' The curtain slipped from one shoulder and she pulled it back into place again. 'They have no idea we are here.'

'They bloomin' well ought to, since I called them before I came looking for you.'

'Sally!' Flora gasped. Abandoning the shelving, she made her way back to the steps, dragging the heavy curtain behind her. 'What do you mean you called them? How?' She stubbed her toe on the bottom step and sat down with a thump, her teeth gritted.

'I used that telephone machine in the back hall.'

'Oh, Sally!' Flora gathered her into a crushing hug. 'Why didn't you tell me? I thought we were going to get battered to death and buried in the garden.' She held Sally away from her, staring in a face that was little more than a grey shadow in the low light. 'How did you know how to use a telephone?'

'Never 'ave before, but I've watched others often enough. It was when Jenks went to fetch the laudanum and Mr Lange was upstairs. But don't go getting too carried away, Missus. They ain't here yet.' Ever the pragmatist, she shrugged out of Flora's hold, grabbed the bottom half of the length of fabric and wrapped it round herself.

'Maybe not, but at least we now have hope.' Flora closed her eyes and sent up silent thanks. She was about to hug Sally again, but her maid must have sensed it and eased sideways away from her.

Minutes passed and Flora's relief dissolved, replaced by the nagging fear that maybe the police might not arrive before John Lange returned to get them? If not, then at least he and that slimy butler would have William and Bunny to deal with. Maybe even her mother-in-law.

'Did you tell the police exactly where we were?' Flora demanded, her nerves on edge.

'I told them where *you* were.' Sally sniffed. 'I didn't plan on being stuck here with you at the time. I wish they'd hurry up, because I need the privy.'

Flora glanced up at the sound of urgent repeated rings of the doorbell was followed by a heavy pounding on the front door.

'Thank gawd for that,' Sally muttered.

Flora scrambled to her feet. 'If we can hear them, then they can hear us. Climb the steps and bang on that door, and shout as loud as you can.'

'What about you? Or ain't it ladylike to pound on doors?' Sally snorted.

'This is no time to argue, just do—' she broke off as the cellar door swung open and Inspector Maddox stood silhouetted at the top of the steps.

'Are you two ladies going to come out, or should I wait until you've finished your argument?' Inspector Maddox stood framed in the doorway, a raised eyebrow above a bemused, mocking smile.

Chapter 32

Flora was about to thank him for arriving in time, but the fact he saw her as a source of amusement froze the words on her tongue. Instead, she stomped up the short flight of creaking steps and swept past him into the hall, leaving Sally to follow.

'You took your time opening the door,' Inspector Maddox snapped at the cowering figure of Jenks, who had retreated to the servant's door. 'Now where's John Lange?' Without waiting for an answer, he bundled the protesting butler through into the rear, followed by two policemen.

'Mrs Harrington!' Harry Flynn's worried face appeared at the open front door. He rushed to her side, his face a picture of shocked concern. 'I didn't expect to see you here, but it looks as if we were just in time. That blackguard hasn't hurt you has he?' He sounded breathless as if he had been running.

Flora shook her head, her teeth chattering too hard to speak, as she took in the figure who followed him in. A tall, angular man in striped trousers and an old-fashioned black cloak that reached past his knees.

She caught sight of her reflection in the mirror by the door and groaned. Her hat had squashed down on one side and she still wore the length of velvet round her shoulders, which she could now see was indeed a curtain in a sickly shade of lime green. No wonder she looked odd.

'I'm very cold, Mr Flynn.' Flora smiled at the inspector's retreating back. 'But quite well and very relieved to be out of that damp cellar.' She summoned her remaining poise along with a tremulous smile which she directed at the man beside Harry.

'My apologies, Mrs Harrington.' Harry recovered his manners and indicated the stranger. 'This is Mr Howard Lange, Evangeline's father.'

'In whose hall you happen to be standing. Pleased to make your acquaintance.' He bowed briefly over her hand. 'We're more concerned for you, my dear. We were very afraid my stepson was about to compound his already vicious crimes.' His gaze left her and darted the hall as if he was looking for someone.

'No, I'm fine,' Flora assured him, though images of the grave in the garden persisted. 'Did you arrive here with the police?' It occurred to her then she had one of his discarded curtains draped round her but he didn't appear to notice.

'I'm sorry to say, no. That was pure coincidence,' Harry said. 'We spotted two taxis and a police van draw up as we entered the square. I must say it made me quite jittery. Thought they'd come for me.'

'For you? He thought *you* had killed Evangeline?' Flora frowned up at him.

'Harry was Inspector Maddox's main suspect up until this morning,' Howard Lange explained.

'Ridiculous. I never really thought of you as a possible suspect.'

'I'm pleased to hear that, Mrs Harrington.' A smiled tugged at Harry's mouth. 'The waiter at the Alexandra Hotel told the police I was there with Evangeline the night she died, even though I hadn't visited the hotel for weeks. As it happened I was alone in my flat, which meant my alibi was not strong enough to convince the Inspector.'

391

Flora nodded, relieved to be able to think of something other than cold, dark prisons and rats. 'I remember that when you took me there for coffee the other day, the waiter said it was nice to see you again so soon.' She ran the incident through her head and something surfaced. 'His spectacles! He had broken them and had to use his spare pair.'

'Exactly. Without them, he mistook John for me.' He glanced at Mr Lange and back again. 'We convinced Inspector Maddox to talk to him again and to our relief, he acknowledged his mistake.'

Flora stared round the hall vaguely. 'Where's my maid? She was in the cellar with me.'

'I'm not sure, but she was here a moment ago.' Harry eased her gently to one side to allow two uniformed officers to sweep past him and joined a commotion taking place in the rear hall, while two more took up positions on the doorstep.

'I'm sure she's fine. I'll find her in a moment.' Flora became vaguely aware of a scuffle taking place on the doorstep. Someone was trying to enter the house but was being forcibly prevented by the policemen.

'Where's my wife? Let me pass you dolt!' Bunny's voice cut through the ineffectual attempts of the policeman who blocked his way.

Flora's heart lifted and she glanced past Harry's shoulder to where Bunny had squared up to the larger policeman.

'I'm sorry, sir, but I can't let you in. My Inspector said no one must enter.'

'If you don't stand aside, I swear, I'll—' Bunny's eyes flashed as he pulled back his arm, his fist clenched and about to land on the unfortunate policeman's chin.

'Bunny!' Flora shouted, horrified but strangely elated at the same time.

He looked up at the sound of her voice, his expression changing from fury to embarrassed relief as he met her startled look. He dropped his fist to his side, and adjusted his spectacles with his other hand.

'Please let him in.' Flora pleaded with the surly policeman, who looked disappointed at being denied the pleasure of fighting back. He gave a brief nod then stood to one side as Flora pulled Bunny into the hallway.

Flora buried her face in his jacket, her eyes closed while tears squeezed between her lids onto his coat. 'What are you doing here?' she mumbled into the wool as she hung on. 'How did you know where I was?'

'First things, first.' He disengaged her arms and held her away from him. 'Are you all right? Not hurt, nauseous or anything like that?' His worried glance drifted lower and then back up again so she knew instantly what he meant.

'No,' Flora whispered. 'We're both fine, truly.'

'Thank goodness.' The worry left his eyes as he gave her his full attention. 'What on earth are you wearing?'

'Oh.' She gave the length of material a grimace and let the curtain slide to the floor with a soft whoosh. 'I had forgotten about that. Never mind, it's not important.' She wrapped both arms round his neck and buried her face in his chest. 'You have no idea how glad I am to see you.'

'Dash it, Flora, I've been in Hell since your phone call last night. I was convinced you were hiding something and William dodged all my questions about what had happened. I caught the first train this morning, but when I arrived at Prince Albert Mansions, Randall told me you were goodness knows where and William was at the police station. I went straight to Cannon Row, which is where I was when Sally's call came in.'

Flora stopped his lips with a finger. 'Slow down. I thought I was the one who gabbled when nervous.'

'Yes, well. I have a good excuse.' He swallowed and hugged her again. 'Maddox arrived here first because it took William and I ages to find a cab.' He half turned to indicate William, who had followed him into the hall.

Impulse sent Flora from Bunny's welcome arms into his.

'I'm so glad you're safe,' William whispered, his voice choked with emotion. 'Why didn't you tell me you were coming here?'

'I'm sorry. It didn't occur to me this matter wasn't all tied up yesterday.' She looked from William's face to Bunny's. 'It wasn't until I saw John's face I finally guessed the truth.'

'Had you done so,' William sounded almost fatherly. All that was missing was a wagging finger. 'I could have told you Maddox had received new evidence that changed everyone's minds about Gordon being the murderer.'

'What evidence?' Flora demanded.

'This.' Harry withdrew a hand from his pocket and held it towards them. In his palm sat a circular brooch with sparkling red and green stones cut through with a row of white ones. The words 'National Union of Women's Suffrage Society' across the centre.

'Evangeline's brooch,' Flora gasped. 'Where did you find it?' She looked from one face to another, where confusion vied with curiosity. 'Oh, I'm sorry. My father, William Osborne, this is Mr Howard Lange and Mr Harry Flynn, Evangeline's fiancé. This is my husband, Bunny Harrington.'

Nods, smiles and brief handshakes followed as the four took each other in.

'The police insisted she wasn't wearing it when she was found,' Howard Lange said. 'I knew a robber wouldn't have left such a valuable item behind, and if my suspicion was correct, neither would John, so I invited our Inspector friend to search the house when he was out.' He released a slow breath. 'We found it in my safe – the last place he expected anyone to look, no doubt.'

'And if we did,' Harry interjected. 'The police would assume Evangeline had put it there herself. We assume he intended keeping it to sell later.'

'John tried to convince me it was imitation, made of semi-precious stones.' Flora ran a finger over the facets that felt warm to the touch, then turned it over. 'I'm surprised he didn't clean it though.' With a finger she indicated a crust of brown on the wickedly sharp pin. 'What does that looks like to you?'

'I'm sorry, my love, but what does what look like to me? Bunny asked, frowning. 'I'm late to this party don't forget?'

'Sorry. It's dried blood. John's blood. 'It was what Sally said about the collars which convinced me he had murdered her.'

'Collars?' Bunny peered at her over his spectacles. 'Would someone mind enlightening me? Or am I to understand Evangeline was killed by her brother?'

'Stepbrother,' Harry and Howard Lange said together.

'When John attacked her,' Flora began, 'Evangeline reached for the first weapon she had to hand. She grabbed this brooch from her coat and jammed the pin in John's neck.' Mr Lange flinched and Flora brought a hand to her mouth. 'Oh, I'm so sorry, I didn't mean to remind you.'

'Please don't distress yourself, Mrs Harrington.' Howard Lange's eyes clouded but his gentle smile remained. 'The truth will never be worse than what I imagined when I was told my daughter was dead.'

'John kept easing his collar away from his throat,' Flora went on. 'I thought it was a nervous habit. Then the maid told Sally he had a wound there which hadn't healed.'

A clatter of footsteps announced the return of Inspector Maddox. Behind him two policemen frog marched John through the hall. Each held an arm firmly behind his back, making him hunch forward as he walked. A hank of his disarranged hair hung over one eye, one sleeve of his shirt torn away from the shoulder and the smears of mud on his trousers; all evidence of a struggle.

Silence fell as the group in the hall turned to stare at him.

'She deserved it,' John muttered, his chin jutted defiantly as he was hauled past Harry.

A low growl sounded in Harry's throat. He strode forward, pulled back his right arm and punched John squarely on the jaw.

John's head snapped back, a look of utter surprise on his face as he toppled slowly backward. Taken unawares, the policemen lost purchase and with no choice but to release him, John hit the floor. His head connected with the marble tiles with a sickening crack and he lost consciousness.

A horrified scream came from the top of the staircase. Mrs Lange swayed on the half landing, both clutching the balustrade as if she needed help to stand. She released a sob and launched herself down the stairs, fell to her knees beside her son and ineffectually patted his face and head with fluttering hands.

'Get away from him, Camille.' At the sound of Mr Lange's harsh voice, her hands froze in mid-air and she cringed away, sitting back on her haunches.

'Howard,' she pleaded in her little-girl voice. 'He's my son.' Her unfocussed eyes filled with tears and her bottom lip trembled.

'If you make any attempt to defend him, you can join him on the gallows.' He glared at her, unmoved at the pathetic figure of his wife, who sat whimpering on the floor.

Harry stepped over the immobile figure, bent and tugged John's collar away from his neck, revealing the swollen and angry scratch Flora saw earlier.

'Very astute of you, Mrs Harrington,' Inspector Maddox raised a brow at her, evidently impressed, if reluctantly so.

'She certainly is.' Bunny hugged Flora closer. 'Impetuous, thoughtless sometimes and definitely headstrong. But she gets there in the end.'

Embarrassed to be the focus of so much attention, Flora brushed down her skirt and adjusted her ruined hat. 'I must thank all of you for arriving so quickly.' Relief made her tearful. She reminded herself to appreciate Sally more for her quick thinking. Maybe another trip to the perfume counter at Harrods might be appropriate as well. Thoughts of Sally made her glance round but there was still no sign of her. Where could she have got to?

One of the policemen helped Mrs Lange up. Passive and silent, she reminded Flora of a ragged crow with her hunched shoulders giving tiny flinches as she shot quick, fearful glances at the activity going on around her. Flora tried to understand what had driven her, torn between her love for her husband and her only child. In those circumstances, who knew what any woman would be capable of? Did motherhood banish all sense of right and wrong in protection of a child? Then she recalled Lydia's words about what a lovely, kind, generous person Evangeline had been and her compassion dissolved.

'How could John have cold-heartedly murdered his own stepsister?' Flora asked sadly. 'She treated him with nothing but kindness.'

'Greed.' Howard Lange spat the word with contempt. 'He was always an acquisitive boy. No matter what he told the world, I treated him well, though I admit I could never warm to him. A whining mother's boy who grabbed all he could: expensive education, fine clothes, a generous allowance. He took it all as his due without a word of thanks.' He nodded towards Flora. 'Now if you'll excuse me. I have to see to Camille.'

'But she knew what John had done,' Flora said before she could stop herself.

He turned sad eyes on her. 'I know, but when all is said and done, she's still my wife.'

Flora watched the tall, stooped man escort Camille into the sitting room. The air of tragic defeat hanging between them an indication of the emotional torture their marriage was to become.

John groaned as he regained consciousness, propped himself up on one elbow and covered the left side of his jaw where Harry's fist had connected with one hand.

No one bothered to see how he was, but stared at him as if he were a specimen in a zoo. Then, at a silent signal from Inspector Maddox, the two policemen dragged him unceremoniously to his feet.

'How did you know Gordon hadn't done it? Flora watched as the officers bundled John out to the Black Maria that waited at the kerb, which resembled a coffin on wheels with its iron grille in the rear door and slits for windows.

'A witness came forward who claimed he was at a poker game in Berwick Street on the night Miss Lange was killed.'

Maddox's tone indicated disappointment. We'll have to stick with the charge of spying and breaking and entering.' At Flora's sharp look, added, 'And conspiracy to commit murder of yourself, of course.'

'I apologize if I've made your investigation more difficult, Inspector.' Flora felt calmer, but shivered as the front door lay wide open to allow a steady stream of policeman back and forth. 'I thought Gordon was the killer or I wouldn't have come here.'

'I can't pretend I'm happy about you poking about where you shouldn't have, Mrs Harrington. That Nurse Bell was a charmer I must say. She offered to charge us only half what you paid for her testimony, but I soon put her straight.' His upper lip curled, though the sparkle in his eyes showed he was amused rather than angry. 'I'll admit your methods produced results. I wish my own officers were as resourceful. Not to mention stubborn.'

'My wife's perseverance will be directed to more domestic matters in future.' Bunny massaged Flora's hand in both of his. 'She needs some peace and quiet after this adventure, which will certainly be her last.'

Flora opened her mouth to correct him but resisted, too grateful for her escape from certain death to argue. There would come a more appropriate time to remind him she wasn't as pliable as most wives.

Sally appeared from the direction of the kitchens with Flora's coat slung over her arm.

'Where have *you* been?' Flora shrugged into the garment, grateful to feel warm again.

'I told you before, I needed the privy,' Sally said in a whisper, then louder. 'I went to find our coats. They were out the back where that Lange bloke had left them. Yours is a bit dirty, Missus, and mine's got a rip in it.' She frowned, twisting to peer at the hem of the faded brown wool.

'I'll buy you a new one, Sally.' Euphoria made Flora generous, followed by a shudder at the thought that John had planned to bury them in their coats, or why else would he take them into the garden? She instantly resolved to replace her own as well.

'I hope my wife's antics haven't made you want to quit her service?' Bunny addressed Sally. 'I don't imagine exposing a murder was part of your duties when you came to work for us?'

'Not me, sir.' Sally sketched a curtsey. 'Not had so much fun for ages.' She hooked a thumb at the corridor behind her. 'And in case anyone was wondering, that Jenks fella didn't grass on Master John for shutting us in the cellar because he was caught filching the silver. Mr Lange threatened to turn him in if he didn't help.'

'Indeed.' Inspector Maddox narrowed his eyes. 'You must share your skill at wheedling information out of people, Miss Pond. We could use you in the force.'

Sally flushed and ducked her head away with a murmured, 'Not ruddy likely,' which Flora hoped the policeman hadn't heard.

'I'll go and tell the Inspector we'll talk to him tomorrow,' Bunny whispered. 'Back in a moment.

William took his place beside her, a wry smile on his face as he looked down at her. 'You're sure you're all right?' He stroked her cheek lightly with a finger.

She smiled up at him, just as the sound of renewed weeping and a low male voice reached them from the next room.

'Poor Mr Lange,' Flora said sadly, placing her hand briefly on William's arm. 'He's lost his entire family.'

'Howard Lange wrote his own tragedy,' William replied. 'If he intended to leave his wife and stepson out of his will, he should have done so in secret, not taunted them with the fact. He made his daughter a target.'

As Bunny returned, Flora interjected. 'Families are difficult things, aren't they? So strong in some ways and yet fragile in others.'

William's eyes bore into hers until she wanted to look away, but couldn't. Nor could she summon a response which wouldn't sound trite and dismissive, so she remained silent. 'My greatest fear is that you and I shall never be able to achieve the closeness I always wanted.' His lips twitched but did not quite firm a smile. 'I haven't helped much by not being around this week either have I? Yet I intended to. I wanted to, it was just-'

'Your work is important,' Flora found her voice at last. 'I understood.'

'I know, but we don't know each other any better now than we did before.'

'That's not entirely true. Before Bunny takes me home, perhaps we can finish our afternoon tea at Princes Ice Rink without you rushing off this time?'

'I would like that,' William dropped a kiss on her forehead. 'Perhaps I shall teach you to skate as well?'

'Surely not?' Bunny looked horrified and William frowned.

'Er no.' Flora grasped her husband's arm. 'Let's go back to the apartment. We've seen enough misery for one day.'

'You take my cab.' William gave Bunny's shoulder an affectionate pat as if they had been friends for years. 'I'll settle things here and make sure Sally gets home safely.'

'Bunny's staying for dinner, Father.' Flora placed a hand on his forearm. 'And afterwards, I'll explain why I cannot go ice skating.' She tugged Bunny toward the door before William could voice the question which had appeared in his eyes.

'Flora?' He called her back when she reached the door. 'I know Christmas is still a week away but I thought we would decorate a Norwegian spruce I have arranged to be delivered to the apartment.'

'You did that as well as catch Serbian spies and murderers?' Flora asked, impressed.

'Well, not until this morning in fact. I made a call and Randall is handling the rest. But the idea was mine.

'That sounds like a perfect start to the Christmas season.'

Inspector Maddox followed them onto the front step, his attention directed over their heads into the railed garden of Connaught Square. 'Were you aware, Mrs Harrington? The Tyburn Tree gallows was once located in this square?'

'No, I wasn't.' Flora shivered, tucked her arm through Bunny's and made a run for the waiting taxi.

*

Flora nestled against Bunny's shoulder as the vehicle chuntered through Hyde Park. 'I'm sorry I barged into the Lange's house the way I did. I thought it would be a kindness to let the family know about Victor rather than have them hear it from the police. Little did I know.'

'I know you better than that, Flora.' He slanted a downwards look at her. 'Admit it, you were proud of the part you played and wanted the Lange's to know how clever you had been.'

'Maybe.' She cuddled closer, inhaling the familiar, spicy scent of his cologne, her head ducked away to hide her blush. 'Did I mention how glad I am to see you?'

'You did,' he drawled. 'Twice.'

'I wasn't clever enough, though, was I?' Flora chewed the inside of her bottom lip. 'I knew something wasn't right about Victor being the killer, but everything pointed to him until today. I'll pay more attention to my own instincts in future.'

'There won't be any more sleuthing for you, my love. Those days are over.' When she didn't respond, his eyes narrowed behind his spectacles. 'William doesn't know yet does he? About the baby, or he would have caught on about the skating thing?'

'Well, er, everything became so busy I didn't have the chance. What with him rushing off after his Serbian spies at every opportunity. Then there was—' she caught his hard look and sighed. 'Um, sorry, no, I haven't.'

'Hmm,' he said. 'We'll address that later. However, I have some news of my own.'

'Really?' Flora shifted backward on the seat, a hand braced on his upper chest so she could look into his face.

'My firm of solicitors intend to open an office in Lincolns Inn and have asked me to head their team there.'

'Oh, Bunny that's wonderful.' She was about to throw her arms around him but hesitated. 'What about your dreams of opening a motor car factory?'

He shrugged. 'I'm going to be a family man now, so perhaps I should rethink that ambition. There are too many risks in such ventures which don't exist in the world of criminal law.'

'It's wonderful news, but the factory was your dream. I don't want you to abandon it for me.'

'Not for you, for us. Anyway, ambitions change. I'm happy with the decision, so don't spoil my surprise. I haven't finished telling you yet. When the news office opens we'll be moving here, to London.'

Flora sat bolt upright. 'Really?' A thought struck her and her shoulders slumped. 'What about your mother?'

'She wants to come too, of course.'

'Well naturally, I just thought-' Her stomach dropped to her boots, but she tried not to let it spoil her excitement. It seemed her hopes to have Bunny to herself for a while were as far off as ever.

'She's been talking to Arabella Greene,' he went on, oblivious to her disappointment. 'She has these supposedly private conversations on the telephone but forgets she shouts into the receiver so the entire house hears every word.'

'Who is Arabella Green? I don't think I know her.'

'Mother's cousin, who was widowed about ten years ago and lives with her daughter in Kingston. However, since their fourth child was born, their house is too noisy for a lady who likes order and naps in the afternoons, retires at nine thirty and likes to hold marathon bridge parties.'

Flora snorted. 'She sounds just like your mother.'

'She is. Now don't look so disapproving, Mrs Green is about to do us an enormous favour.' He pulled her closer. 'Mother and I have decided to sell the Richmond house. With the proceeds we'll buy a cottage in Chiswick village for herself and Arabella and a house for us.'

'A house?' A rush of excitement flooded through her, leaving her literally open-mouthed.

'I thought you'd like that.' He winked.

'Oh, I do. But—' she floundered, suddenly guilty at her display of such obvious pleasure. 'Only if it's right for Beatrice.

I wouldn't want her to feel we don't want to live with her, especially now, what with the baby, I—'

'Stop talking.' He silenced her with a finger pressed to her lips. 'Or I'll tell her you won't hear of her going off to live in Chiswick and want her to stay with us forever.'

'You wouldn't!'

Chuckling, Bunny bent his head and pressed his lips firmly to hers.

We hope you enjoyed this book!

The next Flora Maguire mystery is coming in summer 2017

More addictive fiction from Aria:

 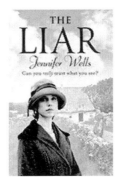 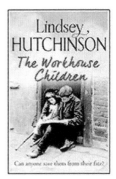

Find out more
http://headofzeus.com/books/isbn/9781784977177

Find out more
http://headofzeus.com/books/isbn/9781786691071

Find out more
http://headofzeus.com/books/isbn/9781786692511

Acknowledgements

With grateful thanks to the dedicated team at Aria for all their efforts in making this series possible. To Caroline Ridding for her vision in bringing Flora to life, Sarah Ritherdon for her enthusiasm for my characters and Jade Craddock for her sharp eye in straightening out my clumsy narrative.

Thanks too, to my agent Kate Nash who always had faith in me even when I did not, and whose encouragement and hard work is what has got me this far.

A special mention also to the Historical Novel Critique Group, great writers all of whom never fail to keep me on track.

About Anita Davison

Born in London, Anita has always had a penchant for all things historical. She now lives in the beautiful Cotswolds, the backdrop for her Flora Maguire mysteries.

Find me on Twitter
https://twitter.com/AnitaSDavison

Find me on Facebook
https://www.facebook.com/anita.davison

Visit my blog
http://thedisorganisedauthor.blogspot.co.uk/

Visit the Flora Maguire blog
http://floramaguire.blogspot.co.uk/

About the Flora Maguire Mysteries

 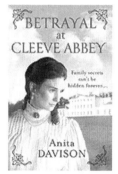 

Find out more
http://headofzeus.com/books/isbn/9781786690814

Find out more
http://headofzeus.com/books/isbn/9781786690821

Find out more
http://headofzeus.com/books/isbn/9781786690838

Visit Aria now
http://www.ariafiction.com

Become an Aria Addict

Aria is the new digital-first fiction imprint from Head of Zeus.

It's Aria's ambition to discover and publish tomorrow's superstars, targeting fiction addicts and readers keen to discover new and exciting authors.

Aria will publish a variety of genres under the commercial fiction umbrella such as women's fiction, crime, thrillers, historical fiction, saga and erotica.

So, whether you're a budding writer looking for a publisher or an avid reader looking for something to escape with – Aria will have something for you.

Get in touch: aria@headofzeus.com

Become an Aria Addict
http://www.ariafiction.com

Find us on Twitter
https://twitter.com/Aria_Fiction

Find us on Facebook
http://www.facebook.com/ariafiction

Find us on BookGrail
http://www.bookgrail.com/store/aria/

Addictive Fiction

First published in the UK in 2017 by Aria, an imprint of Head of Zeus Ltd

9 7 5 3 1 2 4 6 8

A CIP catalogue record for this book is available from the British Library.

ISBN (E) 9781786690838

Jacket Design © debbieclementdesign.com

Aria
c/o Head of Zeus
First Floor East
5–8 Hardwick Street
London EC1R 4RG

www.ariafiction.com